ELENI'S

JOURNEY

The Secrets That Lie Series

Devin Devonne

Sybella Dawn Publishing
Menifee, California

Sybella Dawn Publishing
30141 Antelope Road Suite D PMB 765
Menifee, California/92584
www.sybelladawnpublishing.com

Publisher's Note: This is a work of fiction. Names, characters, places and incidents are a product of the author's imagination. Locales and public names are sometimes used for atmospheric purposes. Any resemblance to actual people, living or dead, or to businesses, companies, events, institutions, or locales is completely coincidental.

Book Layout ©2013 BookDesignTemplates.com
Book Cover: SeflPubBookCovers.com/JayAheer

Ordering Information:
Quantity sales. Special discounts are available on quantity purchases by corporations, associations, and others. For details, contact the "Special Sales Department" at the address above.

Eleni's Journey: The Secrets That Lie Series/ Devin Devonne. -- 1st ed.

For those whose continued support endured

Love recognizes no barriers. It jumps hurdles, leaps fences, penetrates walls to arrive at its destination full of hope.

Maya Angelou

1   Eleni

Eleni stripped off all layers of her clothing, diving naked into the inviting cerulean water of the Anseba River. The cool water splashed over her skin leaving her refreshed, blissful and lost in the freedom of the river. She arose from her dive to hear someone calling her name. Eleni's face tightened, her lips pursed, irritated by the interruption of her aqueous serenity.

"Who is there and why do you summon me?"

"It is I."

She recognized his voice immediately. Why had the prophet sought her?

"What are you doing here?" she asked, diving into the cool water before joining the prophet at the edge of the river's bank. The feathery breeze over her exposed skin sent shivers down her spine.

"Turn around," she demanded. "You should not be gazing at me! My father would not tolerate any man's eyes looking upon the bare body of his daughter!"

"Princess Eleni, I have seen everything on most of the women in this kingdom. I mean no ill intent; it was not my desire to come down here to intrude. I came down the mountain to tell you of the vision I had about you."

The prophet's dark brown eyes narrowed, and his lips flattened into a straight line. "When I reached your study, you were nowhere to be found. It seems as if you are quite skilled in eluding your guards. Your mother informed me the only place you would be was down here at this river."

"What is the nature of this vision?"

"You will experience a life-altering event as I told you before, only this change will occur expeditiously. Eleni, the vision I had of you, years ago will come to fruition this day. You will marry a stranger and gain wealth beyond your ability to perceive. However, your suffering will outweigh all the wealth you will ever know. Despite this, the Creator will be with you always."

Eleni's laughter echoed longer than usual as she peeked her head from behind the massive tree trunk, to get a better glimpse at the prophet who continuously paced back and forth in front of her.

"I understand now why my father instructed me not to talk to you. You trumpet these visions of yours as if they are true. Your stories are worse than the herbs the healers always try to sell my mother in the village."

"What I say to you in these moments will occur. Princess, you must heed my warning," he concluded, falling to his knees in prayer. He sang in an unknown language, nodding back and forth in a trance like state.

Eleni's breath quickened as she glanced uneasily around the tree. The commotion caused her to step out into the open, clad in only her undergarments.

The prophet stopped his motions and focused on Eleni. His eyes encompassed a fire in their centers, his singing quieted.

"Princess, someone is approaching our lands from the south. You must get back to the kingdom; they are coming for you."

"Who is coming for me?" Eleni whispered. The prophet vanished from sight right before her.

Strange, he scares me, disappears, and did not answer my question. Sigh...I am sure he was only trying to tell me some silly story. What he says cannot possibly be true.

Eleni combed her surroundings in search of where the prophet had gone. She wished she could stay down at the river longer, but knew she should return to her chambers before her mother sent the guards after her. Eleni shrugged and picked up her things, leaving the river bank in haste.

As Eleni emerged from the forest approaching the path home. She slowed as she noticed an elderly woman, two men in robust armor, and a cloaked man all on horseback. As they passed her, Eleni gazed into the eyes of the cloaked man staring at her. He held an impenetrable and unyielding stare that gave no clues as he passed, continuing to ride towards the entrance. They halted speaking to the castle's guard who questioned the visitors before allowing them to proceed.

Eleni's stomach churned in pain remembering the prophet's words: *Changes are coming today.* She bit her lip in an attempt to calm her heart, and the pounding in her chest. Mustering her courage, she continued up the long path towards the castle's hall.

Exhausted and out of breath, she reached the room and eased around the side where she eavesdropped on the visitors' conversation through the open door. She peered around the door as her father, King Dabir, commanded the guests to stand after kneeling before him. The arm of his emerald robe was so wide the encrusted jewels on the sleeves slapped his adviser in the face as he hurried past her father. Eleni chuckled briefly; this enjoyment would be short-lived.

"I am Hillina, Servant of Abyssinia. We have come for the princess, Eleni," the elderly woman said to King Dabir.

"We noticed her as we came up the path and believe she would make a good wife for Arkamun, King of Abyssinia."

King Dabir rose from his throne with a gallant stance and piercing stare in the elderly woman's direction.

"Who told you of our kingdom and my daughter?"

He raised his eyebrows as he sank back down on his throne, the sleeves of his robe resting at his sides.

"She became known to us from the spies implanted throughout your lands, your majesty. My ruler, King Arkamun, desired information of other kings in the surrounding areas, to inquire of those who posed a potential threat to his kingdom. The spies reported of a beautiful princess living here in Eritrea; one far more superior than the other ladies presenting themselves to my king."

"Spies in our kingdom?" Dabir roared at his guardsmen. He clenched his chiseled masculine jaw while sweat formed on the brow of his brown skin.

"I will get to the bottom of this. Spies implanted in our lands indeed!" he bellowed again, pounding his fist on the armrest of his chair. King Dabir lowered his voice, calming his demeanor.

"There are other noble women you can take from my lands. I will not part with my eldest daughter. I promised her from childhood she would never leave her home." Dabir planted his legs on the marble floor beneath him. "She is to marry a ruler of my choosing and ascend to my throne as a Queen upon my death," he added glaring at the Hillina.

Eleni drew in a deep breath through her nose. The palms of her hands moistened from wringing them together so hard.

He would not let me down, and send me away from my home.

Eleni diverted her attention away from the conversation momentarily, seeking comfort from resting her back on the warm stone wall. Closing her eyes, she anticipated hearing the moment when her father, in a show of strength, would send the unwelcome visitors fleeing from their home.

"We will have your eldest daughter, the princess, and we will accept no other," Hillina announced projecting her voice above the whispers in the room. "The King offers a bountiful reward for your daughter's hand in marriage.

"Your lands will become prosperous once more. You will become a part of King Arkamun's household in Abyssinia. You shall be given ships, weapons, and gold." Hillina moved boisterously about the room, fiddling with the bracelets around her wrists. "King Arkamun will protect you from those who would attempt to take your land or wage war against you.

"You will never need to do battle again. You will never want or need anything. We will provide you with all things promised, and you will be welcome to visit your daughter whenever you desire."

Dabir sat back on his throne in utter silence, his posture still. His oval eyes scrutinized every move the elderly woman made.

"Bring me my wife, Abrihet. Bring her to me now!" he howled.

Unfortunately, Eleni did not hear the words she wished her father would have spoken on her behalf. She crouched lower behind the door to hide from the guard who went to summon her mother, the queen.

Moments later, Eleni peeked around the corner of the door, running her hands through her raven curls, as her mother Queen Abrihet arrived. She walked as regal as ever, greeting everyone in the room as she passed them.

Her mother's features rivaled Eleni's own. A long crown of raven hair pulled back in a braid adorned with golden jewels, stopped at her waist. An emerald green jeweled necklace hung around her narrow neckline. Her curvaceous body hugged the emerald gown she wore, hiding her firm, slim, muscular figure and rounded breasts. Her caramel skin, still youthful and smooth, radiated with the scent of jasmine.

Mother is such a rare beauty; I only hope one day to be as she would want me to be. I am not ready to be sent away now, not when I still had so much more to learn from her.

Eleni concealed her presence behind the door, listening to the conversation her mother had joined. Hillina appeared nervous as Queen Abrihet entered the room. She fanned herself profusely, bit down on her smile, and avoided eye contact with the queen.

"If you were not the queen of this beautiful land, we would take you to be Arkamun's wife. You are as beautiful as your daughter. We see the source of her loveliness."

Queen Abrihet ran her hand down the side of her gown. She made a choking noise in her throat; her face became flushed after the brazen comment Hillina made.

She joined her husband on the throne sitting to his left in silence. Her throat muscles tightened.

King Dabir shifted in his seat facing his wife.

"These people came to us from Abyssinia and have requested to take Eleni to be the new king's wife. My queen, they offer us land, gold, jewels, and will make Eritrea a part of Abyssinia. We are welcome to join them at court if we so desire. Is this something you would consider?"

Queen Abrihet held her head down momentarily, pulled her chest in, then released a deep breath. "I knew this day would come for her. I must let her go sooner than I desired. However, the thought of our kingdom falling under protection of Abyssinia and raising our other daughters in peace sounds..."

Queen Abrihet's voice trailed off. Her posture perked up as she edged to end of her seat.

Eleni stood behind the door clutching her gown tightly in her hands, the muscles in her neck trembling as she listened to her parents consider the offer from Hillina, to send her away. She continued listening in hopes her mother would redeem her where her father failed, by turning down the offer of her betrothal.

"Will my daughter be honored and respected? What are the guarantees of these jewels and land if we agree to your proposition?"

A wide grin crossed over Hillina's old crackled face; she spoke again with a brazen forwardness. "More gold than you both could ever spend. As a gesture of good faith..." She waved for the men she traveled with to come forward, moving her disheveled strands of gray hair from her face.

The guards brought forward a chest, lowering it. They opened the silver adorned box and placed it at Queen Abrihet's feet. The queen slid even closer to the edge of her throne, leaning forward, and beheld the amount of shimmering brilliance in the chest.

"Elevation in the king's court, jewels, more than you can imagine. Yes, my dear, your daughter will be cared for. All will be well if you agree to our terms of betrothal." Hillina captivated them with her deceptive words cloaked underneath the disingenuous smile across her face.

Queen Abrihet grasped two handfuls of gold, swiveled toward her husband and smiled. "I agree to the terms" Queen Abrihet dropped the gold, grasping Hillina's hand. "You may have my daughter, and we will be at her side for her marriage to the newly crowned king."

Queen Abrihet nodded in the direction of her husband before rising from her chair. She smiled once more as she passed those lowered to their knees in respect of their queen.

Eleni's eyes locked with her mother's as she walked past her. She was stunned her mother did not stop to speak with her.

"Mother!" Eleni called out, her face reddened, her heart sinking as she barreled towards her mother walking down the road to the stables.

Eleni placed her hand on her mother's shoulder, halting her from going any further.

"How could you do this to me, Mother? Why would you sell me for jewels and power? This marriage is not what I want!" Eleni screamed.

Queen Abrihet removed her daughter's hand from her shoulder, stroking her hand with her own.

Eleni snatched her hand away from her mother, taking a breath, holding it in before letting out an internal scream.

"Eleni, this happens in life," Queen Abrihet answered talking a deep, satisfied breath. "The manner in which you choose to conduct yourself in this matter will dictate our future and the prosperity of the kingdom."

"Mother, I do not want to marry this man! I do not know him, and I do not love him!"

"You have no choice in the matter, my daughter; your father and I have spoken on this issue. It is time for you to conduct yourself as a woman, a wife and assume the responsibilities of a queen."

Eleni spun away from her mother in a huff. Tears forming in the corner of her eyes, she ran as far as she could away from the castle and her mother. Eleni heard her mother calling out to her, but ignored her continuing to run as far as possible. She needed to compose her thoughts and what she would do next.

My mother and father betrayed me; I will never forgive them. My life has consisted of lies; they never planned on me staying here in our kingdom.

Eleni ran as long as she could until she felt her legs give out beneath her and she collapsed down into the high grass. Tossing her head back toward the sky, she watched as the sunset gave way to a clear sky with endless stars. All around her bonfires were lit throughout the village, large flames and smoke filling the air. Dancing commenced as word moved throughout Eritrea about Eleni's engagement to the new king of Abyssinia.

Eleni had forgone dinner, staying out amongst her people who came to greet her and give blessings for her upcoming union. Eleni nodded in acknowledgment as she passed them in the pastures, concealing her sadness behind a broad smile. The prophet's words would indeed come to pass.

She would be forever trapped in a marriage and sent to a kingdom she did not want to be in. She watched her people celebrating with a blank stare, her eyes watery with tears at the men and women dancing in her honor.

She could not help but cry. These moments would be some of the last memories of her homeland. She rubbed her temples in an attempt to ward off the pain forming in her head. The throbbing increased, forcing her to return to her chambers amidst her marriage celebration.

The air from the night sky carried a fragrant wind encompassing her. Dimly lit candelabras lined the hall leading to her chamber room. She slammed her door behind her, curled up on her chaise and cried herself asleep to the thunder of the drums giving her praise.

Queen Abrihet ate dinner alone that evening. She barely touched any food on her plate, pushing the contents around with a fork, recounting the day's events and the betrothal of her daughter.

Dabir should be here with me celebrating our daughter's betrothal.

Losing further interest in her meal, Queen Abrihet pushed her plate with its contents across the table, knocking the chalice with wine on the floor.

"Cassia," Queen Abrihet called out to her servant girl. Cassia heard the queen summon her. She appeared in the doorway of the chamber room to await her orders.

"Milady, how can I serve you?"

"Girl, I spilled the wine. Clean up this mess and get this food out of my face, I have lost my appetite," Queen Abrihet demanded, folding her arms. Cassia did what she was told in silence, not making eye contact with the queen.

"Hurry up and get this mess cleaned up."

"Yes, Milady," Cassia murmured, in a hurried fashion to finish her cleaning.

Queen Abrihet placed her hands on her hips, drilling her eyes into the back of Cassia's head as she cleaned. She was relieved to be alone again when the girl scurried the broken glass and food out of the room.

The celebration in honor of her daughter continued well into the evening. Wooden string instruments now accompanied the thundering drums, and flutes created a hypnotic harmony. Queen Abrihet watched from her window as the villagers laughed, danced, and mingled among one another.

As a mother, she should have been overjoyed her daughter was matched with such a ruler as Arkamun. Eleni would have a palace grander than the one they lived in and riches passed down to her children. She was so assured of her decision when she promised her daughter to Hillina.

It was not until she recounted a conversation she had with her husband about their kingdom falling into peril, and what needed to happen for its restoration when the doubt of her decision begin to weigh on her.

Dabir must reassure me about this decision; we mustn't send Eleni away if it is not warranted.

Queen Abrihet slipped her gold robe over her emerald gown and picked up a candelabra off the table to take with her in search of Dabir. She headed down the east wing in the direction of Dabir's private chamber, the train of her emerald gown making a swishing noise on the limestone floor beneath her feet. Abrihet stopped dead in her tracks when she saw a tall shadowed figure at the door speaking with her husband. Curious, she backed out of the hall behind a pillar and watched the man hand Dabir a bag of gold.

Abrihet backed further behind the pillar. Her questions for her husband were now answered. Dabir had sent for the visitors and was paid extra gold for his cooperation in convincing her to sell their daughter into marriage. Adrenaline rushed through Abrihet's body. She would confront her bastard of a husband and demand answers from him. She poked her head around the pillar to find the hall once again deserted.

Alone again I see.

Abrihet moved in haste towards Dabir's chamber room door. Before she could knock, a warm hard hand wrapped around her mouth from behind, sending the candelabra out of her hand and onto the floor with a loud clank. A cold object was placed against her neck. She bit down the on hand, which momentarily released its grip long enough for her to let out a high-pitched shout muffled by the other hand placed across her face.

The shadowed figure she had seen earlier now had taken her hostage. The cloaked man dragged Abrihet bound and gagged through the deserted part of the castle out into the night. The more she fought the tighter the grip was placed on her. Her mind raced with the possibility of escape and the course of action she would take too free herself.

If he is going to kill me, he should do it now, for if he fails to do so, he will be in for the fight of his life.

Abrihet and her captor came to a stop in the high grass not far from the kingdom when without warning, he cut her ties and removed the gag from her mouth, releasing her.

"You are free to go," he said dropping the ropes in the grass, pulling the reins of his horse off the nearby tree.

Abrihet rubbed the areas around her wrists where she had been bound. She had many questions for the man but found it difficult to find the right words. Finally, she was able to mutter. "Why did you take me, only to release me?"

The cloaked man stepped back down from his horse and circled in Abrihet's direction.

"You were not supposed to be in the hall tonight. I took you only to secure my departure from the kingdom." His voice was calm and reassuring, her anger against him subsided.

"Why were you in my home on this evening? Why did Dabir summon you to his chambers? Does the gold have something to do with my daughter's betrothal? Who are you?"

"Those are questions I cannot answer, Queen. I am sure you will learn the answers for yourself in due time. However, you will not tell anyone especially your daughter of what you have seen this night, nor will you inform anyone of our little mishap. If you do, I will have no choice but to come back and finish what I started. You are a stunning woman and a queen. I would be most excited to use my knife to cut away your gown, to see your beautiful silhouette."

Abrihet should have been appalled with what the mysterious man had said about seeing her unclothed, but was more flattered he had noticed her. Her husband had not touched her since they lost their only son and male heir, and sought comfort in the arms of many other women in the kingdom other than her own.

The flattering comment made her face red from blushing, and she was happy he could not see her clearly in the night sky.

"Well if you want what is underneath my gown, I give you permission to do so," she cooed. "I believe you underestimate your chances with me."

The cloaked man let out a boisterous laugh, saddled his horse stopping beside where she stood. He leaned over, lifting Queen Abrihet off her feet, kissing her deeply with his mouth and tongue.

"Well... If my king sends me back to seek you out, I will know you have spoken about this night," he said into her ear, releasing her back into the ground. "Farewell Queen," he scoffed as he rode off into the brush in the cover of night.

Abrihet touched her lips. She could still taste him, the sweetness of his lips lingered. She was not sure if she should laugh or cry by the evening's events. The man did not answer any of her questions, leaving her wondering who he was, and after that kiss, she had hopes of encountering him again. She would heed his warning, and not share the night's events with Eleni.

Abrihet grabbed the train of her gown and through the darkness she walked, the smoke and fire of the bonfires rising in the distance. Her bare feet were caked with the damp mud and grass as she came into the village where the celebration of her daughter continued. She passed by a few villagers unnoticed for they were engrossed in laughter, the drunken men flirting with the women, pulling them into their laps.

Relieved she was not stopped and questioned, she made it back to the castle to her chambers. After cleansing herself, Abrihet sought out her daughter as she wanted to apologize for her actions in their argument earlier in the afternoon.

The west wing of the castle was quiet. The candles lit in the hall leading up to Eleni's room had all but extinguished their flame.

Abrihet knocked on Eleni's chamber room door. There was no answer, and she waited for two minutes before pushing the door open. The room was dimly lit; only a single candle held its flame. Abrihet's eyes adjusted to the room as she stepped inside.

Her daughter was sound asleep on the chaise. Not wanting to wake her, she scooped up Eleni's favorite blue and gold embroidered quilt and placed it over her daughter. Eleni had had the blanket since she was a small child; the embroidery was worn and fading as the years had gone by. It was a bittersweet reminder she would lose her little girl in marriage in a few days.

Abrihet held back tears as she kissed her daughter's forehead and stroked her hair. She now had a secret she had to carry and keep from her daughter; a secret she hoped would not come to the harm her. Abrihet had one more stop to make before retiring for the evening. She withdrew from Eleni's chambers to confront her husband once more.

Abrihet came back to where the night's events had taken an interesting turn. Kidnapped, seduced, and secrets revealed were all things plaguing her mind. This time, as she approached Dabir's chambers, she noticed the door was partially ajar, two silhouettes moving inside the room. She rubbed her arms as she approached. Swallowing excessively, she was unsure of what she would find behind the door. Closer and closer she came until she

peered through the crack in the door, finding Dabir speaking to a village woman standing before him. She knew of all his affairs, but this was the first time she laid eyes on one of the women he had brought into their home.

Abrihet continued to spy and eavesdrop on her husband and this woman in a desire to be a part of something. She held a longing gaze for her husband as she listened to their conversation.

"What is your name, maiden of Eritrea?"

"I do not believe you brought me here tonight in secret to ask questions, King. What is it you desire of me?"

"Before we indulge in why I brought you here, I would like to know with whom I am speaking. I will not ask you again woman; what is your name?"

"Forgive me, my king. My name is Solara."

"Your features nor your native tongue is like the women of Eritrea. What is your native land?"

"Knowing where my native lands are not necessary, my king. Please allow me to fulfill my real purpose for being here. I promise I will not disappoint you."

Solara sashayed moving closer to the king, grabbing his erect penis through his pants.

Abrihet blinked heavily. Trying to see better into the room, she pushed the door slightly, alerting Dabir that someone was outside. She moved behind the nearby pillar again to hide as Dabir checked the hall before swinging the door closed again. The door popped back open slightly, giving Abrihet the opportunity to continue to spy. When she was comfortable he would not be alerted to her presence, she resumed her position by the chamber room door.

Abrihet adjusted her eyes to see back into the room. Solara was now down on her knees, sucking and serenading Dabir's penis with her lips. As she sucked, she made aggressive motions with her mouth and tongue causing Dabir's knees to buckle, singing a chant to his penis in a foreign language.

Abrihet could feel the moistness between her legs. She and Dabir had not shared an encounter such as she witnessed in years. She could see Dabir was pleased; she could tell he was receiving the best oral pleasure he ever had. Abrihet touched herself between her legs again momentarily before she composed herself, continuing to watch her husband's intimacy with the village girl.

Solara pushed the king down into a large chair in the room. Mounting his penis in an equestrian manner, she moved with salacious intensity as she whispered into the king's ear.

"Release your seed inside of me, so I may give you the son your queen never could."

Her vagina massaged and squeezed Dabir's penis as they both clinched each other, each feeling the simultaneous sensation of an imminent orgasm.

Abrihet rose to her feet; she had seen enough and would put a stop to this encounter. As King Dabir and Solara both continued to approach their climax, Abrihet flung the chamber door open and spoke in a smooth voice.

"I hope this not how you intend to spend the wealth of Eritrea, oh husband of mine?" She questioned dropping her shawl in a nearby chair.

"Where did you come from, Abrihet!" screamed Dabir.

Solara, startled by the queen's entrance, grabbed her garments and ran out of the chamber room naked, brushing past the queen.

"Standing in the doorway watching you and that cave beast shame yourselves. I hope you choose to display more wisdom in the leading of our people since our daughter is your means of acquiring this new found wealth and land."

Dabir jumped out of his chair and stood naked in front of Abrihet, who continued to stare firmly at him. "I forbade you to speak of this night to anyone in our court, nor alert Eleni of my exploits."

"Dabir, you make me laugh with such comments. All those who are closest to us see your whores on hand at all hours. I shame you for insulting me so, but if it would put your mind at ease, I will say nothing to your daughter, even though you should know by now I have never given her a reason to fault you. Now since you are finished with your evening tryst, you should remove the stench of your whore and go to bed. There is much to prepare for our daughter's departure to Abyssinia."

Queen Abrihet retrieved her shawl, leaving Dabir standing in the room naked, still stunned his wife saw him with another. Abrihet clutched the wall, her strength leaving, her heart thudding dully in her chest. She felt mentally fatigued and drained from confronting Dabir and what she had seen. Returning to her chambers, she sat near the window in silence and in thought. She was forced in keeping yet another secret from her daughter, this time about the whorish ways of her father. Abrihet took solace in knowing her daughter would be away from the kingdom in the next few days. She fell asleep praying she and Eleni would end up with the happiness they both so deserved.

On the third morning in December, the day of Eleni's seventeenth birthday, she was escorted from the only home she ever knew beginning a journey to the kingdom of Abyssinia. Eleni's heart broke into pieces as her carriage continued to pass by familiar surroundings from her childhood. The Greenland where her mother would walk with her and her sisters. The Anseba River where she would escape her guards and swim for hours. And finally, the healer's shanty where she would spend hours peeking in a small window watching the healer mix many potions to sell in the village. Eleni bore the details in her memory. She would never forget her home.

The carriage bumped along the rocky path out into the open lands. Hot and sweaty, Eleni, her parents and entourage traveled across the desert towards Abyssinia. The solitude in the carriage left Eleni with only her thoughts to occupy her. She played back the images of the conversation her parents had with the elderly woman.

How could they have done this, sold me for position and jewels in a kingdom they never mentioned!

This king she was to marry was a mystery. Her parents kept any details about who he was, how he was built physically, his mannerisms and what kind of a man he was a secret from her. Eleni made up her mind at the first chance she would try to escape. She would rather die in the outskirts of the desert than be sent to marry a man she was unsure she could ever love.

The next morning, she was jolted from her seat as she slept when her carriage came to a sudden stop. She peered from inside the small rectangular window. She saw no guards to the front nor the back of the carriage. She opened the carriage door quietly, slipping past her parents' carriage unnoticed. The guards had removed the horses from their harnesses and had led them down to the nearby watering hole. Eleni cast a glance, noticing the nearby lush green trees not far past where the horses and the guards stood. She would only have one chance to escape.

This is my only chance for my freedom and my life.

Eleni made off, slipping off her slippers in the warm desert sand, behind the guards and the horses she lumbered gaining her freedom with every step she took. She could feel the wind on her back, the sun on her shoulders, the granules of dirt beneath her feet. She had almost reached the shaded trees when something pulled her from behind by her long gown, sending her face first down into the sand.

"Where do you think you are going?" the voice called out behind her.

Eleni twisted her body to one side and saw the guard, still holding her gown.

"Let me go; you are not going to keep me here, let me go!"

She kicked him violently until he released his grasp. He lost his balance falling and hitting his head on a rock. Eleni got to her feet and ran again, this time tripping over a stone hidden in the sand, sending her to land on her ankle. Eleni tried to get to her feet again, before stumbling. She winced in pain, grabbing her ankle; it was sprained. She now could not move far, and realized, that she was helpless out in the open.

"Help me! Help me!" she called over to the guard, still passed out in the sand.

I have to get out of this bright sun.

Eleni pulled herself up on her knees, slowly making her way to the shade of the nearby trees. She detected something was lurking behind the cover of the brush, watching her. Eleni pushed on towards the trees, with the fervent hope she could climb out of danger. Eleni was unable to move any further when her dress became entangled in the brush. She could feel the animal's eyes on her waiting for the perfect moment to attack her.

Eleni tried to rip her dress from the brush, becoming more entangled. She stopped struggling, retreated into a fetal position, curling her knees further into her chest. She could not outrun what was waiting for her in the brush, and she closed her eyes, whimpering, moaning, and waiting for the animal to attack. Silence engulfed her. Eleni felt her body lifted from the ground; she was being carried.

Opening her eyes, she glared at the dead lion not far from where she lay. The guard she had knocked out, saved her from death by spearing the beast with one blow. He had thrown Eleni over his shoulder and carried her back to the carriage where her parents stood waiting, woken by her screams and the guard's scuffle with the lion. Eleni avoided eye contact with her parents as the guard placed Eleni down in front of them. Her ankle swollen and bruised; she struggled to stand, bracing herself against the guard.

"Look at me," King Dabir demanded. Eleni hesitated before locking eyes with him. He had a stony expression on his face, his eyes dull and black. Without warning, he slapped her across the face, sending her small frame into the sand.

"How dare you do this to your mother and me. After everything we have done to secure your place with a grand king, and in a beautiful kingdom."

Eleni focused her attention on her father's mouth. She had the inability to look at him in his eyes.

"I am so sorry, Father," she muttered. "Please forgive me for my actions." Eleni dropped her chin to her chest, her eyes wet with tears.

"You will fix this by marrying Arkamun, and not giving me any more trouble. Abrihet, get back in the carriage. You will say nothing to your daughter."

Abrihet frowned at Eleni and acknowledged her husband before returning to their carriage. Eleni sobbed uncontrollably, her tears multiplied.

"Guard, I am placing you in charge of watching my daughter. Tend to her ankle, and make sure she is locked her in the carriage. I do not want any more trouble from her."

The guard nodded he understood. He gathered Eleni into his arms once more, returning her to her carriage.

Eleni was seated back on the coach bench, the guard leaving her momentarily to collect oils and bandages to tend to her injury. She said nothing to him only shifting when he touched her swollen ankle.

"You will have to stay off your ankle the remainder of this journey."

"I understand, thank you," Eleni whispered as she eased herself further back further on the carriage bench. The guard handed her a blanket closing the door behind him. She found herself alone once again. Eleni heard the guard call out to the lead men. They cracked the whips on the horses pulling off on their journey once more.

I will never forgive him for striking me, I do not know the man who spoke to me the way he did. I can see now all he cares about is the gold, jewels and land. And Mother... what can I say about her? She stood there and said nothing. After my marriage to this King, they both will be dead to me. I will never care to see them again.

The remaining days of the journey to Abyssinia were quiet for Eleni. Enclosed in her carriage, gave her the time to reflect on her parent's actions. Her marriage only days away to a man she had never met, and she wondered what she should expect in her new home and kingdom. The whips cracked once more on the horses backs as the carriages rounded a corner onto the path at the entrance of the new country. Eleni peeked out from behind the carriages curtain gazing at the people of the nation who lined the sides, tossing flowers into the path up to the top of the mountain.

What a beautiful country this is.

The castle sat nestled on the side of the mountain; parts of it built into the rock below and beside it. The kingdom's slaves constructed Eskendar Castle. A white stone resembling marble was used and chiseled into entrancing shapes and sizes. When the sun shone down on the castle's surface, the rock appeared as if it were bathed in beautiful diamonds coruscating in the sun. The statues sat on pillars on the castle tops, and the courtyard and the entryway were all covered in solid gold. Eleni's eyes widened in amazement, unsure of which direction to focus her attention.

I cannot believe how beautiful this kingdom is.

Eleni momentarily forgot everything weighing on her mind, for the brief moment she allowed herself to take in all the beauty swept around her. Her carriage continued up the long path to the castle passing large fruit trees of grapefruit blowing a delectable scent through the carriage.

Heavenly.

She continued to glance out the carriage window, the ocean's blue water spread out over the horizon. The gentle breeze from the water blew the cold air through the carriage window calming her nerves. The coaches continued up the steep path until they reached the opening of the courtyard pulling to a halt in front of the castle. Eleni rubbed the back of her neck and adjusted her clothing. She was not ready for this moment to meet the king. He would know by looking at her; she did not want to be there or be his queen.

2 Arkamun

Within three days of leaving Eskendar Castle, King Arkamun's messenger, Berhanua, arrived back in the kingdom. He sought out the young king in his chambers to inform him of King Dabir of Eritrea's acceptance of his bribe and payment for his daughter, Eleni. She had been selected to become his bride and was due to arrive by carriage within a week's time. Arkamun took the news as a sign of good luck. He would have one woman under his control, and would mold her to be an exceptional queen.

Arkamun had a few days to prepare for his new bride. He ordered his staff to decorate her chamber room with the finest luxuries. He would seduce her with his wealth and hopefully by doing so; she would relinquish control. Arkamun wanted her to be oblivious to the secret lust for women, and the sexual affairs he would continue to engage.

Arkamun sent inquiries into the town and nearby villages ordering women to be brought back to the kingdom for the remaining days of his single-dom. Whores, handmaidens, and servants were paraded in front of the young king. He wanted to experience as many as he could sexually. His need for sex and women increased over time, an unquenchable thirst unable to be soothed. In these days, Eskendar Castle was overrun with naked women at every turn.

Guards, maids, servants all participated in the week long orgy overtaking the castle. Arkamun's mother, Queen Meseret did her best to ignore events happening around her. She finally removed herself from her surroundings and sought refuge in the caverns underneath the castle.

Plush pillows, lush jewel tone blankets, trays of figs and cheese were placed around the curtains of blue silk adorning the cavern walls. The preparations had been made as she had requested. Queen Meseret adjusted the sapphires on the parted braids across her crown, sprinkled lavender oil on her neck, down her chest, and underneath her robe. She anticipated her lover's arrival at any moment and wanted to please him when he arrived.

The secret door to the cavern wall opened. Berhanua whisked himself inside, dropping his cloak to the floor, swooping Meseret up in his arms kissing her passionately.

"I have missed you so much my love," Meseret cooed as she kissed him again, slipping her tongue into his mouth allowing it to dance along with his.

Berhanua wasted no time sliding his hands underneath Meseret's robe; her oiled skin smooth to his touch. His hands moved up her supple thighs pushing her legs open, palming the moistness between her legs. Meseret moaned in excitement releasing her tongue from his mouth, moving his hand deeper between her legs in appreciation.

"I have missed you as well, Meseret. There is much for me to tell you of my journey," Berhanua whispered into Meseret's ear.

"Tell me later, all I want from you right now is for you to show me how much you missed being away from my arms."

Berhanua's fingers found their way deeper into Meseret's moistness, her mound swallowing his long, lanky fingers with each thrust. Meseret bucked her head backward; her moaning increased as she found her way to climax. He released his fingers from her mound. Meseret kissed him gently again before untying his breeches, dropping them to the floor.

Berhanua removed his shirt, smiled and pulled her into his naked body. He kissed her once again lightly on the lips, untied her robe, slipping it over her body to the ground. Massaging her back into the blue silk curtains, he lifted her up around his waist, up onto his shoulders, placing her knees gently on them.

Meseret leaned her breasts and head against the cool silk curtains resting them against the cavern wall.

Berhanua drowned his head in-between her thighs, his tongue flicking her clit rapidly, the moistness dripping between her legs, as he held her buttocks firmly in his hands. Moving slowly, he blew warm air on her starfish, before circling and probing it with his tongue.

Meseret shook from the sensation sent up her thighs. She grabbed the silk curtain, pulling it into her mouth to hide the screams of passion.

Berhanua increased his sucking and kissing her asswhole with each of her jerks until she climaxed again releasing her juices onto his face and into his mouth.

"Please Berhanua, you must put me down. I cannot take much more," she sang between moans.

He obliged her, lifting her off his shoulders back down to his waist. "Wrap your legs around my waist, and brace yourself against the wall," he whispered into her ear once more.

Meseret did as she was told. Berhanua's hard organ pressed again against her buttocks. His penis increased with size and length as he pushed himself in and out between her thighs tracing her clit with the head of his cock. Meseret was excited again, and fluid dripped from inside of her down his shaft.

"It seems as if you are ready now," he mumbled as he pushed himself inside of her, pressing her further against the wall. The warmth of his chest against her. His long cock thrust in and out of her, exciting every part of her as he stroked her steadily. Her thighs tightened around his hips, her feet resting underneath his buttocks.

"Harder, Berhanua," she moaned, "I want all of you."

Berhanua moved his twelve inches into her abyss, his breath deepening as he moved harder and faster. Meseret's skin glistened with sweat. She had never enjoyed sex as much with her late husband. She found enjoyment with only one other man before Berhanua, but his arrogance and cruelty towards women had lessened her desire to be with him.

Meseret's mind wandered out of the moment with Berhanua; her thoughts slipped towards her son, Arkamun. Her focus shifted abruptly back to Berhanua when he turned her around on his waist, facing him, and looked at her tenderly before passionately kissing her again.

"Your thoughts were getting away with you again."

"No, Berhanua, I was lost in reflection for only a moment."

"Your thoughts should only be with me right now your majesty."

"My thoughts are with you, my love," she lamented, kissing him again.

Meseret allowed him deeper into her abyss once more, both of their body's entwining until they climaxed together. Meseret yanked the silk curtain down over them, covering their naked bodies as they continued to embrace. Berhanua kissed Meseret on the forehead as she lay on his bare chest.

"Will you tell me now, of your journey? Is Arkamun to be married?"

"Yes, my love, he is. King Dabir agreed to let his eldest daughter marry Arkamun."

"Splendid, when is she due to arrive?" Meseret asked as she shifted on Berhanua's chest.

"In a week's time, she will be here. I believe the king will be pleased with her. I can only hope he is patient with her. She is quite young."

"Well, let us both hope, he will be pleased with her. Perhaps he will settle down, and discontinue his whorish ways with all the other women he seems to find at his disposal. Is there any other information you need to share with me? Were the princesses' parents pleased with the gold?

"Yes, they were pleased, Meseret. They accepted everything Hillina offered to them, and perhaps even more."

"What do you mean even more? Is there something you are not telling me, Berhanua?" Meseret queried for more information

"No, there is nothing more we offered. I only meant they are quite greedy. If we had offered them more, they would have taken it all. As far as Arkamun is concerned, we can hope he will be pleased with the girl, Meseret...We can hope..."

"Now my love, if there are no more questions, let us not have any more talk about your son. We have limited time to be together; we should be more focused on me tasting you again."

Meseret smiled and drew the curtain over her thighs.

"As you wish, no more questions," she beckoned, pushing his head between her legs once more.

Meseret and Berhanua spent four more days locked away in the caverns before they returned to their separate worlds.

The morning of their departure was an emotional one for Meseret. She watched Berhanua as he dressed: his chiseled chest muscles bulging from his shirt. His breeches, he slipped over his muscular chocolate thighs and buttocks. Watching him made her lust for him again, and she touched herself between her legs.

"There is no more time for touching yourself," Berhanua zinged, falling onto the curtain next to Meseret. He tugged her in for one final kiss before dragging her to her feet.

"Get dressed, my queen; we have to get back before we are missed."

Meseret acknowledged his words and slid her robe over her bare shoulders. "I hate leaving you my love; I would rather stay here among the cold rocks than to return to find my son engaged in some activity with multiple women."

Berhanua kissed her forehead, picked up his sword and his remaining belongings. "I understand, Milady, remember our time here, and all will be well. Now I must go as should you before we are caught together. I shall see you again soon."

Meseret smiled as Berhanua grabbed her hand. He kissed it gently before disappearing through the secret door. He was gone in an instant, leaving her alone. Meseret washed her skin and dabbed jasmine oil once again on her skin. She hoped it would be enough to mask the scent of sex, and keep her son from going into a mad rage.

Meseret made her way back to the castle. There were naked men and women sprawled out everywhere in the corridors of the castle. Meseret's blood started to boil.

Where is my son? He is supposed to be preparing for his bride, not continuing in this orgy six days later.

Meseret came around the corner to her chamber room and stopped in her tracks. There in front of her was her son, Arkamun, beating a servant with a cane as he rammed himself inside of her.

"What is the meaning of this Arkamun? You are supposed to be making preparations for the new princess to arrive here at our kingdom! Why are all of these whores in our castle? If your father were alive, he would be flabbergasted to see what a fool you have become."

Arkamun laughed, increased his thrusting and continued to beat the girl with the cane.

"Give me the rod!" Meseret shrieked as she tried to grab the cane out of her son's hands.

"Not so fast Mother," Arkamun hissed, slapping her hands away from him. "You have no control over what it is I do. I am the king, you are now just a queen, and have no real power."

He released the girl from his control, pushing her away and stood in front of his mother naked.

"This is what my father wanted me to be, is it not? Not to be a weak man, not to show any insecurities, to be a tough man, confident in his skin?" Arkamun challenged stroking his hard cock. "Tell me, Mother, is this what my father wanted, or better yet what you wanted?" he inquired again, smiling.

Meseret could not help but look at her son. Even when she was disgusted with him, he was such a beautiful creature. Although he was depraved and sadistic, he was a marvel of a man.

She reflected on their relationship and how it came to be; her going into his room as a child, hugging him close to her. She tried to comfort him after the rapes and beatings inflicted upon him by his father, her husband.

She remembered their first encounter, and when it went too far. The night he snuck into her chambers when he was thirteen years old, muffling her screams as he raped her it was the start of their incestuous, perverse relationship.

He grew from a scrawny thin little boy, into a strong, muscular, brutal young man. With caramel colored skin, thick thighs like Berhanua, he towered over her. His arms were rock solid; his enormous organ even larger than the twelve inches of her lover.

Meseret remembered her son's embrace and how he touched her. Their encounters were always unique; she tried to make him forget his father's ways. She glanced away when Arkamun bore his chestnut eyes into hers. He took pleasure in her looking at his naked body.

"My son, you know this is not the what your father was trying to show you when he disciplined you. He wanted to make you stronger, not a weak little boy like you are acting like now."

"I suggest you redirect your attitude, Mother. You might find yourself in a situation not becoming of someone like you."

Meseret sensed her son threatening her and backed off. "Well, son, I will heed your advice and do as you ask. Might I suggest you put some clothes on and rest. There is much to be done in the next day before the princess arrives. I shall speak to you when you are calm."

Meseret brushed past Arkamun, returning to her chambers, pleased he did not detect the scent of sex on her skin. She realized she still had feelings for him. They had not been intimate in months, yet she still yearned for his companionship and touch.

Am I like him with the constant need for sex and intimacy? Am I the one who created the monster who is now my son? I pray his bride will win his heart and change his ways.

The next morning, Meseret sought out Arkamun, on what preparations remained before his bride's arrival, but her son was nowhere to be found. Meseret concluded he left the kingdom in search of something to satisfy his sexual appetite. Left to make the final decisions Queen Meseret called all of the servants in, to clean, kick out the remaining miscreants in the castle and finish preparing for the princess's arrival.

Fresh flowers were cut and arranged on every floor throughout the castle. The floors were mopped and dried, fruits and game were brought in for the feasts and upcoming wedding. The castle returned to its' splendor. Meseret clapped her hands in pleasure. The princess should be happy arriving at her magnificent new home.

Arkamun returned to his chambers from an overnight tryst-filled with mad passionate sex and multiple women. He peeled off his clothing, scattering the pieces across the room; before he came to admire the reflection of his naked body in front of his mirror. Chiseled like a god, hung like a horse, and muscular like a Spartan soldier, he stared at himself marveling all of his attributes the women he encountered seemed to enjoy.

I would be a prize to any woman.

He continued to gaze at his reflection.

"Wash me thoroughly," he commanded to the maidens waiting in opposite corners of the room. The women nodded in acknowledgment, meeting him where he stood, sponging his body with scented oils and goat's milk.

Arkamun grinned devilishly as he rocked his face from side to side. He made his body into a steeple. If his father were living and saw how he had changed, he would never be able to call him weak again, nor strike him with the golden rod he used to carry and beat him with.

Arkamun dressed in a robe and went to his mother's chamber room. He wanted to see her before the girl was due to arrive. He entered her room without knocking; the curtains still were drawn. His eyes adjusted to the darkness and made out the outline of his mother's silhouette still underneath the covers as she slept. He removed his robe, kicked off his slippers, and slid his nude body in the bed against hers.

Arkamun wrapped his arms around Meseret's waist pressing his body against her bare buttocks. He was immediately aroused. She stirred; opened her eyes, and was woken by the weight of a body resting against her. She blinked her eyes a few times to adjust to the dim light before she flipped over and saw her son lying there.

"What are you doing in here, Arkamun?" she questioned wrapping the sheets around her bare body.

"I was coming to give you a wake-up call, Mother," Arkamun said, smiling.

"A wake-up call was not warranted, Arkamun. You need to leave," she demanded, nudging his body away from her. Pained, Arkamun retreated from the bed, sliding his feet into his slippers.

"You have never asked me to leave before, Mother. So many times, we have embraced each other, you allowing me inside of you. You know I love you so deeply. Why should I now have to leave your side?"

Before Meseret could answer, the trumpets sounded in the courtyard, and the clatter of horse hoofs on the pavement came to a halt. Princess Eleni had arrived at the white castle.

"Your bride is here, Arkamun. You should take more interest in her than me. Leave me, and prepare yourself for your future wife."

Arkamun came to the bedside and leaned over, kissing Meseret passionately on the lips. He wanted so badly to take her right then in that moment, but obeyed her command to leave her chambers. He could not see his bride until he calmed himself. His mother had made his cock so hard he had no choice but to return to his chambers to release the pressure he felt building.

Arkamun stretched out on his bed, cock in hand. He stroked his member up and down, pleasuring himself with each movement. He thought of his mother, and how he wanted her again. It had been so long since they embraced; he believed she turned him away because of another. But who? What man could have found his way into his mother's arms?

She will be mine again, nor will she belong to another.

Arkamun thought of his sexual relationship with his mother until he climaxed, shooting a load into his hand. Relieved, he wiped the cum from his hand on his sheets. He peered out the window in the high tower in time to see his bride enter the castle. He was curious about her and sought answers to the questions burning inside of him.

The welcoming party led Eleni and her parents to the entrance of the castle. "Welcome to Eskendar Castle," they said, kneeling. Hillina, the same woman Eleni had seen in her homeland, joined the welcoming party at the castles entrance. She greeted everyone and informed them she would take them to their rooms.

Hillina led Eleni and her parents up the back staircase where they climbed the three flights of grand stairs. As they approached her parents' room, the first off the back staircase, Eleni noticed a tall, muscular dark skinned man in armor standing at the corner of the hall. He stood still, his eyes meeting her mother's. Eleni turned and looked at her mother's face, which was red from her blushing.

Had they met before? Who was this mysterious man who stared at her mother?

Hillina escorted Eleni's parents into the room, requested they dress for dinner and informed them a servant would be by to escort them to the hall. Eleni met eyes with her mother one final time before Hillina grabbed Eleni's hand, leading her to another chamber room door.

"This will be your room, my dear."

Eleni opened the heavy door and gasped at the panoramic view of the sea. The solid marble bed against the wall was befitting for a queen. Sheer gold and amethyst drapes hung from all the bed posts. A gold stool sat off to the right, for Eleni's small frame to ease herself into the massive bed. Eleni traced her hands over the gold and amethyst embroidered quilt.

"This is all mine?"

"Yes, it is yours, my girl, and it belongs to your king as well, whenever he wants to visit you here."

"Are there other chamber rooms I will have access? Eleni inquired, furrowing her eyebrows.

"There is only one other chamber room you will obtain access to; it is the place you will spend most nights with your husband. You will come here only if you displease King Arkamun after you are married. I caution you not to displease this king."

She strolled to the armoire in the corner of the room to retrieve an evening gown for Eleni.

"You will wear this to dinner tonight, Eleni," she said, waving the gown at Eleni.

Eleni took the dress from her hands. Stepping in front of the mirror, she held the dress up against her body and smiled.

"It's beautiful! I have never had anything like this at my disposal."

"Good! You will always possess the finest gowns; you must always do your part and be presentable as queen. Now, your servant girl will be in to bathe you. I should inform you, that you will not get a glimpse of the king tonight. You will make his acquaintance tomorrow at your wedding. However, I will tell you, he likes to play games and could be watching you without your knowing. So give him what he wants, please him, however, he may ask, and you shall lead a happy and promising life here."

Eleni hugged Hillina tightly. "Thank you! I will do my best." Hillina was taken aback by the embrace and released Eleni immediately. "Make sure you do." She patted Eleni on the shoulder and left the room.

Eleni sat down on the bed and studied her surroundings further.

This place... I wonder if I can truly be happy here? I still will never forgive them for sending me here; I do not care how beautiful this place is. This was not supposed to be my life.

She crossed to the window and rested her elbows against the window sill. She glanced out at the vast body of water.

While Eleni was in deep reflection, a knocking came from the chamber room door.

"Who is there?"

"Princess, I am your servant."

"Enter please."

The door swung open and in walked a young girl who could not be more than Eleni's seventeen years of age. She was a slim girl with smooth cocoa skin, long straight raven hair wrapped tightly in two buns on the sides of her head, perky breasts, almond shaped dark brown eyes and full lips. Eleni thought she was a charming girl.

"My name is Ayantu; I am to serve you, Princess Eleni."

"It is nice to meet you."

"I'm happy to meet you as well Princess Eleni. You are going to be the new queen!" Ayantu said excitedly. "I am grateful and honored to serve you."

"Ayantu, I am a girl who was brought here, not by my wishes, but my parents. I am doing as I was told. Tell me, what do you know of this king, Ayantu?" She leaned back on the bed watching as Ayantu poured steaming water into her bath.

"Well... He is handsome, muscular, women love him, and he loves them." Ayantu had hesitated for a moment before she continued.

"He is kind, rich, and of high stature; you will be petite under him."

So he is tall... Will I like him, however? Is he a good man?"

"He is a king, Princess Eleni, and kings can be good and bad. Be careful because he scrutinizes everything." Ayantu knelt on the rug in front of the tub, poured dry herbs and a fragrance oil into the water, and swirled them around with her hand.

"Time for your bath, princess," Ayantu announced, standing to assist Eleni with undressing. Ayantu unbuttoned Eleni's dress, unlaced her corset and tossed it over on the water basin on the side of the tub. She assisted with removing the rest of her gown. Eleni slipped her dress off down over her knees, onto the floor. Ayantu picked the worn and sweaty dress from the floor and put it into her basket for washing. Taking Eleni's hand, she assisted her with stepping into the deep tub. Sitting down, Eleni lowered herself into the warm bath.

Out the corner of her eye, Eleni caught Ayantu gazing at her body as she helped her into the tub. She made out Ayantu's hard nipples asking for attention as they poked through the simple green dress she wore. Eleni ignored Ayantu's glances and body language and submerged herself deeper into the water. Scents filled the air moving through her nostrils. Many smells encompassing the room were unfamiliar to her.

Eleni swished her hands around in the water, the oils from the bath beading on her skin. "What did you add to this water, Ayantu?"

"Lavender oil and other herbs which will nourish your skin," she acknowledged, pouring more oil in the tub above Eleni's skin. Eleni caught sight of Ayantu gazing at her again. She noticed her hand slowed in the water above her skin.

"I think that is enough oil, Ayantu, thank you."

Ayantu blushed and removed her hands from the water. "The king will always want to smell a fragrance on your skin, so you must make sure to use oils and herbs daily."

Eleni settled into the tub, her raven curls floating on top of the water.

"I will do anything the King would like for me to do, as long as it results in him wanting to be in my presence. The oils and herbs you used in my bath smell pleasant. With your assistance, I will use them daily. You will show me how, won't you?"

"Of course, Princess, anything you need I am at your service." Ayantu got up on her feet. "You go ahead and relax for a while; I will come and check on you shortly."

Eleni smiled in agreement and taking a deep breath she closed her eyes.

Everything will be all right.

Eleni relaxed and rested her head on the side of the tub. Her eyes fell heavy as she drifted off to sleep.

Arkamun stepped out of the shadows and into the bath chamber where Eleni rested. Entranced by her beauty, he held a strand of her raven hair to his nose. She had the aroma of fresh roses and lemons. Her breasts were the perfect size with dark pink nipples that poked through the bubbles in the tub. Arkamun's cock jolted in his pants as he ran his hand through the water tracing up her thigh. Skin as smooth as silk, she was the perfect choice for his bride. He would break her if she did not become his perfect queen.

The chamber door bolted open, and Arkamun moved back into the shadows of the darkness. It was Ayantu coming to get Eleni out of her bath.

"Princess, wake up, it is time to get you dressed, Milady," Ayantu insisted, shaking Eleni from her slumber.

Eleni yawned and opened her eyes. "I did not realize I have fallen asleep, were you in here with me the entire time?"

"No Princess, as I said before, I was going to come back and check on you. Why do you ask?"

"I could have sworn someone was in here with me. Even though I slept, it did not feel like I was alone."

"You are overly tired from your journey, princess. I can assure you; you were alone."

Eleni slowly released a deep breath, stepped out the bath and dried her skin. She paused as she sensed someone in the corner of the room watching her. She whirled around, but there was no one there.

She closed her eyes, remembering what Hillina said to her: She would not meet King Arkamun that night, but he would watch her every move.

I can feel the king looking at me.

Eleni continued to get dressed. Ayantu brushed her hair until it dried down her back, her raven curls bouncing into place. She put on a long silver gown with crystals sewn into the sleeves, which draped over her shoulders. A crystal headpiece with a single crystal jewel rested on her forehead and long diamond earrings dangled on the lobes of her ears. Eye color, Rouge, and a lip tint adorned Eleni's face; she was bare-faced before coming to Arkamun's kingdom. Eleni could not recognize the woman who stared back at her in the mirror. She clutched Ayantu's arm for support as she held back her tears.

"Eleni..." Hillina's voice called out from behind the door. "Eleni, it is time for you to head down for dinner." Hillina knocked on the chamber room door.

Eleni thanked Ayantu, inhaled deeply and stepped out into the hall.

"You are stunning," Hillina gushed, clutching Eleni's hand as she led her down the long hallway to the dining room.

"Thank you," Eleni spoke in a quiet voice, avoiding eye contact with Hillina and scratched at the sleeves of her gown.

"What is wrong with you, girl?"

"I am nervous about all of this; I hope I am pleasing in the sight of the king," Eleni closed her eyes briefly, taking another deep breath.

"He will love you. However, you will not be seeing him this evening. You have nothing to worry about; you are having dinner with your parents and Arkamun's mother tonight. You need to stop acting so flighty; you will rip your gown pulling on your sleeves as you are."

Eleni calmed herself by breathing deeply. "Arkamun's mother?"

"Yes. You are aware, his father died. Arkamun is the heir and newly crowned king. His mother, Queen Meseret, is alive and well, and who you will be meeting tonight, my dear. So be on your best behavior, my child. You do not want to upset Queen Meseret."

"Yes, ma'am, I will be."

Eleni and Hillina continued down the corridor through the throne room to the dinner hall. Eleni's hands became sweaty, and she rubbed them on the front of her dress trying to calm her nerves as she approached the dining room. She glanced up and noticed the star constellations painted on the ceiling.

"I wish I were able to fly away from here," Eleni mumbled under her breath.

With what she heard about the king, she wondered if everything would turn out all right. As they approached the dinner hall entrance, the laughter of her parents and of another woman which she assumed was the queen filled the air. As Eleni and Hillina narrowed their distance to the hall, Eleni stiffened. Were those footsteps approaching behind her? She circled to glimpse who was behind her, but the hall was quiet except for herself and Hillina.

Arkamun?

Eleni and Hillina approached the doorway and stopped.

"I must announce you now Eleni; wait here until I call for you," Hillina said, leaving Eleni alone in the dim, candle-lit hall.

"Excuse me, my queen; the princess is here. May I now introduce to you, your future queen and daughter, Princess Eleni!"

Eleni, distracted by the sounds coming from behind her, ignored her name being called. She heard the footsteps again and saw a shadow move across the hall, tempting her to follow where it moved.

"I now introduce Princess Eleni!" Hillina announced once again.

Eleni wrinkled her nose and peered down the hall once more. The shadow she believed she saw was gone, and footsteps had quieted.

I must be dreaming.

Eleni shook her head, parted her lips slightly, and proceeded back to the dining hall.

"I apologize for my delay, but I was a little distracted. Footsteps were coming from down the hall."

Eleni drew her gown up over her knees and kneeled in front of Queen Meseret

"Great Queen, I am sorry for my delay. I hope you are not upset with me."

Hillina lumbered over to where Eleni kneeled in front of the queen and yanked her up from behind by her hair. "What are you doing, girl! You are a princess; you do not kneel!" Hillina snatched Eleni's arm and dug her nails into the side. "Get up off this floor and sit in the chair over there!"

The room went silent. Her parents sat there staring at her dumbfounded, their blank faces draining of color.

Queen Meseret shoved her chair out from the table and slapped Hillina across the face. "Hillina! How dare you strike Eleni! She has done nothing wrong, but tried to apologize for her distraction, which I am sure it was none other than my son playing games with her." Queen Meseret picked up Eleni's arm and held it in her hand. Blood oozed from the spots where Hillina's nails had sunk into her skin. Queen Meseret lifted Eleni's face with her finger to her eye level.

Eleni could see Queen Meseret's looks rivaled her mother's. Her tightly woven braids were worn loosely and adorned with different shades of jewel-tone stones. Her high cheek- bones were lightly colored with a pink tint, and a dark red painted her full lips. Her green eyes fastened onto Eleni's, calming her nerves.

"You are a beautiful girl, Eleni, and I am sure you will be an even better daughter to me. I always wanted a girl. Please forgive Hillina for her ignorance; sometimes her age gets the best of her." Queen Meseret wrapped her other arm around Eleni's waist and escorted her back to the table.

Eleni glanced at Hillina, who glared at her with displeasure. Eleni knew she had upset her, and promised herself she would make amends as quickly as she could. She did not mean to offend the old woman nor irritate her.

"Sit next to me my daughter and let me clean those wounds for you," Meseret beckoned. She nudged a chair out from under the table for Eleni to sit. Meseret signaled the servant in the corner and asked for water and bandages to wrap Eleni's arm.

"I am sorry," Eleni said, out of breath and with tears forming in her eyes. "I was trying to say I was sorry for being a little distracted and a little late to dinner."

"My daughter. You do not have to apologize. You did not know, and I am sure the customs in your kingdom are different. Your parents did not know how to advise you." Meseret sent a glare of distaste across to Eleni's parents.

Eleni reclined back in her chair as the queen pushed back the sleeves on her royal blue gown and tended to her arm. The queen's words reassured her, she was in no trouble.

Queen Meseret finished bandaging Eleni's arm and leaned in closer, whispering in a low voice in Eleni's ear. "Come closer to me, daughter; I want to share something with you."

Eleni liked that Queen Meseret called her daughter; it was refreshing to know she accepted her as her daughter and approved of her marriage to her son, Arkamun. Eleni leaned forward so she could understand the queens low tone. She murmured to Eleni in a quiet but cautious voice.

"I am sure those noises you heard were from none other than my son. I am quite sure he has been following you since you arrived here. He has always been very mischievous and a little devilish. Witnessing these events tonight has led me to warn you to be careful of him. You are very young, and even though you are a beauty he will love, I can see you can be very naive as well. Arkamun can love you one moment and despise you the next.

You must keep him happy, Eleni or things will turn for you, remember my words."

Eleni sat up straight in her chair and recalled the conversation she had with the Prophet in her kingdom. A chill shot down her back as she remembered his words of what would happen to her.

Yes, my queen; I will remember, and I will do my best to keep him happy."

Eleni shifted her body forward and eyed her parents across the table. She could tell her mother was uncomfortable. She still had not confronted her mother about the man she saw earlier in the afternoon.

"Is dinner ready to be served now? I am starved," Queen Abrihet remarked.

King Dabir shifted in his seat, studying Queen's Meseret's mannerisms from across the table. "Queen Meseret, your kingdom is lovely, and we thank you for your hospitality and your generosity. I apologize for my daughter's behavior; she knows who she is, and I will never understand her reasoning. However, I assure you she will perform well in all aspects required."

"I am sure she will carry out her duties appropriately," Queen Meseret smiled at Eleni. She then clapped her hands twice.

"Dinner will be served now."

The servants scurried about the room bringing in the main courses. Eleni drowned out the conversation between her parents and Queen Meseret and sat in silence as the meal was laid out in front of her. She thought about all of the warnings she had received and her stomach clenched. She took five bites of food from her plate as bile rose in her throat.

"I need to be excused," she groaned.

"Daughter, are you not well? "Queen Meseret asked.

"No...I am not feeling well, my queen, and I need to lie down. Tomorrow is a big day; please forgive me," She scraped the chair away from the table, and bolted out of the room into the hallway. The ceiling spun as Eleni flew back to her room and slammed the door behind her. She stumbled to the bed and laid down, gazing out the large window to the sea. In an instant, the cool breeze from the water calmed her. As her nausea subsided, she rolled off the bed towards the window, admiring the stars and the moon. The full moon hovered above the glistening water below.

I am so alone here. I wish I could return home.

She looked out of the window once again. Eleni loosened the ties on her dress and without warning, felt the touch of hands on her back.

"Ayantu! I did not hear you come in."

Eleni whirled around to see who was there. There was nothing but shadows dancing upon the walls in the night. She exhaled and pivoted back around towards the window, continuing to unlace her gown. She heard another movement in the room; the door creaked open and slammed closed behind her. Someone had been in her room, but now she was alone bathed in moonlight.

"Arkamun?" she called out, but there was no response. "Ayantu?" Once again, there was no answer. What was happening in this castle? Eleni's hands trembled as she continued to undress and fastened the night clothes laid out for her around her shoulders. She climbed into bed and gathered the covers up to her neck.

She thought of the day's events and wondered if it had been Arkamun who had tried to undo the laces on the back of her dress and watched her bathe. How would their wedding night be? Would she be pleasing to him? Being intimate with a man of his stature made her legs muscles tighten. She had never been touched by a man. She silently prayed over and over as she dozed off that he would be kind and gentle with her, and she, in return, would be a pleasing wife to him.

But more so, she prayed that the prophet's words were not true.

3 Eskendar Castle

The level of tension in the dining hall rose after Eleni's abrupt exit. Abrihet clutched Dabir's arm in embarrassment from her daughter's actions. Hillina stood in the corner of the room gawking at Eleni's parents. The servants had scattered from the dining hall before Queen Meseret responded.

Abrihet released Dabir's arm from her grip and focused her attention on Meseret; her facial expression was one of concern for Eleni. "Queen Meseret, I am so sorry for Eleni's abrupt exit, she is nervous about the wedding. Perhaps I should check on her."

"Abrihet, I hope you do not mind me calling you Abrihet," Meseret said warmly. "I agree. I believe tonight was a bit much for Eleni; she will be fine after some rest. You should check on your daughter to make sure she's settled. Tomorrow is going to be a big day for her. Go now; we will meet again tomorrow."

Queen Abrihet smiled nervously, acknowledged her husband and Queen Meseret, and made her way out of the dining hall. She wanted to find her daughter so she could explain who the man was before Eleni informed her father. Through the castle she went, the dim light shining on her pale pink gown. As she made her way to her daughter's room, a hand reached out and touched her on the shoulder.

A stark chill ran down her spine as she reeled around in the direction of the hand. It was the man she had kissed her in the woods of her kingdom: the man with whom she met eyes with when she arrived at the castle. He was standing in front of her smiling broadly. Abrihet smiled back at him, blushing slightly.

"What are you doing? If my husband catches us, it will be death for both of us."

"I had to make your acquaintance again, to speak with you again. You captured my attention that night in your homeland, Milady."

"You never exactly made your introduction to me. Tell me, sir, what is your name? You did not reveal it to me at our previous encounter."

"I am Berhanua, guardsman to King Arkamun."

"Well, guardsman, Berhanua, show me how I captured your attention that night in the woods."

Berhanua seized Abrihet's wrists, reeling her into a kiss. Excited by his touch, she allowed him to slip his tongue deep into her mouth.

"I want to feel you, Milady," Berhanua offered breaking the embrace. "Will you allow me the pleasure of exploring your body?"

"We should not be doing this," Abrihet panted, stepping away from him. "I was on my way to check on my daughter. I need to make sure she is okay."

"Your daughter is fine. The maid reported she was asleep for the evening. There is no reason to disturb her. I promise she is well cared for."

Abrihet clasped her hands to her chest, nodded then spun around in the opposite direction, saying nothing.

"Where do you think you are going?" Berhanua questioned, stepping on the train of Abrihet's gown.

"Release my dress. I am going to find my husband and the other queen."

"No, you are not, you are going to come to me." Berhanua tugged on her gown until he was able to spin her around and kiss her again.

Abrihet was smitten; she would not turn down any other offers he made. "All right, all right... I will come with you; you've won."

Berhanua took Abrihet's hand, leading her out into the fading daylight sky. The salt ocean breeze engulfed them both as he escorted her to the stone staircase meandering down to the beach. Abrihet surveyed the scenery around her. Over the side of the stairs, the waves below crashed gently on the shore. The sky above them radiated purple and pink streaks as the sun set beneath the clouds.

Berhanua caressed Abrihet's back while she glowered out at the sea. He ran his hands up her back and placed his warm lips against the nape of her slim neck. Abrihet exhaled as he touched her. Caressing her face, he guided her up to his mouth. She parted her mouth permitting him to savor her tongue once more.

Their bodies touched, and Berhanua pressed Abrihet against the stone wall. Abrihet felt her knees give way, and he braced her with his hands, kissing her even deeper. She loved how forceful but gentle he was with her. Abrihet's body tingled. Her nipples tightened to pebble hardness, poking through her gown.

"Such beauty, let me see you." Berhanua slipped the sleeves of Abrihet's gown from her shoulders, exposing her breasts. He drew the velvet peaks into his mouth, savoring her sweet chocolate temples of smooth flesh.

Abrihet moved her hands down Berhanua's body. She felt the ripples of the muscles in his chest, the firmness of his thighs, the roundness of his buttocks and rested on the hardness of his arousal.

"You are such a pleasure, sweet queen; I want to explore much more."

"Yes, explore more, you can explore anything you want," Abrihet panted, engulfing Berhanua again.

Berhanua lifted her pale gown over her thighs as he wrapped her legs around his waist and braced her against the wall. His swollen staff emerged from the opening in his breeches. He played with the curly mound of tawny hair between Abrihet's thighs, and when she was ready, his hot flesh slid inside of her, joining his body to hers. Abrihet arched forward to meet his next powerful thrust, releasing ragged gasps between each. Sweat poured off their bodies until he groaned in blissful agony, releasing his burning hot seed into her. Abrihet felt an explosion of ecstasy, a release she had not felt in ages.

Abrihet opened her eyes and acclimated to her surroundings. The temperature had dropped and the evening sky had turned dark. Abrihet smiled at Berhanua as they straightened their clothing. She noticed a figure not far off in the distance. It was Queen Meseret standing in the courtyard glaring, not a hundred yards away.

"Berhanua, Queen Meseret has seen us."

Berhanua swiveled around, meeting eyes with his other lover. Queen Meseret broke her angry stare and turned away from them both.

"We must leave; I need to get you back to your chambers, my queen."

Abrihet brushed the wrinkles out of her gown and followed Berhanua back to the castle.

"Do you believe she watched us the entire time?"

"Well, Milady, I think by the look on her face answers that question."

"You are right; I will have to speak to her about what happened."

"You will do no such thing. It would behoove you to leave immediately after the wedding tomorrow. I know Queen Meseret; she will not be pleased with outsiders sleeping with her guards."

"Are you sure that is the reason? Her expression reflected she was not pleased with your sleeping with me."

Berhanua glanced away, unable to meet Abrihet's eyes. She knew then she was right, the man she was intimate with belonged to Queen Meseret. Up the path they went in silence, sharing glances and no words. They came to the hall that led up to Abrihet's chamber and stopped. Berhanua attempted to kiss her again, but this time, she turned her head.

"I thought I was going to have an evening to remember filled with enjoyment; I hoped to have been your only one. But to find you have the attention of the other queen does nothing but sour my stomach."

"Please, Abrihet, let me explain. Yes, I am Meseret's lover, but I felt something when I met you in your kingdom. I still feel something for you in this moment. There can be no harm, in caring for you both."

"The damage in your caring for both of us has driven me to plead with the Queen not to turn my daughter away. I shall not see you again nor speak of this night. I hope you find what you are looking for, Berhanua."

Abrihet left Berhanua standing in the hall and sought out Queen Meseret. She did not have to look far before she found her. "Queen Meseret, may I have a word with you?"

Queen Meseret paused, before swirling around to face Abrihet. "What I can I do for you, Queen?"

Abrihet hesitated before continuing. "I wanted to apologize for what you witnessed this evening between your guardsman and myself."

"What do you believe I saw Abrihet, other than you engaged in sexual exploits with someone other than your husband?"

"I am sorry that you had to observe anything at all. Berhanua never explained to me that you and he were lovers until we saw you."

"There is nothing more than can be said. I will make this suggestion to you, Abrihet. After your daughter's wedding, you will leave my kingdom, or I might have to inform your husband of your tryst with Berhanua. I am certain he would slit your throat if he were to find out you were with another man."

Abrihet rubbed her neck and nodded in acknowledgment. She would depart with her husband after the wedding. No other words were spoken between the two women. Abrihet returned to her chamber where she found her husband asleep. She undressed quietly and slipped underneath the covers, never waking him, and laid quiet until she eventually drifted off thinking about her encounter with Berhanua.

Meseret was bothered by what she had witnessed earlier in the evening. She had no right to be jealous of Queen Abrihet, but she could not stop the scenario from replaying in her mind. There was only one person that could remove the thoughts from her subconscious. Her son. She had refused him that morning, but if she were to sneak into his room and get into bed with him as he had done earlier, he would not refuse her.

Berhanua stood off in the wings listening to the conversation unfold between Meseret and Abrihet. Once the women parted ways, he continued to follow Meseret. He hoped he would have a moment to explain himself. She stopped in front of Arkamun's door, knocked then entered when there was no answer. Berhanua crossed the hall and cracked the door quietly to overhear the conversation in the room.

The room was quiet. He could see Meseret's silhouette illuminated by the candles staggered around the chamber. She slipped her robe off, baring her naked body, and slid in the bed with her son. Arkamun turned over and pulled his mother into a passionate embrace, and they kissed. Berhanua made a choking noise; bile rose in his throat. He turned his eyes away from the scene before him. He had seen enough and closed the door retreating to his chambers, shaking his head and murmuring under his breath. He now knew who Meseret's other lover was; it was her son.

Eleni woke to the morning sun beaming through the window in her room. Her eyes fluttered open adjusting to the brightness around her. She threw the covers off herself, bouncing her knee against the mattress. Moving to the side of the bed Eleni gulped down the water left in the glass on the table.

Today is the day I marry a man I have never met, let alone love. I wish I could run away from here. Escape and go home.

A knock on Eleni's chamber room door distracted her from her negative feelings. It was Ayantu who had come to help Eleni bathe and dress for the wedding.

"Good Morning, Princess, let's get you dressed and ready for your big day."

"Oh if we must." Eleni sighed loudly as she trudged over to the vanity where Ayantu was waiting to brush her hair.

"Is something wrong, Eleni?"

"I am not sure about this wedding or this marriage to Arkamun." Eleni plopped down on the chair cushion.

"What is not to be sure of? You are marrying a king, a handsome, rich one. Yes, he might flirt a bit with other women, but I believe he will be good to you. You are a beautiful girl," Ayantu replied softly.

Eleni could feel her hand slowly brush by her shoulder; it seemed to linger at the nape of her neck. She shrugged her shoulders and shifted in her chair. Ayantu's hand returned to work on her hair.

"I appreciate the compliment, Ayantu; you are a beautiful girl yourself."

Eleni watched Ayantu's movements in the mirror. She brushed Eleni's raven hair into an elegant up-do, full of twists, braids, and curls. Ayantu placed gold jewels throughout her hair that sparkled off the walls. Eleni could only think about the events of the night before. She still wondered whose hands had been on her back last night, if it was Arkamun and if it was him, why had he chose not to make himself known?

"Can I ask you a question, Ayantu? Did you come into my chambers last night to undo my gown?"

"No, Eleni, I did not. It sounds as if Arkamun paid you a visit. Hillina did say that could happen."

"I believe you could be right. I thought it could have been him; I just wanted to be sure."

"Well, now you have your answer. Let's finish getting you dressed. Now the veil."

Ayantu clipped the gold encrusted veil onto the back of Eleni's head. Just as she stepped into her gown and was laced up, Eleni could hear her mother in the hall outside her chamber room speaking with the guard. Eleni thanked Ayantu for her help and dismissed her before her mother entered.

Queen Abrihet hurried across the room, pulling Eleni into an embrace before she rubbed her hand down Eleni's cheek. Eleni swatted her mother's hand away from her face and veered around back in front of the mirror. She smoothed her gown as she frowned at her reflection.

"I know this is something you do not desire to do Eleni, but you are doing what is right for our kingdom."

Eleni paused from placing the other earring in her ear, focusing on her mother through the mirror. "Mother, at this moment there is nothing you can say to appease me. You sold me for jewels and land. I told you I would do what was required to secure our home, and for you and Father. I will bear sons for this king, and submit to his every need and command as you asked. Instead of telling me what I am doing is right for the kingdom, how about you explain the guard you locked eyes within the hall when we arrived."

Abrihet's face reddened and, she cleared her throat before she responded. "Eleni, there is no need to worry about the guard. He was one of the men that came to our homeland the day you were betrothed to Arkamun."

"Is that truly the entire story, Mother? The way you two looked at each other, it seemed as if there was something more."

Eleni noticed her mother would not make eye contact with her, and she fiddled with the sleeves of her gown. She could tell her mother was lying. There was more to the story, and she wanted to know what she was hiding. "Mother, I know you are not telling me everything. You need to tell me what is going on."

"Eleni, there is nothing else to say. I only wanted to tell you I love you, and you are beautiful. I hope you find the joy you seek here in your new home. You must, however, produce an heir soon, to keep your place as queen and to ensure your family is happy. I expect these things to happen to keep us all safe and happy." She kissed Eleni on the forehead and left her standing there in a disgusted silence.

Eleni glanced at her reflection one last time.

I hope I please this king.

She inspected every aspect of her appearance. Ayantu worked wonders. She no longer looked like a young girl; the reflection in the mirror was one of a young woman in an unfamiliar veil and bridal gown. She had to admit that the gown was beautiful and loved the way the silk fabric of felt against her skin. If it was Arkamun who indeed saw her last night, she wanted him to be pleased with their first encounter as king and queen, husband and wife.

"It is time, Eleni. You look marvelous." Hillina had appeared in the doorway. "Do not forget what I told you about making Arkamun happy. An heir will be required by you as soon as possible."

"I have not forgotten what you said. Between you and my mother reminding me, I know what I am supposed to do." Eleni pinched her lips together.

"Good! Make sure you do!" Hillina picked up the back of Eleni's dress and train. "Let us go!"

When they reached the door to the throne room, Eleni closed her eyes and took a calming breath. Hillina fanned her gown out behind her. A gold dress accentuated the curves of Eleni's body. Hillina primped the veil covering her eyes and face, and it would only be lifted when it was announced she had become Arkamun's wife. Eleni wished she could hide behind it forever.

The door opened to the throne room. Eleni entered alone, inching down the aisle, the lavender and pink rose bouquet she carried made her hands sweat. She glanced to the left and right through her veil and saw many blank expressions from the people of the court, as they gazed upon her.

Not far up the aisle Arkamun stood. His visage handsome, dashing and tall. The structure of a man who had been crafted by the Creator's hands, with muscles protruding from all over his body. He had a bald head and a radiant smile that caught her attention as she gazed through her veil.

Perhaps this will be a grand occasion. He is handsome and maybe I could learn to love him.

She squared her shoulders as she reached the end of the aisle. Arkamun, breaking with tradition, lifted the veil off her face and smiled again.

"You are beautiful."

Eleni felt faint looking at him. His smile warmed her on the inside. For the first time since coming to the white castle, she felt comfort and believed that their marriage would be a good one, and perhaps she would indeed be happy.

Congratulations and best wishes abounded from the court. Jesters juggled fruit and entertained the guests. Large trays with stuffed boars sat on stone pedestals. Spirits flowed from crystal fountains, and the wedding cake was topped with fresh lavender, blowing through the air. The night was filled with music, dancing, drinking, and laughter.

Eleni eyed her parents having an enjoyable time, despite the stolen glances she noticed continuing between her mother and the guardsman. The dinner passed in a blur. Eleni found herself becoming tired and asked King Arkamun if she could be excused from the festivities.

"Allow me to escort you to our chambers, my queen."

He is so kind to escort me to our chambers.

Arkamun drew Eleni's hand in his and escorted her out their celebration. They went down the hall of the castle and up two flights of stairs before stopping at a door. Arkamun cracked the door ajar and gestured for Eleni to enter the room.

"These are our royal chambers, my queen. Come in."

Eleni stepped inside, closing the door behind them. Eleni's eyes flashed around the room; it was spectacular. She focused her attention on a golden elephant sitting on the table. Before she could ask a question about it, Arkamun clutched her arms and yanked her into him.

"You are mine now!" Arkamun snapped. His face darkened his earlier kindness disappearing.

She backed away. "What are you doing? Let me go!" she screamed.

"Do not waste your voice, my queen!" he said with a devilish calm. "No one will hear your screams, and even if they did, they would not dare intervene on your behalf."

Eleni tried to wrench away from Arkamun. He slapped her face which brought her to her knees. As blood dripped from her nose and bottom lip, she turned towards him with tears in her eyes. "Please stop! Please do not do this to me, my king!" she pleaded while kissing his feet.

Eleni was disgusted in being reduced to kissing his feet, but if she could convince him to stop it would be worth it. All the warnings everyone gave her did not prepare her for the man she kneeled in front of now. Arkamun jerked her small frame from the floor and ripped her dress from her body. He careened her into him again and shoved her up against the wall.

"There is nothing you can, do Eleni. You are my wife, my property, and I will have my way with you and do whatever I desire. If your tears and cries of pain please me, you will experience pain beyond your ability to comprehend." He said with an eerie and sinister calm.

He seized her bare buttocks, bending her over and speared her with perverse, violent, and repetitive thrusts. He ravaged her anus until she bled. She pleaded for him to stop, but the more intense she suffered, begged, and screamed, the more brutal and aroused he became. When he climaxed, he pulled himself off her and shoved her to the floor. "Clean yourself up and get back to our wedding celebration. We did get married after all."

He retrieved his clothing and left the room. Eleni sat in a pool of her blood still leaking from the orifices of her backside, nose, and mouth. She cried and gathered her clothing into a pile. How would she survive this horrific bondage? She would never be able to love, or live in peace or freedom. Her life would consist of repeated brutal rapes while having to pretend the sexual atrocities were non-existent.

Eleni pushed herself up on the floor and found her way to the tub so she could bathe. After drawing her bath, she stepped into the tub and sat down with caution. The water stung her in the places where she had been violated. She cried for her servants to aid her, but no one came to her side. If she did not hurry, Arkamun would return, and she would endure another hellacious rape. Eleni finished washing and fixed herself up as Arkamun commanded.

Eleni returned to the ball. She felt Arkamun's eyes on her as she entered the room. She was seated on the throne, where she watched her new husband flirt and touch women inappropriately. Her body continued to throb in the places where Arkamun had violated her. Ignoring the pain, she brandished a bright smile and did her duty pretending to be the happy wife. The celebration ended in the early hours. Eleni retired to her private chambers alone. After tending to the ravaged parts of her body, she sank into a restless slumber.

Eleni's parents departed Eskendar Castle the next morning. Despite her being angry at them for their actions, she still wished she had the opportunity to say goodbye. They abandoned her in a kingdom where she had no one for comfort.

The beatings and the rapes continued in the following weeks since Eleni's marriage ceremony to Arkamun. Her belly had swollen; her bleeding had ceased. She was informed that she was withchild. Eleni prayed the baby would be the answer to please Arkamun and stop the further beatings she would have to endure.

Not long her pregnancy was confirmed. Eleni sought out Arkamun to share the fantastic news. Eleni arrived at Arkamun's private chambers. She knocked three times before entering.

"Arkamun, are you in here?" Eleni called out, entering the room. She did not have to walk far before seeing her husband sitting on the chaise in the corner; a servant girl straddled on top of him riding his erect rod.

Eleni had heard the rumors of her husband with other women, but it was the first time she saw another woman with Arkamun. She noticed he was much gentler with the servant girl than he was with her. She felt like she was going to vomit and diverted her eyes from seeing anything further.

Arkamun gawked at Eleni furiously for being interrupted. "What do you want?" he screamed, pushing the girl off him. He treaded across the room to his wife. "I told you not to come here if I did not send for you."

Eleni took a step backward towards the door. Her eyes met his narrowing eyes that bored into her. "I thought I would share the news with you; we are having a baby. I was excited. I believed you would have wanted to know."

Arkamun smirked, jutting his chin. "I told you never to come here unless I summoned you. A baby indeed, we shall see."

Eleni tried to evade Arkamun's grasp, but he blocked her from moving with his mass.

Arkamun grasped Eleni by her neck and dragged her out into the hall. "Stay out of my chamber room and do as you are told," he hissed. Releasing his grasp, he flung her, sending her flying down the staircase.

Queen Meseret found Eleni bloodied at the bottom of the stairs. She called to the servants to have her taken to her chamber room. Bandaged and bruised, Eleni remained unconscious for a week. Slowly Eleni regained her strength and opened her eyes. Her thoughts raced while she tried to piece together what happened.

"You were in an accident," Queen Meseret muttered, taking Eleni's hand in hers, and squeezing it gently. Eleni tried to sit up in bed, an overwhelming amount of pain prevented her from doing so.

"Eleni, please relax. You should not be moving around; you need to rest."

Eleni looked down at her stomach. The swelling was gone. "The baby?" Eleni sobbed. "What happened to my baby?"

Queen Meseret stroked Eleni's forehead to relax her. "The baby is gone, Eleni. As I explained before, you were in an accident. You had a fall."

Eleni remembered what had happened. Why would Queen Meseret continue to overlook what her son continued to do to her? What was she trying to hide?

"I remember what happened, Your Majesty. It was Arkamun who pushed me down the stairs."

"I assumed as much, Eleni. I apologize for my son's actions and the harm that has come to you. Arkamun sometimes has a temper, and I believe that if you have patience with him, he will get better. I know we have not spent much time with each other since the marriage ceremony, but perhaps we can start?"

"Perhaps we can, Your Majesty."

"Please, daughter, call me Meseret or Mother Meseret. No need for such formalities. Now get some rest, you will be back on your feet in no time."

Eleni gave Queen Meseret a weak smile. Her conversation was somewhat comforting. Perhaps they would be able to build on their relationship, and she would have a person to confide in.

Life for Eleni continued in this manner for the next two years. Eleni had become pregnant several other times, all resulting in miscarriages by her husband's hands.

Despite her relationship with Queen Meseret improving and becoming a close one, Eleni often found herself wallowing in sadness, loneliness, and missing her family.

The only peace and solace she ever experienced was when she escaped the kingdom walls and be near the forest and the ocean as she did before in her kingdom.

If this is love and my destiny, life is not worth living.

Dusk set in over the calm waves brushing over the shore of the quiet lagoon. Eleni roamed along the beach, allowing herself to dig her toes into the warm sand beneath her feet. A quiet ocean breeze blew across her body and face, providing a serene sensation of peace and tranquility. She gazed up at the sky and saw the sun set beneath the clouds.

Why did she have to be the pawn used in her parents' scheme to secure their prestigious position in the kingdom? Why did she have to forgo her hopes and dreams? How much longer could she pretend to love a man who had never had her heart? How much longer could she pretend to embrace the responsibilities of being queen?

How many nights of abominable and savage intercourse could she endure by diving into the depths of her imagination and seeing her in the arms of a man she desired and dreamed of?

The solitude of the ocean, beach, and the breeze forced Eleni to confront the truth of her feelings she had ignored for years: she had never loved her husband the king, and she never wanted to be his queen.

As her sense of isolation consumed her thoughts and emotions, the visions of her publicly perceived happiness and her private internal misery bombarded her mind. Eleni took several steps leading her deeper into the water.

"Death is my only deliverance from such a meaningless existence," she whispered.

She gazed upon her royal garments becoming saturated, as she descended into the increasing depth of the ocean. The water covered Eleni's head as she submerged herself into the deep, calming waters.

Her soft raven curls untwined from the bun secured at the back of her head, floating around her in the water.

I am so drained of this existence; the afterlife will have to bring me joy and peace. Oh, beautiful ocean, you are where I belong; where I can seize the tranquility which has escaped me all these years. Please take me away to another world, another place: A place where love is ubiquitous and joy are everlasting.

Eleni closed her eyes as she descended into the depths of the dark waters of the ocean. As her lungs filled with water, she felt her body become light as life seemed to leave her body.

The current of the water carried her body farther out into the sea. Her near lifeless figure begins to disappear into the deep.

The journey is almost complete.

4 Westminster Castle

12 Years Later

Westminster Castle in England had found peace from famine and war. King Henry and Queen Anne welcomed three sons during those peaceful times. Keaton, the eldest son, was the first in line to become king. He found he hated living in the castle, the studying, and the constant supervision. His father's nagging left him with little time to blow off his responsibilities from the castle. When his middle brother David came to be, Keaton felt a bond immediately. David scrutinized his brother's every move, and whenever he could, he would follow Keaton everywhere.

As King Henry aged, his temperament hardened further towards his eldest son. Without a valid reason, King Henry had Keaton removed from the castle and thrown out into the wilderness with the expectation of making him into a man, and a stronger prince. Abandoned in the woods with no clothing and shelter, he walked for miles looking for a sign of life outside of his castle walls.

As many times as I have ridden my horse in the forest, you would think I would know how to get home.

Through the mud, dirt, the wind, and cold Keaton trotted until he reached a lush emerald green meadow. Tired and worn, he settled in underneath a large tree, wrapping himself in the thick, dense brush to keep warm.

The cracking sounds the animals made in the forest startled Keaton out of his sleep. He eventually dozed off, awakened the next morning by a rock hitting him on the head. Keaton shot up from sleeping, rubbing his temple in pain. He surveyed his surroundings and rested on a set of blue eyes looking at him from behind a large prickly bush.

"Come out, whoever you are. I can see you over there."

A young maiden appeared: pale with a small frame, beautiful cornflower hair resting at her waist, her turquoise blue eyes beaming at Keaton.

"Who are you? And why are you in my forest?" she inquired.

Keaton brushed the tall grass off his clothing before coming towards her.

"I am Prince Keaton. You are wrong in saying this is your forest. This is my forest, Milady."

"If you are the Prince, why are you out here so far from your castle?"

Keaton rubbed the temple of his head again. A significant bump started to form where the rock had hit him. Everything around him spun. He leaned his body up against a tree and closed his eyes to keep from passing out. He rubbed his eyes and focused back on the girl.

"My father, he put me out here. He said I needed to become a stronger, wiser prince before I become king."

"Well, Prince, I hope you can find your way home." The girl headed in the direction from where she came.

"Wait, please, you cannot leave me out here dizzy and bruised. I do not even know your name."

The girl twirled around and laughed. "Did you believe I would leave you out here to your efforts, especially since I injured you? Come along. And to answer your question, my name is Faerydae."

"Faerydae... I like it, very different."

Faerydae led Keaton through the forest until she came to her windmill home next to a creek bed. Beautiful red, purple and orange flowers surrounded the mill, and the mill's wheel carried water up and around before crashing on the rocks below.

"This place is beautiful, Faerydae. I never knew such places existed in my kingdom."

"Well, perhaps you should consider staying with us for a while. There are many things a prince could never see from the walls of the castle. Come in. Let me get you cleaned up before we enjoy a hot meal."

Keaton glanced around his surroundings again before entering the quaint cottage.

Once inside, the smell of a stew brewing on the fire drew his attention. Keaton relaxed on the floor after Faerydae attended to his bruise, and her mother finished preparing supper. He slapped his knees and smiled. He felt at home with the maiden girl and her family.

Keaton's experience with Faerydae and her family gave him perspective on how a family was supposed to live. Nothing was easy for him in the castle. He sensed his brothers would never know the feeling of being approved of or wanted by their father. His eyes were opened over the next weeks as Faerydae showed him how to harvest plants and herbs for medicines, how to heal the sick, and how to live as an everyday person in an everyday world. The more he experienced, the less he wanted to return home.

Keaton would not have a choice in the matter. As he and Faerydae were gathering mushrooms one evening, his father's men located him and returned him to the castle. Keaton marched into the palace demanding to speak to his father.

"Father, where are you?" He screamed as he continued through the halls. Keaton's mother lumbered towards him with her arms open.

"Son, you are home. I have missed you."

"Save it, Mother; I am sure you were in on Father sending me away from the beginning. Where is he? I was happy I was gone. I did not want to return. FATHER!"

King Henry strolled into the hall, meeting his son face -to-face. "What is the meaning of all this commotion? I am pleased to see you have been returned safely."

Keaton loosened the collar on his shirt, his face reddened. "I am only here because you sent your men after me. I was perfectly content where you left me, Father."

King Henry paced the hall, squeezing the redness out of his hands. "I sent you to the forest for a few days to clear your stubborn head. I see you have learned nothing."

"Don't you think you are rather hard on our son?" Queen Anne asked.

King Henry's eyes narrowed in on his wife. "If I wanted your thoughts on this situation, wife, I would have requested your opinion. I suggest you leave being the king to me."

Queen Anne quieted and said no more. She acknowledged her husband and grabbed her son's hand in comfort before leaving the two of them standing in the hall.

"There will be no further talk of you staying out in the forest with the maiden girl my men found in your presence. I suggest you return to your chambers, clean up and prepare for your lessons tomorrow. You have responsibilities to tend to."

Keaton rolled his shoulders before brushing past his father. Returning to his chambers, he kicked anything not bolted down across the room. Nightfall was not too far off. He would not stay where he was not truly wanted. He declined dinner, remaining out of the dining hall. The servants in the room quieted, and the candles' reflections dwindled under the door.

Keaton cracked his chamber room door to peer in the corridor; All was quiet. A clicking on his window distracted him, and he retreated into his room. He looked down from the two-story window to see Faerydae standing there.

"Help me up," she whispered, throwing a rope up to him.

Keaton secured the rope to his bedpost and pulled her up into the window. He embraced her deeply, brushing his lips upon hers.

"What are you doing here? If someone were to find you here..."

"I came to take you away with me. I did not want to say goodbye."

Faerydae rested her hand on his. She kissed him again, pressing her lips harder into his. Keaton slipped his arms around her waist and tasted the sweetness of her tongue and lips.

"I love you," he whispered to her. "I never want to be apart from you again."

"And you shall never be parted from me again."

Faerydae pushed Keaton down on the side of the bed, lowering herself on top of him. Her luscious, perky nipples protruded from the scant cotton shirt she was wearing.

Keaton had never felt the touch of a girl before, and his erection was throbbing in his pants begging for him to take her. She kissed him again, their tongues finding each other's sweet spot in the other's mouth.

"I want to give myself to you," she mused hypnotically.

Keaton ate the words she spoke like a meal. He pulled her breasts from her shirt, wetting her lush rosy nipples with his tongue.

Faerydae reached down and retrieved his swollen muscle from his pants. Easing herself down on his manhood, they glided together simultaneously until whispers exited shallowly from her lungs and he felt his seed spill inside of her.

"Now come away with me." She rearranged her clothing and smoothed her hair back into place.

Keaton straightened his clothing and prepared a bag. He tousled his room to appear as if it was a struggle. "Wait for me. I will return. I need to say goodbye to someone first."

"Hurry, we do not have much time."

Keaton nodded and hurried out to his brother's room.

"David!" he called out, opening the door in the next room slightly. His brother was covered up on the bed, sound asleep.

"David," he called again, closing in on the bed. Keaton knelt at his brother's side and stroked his hair.

"Little Prince, I wanted to say goodbye. You will make a great king one day."

David rolled on his side; his eye parted open slightly. "Keaton, where were you?" he whispered quietly.

"I was away. This is a dream. Go back to sleep."

Keaton rolled his brother away from him, tucking the blankets back over his shoulders. He memorized his brother's face as he moved out of the room. He scuttled down the corridor back to his chambers. Faerydae had left a note on his bed demanding money for his return.

"They shall believe it was a kidnapping," she hissed as she climbed down the window.

Keaton grabbed his bag, cast one final glance around his room, and disappeared into the night.

Years passed and the rumors of what happened to Keaton faded. King Henry shifted his focus on his middle son David, who grew and prospered as a prince. Keaton never strayed too far from the kingdom. He loved his brother and regularly checked in on him from the outskirts of the palace.

Keaton left his name behind, becoming Jasper, and married Faerydae. They founded a tavern in one of the distant villages of the kingdom and built a prosperous business and life for themselves. A child was born soon after, a son named Taner. All Jasper asked for had come true and he found happiness for a time.

Upon meeting Faerydae, Jasper knew she was different, and her ability to cure ailments and call on spiritual creatures was part of the mystique that drew him to her. But when unfriendly peasants found her pouring milk into the dirt or chanting up at the moon on different evenings, they believed her songs and practices to be evil. They alerted King Henry of her and others they believed to be practicing witchcraft.

King Henry wasted no time in taking action against Faerydae and other peasants accused of these evil practices. He enacted an order to have all those accused of witchcraft presented to him at court for a trial. If those accused were found guilty, they would be burned alive at the stake or hung.

The order spread like wildfire throughout the court, and many fled England for fear of prosecution by the King. Guards entered nearby villages and dragged innocent peasant women to the castle to be prosecuted. As word of the executions and trials made its way through Jasper's village, he pleaded for Faerydae to take Taner away out of the village. She refused his warning and remained in the community, working in the tavern.

All Jasper had feared came to pass. As he returned from his home from spying on his brother David, he observed women ripped from their husband's arms; body's scattered throughout the dirt road, run over by horse and carriage. Bodies burned beyond recognition burst out of nearby structures as smoke billowed up into the cloudless sky.

The remaining villagers were either injured or too old to flee. Jasper sprang into action, jumping off his horse to aid one of the peasant women who was attending to the injured.

"I'm here to help you, Maggie." Jasper coughed through the smoke.

"Jasper, I am happy to see that you are alive. I can take care of the injured. You need to get to your wife." She pointed in the direction of his tavern. "Do not worry about us; we will be okay. Help your wife; she needs you."

"What do you mean, Maggie? What happened here? What happened to Faerydae?"

"The mob of soldiers arrived, Jasper, I heard screams coming from the direction of the tavern. I was unable to get there in time. You need to go and find your wife."

Jasper touched Maggie on the shoulder advancing down the smoky path towards his tavern. He saw no one in sight; the surroundings were quiet. The tavern was in shambles. Table and chairs were thrown all over the place. The pot over the fire was turned on its side. The curtains Faerydae hand stitched were torn from the windows and tossed on the ground. Tears welled up in Jaspers' eyes.

"Faerydae!" he yelled. "Faerydae!" he screamed again.

Jasper squinted around the room through the smoke and his tears. A large framed man was lying on the ground. It was his friend Benjamin.

"Benjamin, Benjamin, wake up," Jasper echoed as he shook him violently.

Benjamin gasped for breath. He clutched Jasper's arm, refusing to let it go. "Help me up Jasper," he cackled opening his eyes.

"What happened here, Benjamin? Where are my wife and my son?"

"Jasper, I am not sure. Faerydae was preparing dinner for us; the baby was over in the cradle. Everything was fine until the soldiers entered the tavern. The other men who were here with me tried to protect her and the baby. We could not protect her; it was too many for us, and I was knocked unconscious. I am not sure what happened to the other men, to her, or your son."

Jasper breathed quietly and avoided eye contact with Benjamin. He rubbed the sweat forming on his hands on his pant legs. Jasper knelt helping Benjamin off the ground and into a nearby chair he turned back on its proper side.

"I have to find my wife and son Ben. Will you be all right here if I left you for a time?"

"Of course, Jasper you must go. Find your family!"

Jasper patted Benjamin on the back and scurried out the side door of the tavern. He surveyed for any sign of his wife and son. He snagged a torch from the bar wall, lighting it on the burning flames in the fireplace before stepping back outside of the tavern.

Jasper swung the light in front of him, illuminating the ground enough to highlight drips of blood leading into the woods. He followed the blood splatter on the ground as it led him deeper into the woods. The air became dense as if the forest was weeping and sad; the birds did not sing above as before. Jasper pressed further and further on until he saw a light up ahead in the meadow where he first met Faerydae.

He slowed his pace and closed his distance to the meadow. Faerydae was ahead of him covered with blood, holding their son in her arms.

"Faerydae," he called out to her as he approached. She ignored his call and kept chanting.

"Faerydae!" Jasper called out again. This time, she stopped, circling to face him. Tears ran down her blood-smeared face.

"I am trying to bring Taner back. I am trying to bring him back to us, Jasper," she said through her tears.

Jasper tread closer to where she stood. He could see the tiny frame of his son in her arms, dead, cold and blue.

Jasper fell to his knees, his spine bowed and shoulders drooped.

"What happened, Faerydae?" he asked between sobbing

Faerydae knelt down at his side, still clutching their son in her arms.

Jasper slid the baby out from her arms and held him to his chest. "What happened, Faerydae?"

Faerydae snatched the baby from Jasper's arms and rocked him again. She looked at him with a fevered stare, her nostrils flaring and her mouth curling up with a sneer.

"It was the mob of soldiers sent by the king, your father," she spewed angrily. "They came to take me to the palace to stand trial as the others. They said my child and I were an abomination to the crown, and I was to be put down. The men in the tavern tried to help the baby and me. I ran over to the crib, picked him up in my arms and tried to run," She cried out. "Our friends tried to fight them, but the soldiers overpowered them. They knocked me to the ground and wrenched him from my arms. They took him outside of the tavern and slit Taner's throat right in front of me, Jasper. They killed our child before my eyes. I can bring him back, Jasper. You must let me bring him back."

Faerydae placed the baby at her feet. Jasper attempted to retrieve him when she lunged at him.

"You leave him there," Faerydae demanded, shoving him out of the way.

"Faerydae, you cannot bring him back, you would be going to a dark place, and against everything you were taught. You are good, you are my wife, and you are not a witch of dark magic or any magic."

"It does not matter what I believed previously. They have stolen all joy, love and goodness from me. They shall pay with their lives for what they have done. I will never return to the village unless it is to be upon my death and death to those who harmed my child and me. Jasper, all those who have inflicted pain on my son and me shall pay."

Faerydae picked up a wooden stick sitting on the forest's ground. Swinging it over her head, chanting and calling out to the gods for her son to be avenged. Jasper was unable to get Faerydae to leave their child's side for six days and seven nights. She had prayed, cried, and worshiped but was unable to get her son to come back to her.

Famished and hungered after days of fasting, she asked Jasper to bury their child. Jasper laid his son to rest under the tree where they first met and often made love. He stayed by Faerydae's side until he felt comfortable leaving her alone briefly. Jasper returned to the village only to find their tavern burned completely to the ground. There was nothing left for them to go back to. The village was defenseless, most of their friends laid strewn out on the street left for the rats to feast upon their corpses.

Jasper knew the soldiers would return to continue their search for his wife. To protect her, he moved them deeper into the forest. They found an old abandoned cottage near a marsh to occupy. Faerydae resented Jasper as the days turned into months. She blamed him for his father's war against the spirited. Faerydae's demeanor changed even further when she encountered a woman named Sema practicing the dark arts in the forest clearing as she gathered mushrooms for her dinner.

In conversation with the woman, she found she could learn a great deal and invited her back to the cottage she and Jasper shared. From the day Sema came to the cottage, Faerydae experimented with the dark side of magic. The magic consumed her, hardening her heart. She was no longer the sweet loving girl Jasper had fallen in love with.

Despite her changes, Jasper still believed she could be redeemed and loved her. She rejected his advances at every turn. Time passed on. Jasper's heart turned cold and would long again for his life he gave up as Prince Keaton. He regretted the actions he took to leave the kingdom and concluded he wanted to return to his previous life and go home. Watching his brother grow into a great prince made him jealous. He wanted to become king and dispose of his father who induced his suffering. He started to devise a course of action.

My lovely Faerydae will have to die if I am to regain my position and my life.

Jasper knew what he had to do. He would lead the soldiers to Faerydae practicing the dark arts. Upon her capture, she would be returned to Westminster Castle and put to death. He would leave the village the first thing the next morning, explaining to Faerydae, he was going to seek information from their village about the soldiers.

He knew that evening would be the last encounter they would have with each other, and he would be sending his wife to her death. He returned to the cottage that night from hunting with the game he had caught. He skinned the deer and prepared the meat for cooking on the outdoor fire. Faerydae saw him through the tiny window of the cottage. She excused herself from her teacher and joined him outside.

"What are you doing out here, Jasper?" she questioned, moving out the cottage door to where he worked. Jasper paused from his cutting and glanced up at her. He noticed her fair hair was turning gray, the youthfulness of her looks starting to fade. She was beginning to resemble the witches in the stories told to him as a child.

"You look unwell, Faerydae."

"I am perfectly fine, husband. Are you going to answer my question?"

"I am preparing the deer for supper. Can you place the pot on the fire for me? We can make a stew for dinner tonight. Faerydae glowered at Jasper. She had lost all trust in him over the months and maintained he was the reason for their son's death. She wandered around him, snatching the pot from the wooden work table, and placed it on the fire.

Jasper finished with the meat and brought it over to where Faerydae positioned herself. She took the meat from him and put it in the pot along with some herbs, mushrooms, and some vegetables. She mumbled under her breath, and the cauldron was filled with a broth instantly. Faerydae wiped her hands on her apron as she passed Jasper on her way to the cottage door.

"You have nothing more to say to me, wife?" Jasper asked as she sauntered by.

"No, there is not much for us to discuss unless it is me bringing my son back from the dead."

"Faerydae, you know bringing him back is not possible unless you invoke yourself into the dark arts you are practicing," he insisted, sighing. "You know he was also my son. I miss him as much as you, wife."

"I am quite you sure miss him, but you have done nothing to avenge his death. You have let me down once again. Now I find, everything is in my hands to get the revenge I seek. What do you believe I have been learning from Sema, Jasper? During the days and the nights of our ramblings, I have learned a great deal, my love."

Faerydae paused at the doorway entrance and pivoted back towards Jasper. "I am almost ready to try the spell on a corpse. If this works, I shall be able to bring our son back from the dead."

Jasper approached Faerydae and tried to take her hand.

"Touching me is something you do not have permission to do, Jasper," she howled, ripping her hand away from his. "I am no longer yours to touch as I have told you previously. You have destroyed my life and your father has taken everything from me, including you."

"I wanted to show you I am here for you, Faerydae. I am your husband and care for you.

Jasper heaved his chest in and out the vein in his neck pulsed. He clenched his jaw and ground his teeth in silence.

She would not be a problem much longer.

Faerydae shifted her stance, crossed her arms and glared at Jasper. "There is nothing you do or say that will change the situation, Jasper. You should leave. Do you not believe you have done enough? Our life together is over. All that remains is my final act against those who have harmed my son and me."

"What do you have planned, wife?" Jasper clutched Faerydae's arm.

"It is none of your concern. I told you not to touch me again." Faerydae snatched her arm.

Faerydae mumbled under her breath and bore her eyes into Jasper. His head pounded in pain like the day they first met.

"What are you doing to me?" he screamed as he doubled over in pain.

Faerydae held her hand out in front of her and continued to chant.

Jasper grabbed his head and started to go black. Before he passed out, he saw Sema out of the corner of his eye come to the door and place her hand on Faerydae's shoulder to get her to stop.

Her chanting ceased, and she retreated into the cottage.

Jasper lay unconscious on the ground for hours. Later, he awoke to a slight headache. He looked around to see where Sema and Faerydae were, and saw them asleep inside the cottage. After quickly eating the remainder of the cold stew left behind in the caldron, he gathered his walking stick and belongings and headed into the village as dawn approached.

The trek through the forest was a quiet one. He made sure that his father's guards would discover every move he made. He believed the trap he was setting for his wife would work. As the village came into view, he heard footsteps behind him. Jasper spun around to see who was there; of course, when he looked back, the forest was quiet.

Good, they are on my trail.

The sun rose as he walked through the village. Slowly, people were starting to return and rebuild. He studied his old tavern looking upon the charred remains. Kneeling in the rubble, he picked up a piece of wood. His dreams for the bar faded, his happy life destroyed in one moment by his father. As he reminisced about past times, one of the remaining women in the village approached him. It was Christine, the woman who owned the brothel a few doors down from the tavern.

"Jasper," she called out as she approached. "You are alive!" she squeaked as she embraced him.

"Yes, Christine, I am well. I came to the village to see what other damage was done and who remained here."

"Oh Jasper, so many of the villagers have been killed or taken. Some have returned to rebuild. Many women have been taken to Westminster Castle to be tried as witches."

"I know, I was followed back here to the village, Christine. I am not sure who was following me, but for your safety and all those remaining, you need to get them into hiding. I cannot protect you if they attack again."

"They have not attacked again Jasper; there have been many knights in and out the village looking for so-called witches. I do not know who followed you here, but you should leave the village and get back to where you came. Protect Faerydae."

Christine embraced Jasper and went off to warn the other villagers of the mysterious men hiding in the outskirts of the village. Jasper placed the wood in his bag. He inspected the village one final time and headed back into the forest. He could sense that he was still being followed.

Time to put my plan into action.

On the long walk back to the cottage, Jasper saw the brush move. Three men stepped out of the foliage, surrounding him. Jasper pulled his knife from his satchel, taking a defensive stance.

Exactly what I want to happen.

Jasper traipsed closer to the three men ready to fight. Before he could strike one of them with his knife, he heard chanting coming from the cottage. Faerydae and Sema stepped out of the door, advancing towards them with their arms raised. Their chanting became louder as they came into view.

The men fell to their knees, wincing in pain. Faerydae's and Sema's approach persisted into the clearing. Men surrounded them from behind, binding their arms at their wrists. Jasper gave an animated performance, pretending he was concerned about his wife being captured. He fought the guards who tried to take her, but was overpowered and hit over the head with the piece of wood that fell out of his bag.

Jasper regained consciousness when snow flurries landing on his face woke him. He touched his head, brushed the snow off his face and rolled over to his knees, getting to his feet. The memory of what happened returned. He knew he had to get to the castle to finish the start of his plan. He staggered into the cottage gathering the rest of the things he needed for the journey, including a vile of a poisonous liquid from Sema's assortment of bottles.

Jasper reached Westminster Castle and was presented to his father, King Henry. Unrecognizable with his long brown hair, and a face full of facial hair, he introduced himself as a stable hand needing work. His father approved him for the job and sent him directly to the stables. The next day, he witnessed his wife and Sema being burned alive. The last remnant of his former life was ended.

5 Prince David

Winter had come sooner than expected to Westminster, and it was a rare day when Prince David was permitted to leave the castle for his ride. He mounted his horse named Steam and headed into the forest. The exhilarating horseback ride made David feel free. The time away from the castle allowed him to reflect on the past and current things in his life. He thought of his brothers mostly. Theron, the youngest, was taken away from the kingdom due to his illness. He left his home at the age of one in the company of a guardian, around the same time Keaton his eldest brother had disappeared twelve years ago.

David had glimpses of his eldest brother Keaton telling him goodbye in his dreams; a memory his mother convinced him was a dream. He still was uncertain. Even growing up as a young boy, David could swear he would see his brother outside darting behind the castle walls. He felt as if Keaton haunted him, always lurking around the corner to play a joke.

David relinquished the thoughts of his brothers and dived into the bliss of the moment. He set his mind free of stress and unwanted duties, the snow blowing over him and his mighty horse as they rode together in sync.

He recalled a conversation he overheard among the servants regarding new ships from Portugal that his father had commissioned. The ships were sailing in and were to be docked that afternoon.

I know I should not go down to the waterfront, but I am dying to see the new ships.

David had dreamed of becoming a sailor and explorer since he was a child. He swung his horse around and headed towards the port.

David pushed Steam to ride faster, and he soon arrived at Ellesmere port. Beautifully carved ships lined each dock, bobbing up and down from the calm waves brushing against them. One ship, in particular, caught David's attention. Pulling the reins on his horse, he stopped in front of the ship called the Lady Fantasy. Jumping down from his horse, he ran his hands over the wood planking on the side of the massive ship.

"What are you doing down there on the docks, boy?" a voice called down from the ship. The captain had spotted David next to the ship and climbed down the ladder, joining David on the dock.

"I am sorry sir," David muttered. "I did not mean any harm I was simply in awe of the beauty of your ship."

"It is quite all right, son. The ship is a beauty, is she not? I am Captain Erikson." He extended his hand to shake David's.

David gave him a firm shake, his attention diverting back to the ship in front of him.

"I'm Prince... Ummm, I am David."

"I know who you are, David. If you are trying to hide the fact you are a prince, perhaps you should not ride a horse displaying the royal colors on it," Captain Erikson replied with a gentle laugh, glancing back at Steam.

David's face became flushed; redness moved across his cheeks. "I did not want people to know I was down here or who I was. I merely wanted to be myself, and not be the prince for an afternoon."

"I understand, son; you do not need to worry. How about you come aboard. I will show you around."

A wide grin crossed David's face, his pulse quickened. "Sounds great, Captain."

The two men ascended the ladder to the ship, and Captain Erikson showed him around. David's eyes widened, and he reached out, touching everything in sight.

"So what do you think of her, David?"

"The ship is beautiful. I would love to sail her out with you." David answered hopefully.

The seagulls danced overhead of the men, as dark clouds formed and pushed in harder waves. The ship rocked from side to side.

"The storm is rolling in, son, so I need make this visit brief. But if I make the arrangement, and your father gives you the commission to sail, I would like to make you first mate, and teach you the ropes myself."

David's eyes widened, and he beamed his heart racing.

"You would offer me, first mate?"

"Of course, I would, son. There are not many young men in your status who find sailing exciting and thrive on learning something new." Captain Erikson lamented, "It would be my pleasure to show you the ropes."

David was lost for words at such a generous offer. Without hesitation, he verbalized his excitement.

"Sir, I would be honored to sail with you and your crew. Yes! I will accept your offer," David gushed, shaking the captain's hand feverishly. "We will need to firm up the details, and I will speak to my father, but I am sure I can make him understand how much I want this opportunity."

The storm blew in faster than anticipated. The ship begun to rock harder as the waves crashed upon the bow and the snow started to fall harder.

"I better be getting back," he said. "The snow is coming down quite hard now, and my father will be sending the guards after me soon."

David and Captain Erikson shook hands one final time before parting. "Be safe getting back to the castle and tell your father of the offer I made."

"I will, sir!" David called out, heading towards his horse. "Thank you again for the offer. I will not let you down."

"You are welcome, David. I will see you soon."

When David returned to the castle, he was met by the stable-hand Jasper, who informed him his father was summoning him for a talk.

"Your father is looking for you, Milord. He seemed rather anxious to speak with you."

"Thanks for the warning, I appreciate your concern." David handed his reins to Jasper.

David could not shake the feeling that he had met the stable hand outside of the castle. Something was familiar to him.

It is nothing. I could not have known him before now.

Soon, David knocked on the door of his father's study.

"Enter," King Henry answered. David opened the door, taking a deep breath. He avoided his father's stare as he entered the smoke-filled room from his father's pipe.

"Father, you wanted to see me?" David sank into the large red velvet chair at the head of his father's desk.

"Yes, David, I called you here because I need to speak to you on a few subjects. The first is that you refuse to take a wife of your choosing." King Henry eyed him from across his desk.

"Father, I am not ready to be married, and besides the ladies you presented to me at the multiple balls did not interest me. Father, you know I always believed you should marry the one you love, with no regard to her station or family." David shifted in the oversized chair, resting his elbows on the armrests.

King Henry pushed his chair out from underneath the desk, stood, and paced back and forth in front of the massive shelves filled with hundreds of books.

"You know you will never marry anyone below your station, and you will not marry anyone other than a woman from a breed of my choosing. This is why I am now in control of your affairs and arranging your marriage. It is all in my hands as of now. You will marry the girl of my choice, and this will be the last discussion on the matter."

David digested every word in silence, shaking his head in disapproval. "Father, you cannot do this me! I am to take my first commission to sail on the Lady Fantasy."

"A commission to sail, on whose authority? I never gave my permission for you to do such a thing."

"Father, it has been my dream, the only thing I ever wanted in my life. Why must you make everything so impossible?" David slammed his fists on the desk, knocking the chair backward.

"You are the one who wants me to become king and caused Keaton to be stolen from us! I never wanted to be king."

King Henry's voice cracked. "There is no choice in the matter my son. If your brother Keaton had not been killed, he would be preparing to be king, and not you. You would, therefore, would be free to do whatever you liked, making you happy. But now you must marry, and take your responsibility to the throne seriously."

King Henry's pace slowed, and he joined David at his side. He returned the chair to the correct position that David had knocked down.

"Sit down, son," he muttered as he sat back in his chair across from David. His son hesitated for a moment looking out the window into the garden. He took in the view of the roses his mother planted and so loved. The red and white flowers reminded him of a time when he and his brother helped her plant them. David gazed over at his father scribbling on a piece of parchment paper.

"My son," Henry called out calmly, his head lowered. "I know about your wanting to sail. Captain Erikson already sent a messenger with a letter of his intent to take you under his wing. Your sailing is the other subject I wanted to broach with you. I am willing to make a compromise with you on sailing on the Lady Fantasy, David."

Confused, David reposed himself back into the chair and stared at his father.

"I will allow you to sail after you marry the princess I chose for you. If you refuse her hand in marriage, I will forbid you to sail, and your privileges outside of this castle will be revoked."

King Henry gave David the piece of parchment. "This is your commission for the Lady Fantasy. The decision is yours, David."

David grasped the paper from his father's hand and unrolled it, reading aloud. David's heart warmed. It was the first gesture of kindness his father had ever shown towards him. He was going to let him sail.

"You are going to let me sail, Father?"

"Yes, on the condition of you marrying the princess I have chosen for you."

"I will marry who you want, Father. Even if it is only for the opportunity to sail, I will do what you ask of me."

"Good, my son, you may leave me now. Enjoy a warm meal and rest. There are many preparations to make."

"Yes sir," David said as he got up from his chair to leave the room. Clutching the parchment in his hands, he paused at the door. "Thank you again, Father." He closed the door behind him.

David ate dinner in the kitchen alone rather than joining his parents in the hall. As he ate in silence, he overheard the servants speaking of the princess his father had chosen for him to marry.

She was the princess of Portugal, and rumors circulated that she was not an attractive woman. David felt a knot develop in his stomach over what he had overheard. But he no longer had a choice with the woman he would marry.

David's twentieth birthday and wedding to the princess of Portugal was marked with the warming winds and blooming of spring flowers. The wedding was to be in a week, and all the preparations were near completion. The final days before the wedding passed quickly. He had to juggle learning the ins and outs on the Lady Fantasy, his studies and complete his father's requirements.

The sun broke through cracks in David's bedroom window, waking him from a restless sleep. He awoke nauseous and light-headed. He was about to marry a woman who did not love and had never seen. He felt weak and had to muster the strength to get out of bed. Having refused his servants' assistance, he bathed and dressed. A knock on the door rang out, but he ignored it and continued dressing. The knocking became harder and more consistent. David heard a voice call out from behind the door.

"David, are you there? David, it is time," the voice said. It was his mother, Queen Anne, who came to wish him well.

David pulled the door open slowly, glaring at his mother and clenching his jaw.

"David, what is it, my son?"

"Mother, did you know anything about Father lying to me?"

Queen Anne's eyes widened in shock. "My son, I had no idea about your father lying to you."

David shifted his stance and crossed his arms. "I only agreed to marry this girl because Father, was giving me the opportunity to sail and nothing else. I do not know anything about her; I have never seen a portrait of her. I have no regard towards her; I do not love her."

"David, regardless of what your father has done, you are beyond the point of saying no. You have no choice in the matter. This wedding is happening now."

Queen Anne grasped David's hand, tugging him out of the room. She led David down the long corridor towards the chapel. David walked in silence with his mother. His shoulders rounded, and he bit the inside of his cheek, as the two of them reached the chapel doors.

Queen Anne stopped and kissed her son on the cheek. "David, this is where we will part ways for now. You will go into the side entrance, and I will enter here. I will see you when this is all over. I love you, my son."

"I love you too, Mother," David replied.

The queen smiled as she entered the chapel.

David heard the steward present his mother. He inhaled deeply and meandered towards the side entrance. David waited at the front of the chapel for the ceremony to begin. He skimmed over all the faces of the lords and ladies of the court. Some of them smiled, and some grimaced and shook their heads.

The music commenced, and the conversations throughout the chapel dwindled until there was silence. The doors opened, and Princess Philippa appeared with a veil covering her head. David tried to make out her appearance. He had found out the night before his wedding about the actual intent of the arrangement. His marriage to Philippa is what brokered the building and shipping of the new carracks brought into port Ellesmere from Portugal.

He betrayed my trust, for ships and peace. Please let me get through this ceremony.

David pushed the anger for his father to the back of his mind. He would confront him at another time about his lies. Philippa continued down the aisle pausing in front of him. David lifted the veil from her face and restrained a sigh as he registered her bloated face, round crooked nose, and acne scars. Her complexion was olive in color not too dark but not pale. Her thin, limp, brown hair fell straight on her shoulders, unlike the thick, lush, full locks of other Portuguese women. David would not have picked her to become his bride. Even if she were attractive, it would not have made a difference because he was not marrying for love.

David grabbed her hand and avoided eye contact, keeping the nausea he felt at bay as they exchanged vows.

I made it through the ceremony.

The chapel bells rang in celebration and the two of them walked out of the chapel arm in arm, and proceeded down the long path to the castle.

"Your Majesty, I hope you are pleased with me," Philippa grinned as they continued to walk up the path.

"Umm yes. I am delighted you are here princess and hope you had safe travels, Milady." David sighed, lying to her.

David's thoughts were consumed with what would come later in the evening. The tradition of the court was for the parents of the bridal couple as well as the key court members to observe the consummation of their marriage. The thought of having to perform a sexual act in front of his parents and other members of the court made him want to vomit. They strolled to the feast celebration in silence.

Numerous toasts from King Henry and Philippa's father during the dinner celebration caused David to wish he could forget the day's events. While dancing with his bride, David fought off the urge to cringe. He plastered a phony smile on his face to hide his displeasure.

The celebration finally ended. David headed to the bed chamber where his servants bathed him and dressed him in his robe. He waited in front of his bed for his new wife. The door opened, and Princess Philippa slowly drifted through the room to David. Her silhouette was visible from the sheer robe she wore.

David was able to get a clear view of her body. Her large stomach poked out from underneath her tiny and flat breasts. Her thighs, thick and unshapely, continued to the back of her body.

How am I going to get through this with her? Ugggghhhhhhhhhhh

As the witnesses to the consummation filled the room, David removed his robe and laid it on the bed. The door closed, and the members of the court took their seats. David lumbered over to Princess Philippa, clutching her hand. Her face quivered, her body shaking.

"You will be fine, Philippa."

I hope I can perform.

David was not quite sure he would be able to achieve an erection to get through his performance. He scooted Philippa over to the bed and untied her robe, dropping it to the floor. Naked before him, her body did not excite David. He longed for the night to be over.

"Come now," he said gesturing Philippa to the bed.

David kissed Philippa gently on the lips to get her to relax. He pushed the unappealing thoughts of her from his mind.

Let me get through this night

Philippa found his penis, stroking it with her hand. David closed his eyes and imagined it was another woman pleasuring him. It was enough to get him aroused. She continued cupping his cock, his engorged flesh hardening with every stroke.

David felt Philippa relax her body against his. Her lips touched his and the daydream he was in vanished immediately. Disgusted, he wanted to rush this interaction along and spread her legs open filling her in one swift motion.

Philippa's breathing deepened. David savagely thrust his erect shaft deeper inside of her.

She whimpered in pain underneath him as he increased his speed and intensity. David felt his arousal failing, becoming soft inside of her.

"Do not separate from me, Milord; you must finish," she whispered, grabbing his buttocks, pulling him deeper into her.

David glided upward. Even though he was no longer erect, he pretended to have an orgasm so the embarrassment could be over. He rolled over on his side, covering himself with the quilt. The witnesses, satisfied with what they had seen, filed out of the room.

"I am sorry I could not do better, Milady," David grumbled.

"It is fine, Milord; I know it will get better. I am going to wash."

Philippa sat up on the side of the bed, picked her robe off the floor, and left to cleanse herself. David lay there alone, with the candlelight bouncing off the wall.

It has to be something more than this. I will never love this woman, nor will I ever want her. I cannot live like this.

David comforted himself knowing he was leaving on the Lady Fantasy in two days. Philippa came back to bed brushing up close to him. She laid her head on his chest and told him she was already falling in love with him. David laid in silence until he dozed off.

For the next two days, David managed to avoid Philippa. His work on the ship kept him away overnight. The last night at the Kingdom was primarily spent with his father. He confronted his father about the lies he had told him to convince him to marry Philippa. Their last conversation was in anger. King Henry made it clear he did not care about lying to his second born son for the good of the kingdom. He demanded David was to produce a male heir as soon as possible.

David thought of his first night with Philippa and wondered if he could ever muster enough energy to make love to a woman he did not want. He left for the port of Ellesmere the next morning. He said his goodbyes to his father and mother and once again completely avoided the princess.

After nine months at sea, the Lady Fantasy pulled back into the port of Ellesmere. David sensed something was different. Something was off, but he could not figure out what it was. The ship docked at the harbor, and the Royal Guard was waiting for him.

How long had they been waiting for me?

David scaled down the ladder to the docks to speak with the Royal Guard.

"Your Highness," one of the guardsmen, said. "We have been waiting two days for the Lady Fantasy to dock. We have word from Westminster Castle. It is your father, he has taken ill and needs you."

"My father? Is it serious? Is he okay?" he blurted, his heart quickening.

"We are not sure, your Highness, but you need to hurry. Time is of the essence."

David swallowed excessively and licked his lips. "Trevor!" David called to one of the men on the ship. "Make sure the lines, and the sails are secure, and the anchor is in place. My father has fallen ill. I must get to him I am sorry for leaving you all like this."

David had been made captain on the Lady Fantasy when Captain Erikson died unexpectedly at sea.

"Aye, captain. Everything will be ready when you return, sir."

Trevor continued to bark orders at the rest of the mates on deck. David picked up his bag of belongings thrown down to the platform for him. He leaped on the back of his saddled horse, Steam, and rode home in silence to Westminster Castle.

"David," Queen Anne called to him as she scrambled out of the castle to greet him. "Son, please you have to hurry. Your father, he... he...is dying David," she said as tears washed down her face.

"Mother, I am here, take me to him." David grasped his mother's hand. They whisked into the castle, up the wide staircase to the king's room.

David swung the chamber room door open. The partially closed drapes let a faint glow of the setting sun into the chamber. Two candles, one on each side of the bed, burned as the candle wax melted and gathered into the bottom of the candelabra. David's father, who was so healthy and fit before David left, now had the frail, wrinkled appearance of an old man. David moved closer to the bed and perched himself on the edge. He rubbed his father's hand.

"Father?" His father did not reply. "Father, I am home," he said again in a low voice.

His father opened his eyes, blinking in the direction of his son.

"David, my son; I waited for you," King Henry said in a shallow voice. "I was riding out with the men, hunting deer. As we stopped for water at the stream, I was drinking out of my flask when I began to feel ill, and suddenly, I was attacked by a bear from behind." King Henry stopped speaking and gasped for breath. "I killed it, but in return, he killed me. I waited for you to come so I can crown you king. son."

"Father," David replied. "I do not want to be king. I want to carry on my life as a sailor. I want to be free, Father, to continue to see the world. I have been given the Lady Fantasy as my ship. Captain Erikson left it to me. He died at sea."

King Henry shuddered underneath the covers. He coughed and gasped for another breath.

"David, I am sorry to hear of the captain's passing, but the time for childish dreams are over. You are now king of England, and there are responsibilities to be had and followed. You will have to appoint another captain. You will produce an heir with your wife who you avoided before you left. You will perform your duties to the court and the people of this land. You are now twenty-one years of age, and you had better start behaving like the man I have raised you to be!"

David listened quietly, clutching his father's hand tighter.

"There will be no more expeditions. Your life is here running your country," King Henry said between shallow breaths.

"But Father, I am supposed to captain the Lady Fantasy with Vasco Da Gama. He asked me if he could sail with my ship and crew personally. I gave the man my word I would sail with him. I will become king as you ask Father, but you will let me sail on this expedition."

David rubbed his eyes to hide the redness. He stared at his father with a vacant expression. While he knew he was about to lose his father forever, David wished he too had run away as his brother had done. By doing so, he could live a separate and happy life away from the court.

David blinked once, returning his focus to his father. He touched his father's face which had gone cold. King Henry VI of England had died.

David fell upon his father's chest in tears. Because of the death of his father, he had to turn down the opportunity to sail his ship to India with Vasco Da Gama. A funeral had to be planned instead.

Nights turned into days and days turned into nights. David felt the loss of his father terribly. Not because he missed his father, but David now realized he was indeed bound to the crown he wore and was no longer able to be free.

Marching into the chapel on the day of the funeral, David was consumed with great sadness.

I wish I had someone to talk to about this. Someone with whom I could share my darkest desires. I have never known what true love is or what it means to be with someone who loves me. My parents loved each other deeply, but my father had the chance to marry the woman whom he loved. Why did my life have to be so different? It was Keaton who was supposed to be king now.

David held his head low and approached the pedestal his father laid upon. He placed a rose on his chest, kissed his forehead and joined his mother and his wife by their sides. The few minutes of his father's dedication seemed like a few hours. He flinched in the fancy garment he wore and longed for his comfortable and simple clothing he had worn while on the ship.

In a moment of fury, he rose during the middle of the prayer and strode out of the chapel. What started off as a slow jog, became a fast run. He felt himself moving faster as if a bee had stung him; he had to get away. In the distance, he could hear Philippa calling out to him.

"David! David, please wait! What are you doing?"

David did not care; he stripped off his top layer of clothing, flinging it behind him, and kept running.

Philippa could not keep pace and stopped where he dropped his cloak. She picked it up and held it in her arms. Clutching his cloak in her hand, she walked back towards the chapel to find his mother.

David reached the lake where he used to swim as a child. He stripped his remaining clothing and dived into the dark, cool water. He felt the water encircle his naked body and sensed the calm he felt when he was near or in water.

Maybe I should drown myself here? Perhaps this should be the place where I let myself slip into an eternal sleep.

He dove deeper into the water and allowed water to fill his lungs.

If this is what death feels like, I welcome it!

David closed his eyes and dove deeper. Moments later, he felt hands jerk him from the water and to the shore of the lake. It was the king's guardsmen along with his mother.

"David, what are you doing? I buried your father today, and I am not going to lose another son like I lost Keaton," Queen Anne cried, her hands shaking as she held her son. "You have to snap out of this," she said firmly, wrapping him in blankets. "You are now the king of England. You must start acting like a king! I will not have this in our household or our kingdom."

David, barely coherent, became unconscious and slipped into a coma.

6 Brink of Death

Weeks passed, and David slipped further into a coma. His condition became critical, and neither the doctors nor the Queen understood the source of his ailment. In the darkness of his dreams, David found himself in a new land far away from home. He encountered a woman who invoked his emotions on a deeper level. This woman was everything he wanted. She approached him, touched his face, and told him it was time for him to wake up and come back to the light. Although her face was not clear to him, he did not believe she was a British woman. She was something more exotic.

"I do not want to wake up, I want to stay here with you," he said to her.

"It is time for you to wake up," she softly whispered again, gently kissing his lips.

David woke up in his room covered with blankets, disoriented. His vision of the woman in his dreams made him feel guilty for leaving her in his dream world. He had wanted to stay there with her, where he sensed he was safe. A breeze from the open window brought the faint scent of the sea into the chamber room. David inhaled the scent and tried to sit up in bed, yet he was still fatigued, and it washed over him again. David saw Philippa through his blurred vision, seated in the corner of the room reading. Philippa noticed him stirring.

"David, you are awake! How are you feeling?" she dropped her book on the floor and rushed to his bedside.

"I am fine." David's voice wobbled as the room dipped. "Where is my mother? I must speak with her immediately. I need to explain what..." He was cut off in mid-sentence.

"You mean you must explain why you were trying to kill yourself?" Philippa barked, her voice rising. "You almost died that day. David, you have been unconscious for weeks. You were on the brink of death."

David tried to focus on other objects in the room to avoid Philippa's gaze. "I was only going for a swim. I was not planning to kill myself. I wanted a moment to myself, not something I get when I am here surrounded by all of you."

Tears welled in the corners of Philippa's eyes. "You expect me to believe what you are saying to me? I realize you do not love me, or care to touch me. I see it in your face each and every time I come within a distance of you. But I want this to work. I am in love you, and want to give you princes," she muttered, reaching to touch his hand.

David snatched his hand away from hers, placing it underneath his blanket.

"I am aware now I was not your first choice, perhaps not even your second. But your father wanted this marriage, so we are going to do our duty, and do what is right for England." Philippa rose from his bedside, retreating to the door. "I will send your mother to you. I hope she can talk to you in a manner in which you will respond." she closed the door behind her.

David laid back in the bed reflecting on what Philippa had said; she was making the best of this marriage. She loved him and wanted to give him sons.

This is not what I want.

His chamber room opened again, and his mother entered, walking briskly to his bedside.

"Darling boy! You are finally awake! Philippa told me you wanted to see me," Queen Anne gushed as she sat down on the bed, rubbing his hand, and kissing him on the forehead.

"Mother, I want this marriage to Philippa to be annulled. I want to be released from this sham of a relationship in which I am living."

The excitement on Queen Anne's face drained and her expression turned cold as if the words he had spoken stabbed her body like small shards of glass cutting her deeply. She slapped him across the face.

"David, you will stop speaking this blasphemy against Philippa! Nothing can be done about this situation! There will be no annulment! It was your father's wish, and he who arranged for you and Philippa to be married. This marriage is not for your feelings, but for the sake of our country and peace. I understand it is not what you wanted, and you wanted to marry for love, but unfortunately, my son, we cannot always have everything in life we want."

Queen Anne exhaled and calmed her demeanor. She leaned over and stroked David's face with her hand. David held his mother's hand close to his face. He sighed heavily. He would never be able to leave his wife. Only one choice remained: succumb to his father's wishes, become king, and to stay with his wife.

"Mother, I am not happy with this situation. But if this is what you want for me, I will remain in this sham of a marriage," David muttered in a softer tone. "However you will grant me one last wish before I commit to the misery becoming my life."

Queen Anne laughed out loud. "What misery, my dear son? Your life is better than most. You should be grateful for what you are blessed with. Make the best of the situation with your wife and life. I understand how you feel, but you must put these thoughts behind you and out of your mind." She chuckled once more at David.

David let out another heavy sigh before pinching his lips together.

"What is it you would ask of me, my son?"

"Mother, I need your blessing for my expedition to India. I will make it my last voyage, and I promise to come back and do what is expected of me as a king. But please grant me this last freedom."

"David!" Queen Anne exclaimed. "Your father would not allow such a voyage for you to undertake. It is dangerous; you could be killed." Queen Anne tilted her head downward and frowned.

"Mother, I will return. And when I do, I will become the king you want. Allowing me to take this voyage is my one condition to keep the peace of this kingdom. Grant this to me, Mother, I need to do this."

David lay quietly as his mother pondered his request. Reluctantly, she gave her permission.

"Yes, my son, I will give my blessing and take whatever you need to make this journey successful. Upon your return, you will be crowned king officially, and take over as ruler of England."

Queen Anne kissed David one last time on the forehead and left him alone with his thoughts.

David stretched out his body in the bed. He had won this battle with his mother: he would be able to take this journey. But what did he sell himself into? What would be the cost? He promised himself he would never forget who he truly was, a sailor, and a man who loved to be free.

In the coming weeks, David's health returned, and he prepared again to leave Westminster for his final adventure before his coronation as king. His mother would rule as Queen Regent while he was away, his inauguration taking place when he returned.

David found himself restless the night before his voyage. Unable to sleep, he decided to get some fresh air. He had not slept in the same room as the princess since they performed the consummation ceremony, so there was no one lying next to him to disturb. He jumped up from the bed, slipped on his boots, and slid his sword into its holder. He went down the stairs in the back tower, avoiding his guards. David opened the lower tower door and stepped into the quiet surroundings of the courtyard. The large moon bathed his skin in a soft pale glow. He wandered the grounds of the kingdom relishing in the roses, bushes, and shrubs in the garden he would not see again, for the months to come.

I shall see my good old Steam.

David deserted the garden in the direction of the stables. A sound rustled in the bushes. Retrieving his sword from the scabbard, he charged forward in the direction of the sound.

"Who is there?" David called out as he neared the bush. He called out again, "Who is there?" Still, there was no answer.

Maybe the sound was in his head? David returned his sword to its scabbard. As he wheeled around back towards the direction of the stables, he heard the rustling again. He jolted around to find Philippa in his path.

"What are you doing out here Philippa?"

"I was unable to sleep, Milord. I came out here to get some fresh air. What are you doing out here?"

"I too was also unable to sleep. There has been much on my mind with the upcoming voyage."

"I see, Milord. I have not seen you since you recovered from your illness. You have not come to my chambers since our wedding, and you do not join me for meals. Did I so something to displease you?"

David knew he would have to confront all the questions his wife had in time. But he never expected being examined so thoroughly while taking an evening stroll in his courtyard.

If David had known he was going to receive this line of questioning, he would have remained in his chambers. He glanced up at the night sky, down to the ground and finally back at his wife.

"No, you have not done anything wrong. I have been away from the castle. Preparing for the journey kept me in Ellesmere many late nights. I have been too tired to ride back here in the late evenings. So I have been bunking on the ship."

"I see." Philippa stepped closer. "Well, I think if there is not a problem, I believe we should share in an intimate moment."

"A private moment?" David asked. "Are we not talking now Milady?"

"We are talking, but I thought since we were out here on the grounds, we could share a moment together. I never get to lay eyes, on you Milord. I miss you." Philippa continued pressing towards David until she was directly in front of him. "We have expectations that need to be met, we must conceive an heir to the throne. I believe this would be a great place to start."

Philippa began to unbutton her robe, letting it drop to the ground. She stood before David naked bathed in the light of the moon.

"Milady! What are you doing?" David turned his glance away from Philippa's body.

"You never come to my chambers; you never send for me."

Philippa tugged on his breeches until she unbuttoned them. She crouched down in front of David, swirling his cock around her lips. She began to suck deeply on his manhood, taking the entire head of his rod in her mouth. Her lips eventually moved down the shaft with a strong desire to make him erect. She kept licking and sucking his penis, and glancing up at David to see if he was enjoying what she was doing to him.

David resisted at first but started to daydream again about the woman from his vision. He gave in to the sensation of his penis being sucked.

David's manhood became swollen as he fantasized about the other woman coupled with the cold air encircling his buttocks. He shifted, thrusting his thick hardness further into her mouth. Philippa choked for a moment and adjusted to the force of him, as she continued to please him orally while using a swirling movement with her tongue. David moaned in the enjoyment of the moment; it almost felt to him as if his dream woman was there pleasuring him. He opened his eyes and reality sunk in that it was Philippa who was pleasuring him.

Disgusted, he immediately removed his cock from her mouth. Clutching her arms, he lifted her up off her knees onto her feet. David wheeled her around, crushing her body against the tree. David avoided eye contact with his wife. He hoped he could immerse himself back in the vision of the mysterious woman.

David bent her forward, her breast rubbing against the trunk of the tree, as he entered her heat with a driving thrust.

"Oh, you like it rough," he hissed.

He plunged his penis harder and deeper inside of her. Philippa moaned in more pain than pleasure but allowed David to continue. David felt Philippa's body tense the deeper he went. his roughness was savage and cold, but he continued.

"Is this the particular moment you wanted, Philippa?" David inquired between his increased tempo.

Philippa panted between the pain. "A lady should not be treated like this."

"How should a woman be treated, when they provoke someone?"

Philippa did not respond. She should not have provoked him. She continued to endure the agony of the sexual act.

David proceeded with his savage thrusting, his movements faster and his erection harder with each passing minute. He had no concern of pleasuring Philippa; he only wanted it to be over. David finally found his release, emptied his semen inside of her, and retracted his penis. He buttoned his breeches and rotated towards Philippa.

"I hope this was the intimate moment you wished for. I will never be the man or husband you want, but I will do what I am required to conceive an heir. That is all I can give." David picked up his boots and headed back towards the castle.

Philippa was left alone in the moonlight. She had believed David would grow to love her. However, the savage nature of their sexual encounter made her realize he never would. She gazed down at her breasts. They were red and blisters had started to form from the skin rubbing against the bark of the tree. She touched them slightly and breathed deeply. They stung to the touch and were painful. Tears welled up in her eyes as she gathered up her robe, still laying where she dropped it on the ground. She reached down to pick it up, lost her footing, and fell to the ground sobbing.

Her husband did not want her. She vowed to herself she would do her duty of being queen. Her life at court would solely be to produce an heir to the throne.

Philippa heard a rustle coming from the side of the stables. She threw her robe up over her shoulders covering her extremities. A handsome bearded man appeared before her.

"Who are you?"

"I am Jasper. Milady, I work in the stables. I heard crying, and I came to see if everything was all right."

Philippa rose to her feet and moved a little closer to the man standing in front of her. He had dark brown hair, a dark bearded face with high cheekbones, and deep blue eyes like the ocean. He had broad shoulders. She made out the corrugated leanness of his flat abdomen through his shirt. He seemed familiar to her like they had met before.

"I'm fine Jasper, thank you," Philippa replied. "I only slipped, and I am better now. I should go." Philippa steadied herself, brushing past Jasper as he ran his fingers over her hand. It caught her by surprise. No one had ever touched her in such a sweet, kind manner before.

"Like I said, before Milady, I wanted to make sure you were okay." Jasper squeezed her hand a little tighter, drawing her closer to him. "It seems that you are a little out of sorts, Milady. I wanted you to know my services are yours when you need them. I am always here at the stables if you need a listening ear. You seem quite alone here in this castle."

Philippa blushed, her cheeks infused with a bright cherry red. She glanced away, hoping he would not notice.

Jasper took it as a sign to leave. He bowed slightly returning in the direction of the stable.

"Wait, Jasper!" she called out softly.

Jasper circled towards Philippa's direction.

"Thank you again, Jasper. You seem to know more about me than I about you. I would like to know more about you, but I cannot. I thank you for your offer of friendship, but with my duties to the future king, I cannot accept your offer of friendship. I do, however, still thank you for saying it."

"As you wish, for now, Milady" Jasper answered. "When you change your mind, you know where I will be waiting. I bid thee goodnight."

He pivoted around heading towards the cottage near the stables. Philippa paused in mid-step and decided to follow Jasper back to the stable cottage. He was already inside when she arrived at his doorstep. She was hesitating at the door when she noticed the faint glow coming from the window. Curious about the mysterious stable hand, she avoided knocking on the door and crept on her tipsy toes over to the window and peered inside.

Jasper stood in front of the hearth of the fireplace and removed his smock, exposing his bare chest, his muscles rippled. He retrieved a pallet from the side of the cottage, dropping it in front of the fireplace.

Philippa lost her footing, knocking her head on the outer window. She hunched down so Jasper could not see her staring at him. Jasper surveyed the window, and seeing nothing; he continued to undress, removing his breeches exposing his large swollen organ.

Philippa peeked through the window again just as he laid down on the pallet on the floor, and started to stroke his penis up and down. She trembled and fanned herself as she watched Jasper's organ increase in size as he touched himself.

Philippa felt her cheek, her was face warm and red again from blushing. She felt a tingling sensation between her thighs and reached her hand down in between them to calm it.

Jasper's penis grew becoming more erect until the point of orgasm. He let out a loud moan as his seed erupted into the air.

His eyes met Philippa's glance. He smirked at her, stroked his cock a few more times, then rolled over on the pallet and went to sleep. She covered her face with her hands, resting her back on the window, and let out a sigh.

Philippa composed herself, and wiped her dried tears from the corner of her eyes. She smoothed her hair and made sure she covered her bruised breasts completely with her robe.

No wonder he looked at me the way he did.

She became conscious that her nipples and breasts were still exposed when she had spoken with Jasper. The tingling remained and gave away to the moistness between her legs when she thought about it. Philippa shook her head.

He is a stable hand, and I should not be attracted to him. There is no way he should be attracted to me. David never studied me like he did. There will not be any friendship of any sort.

She glided back down the path to her chamber room in the castle.

Up the stairs and through the halls she crept, back to her chamber room. Philippa slid the door open, dropped her robe to the floor and bathed herself in the basin of water. She reminisced about the mysterious Jasper, the moistness flowing again from between her thighs.

Aroused, she lay on her bed and opened her legs. She used her fingers to find her clitoris and imagined it was Jasper's fingers touching her. She rubbed harder and faster with her right hand and moved her left hand to the hole in her mound. She was so moist and desperate to quench her desire. She inserted two fingers inside of her and let her body slowly gyrate against her fingers as she fantasized that Jasper was the one giving her pleasure. Moaning loudly, Philippa experienced an aqueous climax, releasing orgasmic fluid on the bed covers. It was the first time she had enjoyed any sexual pleasure. As she lay back on her pillows, she regretted telling Jasper they could not be friends.

The remainder of the twilight hours was restless for both David and Philippa. David arrived back to his chambers and bathed himself immediately. He felt the need to be fresh once more.

I hate having that woman's scent on me.

He threw back the covers back on his bed and climbed in. Staring up at the ceiling, his mind wandered. David was leaving Winchester for his final voyage tomorrow, a much needed time away.

He feared that upon his return, he would have to continue living the facade: that he was happy in his marriage and life in the kingdom.

I now regret having treated Philippa so poorly. She is an innocent victim in this situation my father has created. Maybe I will be able to redeem myself upon my return.

Chills shot through his chest. David tried to empty his brain of thoughts. He pulled the covers up over him and drifted off into a deep dark sleep.

Philippa flipped and flopped on her bed, unable to sleep even after pleasuring herself. Her breasts were still sore, bruised, and began to turn purple in spots. The encounter between her and David made tears well up in her eyes. She felt remorse for provoking him.

I forced myself on him. He will hate me for my actions. I will never make another move unless he asks for me. I will never tell him how I feel, and will keep my distance. I will only be his queen when he needs me to be his wife.

Philippa understood he would never love her. She would be alone in her marriage to David. She smiled again, reflecting on Jasper's offer of friendship. Maybe, just maybe they could be friends. Meeting Jasper was the only bright spot during that horrible evening. She turned into her pillow and cried the rest of the night.

The next morning, David awoke to the excitement of leaving on his final voyage. He rose from bed, forgetting the previous evening, and got ready for breakfast with his mother. When he reached the dinner hall, the table was not set. David inspected the room and called for the servants, but not one came.

Where is everyone?

He continued around to the throne room, but still there was no one in sight. He meandered out onto the grounds where his mother had assembled everyone to wish him a proper farewell. The garden was a lovely lush green, and the roses had bloomed that morning. The aroma of the freshly baked bread filled the air.

David was choked up. He hugged his mother, lifting her off the ground.

"Mother, you should not have gone through all of this trouble. I just wanted a simple breakfast with you."

Queen Anne smiled at him warmly. "David, you are going to be crowned king. You will have a fitting farewell and a welcome celebration upon your return. I love you, my son, and I shall miss you while you are away." She held back her tears and kissed him on the cheek. "Now you eat something before you go. I am not good with goodbyes as you realize," she squeaked, backing away.

David hurried after her, tugging gently on her arm. Queen Anne paused, returning her glance towards David. He hugged her tightly to him.

"I love you, Mother! And I promise I will return," David whispered in his mother's ear.

Queen Anne released herself from his embrace and smiled again. "You will," she said, joining some of the other ladies of the court.

David ate breakfast. Wandering around the grounds, he said his goodbyes to the other members of the court. As he was preparing to leave, Philippa came from the entrance of the castle. She peered in his direction from across the lawn with a sullen disposition. The court watched David's every move. With no choice but to speak to her, he sauntered over where she waited, taking her arm to escort her back to where the feast was being held.

"Good morning, Philippa," he said as he reached out his arm.

"Good morning, Milord." She had a somber look on her face.

They proceeded across the lawn, joining the other guests.

"I wanted to say goodbye to you before I left for the docks. I am sorry about what happened last night. I hope you can forgive me for my actions," David stated in a stern but calm voice.

"Milord, I accept your apology for what happened last night. I know now I am not your choice, but I will continue to do my responsibility as your princess and future queen."

David narrowed his eye and surveyed her face before he responded. "I am pleased you will continue to perform your responsibilities as I will continue to do mine. Be well, Philippa," he said, releasing her arm. He kissed her on the cheek, retreating towards the stables.

Philippa glanced in the direction David headed. Jasper was preparing his horse off in the distance. She smiled. She was looking forward to having an opportunity to get to know more about the stable hand while David was away. She remembered Jasper's manhood from the night before. She desired his massive cock; it was more than she could ever have imagined. She pondered if there would be an opportunity to see it up close and personal. Her nipples hardened and poked through her corset.

I have to stop thinking about that man.

Shaking the perverse thoughts from her mind, she watched as David took the horses reins from Jasper, climbed into his saddle and sped off out of the kingdom. Her eyes locked with Jasper's. He smiled and gave a little wave in her direction. Blushing again she waved back, then joined in conversation with the remaining guests.

7 Voyage

David's journey at sea started on the North Atlantic Ocean. The journey led David and his crew to many places after leaving Europe, making stops in every port while en route to India. Only one expedition before David's voyage had made it to India and was led by Vasco De Garma, the explorer whom he was supposed to have sailed with. David admired De Garma after meeting him and had wanted to attempt the same feat. He wanted to make it to India before his coronation and assuming the throne.

Ten months had passed since they left England. At every port David visited, he thought of his mother and wondered how the affairs of England were handled in his absence. He gave little regard to Philippa, but when she did cross his mind, he would only reflect on the last night before his departure. He longed for a woman, who could understand his wants, needs, and feelings.

Days when the sea was calm, and the sun's luminance broke through the clouds; David found himself lost in daydreams about a woman who could invoke his inner being. In those moments, he wondered if the woman of his dreams existed. She would appear in his mind so vividly, he could reach out and touch her. She faded to his unconscious when he opened his eyes and emerged from his vision, back to his reality lying in his bed.

The ship made stops to the coasts of Portugal and Spain for supplies before heading around the Cape of Africa. Portugal was also the home of David's wife, Philippa. The day they arrived at the Lisbon port, David made sure his crew understood their stop was to be brief and quiet. He also did not want Philippa's father to find out he was there. He knew many questions would be raised as to why the future king of England was taking such a journey, especially so recently after his father's passing.

Luckily for David, his ship and crew were undetected in Portugal, and he was able to enjoy a few of the spoils the country had to offer before resuming their voyage. Three months later, they reached their next stop, the Canary Islands. David was stopped by an older man who sat in the local tavern drinking a cocktail in a coconut.

"Sonny, come over here and sit next to me."

David acknowledged him, pulling a chair up to the man. "How can I help you, sir," David questioned, waving his hand at the servant girl for a drink. She brought over a large glass of ale placing it in front of him.

"Thank you, miss."

She nodded, taking the coins David dropped on the table.

"How long are you and your men here for?"

David gulped his ale and shrugged "I am not sure how long sir; I suppose a few days before we continue. Have a little time to relax."

"A few days is good. So tell me, young man, have you heard the rumors that have been traveling throughout this island?"

David had overheard the stories in passing from other sailors. "Why yes sir, I did hear from some of the other sailors around the island of a place that consisted of beautiful women."

"Well, those are not rumors." The old man sipped the contents of his coconut. "There is an island made up of women. "He paused before continuing. An island of beautiful women... They wait until a ship approaches full of sailors, and when one does, they send out small boats to the greet the passing ships.

David let out a boisterous laugh. "Old man, you have got to be kidding, an island full of women, who come out on boats? Who are you joking?"

"Young man this is not a joking matter...what is your name son?"

"It's David; my name is David."

"Well, David, let me finish," the old man crooned. He slapped David on his back. "Drink up son."

"Yes, sir." David finished his first ale, signaling the servant girl once more for a refill.

The servant girl scurried over to the men, refilling David's mug.

"Fill me up too, girly, I got this round." The old man slammed a handful coins down on the table. She took the money and the coconut.

"Now, back to these beautiful women. Once they row out to the ships, they sing with their beautiful voices to lure sailors back to their shores."

David shifted his weight in the chair; he did not believe one word the man was saying. But he admitted to himself that it was an entertaining story. "So what is your point of telling me this old man?"

"My point is; you are in danger as you continue on your journey. Heed what I say. When sailors are on their island, they are
robbed blind, then slaughtered in their sleep.

David laughed off the warnings of this mysterious island. He
did not believe these myths. He thanked the old man for his drink
and headed back to the ship.

The remaining time spent at the port on the Canary Islands
was uneventful. The crew loaded up on new supplies and made
repairs after coming through the previous storm, leaving part of
the rudder of the ship unusable. The extent of the damage extended their time on the Canary Islands for a week due to repairs.

Back out at sea, the voyage continued smoothly. The day was
clear and blue. The birds were out flying high above the ship,
and the dolphins escorted the Lady Fantasy into the depths of
the ocean.

A great day to be at sea.

David paced up and down the deck, checking his list to make
sure his crew were on task with their duties. As he performed his
inspections, the sky filled with dark clouds turning gray and his
ship rolled into a dense cover of fog. The ship shifted course on
its own, steering itself into the path of the thick fog. David barked
orders for his crew.

"Get this ship back on course, and watch out for the rocks!"
he yelled.

As soon as the fog appeared, it dissipated, disappearing into
thin air revealing an island with jagged rocks on the beaches surrounding it. As the ship came into the lagoon, one of the sailors
pointed at a figure off into the distance.

"Captain, over there on the rocks!"

David circled the surroundings with his binoculars, then towards the direction his crew member was pointing. Standing on
the rock formation, was one of the mysterious women the old

man on the Canary Islands had mentioned. David dropped his binoculars to his chest. A wave of heat closed over him.

Her long raven hair hung past her waist. She had a darker olive skin tone, a firm body, and a beautiful smile. She stared in the direction of David and his crew. The woman smiled, then lifted a horn from its resting place on her hip and blew into it. In the distance, small boats appeared out of the fog. Sweat formed on David's brow and his chin quivered. He should have warned his crew.

Before he was even able to mutter a word, two women popped their heads up from under the waves. They joined the first female in singing the trance-like song.

"You must not listen to them! Turn away from them, do not listen to their songs. They will lure you to their shores!" David screamed frantically.

His words did not help. Two members of his crew slipped off their pants and shoes and dived overboard. The women riding the waves in the water clutched their shirts and led them back to the shore. A third sailor bent over the side of the ship. He reached his hand out to one of the remaining women. She took his hand, yanking him into the water.

Without warning, the ship shifted to the left. One of the sailors had cut the anchor restraints dropping it into the bay, diving into the water after one of the women signaled to him. The ship lodged itself up on the rocks with nowhere to go. Raven heads appeared at the top of the deck, and their bodies followed after. The ship had been boarded. The women continued to sing their hypnotizing songs luring more of the sailors to follow them back to the island.

David dodged around in horror; most of the men had been taken. When the women had their fill of sailors to leave with them, their songs quieted, and they retreated from the ship leaving David with a handful of men.

"We have to retrieve our men," David declared "We cannot leave them on the island. If we do, they will all be slaughtered."

"What is the plan, Captain?" one of the sailors responded.

"We shall wait for the cover of nightfall, and proceed to shore. We will have to be quiet and move with the night. You cannot alert these women to our presence. We will only have one shot of retrieving our men. Prepare our weapons; we shall leave the ship at dusk."

Over the next few hours, David and his men sharpened their swords and loaded their guns in preparation of what they would find on the island. None of them knew what they would find, or even if any of their fellow sailors were alive. They all knew, if they had any chance of leaving this place, the crew members had to be saved.

The sun set over the bay, initiating the mission. They lowered the dinghies into the dark water, boarded the boat and rowed to the island's shore, dragging the empty dinghies on the sand behind them. Dark foliage covered the island, and strange bird songs rang out overhead. David studied the beach for movement, making sure it was deserted.

Signaling with his hand, David and his men spread out and descended in the direction of the faint color of orange off in the distance. As the men closed in on their destination, tall totem poles with strange carvings and flames towered above them. Skeletons swung in the trees from the wind blowing all around them.

Shadows of the women moved around inside the huts. They also heard men's screams and moans coming from various areas of the village. David moved in a soft jog; time was of the essence, and his crew's lives were in danger. David and his men lowered themselves to the ground to pass the huts unnoticed. His crew members obediently followed his order, proceeding into the village on their knees and stomachs under the cover of darkness.

David came upon an open hut and squinted through a hole on the shelter's side. One of his sailors was strapped down on the bed by his feet and wrists. Naked and bare, the native woman performed a serenaded dance over the sailor. She picked up a large scaly object, a snake so large it exceeded imagination and shifted in her hands. The snake's form changed, slithering down her arm towards David's crew member.

David sprang into action. Drawing his sword from his scabbard, he crept forward and using a quick hand action, beheaded the woman with one clean movement, sending her head in the air landing in the lap of the bound sailor. He swiped his sword again, removing the head of the giant cobra.

David released the sailor from his bindings, threw him his clothes and instructed him to assist in the recovery of the rest of the crew. The sailor was speechless, embarrassed for his actions which landed him in the hut. David nodded in understanding, drew back the burlap on the hut and headed back into the night to continue with the mission.

David and the crew continued to creep into the shelters killing off the women and saving their comrades until only three missing sailors remained. David and his team gathered in the center of the village; they heard loud screams coming from one direction they had not gone in.

"You four men with me," David whispered to a few of his men. "The rest of you head back to the ship and get us off those rocks."

"Yes Captain," they all answered simultaneously.

The band of sailors broke into two. The four sailors with David headed towards the screams with their swords drawn. Through the foliage they went, spanning out into the clearing. Images they never would forget surrounded them.

David's three remaining sailors were held and tortured by the leaders of the women pack. Eight bare-breasted women donning long headdresses, concealing their naked buttocks, performed their rituals. These women were so consumed in their actions. David and his men's presence did not startle them. Two of the women had one of David's sailors strapped down to a wooden circle contraption. His legs and arms were spread open and bound. Another woman was riding her vagina on his face while an additional woman rode his penis in a hard and fast fashion.

He moaned in pleasure until the woman riding his penis pulled out a long knife, plunging it into his chest. His screams were muffled by the woman riding his face. She smothered him with her vagina and suffocated him until he was dead. Dismounting his face, she walked to pick up a bowl, joining the woman who had sliced open his chest.

She removed his heart, liver, and other pertinent organs and placed them in the bowl. She dismounted his penis and with the same knife, sliced it off and put it into the bowl. David covered his eyes to obscure his view. His sailors all turned their faces from the horrendous scene before them. Once the women finished cutting body parts, they released his body, dragging it over to the giant bonfire, tossing it into the flames.

David and his men uncovered their eyes watching the scenes around the clearing continue to unfold. They realized they would not be able to save the other two men from the same fate as the other experienced. Four women stood at every side of the second sailor's body. Holding his legs and arms, they retreated in opposite directions and pulled until his body began to break.

David could sense the sailor's pain and knew he wanted to scream. His face was also covered by one of the women, who violently rode his face with her vagina. She muffled his screams to the point of orgasm, as his limbs were ripped from his torso.

The sailor stopped moving, and the woman with the knife once again cut him open to remove his organs, and his extremities. The last remaining sailor was pinned to a wall screaming and praying to God after all he had witnessed.

"Please, Lord, let death come swiftly," He sobbed. He moved frantically until he noticed David and the others. He stopped his movements and smiled. "Get out of here!" he whispered over and over.

The women threw spears into his bound body. The force from the spears caused blood to spurt and ooze from his chest. He smiled at David one final time and died. The women released the body to the ground and removed his heart. David had seen enough. He gestured for the group to head back to the beach. The men in front of him disappeared into the foliage; he gazed back at the clearing one final time, and taking a deep breath, he spun around to enter the brush.

A woman was standing right before him. She tried to kiss him, but he evaded her advances, thrusting his drawn sword into her chest. She fell back on the ground but managed to let out a call alerting the other women in the village who swarmed into the clearing.

David gawked back at the women coming after him. Taking off in a sprint, he made his way through the foliage back to the beach. The crew members observed David and the women coming in their direction. Panicking they all removed their boots, and scurried into the water, swimming back to the ship. The women did not pursue them, but chanted songs and danced on the sand of the beach.

All of the remaining crew made it back to the ship and worked through the night preparing to set sail from the island. The next few weeks at sea remained somber for the Captain and his men. They occasionally laughed and joked, but more often than not, they thought of those who were killed. David would sit on the bow of the ship when it was quiet, and the crew was bedded down. He would find himself staring out into the dark water reminiscing of time past.

It is my fault that I lost three men on this voyage. I should have warned them and listened to the old man.

He documented everything in his journal. He knew no one would believe him back in England. But perhaps one day he could share such voyages with his future son, and tell him about his adventures.

Time moved fast and another three months at sea went by. Finally, David and his crew saw land. They all clapped and sang and danced before making port.

Cape Verde Islands produced exotic fruit David and his crew had never seen before. They enjoyed the spoils of the land: good rum, and good food. After the tragic events on what David coined the "Mysterious Island," his crew found enjoyment in the sexual spoils the island women provided to them for a minimum charge. David, however, was not in the mood and did not want to partake in the sexual exploits of the naked native women.

David found himself consumed heavily in thought one day, as he made his way alone on the beach. He reflected again about the three the sailors he lost and what he could have done differently.

A heavy burden to carry. But I will carry it for life. No one can ever know.

David slumped his shoulders, and his mouth felt dry. The soft waves washed up over his feet as he stared out into the horizon. As his thoughts drifted away again, off in the distance, he noticed a beautiful caramel skinned girl with long hair. Her linen shirt draped, off one of her shoulders.

As she approached him, she smiled gently, "Hello Mister, voulez-vous un verre de rhum?" (Would you like some rum?)

David understood her language. Smiling, he answered her in his best French accent.

"Oui milady je voudrais un verre de rhum" (Yes milady I would like some rum)

She retrieved a cup out of her bag and poured him a drink of rum. David sat down on the beach, the waves brushing over his ankles.

"Parlez-vous anglais" (Do you speak English?), David asked, twisting towards the girl.

"Très peu Monsieur le Président, je vais essayer de vous" (Very little sir, I will try for you), the girl mumbled sitting down next to David.

"What is your name?" David asked, reaching for the rum bottle in her hand.

"My name is Lourdes, sir."

David scanned her silhouette. She was a lovely creature with long, wavy, blondish brown hair, soft caramel skin, and shapely legs. When she uncrossed her legs, David noticed she was not wearing underwear. The softness of the hair from her mound brushed against her thigh, from underneath her blue linen shirt. The hardness of her nipples protruded through her shirt, as the wind blew across them. David instantly became aroused, which he did not want.

It was too late he thought as his erection began to poke through his trousers. David was determined to keep his thoughts private. He avoided looking at her any further and prepared to get back to the ship.

"Sir, where are you going?" Lourdes wondered. She spun around in the direction he headed.

"I have duties back on the ship," David said, straightening his clothing.

"You are not leaving me here tonight sir; I will make you stay here with me."

She stepped in front of David, and untied her shirt, dropping it to the ground. The blowing wind made her nipples hard once again. David's penis started to bulge again, poking through his trousers from seeing her nude. Lourdes moved closer to him and kissed him on the lips. She slid her hand down his pants, grabbed his crotch and began rubbing his hard erect penis in her hands.

David enjoyed how her hand moved stroking his hard cock. He leaned his head back into the wind and exhaled.

This is not happening.

He was waiting for the woman he dreamt of to be real. He so desperately wanted to know what true love felt like. The thought of his crew members also came to mind. He knew he could not go back to the ship and listen to their stories about the women they ravaged all night and all the rum they had drunk. David decided to allow himself to indulge in the moment with Lourdes.

"Me frotter plus difficile" (Rub me harder), David whispered into Lourdes's ear.

"Oui, sir."

Lourdes increased the tension of her hand stroking David's cock. She tightened her grip and pulled his penis firmly.

David moaned in appreciation and once again whispered, "Me frotter plus difficile" (rub me harder).

Lourdes listened to his command and again stroked harder. David snatched her hand out of his trousers, licking her fingers before placing her hand on her side. He unbuttoned his pants, kicking them off to the side. He jerked Lourdes close to him, and tilted her head to the left, placing his lips upon her neck. She let out a moan as he kissed her. His kissing led to bites and nibbling increasing when Lourdes winced in pain. She pulled his head closer to his neck begging him to continue. He continued to bite and nibble down her collarbone, shoulder, and onto her perky nipples, rolling one in his mouth and around the tip of his tongue.

Lourdes moaned in pleasure, grabbing David's head once again and tugging it in closer to her chest. David moved over to her other nipple, suckling it, like a hungry baby searching for milk. He did not abandon her other nipple. He pinched it while he rubbed it around between his index finger and thumb.

Lourdes moaned more freely. David lifted her in his arms up around his waist. He plummeted his fully hard erection between her creamy hips, impaling her on his straining shaft. Lourdes wrapped her legs around his narrow waist and fell back, her hair sweeping against the sand. She moaned louder and grabbed her nipples, rubbing them. David's pulse quickened as he broke a sweat.

David lowered Lourdes down on all fours and entered her from behind, riding her as if she was a stallion. He raised her hips and continued thrusting harder and deeper against her bare ass. He pressed her hips frantically against his, becoming rougher, but he did not care. David yanked her hair and head back and continued to pulse into her excitedly. David's shallow pants led him to pulsate inside her. David became woozy, the exhaustion of the sexual experience had taken its toll, and he passed out, head first, in the sand.

The next morning, David woke up on the beach with sand hugging all of the exposed parts of his body, and in his mouth and nose. He coughed to expel the sand from his lungs. He rubbed his head as a headache formed from the amount of rum he consumed the previous evening. As he got to his feet he immediately felt dizzy.

I need to sit down.

David fell back down in the sand. Visions of his night with Lourdes returned.

"Lourdes!" he called out, looking around. But there was no one on the side of the beach he sat upon. "Lourdes!" David called out again, thinking, this time, she would appear in front of him, but no one came.

Was it a dream?

David leaned over, gathering his trousers in his hand, slipping them on. Pain shot up his thighs to his cock, serving as a reminder, that the night before was not a dream.

Damn, I was rough with her; I hope I didn't hurt her.

He threw his boots over his shoulder, gathered his other belongings and waded up the sand back to the docks to his ship. David reached the Lady Fantasy and crossed the wooden plank.

He found his crew naked and spread about the ship with their whores from the night before. He sensed some partner swapping on board. Whores laid over the men in every direction, some of which still had their mouths around the privy members of the crew. All David could do was smile. He was happy he was not on board the ship last night. He climbed over the crew members on the deck and into his cabin. Opening the door, he saw the girl from last night sitting on his desk.

Lourdes's breasts were exposed; the shirt she wore from the night before, draped around her waist. Her legs were spread open as if she were waiting for him. David was dumbfounded! The sexual urge to ravage her again returned.

"I waited back at the ship for you, sir," Lourdes said in her broken English. "I hope you didn't mind me coming."

"Not at all," David admitted, springing forward, entangling her hair with his fingers. He tugged her head back with force, her eyes resting upon him. He stared back at her, pushing her mouth open as he inserted his tongue.

Lourdes encircled David's mouth with her tongue. As their tongues intertwined, David's erection returned. He released

Lourdes's hair and unbuttoned his trousers once more. He wanted her, and he wanted her now. He spread her legs wider, his penis diving into the warm dark haven of Lourdes's wetness. David jolts were slow and steady until Lourdes moaned grabbing his buttocks and his chest into her. David felt electricity radiate down to his toes. His tempo increased and became fast and hard.

He lifted her buttocks off the desk pushing her back down against the cold wood and sunk himself into her again and again. David's mind wandered once more. He found himself thinking of the woman who came to him in his dreams. Believing it was his dream girl on the desk, he moaned loudly, releasing his moistness onto her sweaty breasts.

Lourdes sat up on the desk and smiled. She stepped down off the desk and covered her sweat and semen-splashed chest with her shirt.

"Je pense que vous devriez laisser maintenant, Lourdes" (I think you should leave, Lourdes), David said, backing up, tying his trousers.

"Est-ce que vous n'êtes pas convaincu, Sir? (Are you not satisfied, sir?), Lourdes said, defeated.

"I am not disappointed, Lourdes. We are leaving today, and I must get the crew prepared."

David picked up his coin pouch off the floor and opened the cabin door, showing Lourdes out.

"Thank you for last night and this morning, I hope this takes care of the fees I owe you."

David opened the pouch and handed Lourdes twenty gold coins. Lourdes snatched the coins out of David's hand.

"Adieu sir," Lourdes cried, rushing past.

David hung his head momentarily. He felt remorse for hurting the girl. He could not let the guilty thoughts consume him. He paced continually back and forth in front of his mirror until he could pull himself together.

Get yourself together man; you have to do better.

He pushed the thoughts from his mind. He headed out to the deck where he kicked one of his crew members. "Get your asses up and get to work, I want these whores off of my ship. We set sail in an hour."

David's voice bellowed throughout the ship, waking his entire crew. They scrambled to put the whores off the ship and compose themselves for duty. Within the hour, the crew had the ship cleaned, stocked and ready to go. They pushed out from the port and let the current from the sea lead them out to the deeper ocean water.

David and his crew never made it to India. After stopping in Malindi and another three months at sea, a second severe storm killed an additional ten men of David's crew. A broken compass led the remaining crew in the wrong direction. The ship sailed up a body of water which was now called the Gulf of Aden, which led them to the shores of Abyssinia. David realized the error and wanted to turn the ship around, but thought if the lands, were uncharted, perhaps he and his crew would make a historical discovery.

David took his telescope out from his side pocket to scout the far off beach when he spotted a young woman in the water away from the shore. Her head was submerged in the water. David removed his boots and shirt, diving from the ship into the frigid water below. Despite the initial chill of the cold water, he swam with speed to the woman, lifting her head up back above water. David's crew let down the dinghy and piled into the boat to retrieve the two of them.

They reached David and the woman, and strained to lift her lifeless body into the boat. David climbed in behind them and rested the woman's head on his knee. The dinghy rowed back to the ship, and David lifted the woman's lifeless body over one of his shoulders. He climbed the ladder onto the deck and laid her body gently down. Tilting her head back, he tried to breathe life back into her lungs.

David pumped her chest with compressions until she started to breathe and cough the salt water out of her lungs. She inhaled deeply and slowly opened her eyes. David's eyes met hers, and a feeling in his gut told him she could be the woman from in his dreams.

8 Abyssinia

Scared and unsure of her surroundings, Eleni gathered what little strength she had and pushed through the crowd of men looking down at her. The crew stood back in shock and amazement at her features. Eleni quickly moved away from them to the side of the ship, climbing on the ledge like she was going to jump overboard.

"Get away from me! Do not touch me!" she screamed at the men below who glared back at her. She jumped down from the ledge of the ship, seizing a piece of plank wood, and swung it. "Do not any come any closer,"

David came out around the group of men. "Please calm yourself, Milady," he stated coming closer. "No one on this vessel is going to hurt you."

"Stay away from me!" Eleni screamed in her exotic English accent, swinging the piece of wood.

"No one is going to hurt you, I promise, "David said again, reaching for the piece of timber. "Are you going to hit me with a piece of wood?"

She swung violently at him, narrowly missing his head. "Yes, I will hurt you if you come any closer."

Everything around her began to spin, the wood became heavy in her hand, as she felt warm and weak. She dropped the wood at her feet. Her eyes rolled back in her head, and she fell, hitting her head on the deck of the ship; she was unconscious once again.

Eleni felt the man splashing cool water down her face.

"Come on, Milady, wake up." He whispered in her ear as he dabbed her face with a rag.

Eleni opened her eyes; a set of vibrant blue eyes stared down at her. "I am still a little light-headed," she stated, starting to sit up.

"If you are still dizzy, it is because you hit your head rather hard. Take your time getting up, Milady."

Eleni reached out to the extended arm. The man helped her to her feet. She rubbed the back of her neck, instantly regretting her actions.

If he wanted to hurt me, he could have left me in the ocean to drown.

Their eyes locked again. It was as she had met him before, a connection, a feeling; she was not sure.

"I am Eleni," she said

"My name is David, Milady. You speak English rather well. How did you learn if you do not mind me asking?"

"Yes, I guess I do speak English quite well. I learned from the pale men like you, who visited my kingdom in past times. My father believed it was something I needed to learn so I could translate for him. I am well versed in many languages, Milord."

"Well, I am impressed. It makes things much easier for us to communicate," David chuckled. "Now if you don't mind, let me get you something to dry off with."

He gently took hold of her arm and led her across the deck, through the multiple sets of eyes resting on her. David walked closely by her side and escorted her to the cabin at the back of the ship. He nudged the door open, resting his hand on the small of her back, guiding her into the cabin and closed the door behind them.

"Please take a seat over there," David said, pointing at a chair.

Eleni settled into the chair. Her wet gown clung to her skin making her shiver from the cold. "This room is for the captain?" Eleni said, casting a glance around the stateroom. "Who is the captain, where is he?" she focused her attention on David.

"Well, Milady, I am the captain."

Eleni eyes widened. "You are so young to be a captain of such a big ship. I expected someone much older, and more distinguished."

"Yes I am quite young," David said, laughing. "However, there was little choice in the matter. The captain before me died at sea on our last voyage; I was made captain in his stead. "David brought a blanket and wrapped it around Eleni's shoulders.

"Thank you," she said, wrapping the blanket tighter around her.

David rounded the desk and sat down, facing Eleni, his face intensified. "How is it I came to find you in the water, Eleni?"

"I was in my place of peace, and I wanted to be near the water."

"Your place of peace was in the water?" David asked intrigued. He picked up a goblet off his desk and offered it to Eleni. She clutched the cup in her hand, drinking the water slowly.

"Yes, I always felt at peace near and in the water. I cannot say why. Ever since I was a child, it attracted me. Sometimes when the wind blows, I can hear it calling out to me." Eleni watched David closely.

"Why do you ask me such questions? I am sure you find it is odd for me to say such things?"

"No, I do not believe it's strange at all. I happen to find peace in the water as well. My family never liked me becoming a sailor or understood me having a need to be out on the open water of the ocean."

Eleni finished her water and placed the goblet back on the desk. She pulled her wet gown over her knees, the blanket warming her skin. "I see. But here you are at sea. So your family accepted it?"

"Not exactly," David said. "I bribed my mother into letting me sail."

Eleni shook her head. "What is the word bribe? what does it mean?"

"Well, it means, influencing another person to do what you want."

"I see, well bribe is an interesting word."

Eleni dropped the blanket in the chair and made her way to the window, taking in the dark blue water. David observed her movements. He was able to tell she was not a slave; her gown was beautiful even though it was soaked with water.

Maybe she is a servant girl.

Regardless of what she was, there was a genuine connection. He wanted to study her, to ask her more questions. He rummaged his fingers through his jet black hair as his eyes laid upon her. Never in his walk of life had he met someone like himself who loved the water of the sea or river as he did. Eleni smiled at him again before returning her glance back to the window. The connection between them become more evident. David believed she was the woman from his dreams, the one he had been searching for.

The hour had become late, and the sun's pink and orange rays brightened over the blue horizon. Eleni shifted her glance back to David.

"Can you please get me back to the shore? I will be missed if I am not back soon."

"Wait, so soon?" He took her hand in his.

"Yes, I am sorry, but they will be looking for me."

Eleni closed her hand around his, holding it tighter.

"Who will be looking for you?"

Eleni did not give an answer, but her eyes told him everything he needed. The fear reflected off of her eyes like an endless pool. He could not hold her there much longer.

"I will return you under one condition" David rounded the desk again. Laying his firm hands on Eleni's small shoulders, he studied her carefully. "No more attempts of wanting to find peace in the water. At least not before we meet again." David swung the cabin door open.

"Perhaps we will meet again," she lamented. Eleni's face beamed as David escorted her back onto the deck.

David signaled the crew to lower the dinghy into the water. He took Eleni's arm once more and led her to the ladder. They both descended the side of the ship down into the boat. The dinghy moved across the gentle waves at a quick pace. David found himself lost in Eleni's beauty; she was still wet, but something about her demeanor and her presence were familiar.

The dinghy glided as close to shore as possible without hitting the rocks below and came to a halt. David rose off the bench, grasping Eleni's hand, bracing her.

"This is as close to shore as we can come. If we come any closer, we will have to rope the boat in. We will let you out in the water here."

"It is okay; I will be okay. Help me into the water, please."

David and another crew member lifted Eleni's frame into the water. The water rested on her chest and weighed down her flowing tresses.

"Thank you again, David, for saving my life. And for the conversation." She waded through the water back to shore.

"Eleni, wait!" David called out to her. "Will I see you again? Where do you live in the kingdom?"

"If it is meant for you to find me, you will." She gave a little smile, turned and continued to wade through the water.

Will I ever see her again?

David made it back to the ship and went back to his cabin for the evening. He removed his clothes, splashed himself with water and reflected on the day's events. He had never seen anyone quite like Eleni, and he hoped the opportunity would present itself to meet her again.

I will go on shore to find her.

David laid his lean, steely-muscled physique across the sheets. It was going to be a long sleepless night; still he tried to close his eyes to rest, but all he thought of was her and the special connection they had formed in one afternoon.

Eleni picked up the wet layers of her drenched gown and scurried out of the water. She glanced one final time at the small boat paddling back to the massive ship anchored in the bay. For the first time in her life, she encountered someone who was similar to her, a person who could be her friend.

David was incredibly handsome. She had never seen anyone like him before jet black wavy hair, turquoise blue eyes, chiseled high cheekbones, and the calm yet firm tone in his voice.

She tingled remembering how gently she spoke to him. Eleni shook her head and shifted her focus to getting back to the castle. She pulled her soaked gown up into her right hand exposing her thighs and ran as quickly as she could up the stone stairs on the cliff to the palace.

Eleni heard the king's guards sounding the horns giving everyone the warning there was a foreigner's ship anchored in the lagoon off the coast. Eleni reached the top of the cliff, stopping to calm her heart and catch her breath.

She tried to think of a story to explain to Arkamun of how she ended up wet, and why she was gone so long. Before she could formulate her story, she could hear her husband behind her.

"Eleni! Where have you been?"

She wheeled around to face him, his face dark and grim. He was displeased.

"I was walking on the beach when I saw the foreigner's ship in the distance. I was not expecting a massive ship to be docked in the lagoon. I tripped over some stones. I came to warn you. I waited to see if anyone was going to appear on the ship."

"And did anyone appear, Eleni?" Arkamun grunted.

"Yes, Milord." Eleni bit her lip. "Some crew members appeared on the deck of the ship and surveyed our land with a telescope. They never rowed ashore."

"Why do I get the impression you are hiding something from me? I am finding it hard to believe you." Arkamun yanked Eleni's wrists with force, closing in on her face.

"You disgust me. A queen is not supposed to offend her king at any time," Arkamun barked, squeezing her wrists tighter.

"Your gown is ruined, and you are soaked! A queen should be at her best at all times!"

Arkamun flung Eleni down to the ground. "You will be bathed and presented to me accordingly" he scoffed, kicking her in the stomach. "Come to me when you are ready," he yelled, sauntering away.

Eleni held her stomach as she gasped for breath. She was going to have a long night. Pleasing her husband sexually was the only way to procure decent treatment. Eleni knelt. Ayantu rushed to her aid, helping her off the ground.

"Milady are you, all right?" Ayantu asked.

"Yes, I am okay. "Eleni's stomach was in knots after the kick Arkamun bestowed on her.

"You would think he would stop hitting you, Milady," Ayantu stated. "Especially if he wants you to bear an heir. How many late term miscarriages have you had now?"

"It has been four times now, Ayantu," she echoed as they walked back to Eleni's chambers.

Eleni knew Ayantu was right. If she were not abused by the hands of her husband and allowed to carry to full term, she would have been the mother of four children, three sons, and a daughter. She had reached her breaking point. She was able to hold each fetus. All of them taking a breath. She prayed to the creator, despite the abuse inflicted by her husband that her children would survive being born so early. None of them did, and she buried each one of them in the royal tomb. The last couple of years started to take a toll on her. She was inconsolable, and her hatred for Arkamun and her parents grew.

Eleni and Ayantu wandered through the castle cautiously. Eleni did not want to face Arkamun or encounter anyone else. They could not move fast enough to avoid Meseret.

"Eleni, what has happened?" Queen Meseret called out.

Eleni and Ayantu slowed, Ayantu lifting Eleni's arm from around her neck. Eleni veered around at Meseret, weary.

"How about you ask your son what happened."

Meseret approached Eleni and touched her face. Eleni's eyes appeared dark, and she looked tired and frail.

"I know my son can be a handful. Perhaps this was not an advantageous match between the two of you? Have you heard from your parents, Eleni? Have you told them about what is happening to you?"

"Yes... perhaps this marriage between myself and your son is not the best arrangement. No, I have not heard anything from anyone back home since I came here. I have given up on them."

"I care for you Eleni; you know this. I assumed things had gotten better from the abuse Arkamun had inflicted and the loss of your children. I will speak to my son again about how he has been treating you. He should not be continuing to put his hands on you. I hope things will change going forward.

My son should not be putting his hands on Eleni, especially since we are still lovers. I had pleaded with him before about his behavior and transgressions with other women. I will speak to him again, and perhaps I can try a different sexual technique to appease him.

Now go, get some rest and bathe. Ayantu, make sure you take good care of our queen."

The two young women arrived back at Eleni's chambers. Ayantu helped Eleni ease into the nearby chair.

"I shall draw a bath for you Milady," she said, leaving Eleni to gather water. Eleni broke down crying in her hands.

It must be a better life than this. I must leave this place.

Eleni could only see the years of her life wasted being a queen to a king who used her on occasion, his concubines to be called

upon when he grew bored with her. If things did not change Arkamun would eventually take her life if she did not take it herself.

Eleni sat up and dried her tears with her hands. She yanked
off her drenched gown and undergarments, standing in the window nude. The sea breeze enveloped her body leaving her at ease.
She reminisced about her meeting with David. Her nipples hardened envisioning his physique; a moistness trickled down her legs.
She laid down on her back and daydreamed more about him.

Eleni wondered what he kissed like, and how his lips tasted.
He was a kind man and no man, including her father, had ever
shown her the level of compassion he did. She brushed her hands
over her body rubbing the areas where the sensations grew. Her
self-pleasuring was averted when Ayantu reappeared and told her
it was time for her bath.

Eleni opened her eyes and exhaled. The palpitations in her
heart ceased, her pulse slowed. She got to her feet and made her
way over to the tub.

"Milady, what was it you were thinking of when you were
lying on the bed? Ayantu asked as Eleni stepped into the tub.
"You seemed deep in thought."

"I was not thinking of anything." Eleni sat back, the water up
to her neck.

"I never see you like that, Milady." Ayantu soaked the sponge
in the water. "Sit up please so I can wash your back."

Eleni was hesitant for a moment but shared her encounter
from earlier that afternoon. "I was thinking about a man I met
today, down at the beach. He saved my life today Ayantu."

"A man? You mean one of the men on the ship docked in the
lagoon?"

"Yes, I was on board that ship today, "Eleni answered, resting
on her thigh. Ayantu, you must not tell anyone."

She relaxed again and laid back against the tub. "He saved my life, Ayantu. Something came over me that I had not felt before."

Ayantu kept bathing Eleni slowly and listening to her story. "I do not want to hear anymore, Eleni. If Arkamun finds out, he will kill you."

"Why not, my sweet Ayantu? You always listened to my stories before."

"You never spoke of another so highly, as you do now," Ayantu spewed getting up off her knees to grab a drying towel for Eleni.

"I never had feelings for anyone like this, Ayantu; I cannot help what I feel."

"Get up out of the bath, Eleni," Ayantu commanded. "I need to dry you."

Eleni rose out of the tub. She did not care for Ayantu's tone, but obeyed her command, stepping over the side of the tub.

Ayantu dried Eleni's body with the towel and wrapped it around her. As she closed the towel around shoulders, Ayantu leaned in and kissed her on the lips, trying to part them with her tongue. Eleni shoved Ayantu away from her so forcefully it almost made her slip.

"What are you doing, Ayantu?" Eleni screamed, horrified

"I wanted to be near you again, I wanted to share a moment again with you," Ayantu answered, finding her footing on the floor.

"Nothing has ever happened between us for you to think that kissing me was okay!"

"But our bath times, you let me pleasure you with my hands," Ayantu retorted," I assumed you wanted more? I thought you wanted me?"

"Those were only times where you showed me what to do to please my king. I never wanted to be with you in a sexual way, Ayantu. I am sorry if this hurts you, but you should know better. Please never attempt such a stunt again or I will dismiss you from my service."

Eleni covered her breasts, her face aflame. What had she done to cause such emotion from her servant?

"Yes, Milady, I understand," Ayantu muttered "I apologize for my actions. They will never happen again."

"Let us hope it does not. Everything is forgotten, help me dress for my night in hell with Arkamun."

Ayantu had laid out a flowing sheer robe with emerald stones on it. Meant to be worn for one reason, giving pleasure to the king. Eleni's breasts sat firmly under the sheer material. Eleni wished she was wearing it for David. Perhaps her luck would change, and the two of them would meet again.

Eleni saw Ayantu's reflection in the mirror. Her face was puffy and eyes red from tears. "I am sorry for being so firm with you earlier, Ayantu." Eleni embraced Ayantu, the sheer robe falling off her shoulders, her naked body pressing against Ayantu's chest.

"You have always been such a good friend since I got here. I do not want to lose you." Eleni did not want the one person she could confide in to turn on her. She would give in to Ayantu's advances to keep her confidant.

Eleni kissed Ayantu softly, her lips parting her mouth with her tongue. Ayantu engulfed her embrace, and they shared a deep passionate kiss. Ayantu wrapped her arms around Eleni tighter. The kiss lasted for a few moments and was interrupted by the guard sounding the night horn.

Eleni broke their embrace. She had little time to finish preparing before Arkamun sought her out. She wiped the evidence of the kiss from her lips. It was a pleasant interaction; one she would have rather shared with David.

"Let me help, Milady," Ayantu said, beaming from their kiss.

"I have to hurry; you know what the night horn means."

"Yes, Milady! dinner is done, and it is time for the castle to shut down for the evening, and for you..." Ayantu's voice trailed off.

"You do not have to say it; we all know what it means."

Eleni picked up the robe off of the floor, throwing it back own, over her shoulders. She slipped her emerald footless sandals around her ankles and toes

"You are stunning, my queen. You better go, or else."

"Thank you, Ayantu," Eleni said, pausing at the door.

Eleni tiptoed down the marble floor to Arkamun's chamber, knocking on the door.

"Milord.".

"Enter, Eleni," the voice responded back from behind the door. Eleni cracked the door wider, sliding through the opening and closing the door behind her. Arkamun stood before her in all white. His rippling muscles pulsated from under his shirt. He was so handsome. Eleni wished he was different, but it was the darkness in his eyes that scared her.

The sun beamed rays of light through the curtain panels, waking Eleni from her abbreviated sleep. Arkamun's arm was strung over her small frame as she laid beneath him. Desperate to get away from him, she positioned a pillow under his arm and slipped out of the bed.

Eleni gathered her tattered robe and left Arkamun's bed chamber, blanketed in bruises once more. She touched her right eye beginning to swell from her husband's strong fists punching her in the face, and flinging her down on the bed.

Eleni reached her chamber room and swung the heavy wooden door open. Staggering through it, she closed the door with her back, causing her legs to give out from under her. Eleni's energy was all but gone, and using her arms, she crawled across the floor making it to her bed. She lugged herself up and into it.

She spread herself across the bed, tears flowing from her eyes. Staring at the ornamented ceiling, she reflected on the events of the past night. Arkamun looked so handsome and so malicious. She had not seen the benevolent side of him since meeting him on their wedding day and never understood why he treated her the way he did.

I could have loved him once. If he had shown me the slightest sympathy, I could have loved him.

Eleni closed her eyes tears, continuing to stream down her face.

Let me wash myself; I need to remove his smell from my skin.

She sat up on the bed and expelled what was left of her robe onto the floor. She advanced over to the mirror, fixing on the likeness staring back at her. Her nude body bruised so easily that she turned black and blue in places.

Her breasts bled from the scrapes Arkamun's rings gave her as he dug into her skin, ripping her robe from her body. Her swollen right eye started to close up. She inhaled a deep breath. Her looks were starting to fade from all the beatings she had taken by her husband's hand.

I'm so tired.

Eleni made her way to the basin. Ayantu had left water for her and ran her a bath. She knew Eleni far too well by this point. Eleni used the sponge in the basin to splash water on her face. She held the sponge up to her swollen eye. It stung her face for a bit but finally started to soothe her skin. Ayantu also left the healing oils out for her. She knew those would help her feel better.

She placed the sponge back into the basin and picked up a familiar looking bottle. Opening it, she smelled the contents.

Lavender.

Eleni poured some into her bath water. She retrieved the second bottle labeled healing oil from the basin. It was composed of various types of herbs and oils. She dabbed a little on her finger and rubbed it on the contusions as well as her bruised eye.

Everything on my body stings.

Eleni finished the applications of the oil and sank in the tub. The warm water hit her legs as the water rose over her. Eleni tilted her head against the back of the tub and closed her eyes. Visions of David came to the forefront. The sensations she felt the day before about him resurfaced. She was swept up by how he touched her. She wanted to be touched by him once again, only this time on a more personal and intimate level. The minutes turned into an hour, and soon, another hour had passed.

Eleni's eyes fluttered. Ayantu was standing above her.

"Eleni! Are you okay?"

"I am fine, Ayantu, I must have dozed off," Eleni said, sitting up in the tub. The water had become chilled, and her body had pruned up from being exposed in the water too long.

"How long did I sleep for?" Eleni asked as she stepped out the tub.

"Had to be for at least a couple of hours, "Ayantu answered retrieving her robe, draping it around her shoulders. "I checked on you briefly. I did not want to disturb you; you seemed very relaxed."

"I lost track of time, I was in pain, I guess my body needed the good soak." Eleni examined her face in the mirror. The swelling and the redness had completely gone away. Her cheeks even had a little pink to them, which had never been there before.

"You look different, my queen," Ayantu said, standing behind her.

"What makes you say that?" Eleni still watched her reflection in the mirror.

Ayantu wrapped her arms around Eleni. "Your face is glowing Milady. You had thoughts about something happy."

Eleni immediately knew it was because of David, but she kept that to herself. She would not bring up her encounter with David again to Ayantu.

"You must have been thinking about me." Ayantu moved her hands up Eleni's body under her robe and cupped her breasts with her hands.

Eleni inhaled, facing Ayantu. "Of course, I was thinking about you. "Eleni lied. Ayantu kissed her on the lips softly, then kissed her again deeper, this time, allowing her tongue to part Eleni's mouth and dance around inside. Eleni could not deny her body becoming aroused by Ayantu touching her and kissing her.

Eleni would continue with the charade and let Ayantu have her way. She felt vulnerable and so unloved after her night with Arkamun. Any amount of affection helped her forget the painful experience.

Ayantu removed Eleni's robe, stripping her naked. "You are so beautiful, Eleni." Ayantu removed her arms from her dress. Before she could go any further, there was a knock at the door.

"Your Majesty?" a voice called out from the opposite side of the door, it was Hillina.

"Just a moment, Hillina," Eleni answered, gently moving Ayantu to the side and covering her waist and shoulders with her robe. She cracked the door, peering at Hillina.

"How can I help you, Hillina?"

"The king sent me to find you. He is waiting for you in the throne room. Did you not remember today is when he opens the court for all to speak to him?"

"I had fallen asleep in the bath. I had not realized how much time had passed."

"You have always been and continue to be such a stupid girl," Hillina said in a hostile tone. "You need to get dressed and get down to the throne room quickly. Arkamun will not be pleased with your lateness."

"Please apologize to the king for me, Hillina, I will be down as soon as I can. This will never happen again."

"Make sure it does not or I will have you whipped myself." Hillina turned away from the door. Eleni closed the door, with her back against it. She was tired of the verbal abuse inflicted on her by Hillina.

Tears once again welled up in her eyes. Arkamun would get his revenge for her being tardy; she did not know when. Ayantu grasped Eleni's hand and kissed it.

"It will be okay, focus on the here and the now."

She led Eleni over to the chair by the window and eased her down into it. Ayantu got on her knees and spread Eleni's legs open, lifting her robe up over her knees. "Just relax," she said as she kissed her thighs.

Eleni leaned her head back and closed her eyes. She felt the moistness between her legs return. She dreamt about David being between her thighs. Ayantu took advantage of Eleni's vulnerability.

She licked Eleni's soft mound, moving the lips with her tongue as she made small circles around her clit.

Eleni moaned, imagining David in between her thighs. The intensity of the licking against her clit had her at the point of orgasm. Eleni's cries made Ayantu intensify her motions with her tongue and lips. She dug her face deeper into Eleni's mound, her tongue finding her hole. Eleni's moistness trickled down her face. Ayantu's tongue plummeted even deeper, stroking in and out. Eleni moaned loudly until she released her moistness on Ayantu's face.

Ayantu moved her head back from her mound, leaned up and kissed Eleni again on the lips. She got to her feet and headed over to the basin to wash her face and clothing.

Eleni was so deep into her vision of David; she did not realize Ayantu had stopped pleasuring her when she reached her orgasm. She opened her eyes and gazed around. Ayantu stood at the basin washing her face.

Eleni felt awkward. Ayantu had pleasured her, but she pictured David in her mind.

"Eleni, were you not pleased?" Ayantu asked.

"It was enjoyable."

Eleni lowered her robe back down over her knees. She Joined Ayantu over at the basin. She took the sponge from Ayantu's hand and used it to clean between her legs to freshen up.

"Ayantu, please bring me my gown," she ordered.

She began brushing her long curls up into a bun on the top of her head.

"Which one, are you wearing today?" Ayantu opened the armoire.

"I think I will wear the ocean blue gown today. And the pearl slippers."

"Should do nicely, you always looked sinful in this gown." She released the dress from the hanger and it up to the light.

"Made me yearn for you all the more," she murmured to herself with a mysterious laugh.

Eleni's neck muscles tightened, and beads of sweat formed on her forehead. She let things go way too far with Ayantu. She could see her becoming a problem in the future.

No time to think about it further.

Eleni draped her robe over the bed and was met by Ayantu with her gown in hand. Ayantu helped her dress, and Eleni glanced in the mirror one final time before heading to the throne room.

9 Meeting Again

Eleni once again looked beautiful. The ocean blue color of the gown radiated on her soft skin. Her hair was perfect, lip stain was perfect, and she had done an excellent job of hiding her ailments. Queen Meseret met her in the hall.

"My daughter, you look lovely."

"Thank you, queen mother," Eleni answered quietly.

Queen Meseret reached out her hand to Eleni. They walked hand in hand until they reached the throne room. Two guardsmen stood at the entrance. Queen Meseret signaled for them to open the door. The same guard Eleni had seen years ago staring at her mother stood before her. Where had he been all this time?

Eleni smiled at the queen mother before she entered the room. She could see the queen and the guardsman locking eyes.

The same situation again. I wonder what is going on. First my mother, and now her.

"I will see you after your duties for the day are done," Queen Meseret whispered. She kissed Eleni on the cheek.

"See you shortly," Eleni grinned.

Eleni glided into the throne room, smiling at the villagers who had come to speak with the king.

This was going to be a long day.

The steward caught Eleni walking in; he whispered to the king that she had arrived, both sets of eyes resting on her. Arkamun's face was red, and he glared at Eleni. The steward continued to smile as he scampered across the room, taking her by the hand. The villagers' gossip quieted when the queen was escorted in.

"Her Majesty Queen Eleni!" was announced as she strolled passed. The eyes of the members of the court rested on her, and they bowed down as she nodded. Up the aisle she went, Arkamun taking her arm from the steward escorting her to the chair. They both sat down, and Arkamun leaned over and whispered into Eleni's ear.

"You will answer for your tardiness this evening. You are embarrassing me and coming to court late is unacceptable."

"I am sorry, Milord; I had to make myself presentable, that in itself takes time."

"I do not care what you were doing. You are to be on time; I will have to teach you better manners," Arkamun said through a smile, pretending as if they were enjoying each other's company.

"You will learn," he mumbled.

He kissed her on the hand and cheek before returning to his seat. Eleni's eyes glazed over. It was going to be a long day and even longer night

David awoke that morning, with his heart racing. He slept wildly, his dreams consumed with Eleni. He wanted to see her again and wondered where she lived.

I have to find her.

Smiling, he jumped out of bed and threw on his clothes. He ate a light breakfast and encouraged everyone going to shore to do the same.

"Light is on our side this morning, comrades; we need to get to shore, to explore and get back to the ship before nightfall."

"Aye Aye, Captain," The crew responded, looking at each other with confusion. Why were they in such a hurry that morning?

"Lads, finish your grub and let's get going."

David finished his plate and tossed it in the wash bucket. He stepped out on the deck of the ship. The fog started to dissipate and reveal the morning sun. The crew finished breakfast and the few men accompanying David to land met him on the deck of the ship.

David and a small team of eight set out on the dinghy. The day was a glorious one, the sun was shining, birds were chirping, and the wind was filled with a scent he had never smelled before. A magnificent castle sat perched on a cliff.

Could this be where she lives?

David was so captivated he did not realize his first mate was speaking to him.

"Captain... Captain... are you alright."

"I'm all right, Cristopher, "David answered, "I was lost in thought."

"Well, you need to snap out of your thoughts, sir we are as close to land as we can get. We will need to get out and bring the dinghy to shore."

"Fine! Let's get it done, men."

David jumped out of the boat, landing ankle deep in the cool water brushing against his boots. The rest of the men followed suit, and they lugged the dinghy up to the shore.

"Make sure you tie the boat up over there, lad," Cristopher said, pointing over to one of the ships' boys who had accompanied them to shore.

David surveyed his surroundings. The beach was composed of white sand filled with flecks of gold. Tall palm trees lined the perimeter of the beach. The sweet scent that filled David's nose blew over him again.

What is that sweet smell?

David gazed around, and his eyes rested on women pulling the fruit off trees. They peeled the fruit with their bare hands and poured the contents into large pots on an open flame.

The fruit was what was creating the lustrous scent.

David yelled over at Cristopher, pointing down the beach to where the women were working.

"I'm going to get a closer look," he stated.

David trotted in the sand up the beach in the direction of the women. One woman saw David out of the corner of her eye. She screamed out loud, alerting the other women to his presence. They all dropped bowls of fruit onto the sand, moving the opposite direction as David approached.

"Wait, wait, wait!" David yelled out.

The women hurried down the beach to the stone stairs leading to the cliff.

"Wait, please wait!"

But the words did not stop them from running away. The women climbed the stairs, leaving their pots and the contents unattended. David caught his breath and seized the opportunity to see what the women had left boiling on the open flames. He peered over into the pot; a red liquid in color was bubbling.

David removed his sword, dipping it into the fluid. The liquid stuck to the end of his sword. He swiped his finger across the blade and tasted it. The liquid was sweet, almost the consistency of preserve.

Fruit laid in the sand around his feet. He picked one up and cut it open. He held the fruit to his mouth, tasting the flesh. It too had a sweet taste, an orange colored flesh and was round. David nibbled on the fruit further. He proceeded up the beach, behind the trees and found the stone staircase leading up to the top of the cliff above.

This must be the way Eleni came.

He did not know where she had disappeared to the day before. David signaled to his crew, and they began to climb the long staircase to the castle. Each flight of stairs they climbed led into a clearing, where many people stopped their work to stare.

The women from the beach must have warned the natives that there were strangers on their shores. David smiled at the strangers and kept climbing. They finally reached the last flight of stairs taking them to the top.

David looked down and saw from their location that they were high up off the beach, clouds hovering below them. The last flight of stairs led them to an open courtyard where a beautiful white castle stood before them. Specks of a glistening stone sparkled in the walls.

David was in awe of the marvel and stood back to take in the splendor. He had never seen something so magnificent. He ran his hands over the castles smooth walls.

I wonder what this castle is made of?

He was met by two guards wearing gold armor. Their staffs were drawn, blades at the end of them, pointed in David's direction.

"What are you doing here?" one of the guards asked.

"We are sailors from the country of England. We were brought here by a storm and upon leaving our ship to explore, we came upon this castle."

"I would like to speak to the person in charge of this place." David moved out around in front of his crew.

"You are in the Kingdom of King Arkamun. He is king over these lands. You are in Abyssinia."

"I am King David of England. Announce me to your king, guardsman."

The guardsmen looked at each other and back at David. The first guard took a step back and turned his staff at a slant, allowing David and his crew to proceed.

The second guard looked at David "I will take you in to see the king."

Through the courtyard garden they went. Exotic flowers in pots lined the path and jewel encrusted decor adorned the many pergolas. They stopped at two massive doors leading into the castle. The guardsman slid the heavy door open to the throne room and led David and his men through the opening.

David gawked around the throne room. The floor was lined with gold, and every chair had an ornate design and gleamed in gold and jewels. Two chairs sat at the head of the room, one with the king sitting in it and the other, his queen. He could not see either of them clearly from the back of the room.

"Wait here; I will have you announced to the king" The Guardsman signaled his staff at the steward who joined him by his side. He whispered into the man's ear and, they both glared back at David.

David felt uneasy and shaking it off he returned his gaze to the king.

The guardsman left the stewards side." You will be announced in a moment, wait here."

He bowed, leaving David and his crew alone. It seemed like they waited hours to be seen. Many peasants lined the doorway waiting to see the king and queen. Each of them needed a solution for their many problems.

David became frustrated and ready to leave.

"We are going to leave," he whispered over at his first mate, Cristopher.

Cristopher gave the command to the rest of the crew to prepare. Before they could make their way out of the castle, David heard his name announced.

"Now presenting, King David of England."

The room grew silent, and many of the people at court were stunned to see such a young foreign king. David swiveled around and scuffled across the long hall, and up the aisle. He observed the king sitting on the throne was quite young himself. The woman sitting to his left, the queen, was none other than the young lady he plucked out of the ocean the day before.

David's cheeks flushed; he was at a loss for words.

She was truly a beautiful creature with her caramel skin, a tight body, and perky breasts. Her cheekbones intrigued him. Her long curly hair, sopping wet the day before, now lay smoothed into a regal bun with a headpiece resting on her forehead. The ocean blue dress she wore hugged the curves and contours of her body.

He had never seen such ornate and tightly fitted gowns on any women back home. David also noticed her lips were not overly full, and wanted to taste them. His cock started to get erect in his trousers.

I have to stop looking and thinking of her.

David shook the impure thoughts out of his mind.

Why did she want to harm herself?

He was plagued with more questions than answers and hoped he would get the chance to see her alone and receive answers to those questions. David had a hard time containing his excitement. He fiddled with the buckle loops on his trousers, avoiding eye contact.

The English king came to the end of the aisle and stood before Eleni and King Arkamun. His eyes locked with hers. She was indeed the woman he saw in his dreams.

Eleni had enough of sitting through the endless hours of speaking with the peasants and wanted to get away from Arkamun, and go back down to the beach to wade in the water. She wanted to let her emotions take her away to another place.

She noticed the guardsman open the throne room door on the opposite side of the room, escorting a large group of men into the hall.

I wonder if David is in that group of men... No, it could not be him.

The peasants continued to enter and after the last one, exited she leaned over to Arkamun. "Arkamun, I am quite tired, might I be excused?"

"You will sit here," he snarled back at her." There is one last guest today."

He caressed her hand, holding it affectionately. The steward made his last announcement, asking for King David to come forward.

Eleni stiffened a wave of shock jolting her upright. The man who saved her life continued down the aisle towards her. He was more handsome than the day before. She loved his raven black wavy hair and his ocean blue eyes she could get lost in; he was looking right at her.

Eleni avoided his gaze and stared at him out of the corner of her eye.

I hope Arkamun does not realize we have met before; Eleni prayed silently to herself.

Arkamun paid no attention to Eleni or her reactions toward the stranger. He squeezed her hand tighter. Her fingers turned purple under his grip.

She sat quietly and did not move. King Arkamun slid to the end of the chair and released Eleni's hand.

"So fellow king, what brings you to my kingdom?"

"We are explorers, my lord, we got lost heading to India and reached your shores instead. We are from the country of England and I am King David."

"Well, well, well, King David, I have heard of England; we have had your kind here before, never a king, however," Arkamun answered smiling.

"You and your men are welcome here" Arkamun crossed over to David and clamped a hand on his shoulder. "I will personally show you to where you can stay. I want to know more about you and where you come from, King David."

"Thank you, I appreciate your hospitality.

Arkamun veered around and tilted his head at Eleni. He signaled for her to come to him.

"You will have your servants escort the rest of these men to where they can sleep and make sure they are well taken care of."

"Yes, Milord," Eleni responded, joining Arkamun at his side.

"This is my queen and my wife, Eleni meet David."

"It is my pleasure to make your acquaintance, Milady." David took Eleni's hand and kissed it. The kiss sent shivers down her legs.

"It's nice to meet you, Milord."

Eleni smiled meekly, taking a step back from him and Arkamun.

"And this other lovely lady is my mother." Arkamun signaled for his mother to join him by his side.

Meseret made her way from the back of the hall reaching her hand out to David. He kissed her hand gently as well.

"It is nice to make your acquaintance, King David. I hope you enjoy your visit in our small and quaint kingdom.

"It is very nice to meet you as well; I thank you all for your warm welcome."

Arkamun held Eleni close like a prize. Eleni felt uncomfortable as Arkamun tightened his grip around her waist.

"Women are beneath men; they are to be played with. You must always put them in their place and have them submit to you; then you can have your way with them." Arkamun kissed Eleni forcefully and pushed her away from him. He then caressed the back of his mother's neck and kissed her gently on the cheek. She too said nothing.

"I see what you mean, Arkamun," David answered uneasily.

"Come, King David, let me show you where you will be staying." Arkamun held his arm out in front of him to lead the way.

The men filed out of the throne room. David glanced back at Eleni and Meseret. His eyes rested on Eleni.

"It was nice to make your acquaintance again, Milady."

"Thank you, Milord." She blushed and avoided his eye contact.

"Eleni, there will be a feast in King David's honor tonight. Make the preparations; the English need to know we know how to entertain here as well."

"Yes, Milord."

Eleni called out to her servants and gave orders to escort the rest of David's men to their rooms. The throne room emptied out, and Eleni was left with Meseret.

"Now that we are alone, my dear, you mind telling me what that was all about? I saw you blushing at that man."

Eleni's face reddened. "I do not know what you mean; I just met the man."

Meseret rested her hands on the sides of Eleni's face and studied her eyes. "Eleni, a woman knows those looks. I am not angry with you for having them. Just be careful of my son, he will have us all killed for our indiscretions."

Meseret moved her hands from Eleni's face and crossed her arms across her chest.

"Indiscretions? Is that why you avoided contact with the guardsman? I saw you two make eye contact. He is the same man that my mother was acquainted with.

"Never you mind yourself with that situation. You have a celebration to prepare for. I will handle my problems, and you should handle yours. Now I will leave you to prepare."

Meseret kissed Eleni on the forehead and scurried towards the entrance. She cast a glance back at Eleni.

"I will see you this evening; I look forward to seeing how you planned your first feast Eleni, do well."

"I promise I will do my best."

Eleni felt like she was out of breath. She grabbed the side of her chair and allowed herself to fall to her knees. She exhaled and looked up towards the ceiling.

I cannot believe he is here.

Before Eleni was able to compose herself fully, Hillina entered the throne room. "Eleni, the King told me in passing we are to prepare for a feast this evening, and you were in charge," Hillina sneered.

"That is correct, Hillina, I am." Eleni got to her feet, taking a deep breath. "I am in charge of tonight's gathering."

"Well, if you are indeed in charge, you need to get off of your hind parts and get to planning! A lot is needing to be done!"

"I most certainly will, Hillina! I do not need anyone else telling me how to do something. I believe I have been queen long enough to perform my responsibilities here!" Eleni screamed.

Eleni left Hillina standing there dumbfounded and headed down to the kitchen staff. She planned the feast for thirty guests including David and his crew.

She summoned the staff to make preparations for the entertainment and instructed them on how Arkamun wanted the decor presented. The day flew past Eleni's eyes; all her planning and executing orders was done. She finished instructing the servants and left the castle garden where the feast was being held to dress for the upcoming evening.

King Arkamun showed David around the kingdom. David was impressed by the upkeep of the grounds and the castle. In his previous voyages, he never encountered such a place rivaling England in beauty. They stopped at the garden outside the castle. The last of the preparations were made for the evenings feast.

Large glowing orbs of different colors shimmered around the garden, and the servants lined the walkway with tall candles. They draped flowers over any surface that allowed a flower. The musicians were setting up, tuning their string instruments.

David, in awe of everything, knew this feast was going to be a miraculous occasion.

"How did all of the people of Abyssinia come to speak English so well, King Arkamun?"

"We have had many visitors to this country, King David. We have had to learn many different languages. French, Italian, English. There may be some variations of the speech, but we all have learned. I make it mandatory for everyone in my kingdom to learn all the languages. We do not want outsiders thinking we are uneducated."

"I am impressed, Arkamun. It is okay if I call you Arkamun, isn't it?"

David glanced at Arkamun and back at the garden display.

"Why, of course, is it okay if I call you David," Arkamun grinned.

They both let out a laugh and continued their conversation. "This will be a night a splendor for you, my friend. We Abyssinian's know how to give a great gathering!"

"I think it will be, Arkamun. I am looking forward to tonight immensely."

"Good! My friend, now let me get you to your room; the hour is getting late, and you must prepare."

"Yes, but I must get my back to my ship before the night's festivities start. I must let my other crew members know we are safe, and we have not been captured."

"Awe, I see," Arkamun noted "I will send word to your ship inviting the rest of your crew to the feast now come it is time for you to get dressed. I will also have something laid out for you to wear." Arkamun paved the way, leading David in the direction of the castle doors. Back through the courtyard to the castle they went. Arkamun paused, closing another door. David could only make out some sort of ritual room, with a pentagram on the floor, and an altar standing before it.

"What do you have there?" David questioned.

"Awe, my private praying room, nothing to worry your mind about."

"I see, well Arkamun, you are a man of mystery."

Arkamun let out a boisterous laugh. "Come, David, let me get you to your room."

They continued down the hall, reaching a solid wooden door.

"This will be your room for your duration of your visit here. My room is across the corridor. There are servants at your beck and call whenever you need them. Pull the white rope in your room, and it will sound the bell. I must get myself ready. I will see you tonight at the ball."

Arkamun crossed the hall to his chamber room. He circled towards David. "When you are ready to be taken back down to the garden, pull the rope twice, and someone will be there to walk you down. See you tonight." He pushed his chamber room door ajar and slid inside.

"Thank you, Arkamun."

David was not sure if he heard him or not but was happy to have a few moments to himself. He shut the door behind him, gazing at all of the impressive decor. The view from his window faced the garden. The servants were working hard to complete everything before the evening's festivities.

Emerald green and gold covered his room. It seemed to be a theme throughout the castle. Mini statues of golden elephants glinted on tables around the room, staring at him with their ruby eyes.

This kingdom is very wealthy. He picked up the figurine in his hand. Or could it be the king who liked to embellish everything?

A knock on the door distracted him. He placed the figurine back into its place.

"Milord?" the voice called out at the door. "Milord? It is Tabetha, your servant; I have come to get you bathed for the feast tonight."

"Come in, please" he answered, stepping out of the way so she could enter the room. She was a petite girl, no taller than his shoulder. She pushed past him and hurried over to the tub with the large kettle of water she was carrying, poured it in, as well as contents from two bottles. Tabetha mixed them with her hand releasing a sweet aroma in the air.

Intoxicating.

David removed his clothes, laying them on the bed.

"You can get into the tub now."

David stepped into the water and sunk down. Herbs and flower petals swirled around his body, softening his skin. He leaned back against the tub, allowing Tabetha to bathe him with the sponge, her hands working to massage his whole body.

David relaxed and closed his eyes. He looked forward to seeing Eleni at the feast. He wanted to speak with her no matter how brief the moment was. Tabetha finished bathing David. She helped him up and gave him a robe. It was soft satin with Arkamun's family crest on it.

"This is not like home, Tabetha," David whispered.

She smiled and kept working. After drying his hair, she led him over to the bed where proper attire was laid out for him. A thick satin embroidered jacket with gold detailing, and a pair of gold satin pants were spread out. Instead of boots, gold satin slippers lay next to the clothing.

"You are to dress similar to King Arkamun." She removed his robe and rubbed oil on his skin. "To moisten your skin Milord."

She continued her movements down his chest, thighs and to his feet. She wiped her hands on a towel and picked up the jacket, unbuttoning it. She asked David to bend down a little so she could help put it on him. David obliged her, bending down and sliding the jacket over his shoulders.

"Now, time for the pants."

She moved with haste, snatching them off the bed and handing them to David. David took them out of her hand and slid them on.

"You are ready to go down to the feast, Milord. Ring the bell and someone will come for you." Tabetha grabbed everything she came with and proceeded out the door.

"Thank you," he said, closing the door behind her.

David pulled the rope twice next to the bed as King Arkamun commanded. A guardsman arrived a moment later.

They walked down to the feast in silence. The corridor was dark except for the few candles lighting the way. They reached the courtyard; it seemed as if more than thirty members of the court had turned out for the feast. The women whispered to each other and giggled, enamored with David and his men.

David glowered around at all of his crew members. They too were dressed in the appropriate garments. All of them seemed like they were quite uncomfortable in the satin garments they donned. David laughed to himself as he passed them.

The women and the men of the court were stunning. He had never seen such vibrantly colored dresses, silk trousers, and jackets. The style in King Arkamun's kingdom was so different from his own.

Even with all the beauty dancing around him, David could only think about the beautiful girl Eleni. He searched all over for her but had yet to see her make an appearance.

The horns sounded. Everyone dropped to their knees as she stepped out of the corridor and through the courtyard making her way to the garden. David held his breath.

Eleni was glistening. She wore an amethyst jeweled gown with a five-foot train. Diamonds and Amethysts crusted the sheer back of her gown. She wore her hair down that evening. Her curls cascaded down her back, and once again, a headpiece rested on the center of her forehead. This time, it too was crusted in diamonds and amethyst stones.

Eleni walked into the feast feeling the eyes on the nape of her neck. She did not care. She was only interested in seeing one person that evening, David. He stood over in the corner next to the colored orbs. Her eyes met his again, and she smiled. A chill ran down the small of her back.

He looks beautiful.

Eleni proceeded, meeting Arkamun in the middle of the garden. The servants immediately gathered her train and handed it to her. The horns sounded one final time, and the queen mother was escorted into the feast and was seated next to the musicians. She gave two claps and the music started.

Arkamun held Eleni around the waist and began to dance slowly. The steward stepped forward and escorted another lady to dance and soon after dancing couples filled the garden. Some of the women without partners accompanied David and his men out onto the dance floor. None of them knew the movements of the rhythmic dance, so they all stumbled for a moment, but eventually mustered through the moves.

Eleni finished the dance and let Arkamun attend to the women she noticed him flirting with. Slipping out of the feast, she lumbered out further into the garden away from prying eyes to catch a breath of fresh air. She made her way over to a bench and settled down on it.

The ocean was clear and the stars shone bright overhead. David kept dancing until he glanced at Eleni sneaking away from the celebration. He excused himself from his dancing partner and went after her. David hiked up the path to where Eleni was sitting and stood behind her.

"It is a beautiful night out tonight; you should not be alone on this nice of a night." David hovered behind her, the dark ocean water bobbing in the shadows.

Eleni whirled around, and relief passed across her face. "David, you startled me."

David crouched next to her.

"Why did you follow me here?" Eleni murmured.

"I wanted to make sure you were okay. You left suddenly."

"I see." She rose and shuffled to the edge of the cliff.

"I needed to get some air, David; feasts tend to get stuffy. As I said before, I enjoy being closer to the water."

"I understand completely." David joined her by her side.

"Somehow I knew you would. I looked forward to seeing you, David."

"As did I. There are so many questions I want to ask you, Eleni."

"Shhhhhhhhhh, no questions tonight, David, I want to listen to the ocean and enjoy being here with you."

David quieted, taking Eleni's hand in his own, caressing it. They both stood hand in hand and listened to the waves crash on the shore beneath them.

"Even though we did not converse this evening, I enjoyed the time I was able to spend with you, David. I hope we will see each other again."

Eleni stepped on her toes and kissed David on the forehead as he leaned down. Eleni released his hand and started up the path back towards the gathering. Before she moved too far away, David touched her shoulder, whisking her around into an embrace, brushing his lips against hers. He wrapped his arms around her tiny waist, drawing her closer to him.

He kissed her deeply, parting her mouth and absorbing her essence into his very cells. Eleni stepped back, touching her lips. She smiled and made her way back to the feast. The guests had dwindled to few, and the servants had started blowing out the candles and gathering up the leftover food.

Eleni gave her instructions to the remaining servants and headed up to the path to the castle. She had not seen Arkamun anywhere and hoped he had found another woman to exploit for the evening. Eleni blew out the candles as she passed through the courtyard into the corridor of the castle.

A tug from behind knocked her down on the pavement. Arkamun kicked her in the stomach knocking the breath from Eleni. He yanked by her hair and dragged her to his room. Arkamun grabbed Eleni by the neck and pushed her body into through the entrance, crashing her against the wall. With his opposite hand, he ripped her dress from the knees up. Eleni screamed, and Arkamun released her neck only to slap her across the face. He forced her down on the bed, pressing her face into the quilt. Arkamun pulled his pants down and forced his phallus inside of her. He ravaged her frantically with his engorged shaft until she was unable to breathe.

He finished raping her and shoved her out into the corridor hallway, closing his chamber room door. Eleni sank to the floor, crying. She was too sore to move.

David made it back to his room from the feast reminiscing on the embrace he had shared with Eleni. He finished bathing himself and had settled in bed when he heard screams from a woman coming from across the corridor. He knew those screams were from none other than Eleni. He struggled with wanting to get out of bed and burst into Arkamun's room to save her.

Not sure about the customs of the land he stayed put and tried to ignore the screams.

He went to the door and listened. The screams and the moans continued for a few more moments before subsiding.

David pried the chamber room door open. Peeking into the hall, his eyes fixed on Eleni. She was huddled over in the corner near Arkamun's door. Lifting her up off the floor into his arms, he carried her back to his room. David kicked the door closed with his leg and stretched Eleni out on the bed. He retrieved a damp cloth from the basin and dabbed it on Eleni's forehead. Eleni stirred a bit and opened her eyes.

"David. What am I doing here?" she whispered.

"I found you in the hall, Eleni. You were hurt, and I came to help you."

David continued to dab her face with the cloth.

"Thank you." Eleni dozed off again.

"You are welcome," he whispered in her ear.

David covered her with the quilt on his bed. He stayed awake and kept watch over her. He wanted to protect her from Arkamun hurting her again. He leaned back in his chair, deep in thought until he dozed off.

10 FINDING EACH OTHER

Eleni left David's room as soon as he dozed off and went to sleep. She could not risk being caught there the next morning by any of the servants, and did not want to risk angering Arkamun if he would have found her there. She left despite the fact she felt safe in the presence of David and wanted to remain there with him.

She prodded her bedroom door open, slamming the door behind her. She wanted Arkamun's smell off her. It was so early in the morning; Ayantu had not been there to prepare her bath. She did not care. There was still enough water in the bucket next to her basin to get the job done.

Eleni struggled with the bucket and managed to pour the cool water into the tub. She dropped another ruined gown on the floor and eased into the water. Her mind and body were drained. She went to work using the same oils as the day before on the bruised parts of her body. She washed in a hurry and stepped out of the tub.

She slipped on her sleeping gown and climbed on her massive bed. As she laid on her pillow, she reflected on how kind David had been. How effortlessly he lifted her off the hallway floor and placed her so carefully on his bed. How he stood guard, protecting her. She believed for what seemed like the first time she had someone who cared about her wellbeing, and made her feel safe. Eleni fell asleep while in the midst of her thoughts. She slept so soundly and peacefully. It was the best sleep she had since she came to Abyssinia.

David wasn't sure where Eleni had disappeared to during the early morning hours, but he could not help but be worried about her. He changed out of the formal attire he had slept in. He splashed water on his face, grabbed his boots and prepared to leave his room to seek out Eleni.

Tabetha entered with a breakfast tray. She seemed to be in quite the hurry to finish her chores. She put the tray down on the table and sped around the room tidying up everything; picking up his clothes from the night before, bringing in clean water for the basin, and making sure everything was in order. She did not say a word until she reached David's bed and saw the blood on the sheets.

"What happened here, Milord?" Tabetha gasped. She held the sheet up in her hand. David dropped his fork on the table and glanced at Tabetha dumbfounded.

The secret is out.

"Well, are you going to answer me?" Tabetha asked again.

"Yes, Tabetha. I was going to answer you. I found Eleni out in the hall last night. She was beaten pretty bad, so I brought her back here to my room. I treated her bruises on the bed; she left my room when I fell asleep."

David stepped in front of Tabetha and grasped her hand. "Would you happen to know where her chamber room is? I need to find her and make sure she is okay. Can you help me, Tabetha?"

Tabetha snatched her hand back from David and shook her head. "We servants are not supposed to talk about what goes on with the king and queen."

She removed the remainder of sheets off the bed and stuffed them into a basket. "I cannot tell you what room she is in. I could be whipped if the king found you in there with her, and I was the one who told you where her room was located."

Tabetha hurried over to the armoire, pulling out a fresh set of sheets.

"Please," David persisted "I need to make sure she is okay. I would not stay long. No one would ever know you were the one who told me where she was."

Tabetha paused from making the bed and gazed at David, her eyes softened. "To get to Eleni's room, you have to go out of this room, make a left. Go up the flight of stairs and when you get to the upper corridor, her room is on the right-hand side. King Arkamun will kill you if he finds out you are communicating with his queen. From what you saw last night, you should realize he is a very jealous and brutal man."

"He will never know I was even there."

"Let's hope he does not find out." Tabetha gathered her belongings and scurried out of the room.

David waited momentarily before he ventured out of his room to find Eleni. The last thing he needed was to be caught by Arkamun. After time had passed, David yanked his boots off the floor and slipped them on.

The sunlight pouring in the hall's window blurred David's vision a bit as he made his way to the stairwell.

"Good morning, David," Arkamun said, stepping out into the hall.

David felt sick to his stomach seeing the man, knowing what he had done to Eleni.

"Good morning, Arkamun. "David crossed over the hall, shaking Arkamun's hand.

Arkamun smiled, ignoring the look on David's face. "I'm glad I caught you this morning, David. I wanted us to continue our conversation about our two countries trading with one another. Come, David, let us take a stroll and continue our talks."

Arkamun kept David occupied all morning, afternoon, and evening; he was unable to sneak off to see Eleni. He received the complete tour of Arkamun's kingdom, seeing everything from the beaches, pastures, hunting grounds and even where some of the members of the court lived.

David returned to his chambers, excited once again. He would see Eleni at dinner. He wasted no time washing and dressing and getting back down to the dining hall. The steward announced dinner, and everyone who ate at the king's table was assembled to be seated. All were escorted into the dining hall and seated according to their status. David looked around the room and saw every seat was taken except the one next to Arkamun's chair.

Where can she be?

He did not have an appetite and barely touched anything on his plate. Meseret glanced over at David during dinner. "Is everything all right young man?"

"Why yes, everything is great."

"It seems as if you are not that hungry this evening. I see you have not touched anything on your plate."

"Everything is fine, thank you."

Arkamun patted his mother's hand. "Now... now... Mother, let the man enjoy his meal. It has been a long couple of days. This could be overwhelming for him."

Meseret smiled and agreed with Arkamun. "I will let the young man be. Now Arkamun. Where is my daughter, is she well?"

"I have not seen her today Mother; she should have been here for dinner. If you would not mind, can you please find out why she is absent from dinner?"

"Why of course, my son, I will go immediately. If you all will excuse me," Meseret said to everyone at the table.

David was glad that she was going to find Eleni. He assumed a brave face and mustered through dinner, engaging in conversation he deemed boring.

Meseret left the dining hall in search of her daughter-in-law. Eleni stayed away from dinners most nights. She assumed it was from the abuse at the hands of her son.

The years have been bad for that girl. I should alert her parents that something is wrong.

Meseret felt responsible for Eleni's torment. Perhaps this David character was Eleni's key to freedom. She saw the way they glanced at each other at the feast. If there were a chance she could help the two escape together, she would.

Meseret searched the garden, the courtyard, and the stables for Eleni. She headed in the direction of Eleni's chamber room when Berhanua stepped into her path.

"Good evening, my queen."

"Berhanua, what are you doing out here this evening?"

"Waiting to see you, Majesty. You have not sought me out since I returned from my voyage with the other guardsmen."

"There is not much to say, Berhanua. I had said all that needed to be said years ago: when you decided to discard me for Eleni's mother, Abrihet. "Meseret folded her arms; her voice became strained.

Berhanua stepped closer. "There has not been another. I have not seen Abrihet since she left our kingdom. However, that is not the case with you."

"What are you trying to say? I am in a hurry."

"I have a secret about you. Perhaps I should tell Eleni and the entire kingdom you are sleeping with your son."

Meseret muttered under her breath, her mouth twisted with disdain. "How do you know this? What you say is blasphemy!"

Berhanua smiled and pulled the queen into him. "I know this because I came to you that night after you saw Abrihet and me at the cliff. You snuck into Arkamun's chambers. I watched you get into bed with him. I saw you on top on him. I watched you..."

Meseret's mouth dropped. There was no rebuttal she could give. "What is it you want from me?" she whispered.

"I want you..."

Berhanua yanked Meseret closer and bore his face into hers. He captured her mouth with hungry urgency, devouring her tongue with his. He nudged her back against the castle wall, ripping her dress up to her thighs. Meseret's nipples swelled as he cupped her breasts in his hands. She extracted his cock from his pants stroking his throbbing manhood until he glided himself inside of her moving in a sensual rhythm. Entwined, they reached an instantaneous climax.

"Put me down, Berhanua."

He released her to the ground. Meseret straightened her dress, turning the rip of her dress to the side. Berhanua slid his pants up over his thighs and tried to kiss her again.

"No..." She backed away. "I have to go. Find me later."

Have I protected this secret that I carry? Will he tell anyone?

Meseret could not be sure. All she could do now was to change her dress and find her daughter-in-law. She headed up the stairwell to her chamber room to change.

Eleni slept all day with no interruptions. The sun had already started to fade into the night sky when she opened her eyes. She rose from the bed and approached the table. Ayantu had been in earlier and left a tray with some fruit. She was so happy Ayantu did not wake her.

I do not know the last time I rested so wonderfully.

She was still a little uneasy from the night before. She gazed at her reflection in the mirror surveying the damage her husband had done. Her bruising was at a minimum, and she had no facial bruises.

David took care of me, thank the heavens for him. I did not want to use those oils again.

Eleni snatched the fruit off the tray and devoured it as if she had not eaten in days. Her thirst was unquenchable. She drank the entire pitcher of coconut water next to the tray.

The warm breeze flooded through the window and swirled up and around Eleni's night garment. It was a beautiful evening. She yearned for the ocean as it softly called to her.

She wanted to erase the horrible thoughts about last night from her mind and body and escape her cage. But where could she escape to where no one would be looking for her?

The salt streams.

Ayantu was the one who showed her the private lagoon when she first came to the white castle. She had been able to escape there for a few hours on occasion and go unnoticed. Eleni stripped off her night clothes and put on a satin rose- colored long robe. She left her hair down, her curls streaming down her back. Eleni cracked open her chamber room door.

No one in sight.

She headed down the back stairwell and had to pass Arkamun's chambers on the second floor. As she got closer, she crept slowly, peering around the marble column to see if anyone was in the hall. Before she could move, she heard conversation drifting down the main corridor.

Eleni froze, squatting down behind the column. She overheard two voices: it was David and Arkamun, coming back from dinner.

"I'm sorry we missed Queen Eleni at dinner."

"She was feeling ill and took dinner in her room tonight. I will let her know she was missed."

Lies...

Before they came any closer, Eleni darted across the hall to the next flight of stairs.

Made it.

She continued down the flight of stairs.

David was distracted from the conversation by a splash of color he saw move past the back stairwell.

Eleni...

David blurred out the conversation with Arkamun.

"I am happy we were able to make a treaty and allow our countries to trade with one another. David, it is nice to do business with an outsider." Arkamun let out a bellowing laugh.

David diverted his attention back to Arkamun. "Yes, I'm sure the trading will be most lucrative. Well Arkamun, if there is nothing else for the evening, I would like to retire to my room."

"Why of course, David, you can most certainly retire for the evening. Let me ask you this: is there something or someone I can get for you to pass the time? You are my guest here, and I want you to be taken care of."

"No, Arkamun, there is nothing. I thank you for the offer, however," David responded casually.

"You are most welcome, David." Arkamun lumbered over to the door of his chamber room. He widened it enough for David to see three women waiting for him. Arkamun gazed back at David.

"I hope you have a good night. I know I will." Arkamun laughed and kicked the chamber door closed behind him.

David's attention immediately turned to the splash of color he saw at the end of the hall. He looked down the stairwell and spotted the train of her robe rounding the corner. David hit the stairs in a hurry and tried to catch up to Eleni.

Eleni reached the last staircase and made it out of the castle unseen. The sun had set and the sky filled with bright stars giving her skin a soft glow. She had no idea David was right behind her. She ducked down behind the castle wall until she reached the stone staircase of the cliff and descended to the beach. Making it down to the sand, Eleni came upon a group of tall brush. Parting the brush, she climbed through the small opening.

"The salt streams," she said out loud.

The salt streams had healing powers, and she often found herself going there after she had been violated by Arkamun. Steam rose off the water, creating a dense fog. She walked over to the edge of the stream and dipped her toe in.

"Perfect," she said out loud, dropping her robe from her body.

She waded into the warm water and dove under. Eleni came up to catch her breath and flipped over, diving under the water once more.

David made it out of the castle past the walls. He saw the tail end of Eleni's robe heading down the stone staircase to the beach. He continued jogging trying to catch up with her at the base of the stairs. She was still too far ahead of him. He moved in heavy strides to get down the stairs to the beach.

I cannot lose sight of her.

David continued to speed down the stairs. He made it down to the beach unsure of what direction she had gone in. He glanced around both ways, but the beach was deserted. Frustrated, he plopped in the sand and stared out at the water.

There were no waves; the water was calm, yet he heard splashing in the distance. David listened and heard the splashing sound again. Off to the right, he noticed a tall bush further down the beach. The fog was rising into the sky behind it.

David got to his feet, trotting his way towards the mist. Stopping at the brush, he noticed a small opening where someone had gone through. He peered through the hole, finding a stream, and glowing green steam rising off the water to the sky. To his left, he saw the robe laying on the bed of sand. David climbed through the hole and rested on the sand of the private lagoon.

Eleni continued to swim underwater. She did not notice him, so he removed his clothing and quietly walked into the water.

So warm and inviting.

He waited for her to resurface.

Eleni resurfaced and laid her head back against the cool stone and looked up to the night sky. She felt the water splash up over her shoulders and opened her eyes. David was staring back at her.

"What are you doing here?"

"You left in the middle of the night, and I wanted to make sure you were okay. I saw the train of your robe in the hall back at the castle. I knew it was you, so I followed you here. I wanted to see you." David moved closer to Eleni's naked body.

"I am okay, David. I did not want you to be caught with me in your chamber room, so I left. Arkamun would hurt you if he had found me there with you."

Eleni avoided eye contact and ran her fingers through her hair. David put a finger under her chin, lifting her face up to meet his eyes.

"You are so beautiful, Eleni," he said, their bodies touching. "I feel something for you that I have never felt for anyone before." David kissed her forehead and gleamed down into her eyes.

"We cannot do this, David. If Arkamun finds out..." Eleni retreated and covered her breasts with her arms.

"He won't find out, Eleni."

David freed her arms and tugged her gently closer to him. Her nipples against his bare chest caused his penis to get erect instantly. David leaned his head closer to Eleni and kissed her again, this time on the lips. She resisted for a brief moment but had yearned for him to kiss her again.

Eleni relaxed, embracing his kiss, and wrapped her arms around his neck. David draped his arms around her small waist, her naked body brushing against him.

Her nipples became perky and hard, the delicate softness between her thighs moistened. They kissed passionately, David's tongue stroking her mouth to ecstasy.

He kissed her down to her neck, tracing circles on the sensitive part of her neckline with his tongue, stopping to suck the area lustfully.

David's hands caressed up and down her spine, moving from her neck to her breasts. He flicked his tongue around the right breast and settled on her stiff nipple. He pinched her left nipple with his index finger and thumb.

Eleni moaned with excitement, leaning her head back as she enjoyed the pleasure David was bestowing on her. He moved to the opposite breast, his tongue dancing on her throbbing nipple. Eleni felt as if she was going to have an orgasm before they even made love. Her moans grew louder.

She clutched his head into her even more. She had never experienced such pleasure from a man's touch. David continued to kiss and lick down her body. He reached her bellybutton and allowed his tongue to explore and taste around her stomach.

Dave stood straight in the waist deep glowing water, lifted Eleni from her waist and sat her on the rocks next to the salt streams. He kissed her passionately on her lips again and slid his hand in-between her thighs, spreading her legs slightly. Eleni felt his hand in-between her thighs rubbing his fingers over her clitoris. She squirmed a little. She had never been touched so gently there by Arkamun.

She opened her legs wider and allowed David to continue. He stopped kissing her and kneeled down in the warm water splashing over his shoulders. He spread her legs wider with his hands and kissed her gently between her thighs. Moving from one thigh to another, he eventually came to Eleni's clitoris and gently began sucking and licking it. The sensations Eleni felt from David's tongue made her hot and squirm on the rocks.

David's licking persisted, taking his index finger and gently pushing it inside of Eleni's warm and wet golden flesh. Eleni moaned in great pleasure allowing David's tongue and fingers to plunge deeper. David stopped, replacing his fingers and tongue with his even harder manhood.

He surrendered himself inside of her while holding her hips; Eleni wrapped her arms around David's neck, holding on. They looked at each other, both shuddering in breaths of gasping completion. Neither of them had ever experienced what they felt in each other's arms.

Their intimacy was so intense they both reached the point of orgasms multiple times. Eleni screamed against David's chest. David poured life into her time and time again.

Exhausted, David and Eleni collapsed on the sand, watching the shooting stars overhead. David rolled over on his side and admired Eleni. He was smitten with her. He knew he loved her. He reached over and ran his fingers through her hair.

Eleni swiveled her position, glaring into David's eyes. David wondered what was going through her mind.

If only I can read her thoughts.

He had enjoyed the evening with her and wanted to savor every moment. Eleni's eyes welled up with tears, and she began to sob.

"Eleni, what's wrong?" David scooted closer to her in the sand, resting her head against his chest. "What's wrong, Eleni?"

Eleni wiped her tears and admired his handsome face. She inhaled a deep breath, then released it.

"I have never had anything like this before, David. I know this is going to come to an end, and I might never see you again."

"Do not say never, Eleni," David insisted, sitting them both up in the sand. He twisted her body towards him so she could see him clearly. "I never want to hear you say never again. We have to believe will see each other again someday, especially since we have this trade route established between our two countries. You can come to England, Eleni."

Eleni sobbed, as David held her close to him.

"Eleni, I need to say something to you," he whispered into her ear.

He rubbed her hand and kissed her on the forehead. "I am in love with you Eleni. If there were a way to take you back to England with me to become my queen, I would do it."

"You would want me to come back to England with you?"

"Yes, Eleni. I want to figure out a way to take you back with me. I do not want to be parted from you ever again. The thought of you being touched by Arkamun angers me. I would kill him if he harmed you again."

Eleni grabbed David's hand tighter and released it. She got to her feet and dove head first into the water. Eleni resurfaced after a few moments and swam over to the rocks near David.

"How would you get me out of the kingdom, David? Everyone is watching everything I say and do. I do not know how this would possibly work."

David dove into the water over Eleni's head. He re-emerged behind her and swam up to her side.

"We will find a way to do this Eleni, trust me."

David lifted her up into his arms again. He kissed her lovingly, sliding himself back into her. They made love another five times, well into the early hours of the morning. Their bodies became so entwined from the intense connection they felt for each other, which led to them falling asleep on the sand.

The sun rose, and Eleni felt the warm rays on her skin. Her eyes fluttered open, and she could see David was still asleep next to her. she hated leaving his side but knew if she did not get back to the castle, suspicion would arise. She removed David's arm from around her waist, brushed the sand off her body and hair, retrieved her robe, and put it on. Eleni walked over to the tall brush separating them from the main beach and pushed it open, glancing one more time at her handsome man lying in the sand.

David awoke some time later and realized he had slept well into the early evening. He noticed Eleni had left hours ago. He rolled over on his back and gazed into the sky as it started to fade from blue to sunset. He reflected on the deep connection he felt with Eleni.

Eleni was everything he could have ever wanted in a woman. He realized after last night; he wanted her to be his wife. David knew his mother, and his country of England would show opposition to divorcing Philippa and making Eleni an English queen.

He was determined to come up with a plan to get Eleni out of Abyssinia, the white castle and away from Arkamun.

The next five weeks of David's visit came and went like a blink of an eye. Arkamun kept David busy most days with concerns of the kingdom, limiting the individual contact between himself and Eleni.

But on the nights Arkamun had thrown feasts and was occupied with his concubines, Eleni and David were able to meet at the beach to spend time together making love. They discussed how to get Eleni out of the watchful eyes of the guardsmen, and onto the ship when David was due to set sail for home.

It was the evening before David was due to leave on his voyage back to England. Eleni had noticeably been out of court again because of another brutal beating inflicted on her. Eleni awoke with the sun setting four days later, not sure if the plan she and David devised was still going to happen.

Eleni was desperate to see David again, even if it was for one last time. She got out of bed and sat down at her desk, composing a letter with her intentions and questions about the plan to smuggle her out of the kingdom. Eleni sealed the letter and placed it on the table. She was about to rise from her chair when there was a knock on the door.

"It's Meseret, can I come in daughter?"

"Yes, please come in."

"I wanted to check to see how you were doing and hoped you would be able to join us for dinner. You know King David is leaving for home tomorrow."

Eleni burst out into tears. Meseret came to her side, wrapping her arms around her "I am quite aware that David is leaving tomorrow."

Eleni released Meseret's embrace and stumbled over to the window. A chilly wind blew through the room. Eleni rubbed her arms and glanced back at Meseret.

"Eleni, my dear, I have seen how you look at King David. I know you have feelings for him."

"You do?"

"Yes, dear, I do, just like when you noticed me looking at the guardsman. I have noticed the way you two look at each other. You are in love with the young man."

Eleni blushed. Had she been so careless with her feelings? Could Arkamun know how she felt about David?

"Does Arkamun know about this?"

"I do not believe he does. What is your plan with David?"

The two women continued to talk about the situation with David and Eleni. Meseret promised to help Eleni leave the kingdom.

Meanwhile, Ayantu approached Eleni's door with her new gown straight from the seamstress. She heard the two women talking from behind the door. Declining to enter Eleni's chamber room, she eavesdropped on the conversation.

"I want to leave the kingdom with David. I want to go to England and become his queen."

Meseret folded her arms and paced back and forth.

"I wrote this letter for David. Can you please deliver it to him?"

Eleni grabbed the letter off of the table and handed it to Meseret.

Meseret took the letter from Eleni and smiled. "Yes, I will deliver it and hope that you will be able to leave the castle. I cannot protect you if your plan goes wrong. I will do my best to keep the guards busy, giving you enough time to slip away. Now, my dear, you have to get dressed. Where is your servant girl?"

Eleni hugged Meseret tightly.

"Thank you, thank you. I will never forget your kindness; you have been truly wonderful. I am not sure where Ayantu is. She should have been back by now."

"Well, let me get this letter to David's chambers. I will see you this evening." Meseret left Eleni's chamber room bumping into Ayantu. "There you are girl, get that dress to Eleni. She needs to get dressed."

"Yes, Milady. "Ayantu stomped into Eleni's chamber room, tossing her newly made gown on the bed.

"Shall I prepare a bath for you, Eleni?" Ayantu asked with a hostile attitude.

"No, not at the moment. Tabetha assisted me with my bath earlier.

"Well, then, let's get you dressed. "Ayantu stepped behind Eleni and removed her robe. She placed her hands around Eleni's waist and started to kiss her neck.

"Ayantu, please stop, we cannot do this again."

"Why not? We did all the time right up until that king showed up here."

"I have told you before; I love you only as my friend. I needed someone at that time, and I appreciate what you have done for me."

"Why cannot I not be enough for you?" Ayantu huffed. She plopped down on the bed glaring at Eleni. Her eyes grew darker as the color from her face departed.

Eleni realized what was going on. Ayantu was jealous of what had developed between herself and David.

How did she know about David and me? Was she listening at the door?

"Ayantu, what is going on with you? Did you overhear the conversation I was having with Meseret?"

"Of course not. I feel like you are pushing me away. I care for you, Eleni. I would never hurt you. I love you."

"I hope that is true. Now help me get dressed."

11 Jealousy

Ayantu left Eleni's chambers and hurried down to David's room, where she retrieved the letter Meseret had left on his nightstand. She wiped the tears from her face and headed towards the stairwell. King Arkamun was right in front of her, locked in an embrace with one of his concubines. Ayantu could have avoided Arkamun by going in the opposite direction, but she chose not to do so.

Eleni will pay for hurting me this way.

She slowed her pace and continued on her path towards the king.

King Arkamun, jostled his concubine to the side, approaching Ayantu. She immediately dropped to her knees and bowed.

"What are you doing down here, peasant? Why are you not by the queen's side?" Arkamun smirked and folded his arms.

"I followed Queen Meseret. She left a letter from Eleni in King David's room, Milord."

"A letter? What type of message? Give this letter to me!" he yelled.

Arkamun grabbed Ayantu off the floor onto her feet and ripped the letter out her hand. He opened the letter and read the contents. His face became red, and his eyes darkened into slants. He folded the letter and handed it back to Ayantu.

"Well, servant girl, you better put that letter back where you found it."

He took his concubine by the arm and continued down the hall. Ayantu was not surprised he did not question her more thoroughly. She knew he would take his anger up with Eleni and follow her.

Ayantu smiled to herself. David and Eleni would be no more. She hurried back to David's chamber room and knocked. He had since returned to his room and opened the door with a smile.

"Why hello," He said in a welcoming tone.

"This letter is from Eleni. "Ayantu placed the letter in his hand and retreated towards the stairwell.

Eleni was nervous about seeing David after four days of seclusion. The bruises Arkamun had inflicted on her were a relief from the previous rapes she had endured. He left her so black and purple that she was unable to be seen by anyone. It was his punishment for being late for dinner.

The dress Ayantu helped her into was designed in the English style standards. She wanted David to see that she could fit in by his side as queen.

Dinner was served in the garden for David's final evening. The hanging lights swung gently in the wind over the heads of the guests. David and Eleni both sent glances of admiration to each other as the night progressed. The evening winded down after three hours with a toast from Arkamun, wishing David and his crew a safe voyage back to England and thanking them for their friendship.

As the dinner guests dispersed, David and his team shook hands with the men, kissed the hands of the women, and said their farewell. After all of the goodbyes, they gathered their belongings and exited through the courtyard down the stone staircase back to the beach.

Arkamun excused himself from the table to escort some of his other prestigious guests to their rooms for the evening, leaving Eleni and David alone for a moment to speak. As soon as Arkamun rounded the garden wall, David walked over to Eleni and clenched her hand.

"I got your letter, Eleni, and I still want to put the plan into action. I see you had your dress made to the standards of the English court, and I am pleased to see you would fit right in as my queen."

Eleni clutched David's hands tightly in return. "I was not sure if you would notice, David. I am glad you are pleased, and I too want the plan to go accordingly. We do not have much time before someone comes back here to the garden. I will meet you at the beach after I have had the servants clear away all of this food and decor, and I make sure Arkamun is settled where he is going to be for the evening. Queen Meseret is helping clear the guards."

"I will be waiting for you, Eleni." David captured her mouth with hungry urgency. "Please hurry. "He kissed her briefly on the hand.

Eleni held his hand for a moment before releasing it.

David made his way across the courtyard, caught up with his men and headed down the stone staircase.

"I will, David!" Eleni yelled out to him.

Eleni and Meseret had the servants clear away the dining decor, leftover food, and wine from the table. She was grateful to know it would be her last night in the white castle. She and David would have a fresh start at his kingdom in England.

Eleni glanced up from her duties and could see Meseret signaling her from the overlook. She placed the vase on back on the table and scurried over to where Meseret stood.

"My daughter, I wanted to let you know that I have the guardsmen handling other duties this evening. Everything should be clear for you to make your escape with David."

"Thank you, I promise I will be gone by sunrise. I thank you for your kindness."

"Now hurry along, there is not much time. David will be waiting for you at the beach."

Eleni embraced Meseret one final time before departing towards the castle entrance. She dashed up the path, when Arkamun met her met her at the doorway.

"And where are you on your way to, my wife?"

Eleni retreated backward, stepping out of his way. "I was heading to my chambers. I am tired and wanted to get some rest after all the festivities."

"Well, then I suggest you get some rest, my queen. I will want you brought to me in the morning hours. I am going to be away from the castle this evening. I have a pressing engagement."

"Yes, Milord."

Arkamun kissed Eleni on the cheek and left her in the doorway. She hurried to her chamber room, gathering as many belongings as she could for her journey, but packed what she could carry. She freshened up her hair and bathed her face in the cool water in the basin. Eleni dried her face and took one more glance around the room.

I will not miss this place.

Eleni reflected on the events leading her to that moment: her parents throwing her away to such a man and relieving money and land; Ayantu becoming jealous of David and hating her; Arkamun's repeated abuse; And finally David saving her and taking her away from it all.

She inhaled and closed the chamber room door behind her. The halls were quiet, and the lights dimmed. Queen Meseret did her job in getting the guardsmen away from door and floor for the evening.

Eleni lugged her bag onto her shoulder and made her way to the back stairwell. Her goal was to avoid the servants and guests wandering through the castle. She slid off her slippers, placing them in her bag, and tiptoed out of the castle. She ran through the stables, past the garden, and through the courtyard, reaching the stone staircase.

Eleni descended the stairs and stopped at one of the pillars, hiding her belongings behind it. She scouted behind her, believing she heard footsteps. There was nothing there except the thick fog closing around her.

It was all in my mind. No one is there.

Eleni proceeded down the staircase until she reached the beach, peering around for David.

Where is he? He should have been here.

She dug her toes into the sand and pulled her gown up over knees, wading deeper into the water. The water brushed up against her thighs. She gazed overhead into the night sky. The moon was full and shining brightly in a cloudless sky.

David had been back at the ship for hours preparing to set sail for the voyage at dawn. Dusk had set in, and he hurried to the dinghy to meet Eleni at the beach. He paddled slowly and swiftly, rowing the boat up on the sand.

David trudged up the beach where he observed Eleni playing in the water. He was in awe. She looked like an angelic being. He loved her more each time he saw her and knew if their plan did not go accordingly, it would be the last time he would see her.

Do not ruin tonight.

David removed his boots and threw them down on the sand. He waded into the water, wrapping his arms around her waist.

Eleni placed her hands on David's and let her small frame relax on his chest.

"You came," she lamented. "I was not sure you would."

"There is no place I rather be than here with you."

Eleni dropped her hand to her side and weaved her body into his chest. "Is this plan going to work, David? What if Arkamun finds out or discovers us here? "Eleni started to sob. "I cannot be alone if this fails. Please do not leave me here David, no matter what."

David hugged her tightly, caressed her hair and kissed her forehead. "My love, I do not plan on leaving you here. You will join me in England as we have planned. You have truly shown me you can take my side and become my queen. I love you Eleni, and we will be together. We set sail at sunrise."

"I'm ready to leave this place and start my life with you at this very moment. Shouldn't we get on the ship now?" Eleni dried her tears and gazed into David's blue eyes.

"So am I, Eleni. Everything is situated my love; we are prepared to set sail. We, however, cannot leave until dawn."

David and Eleni waded back into the water hand in hand.

"I hope that Arkamun does not find out. If he does before we set sail..." Her voice trailed off.

"Let's not think any more about Arkamun for tonight, Eleni. He will not find you here."

David unlaced the golden threads on Eleni's gown and corset, letting them both fall into the shallow lagoon water. Her body was bathed in the pale moonlight. Eleni was such an exotic creature; she enticed him, and he yearned for her each time he saw her.

David removed his shirt, dropping it into the water and brushed his chest upon her back. Goosebumps formed from the cold breeze engulfing them.

Eleni felt David's chest on her back and sighed. She felt his soft lips fall at the nape of her neck, kissing her until her nipples throbbed. "I want you again and again and again, David. Please take me, and make love to me," she pleaded.

Arkamun waited behind the castle wall for Eleni to pass and watched from the shadows to see exactly where she had been sneaking off. After she had passed him, he followed her, hiding behind one of the pillars on the staircase.

She has betrayed me and everything I have given her.

Eleni almost caught him when she spun around. She resumed her descent down the staircase with Arkamun following closely behind.

Arkamun paused when he saw David pull his boat up on the sand. The bitterness of seeing his wife with him rose in his gut. He felt his blood boil and let out a growl in his throat.

Arkamun waited a few moments before he proceeded behind Eleni again. He did not want to get too close, or give away his vantage point. He reached the beach and hid behind some foliage. His anger intensified as he watched Eleni and David make love on the sand.

David's hands ran up and down Eleni's body. Each kiss he gave her electrified her soul. His very touch was all she needed to be complete. She could imagine them being back in England as king and queen. Her body temperature rose, and she slipped her tongue into his mouth, lingering inside of it.

Eleni pulled them down into the sand and let the water brush over their bodies as they kissed. David kissed her neck, nipples, and her breasts, allowing the salt water into his mouth as he nibbled on her skin. Eleni opened her legs and David drove his manhood into her.

His hard shaft conformed to her moist and satin flesh allowing him to press himself deeply into her sweetness. Their bodies rocked back and forth in the wet sand. The deep shuddering of their breath turned them on even more. They both reached the height of orgasm and David released his seed into Eleni.

The deep breathing stopped, and they laid entangled in each other's arms. Nightfall began to fade, and dawn was upon them. David rolled off her body to fetch his clothing. Eleni followed suit, retrieving her damp gown. They both dressed in silence, catching each other's glances. After they had each dressed, they held each other.

"It is time, Eleni." David rested his chin on her forehead. "My crew is sending another boat to fetch you and your belongings."

David pointed to the small dark figure on the water. "Eleni, you need to gather your things and get back down here to the beach. When you are ready and back here on the sand, the boat will be here to bring you aboard."

David took her hand and escorted her over to where his one-person boat rested in the sand.

"I have to get back to the ship, Eleni. I have to wake the rest of the crew. I will be waiting for you." David untied the boat and pushed it into the water. He snatched his boots out of the sand and tossed them in the boat.

"I love you, Eleni. "David kissed her deeply, then waded out into the water before jumping in his boat.

"I love you too! I will be ready when they get here. I just need to retrieve my bag. It is still too early for the guardsmen to check on me, so no one will know I am gone.

"I will be waiting for you on the ship. Eleni, please hurry, the tide will be going out soon, and we need to get out of the lagoon!" David yelled further out from the shore.

"I will be back soon." Eleni, ran up the beach to fetch her belongings.

This is it. I am getting my happy ending and the man I love.

Eleni rounded the corner of the beach to the stone staircase and up the stairs. She pulled her bag from behind the pillar and threw it over her shoulder. A shadow stepped out from behind the second pillar into the early morning sky; it was Arkamun.

"So my Queen, I see you were planning on leaving me this dawn." Arkamun peered at Eleni. His eyes had narrowed, and face had hollowed. She could see he was intent on hurting her.

"No, my king, I was taking a stroll on the beach and was coming back to the castle. "Eleni backed up towards the stairs and dropped her bag over the side down to the beach below.

Maybe I can run and get into the water and swim.

"Stop with the lies, my queen. I saw you here with King David this past evening, and your whore of a servant filled me in on all the little details of your plan to leave and your relationship with King David. The little bitch was persuasive. She told me everything."

"She could not tell you anything; she did not know anything Arkamun. What did you do to her?" Eleni screamed.

"Awe, you are such a stupid girl. She told me everything. I read the letter that she stole out of David's room. And the assistance you have gotten from my mother." Arkamun smirked. "You should tell me the truth, Eleni. What are you doing down here on the beach with King David?"

"I was saying goodbye, Arkamun. His ship is leaving at dawn, or do you not remember from the conversation at last night's dinner? "Eleni stepped down onto the stairs.

"Once again, lies, Eleni. You were leaving me for King David. No one leaves Arkamun for another, not while they are still breathing." Arkamun lunged at her.

Eleni screamed out for David, but no one could hear her. David was already back on the ship, and the dinghy coming for her had not yet reached the shore. Eleni tried to scream again and tried to run down the stairs.

He yanked her hair back, and grabbed her small frame in his arms, throwing her against the cold stone.

Eleni hit the stone with such force her head split open, a puddle of blood pooling underneath her. Eleni fell into an unconscious state and was unaware the crew had made it to the beach and were waiting for her return.

David waited on the deck of his ship for Eleni to come. It was sunrise, and the tide would soon be high enough to lead the ship out of the lagoon back to the ocean. The dinghy David had sent out with members of his crew to fetch Eleni returned without her. She was nowhere on the beach. David wanted answers, and he knew he only had a brief time before they would be forced to leave.

David did not want to leave Abyssinia without finding Eleni, so he rounded up a few crew members who were not occupied with chores and set off in the small dinghy to return to shore. As David and his crew approached the shore, he looked around to see any traces of Eleni.

Nothing.

David and his crew landed on shore and pulled the dinghy up onto the sand. Immediately on alert, he removed his sword from its scabbard. He had no idea what could be lurking around the corner. David and his crew spread out over the sandy beach calling Eleni's name, to no avail. There were no signs of her.

"Sir, we have to hurry, the tide is coming in," One of David's sailors said to him.

David turned and looked out at the lagoon water. He was right; the tide was coming in. "You men get back to the ship and get ready. I have to find her. I am not leaving without her."

All but two of his small crew returned to the ship.

"You two men, with me."

David and the two men mustered through the thick sand to the stone staircase. David noticed a bag resting in the sand. He examined it; It was Eleni's. The three men continued up the stairs, coming to a puddle of blood seeping into the stone. David knew the reason why Eleni was not on the beach. Someone had taken her. It could be none other than Arkamun. David's vein in his forehead pulsed, his arm muscles flexed. He wanted to kill Arkamun.

David signaled his men to be on alert. They ascended the stairs, swords drawn, ready to attack anyone who came across their path. The courtyard was quiet, no guardsmen in sight as they proceeded to the castle doors.

"Wait here," David whispered to his men.

He swung open the tower door and ascended the back staircase to Eleni's room. His adrenaline pumped, and his heart thundered in his chest. He placed his ear against the door. The room was quiet. David burst through the chamber door and found the room in shambles. Blood covered Eleni's bed, the floor, and the desk. All that remained was the gold locket she wore around her neck, laying on the ground covered in blood.

David retrieved the locket and placed it in his pocket. He made his way back out into the hall and was heading towards Queen Meseret's chambers when his first mate Cristopher called his name.

"David, we have to get out of here. The guardsmen are coming in our direction, sir! "Cristopher yelled, running up the stairs after David.

"I have to find her, Cristopher. I promised her I would not leave this kingdom without her."

"Your Majesty, I understand you did not want to leave her, but look at all of this blood. It would be a miracle if she survived an attack like this." Cristopher glanced around Eleni's chamber room.

"I have to find out, Cristopher; I need to know if she is dead or alive. If she is alive, I have to save her."

David and Cristopher heard the sword fighting at the bottom of the staircase. Loud screams came next. It was their other crew wincing out in pain, gasping for his last breath of air.

"Sir, we have got to get out of here."

David and Cristopher could hear the footsteps on the staircase. David directed Cristopher to where Eleni hid when she snuck out of the castle. Quietly they waited until the Guardsmen past and fled down the staircase back out into the courtyard. A trail of blood was all that was left of their fallen comrade.

David and Cristopher whisked across the courtyard and back down the staircase to the beach. Three guardsmen were waiting for them. Swords drawn, Cristopher and David swung, slashed, and stabbed killing two of the men.

They tossed their boots onto the sand and dove into the water. The two of them swam tirelessly towards the ship. Their energy was spent, but they made it just as the ship sailed out of the lagoon.

David staggered to the back of the deck, taking in the last view of the bay where he met his true love, Eleni. He retrieved the heavy object in his pocket. It was Eleni's golden locket caked with blood. He carefully opened it; a small portrait of Eleni was inside.

I wonder when she had this commissioned. Such a small painting. It looks just like her.

David clicked the locket closed and secured the necklace around his neck. He would carry the necklace with him until the end of his days.

"I will never forget you, Eleni," he whispered.

He grasped the chain around his neck and bowed his head in tears, as the vast body of water opened up in front of him.

Eleni was in and out of an unconscious state due to her head injury for days, chained in the adjoining chamber to her bedroom. Hillina had dressed her head-wounds. When she woke, she found she was resting on dilapidated furniture and old rags for sheets and bedding. Her once glamorous wardrobe replaced with servant's clothing.

Eleni's hands and feet were shackled with heavy chains, and she was unable to move. "Help me!" She called out. "Can anyone hear me?"

"I see you are awake." Hillina shuffled into the room, closing the door behind her. She dragged a chair in the corner across the room and plopped down, attending to Eleni's wounds.

"Why am I chained up like this?"

"Why, Eleni, you should already know the answer," Hillina snickered. "I told you that you must always please your king, or you would be disgraced. You have disgraced your king, Eleni."

"But I did not disgrace my king; he disgraced me," Eleni retorted.

"Shut your filthy mouth," Hillina hissed. She slapped Eleni across the face, leaving a hand print. "You will not make blasphemous statements against his Majesty, King Arkamun."

Eleni laid there, staring coldly at Hillina. She knew there was nothing she could do to free herself.

"How long have I been unconscious, Hillina?"

"You have been unconscious for four days, you, stupid girl," Hillina muttered." You will disgrace your king and husband no more." Hillina laughed again under her breath.

Eleni bore her eyes into Hillina's skull. "You never liked me." Eleni pulled her arms, trying to loosen the chains around her wrists.

"You are right stupid girl. "Hillina kicked the chair out from underneath her and placed the rag and basin back on the table.

"It seems as if you have healed enough to be moved."

"Moved where?" Eleni screamed. She laid still, exhausted from the weight of the chains.

"Oh, you, stupid girl, you will be moved out of this castle, away from Arkamun and his new... You will be moved out of this castle, into more accommodating surroundings, Eleni. Or at least until more permanent arrangements can be made to deal with your disobedience, you shall see." Hillina crackled.

"Why not just let me die... Why keep me here?"

"Because, you stupid girl. King Arkamun says death is too good for you. He has a better plan for you. You shall see!" she yelled again as she shuffled out of the room.

"Moved where?" Eleni screamed again.

Eleni was completely alone once more. She glanced around hoping to find a way to pry the chains from her ankle and wrists. The chains were not forgiving. Every move she made increased the tension in them. There was nothing she could do. She was not only a prisoner in her previous room and home, but she was also not on a ship with her true love, David.

Eleni understood her life as she knew it and as she had planned with David was not going to happen. She knew she would never become the queen of England, nor would she see David again.

12 Punishment

Meseret awoke to her son screaming and kicking statues off their pedestals in the hall outside of her chamber room. She slipped on her robe and slippers, stepping out into the hall. One of the servants hurried across the corridor in the direction of her son's room.

"Girl..." Meseret called out to the servant "What is going on? What is all of that screaming?"

"It is the king; he is furious with Queen Eleni. She was preparing to sneak away from the castle last night with that captain from England.

Meseret's eyes widened, and she crossed her arms over her stomach.

How did Eleni not escape last night when everything was planned perfectly?

"Where is my son now?"

"He retreated to his ritual room."

"Thank you, girl. You may go."

The servant girl bowed at Queen Meseret and continued down the hall. Meseret returned to her chamber room and dressed. She had to warn Eleni's parents of what happened to her. Through the castle, she went in search of Berhanua. If he could get a message to them, there might be a chance to save her from the hands of her son.

Berhanua was out beyond the walls of the castle. Meseret could see him in the distance shoveling grain into buckets for the horse feed. The hard ripples of his muscle gleamed in the sun. She could not help but lick her lips.

Not now Meseret, not now.

"Berhanua," she called out, scurrying towards him.

Berhanua glanced up at her, stopping his work. "Well, hello, and good morning, Milady."

"Good morning, Berhanua," Meseret answered, out of breath.

"What is wrong, my love? You are out of breath."

Meseret steadied herself and calmed her heart palpitation. "I need you to do something for me. Eleni is in danger, and I need you to ride to the kingdom of Eritrea to warn her parents."

"What kind of danger do you mean, Meseret? What did you do?"

"I tried to help her get out of the kingdom with King David. Somehow Arkamun found out about the plan and intercepted her on the beach. She is locked up as we speak. I am not sure what my son's plan is."

Berhanua dropped the shovel in the dirt, shaking his head. "Does Arkamun know that you are involved?"

"I am not sure, Berhanua, time is of the essence. Please, you have to help me." Meseret coaxed Berhanua in the direction of the stables. Berhanua saddled one of the horses and gathered a few supplies.

"You will have to ride hard and fast. Be careful on your journey there. I will cover for you with Arkamun."

"I will be careful. I love you Meseret, and I will hurry."

Meseret and Berhanua kissed deeply one final time before he saddled his horse and raced out of the kingdom.

In the eyes of King Dabir, his daughter's marriage to King Arkamun had proven to be successful. The gold, jewels, and land he received helped him fund the war against Bahri Negassi Yeshaq. King Dabir won his quest. He retook his kingdom and removed his land from under the control of the Provence of Medri Bahri.

The kingdoms' restoration of property and wealth led Queen Abrihet to come out of her isolation and to reconnect with her husband and king. Not long after Queen Abrihet's isolation ended, she bore the kingdom a son and new heir.

King Dabir's life could not be better: a new child, wealth restored to the throne, and his wife returning to his side after her long absence from court. King Dabir tried not to think of his daughter Eleni. They had left Abyssinia abruptly and never had the chance to say their goodbyes. Whenever the thought of her passed through his mind, he quickly dismissed it.

The happiness of the kingdom was short-lived. One evening as King Dabir and Queen Abrihet were taking a stroll through the lands of the country, a servant ran up to them, getting their attention.

"I beg your pardon, sir, and miss, but there is a man here seeking an audience with you. He states he is from the white castle and says he brought urgent news of your daughter Eleni."

"Eleni!" King Dabir yelped. He looked at his wife, his eye widened and mouth his slackened.

"You must go, Dabir; I will catch up to you."

King Dabir kissed Abrihet on the forehead and took off with haste towards his throne room. He entered his throne room, and thoughts ran through his mind of his daughter, and what information this stranger had about her. It had been two years since the King had last seen or even spoke to his daughter.

As he rushed towards the throne room, he reflected on the anger in his daughter's voice during their last conversation. He could visualize the despair and resentment in her eyes. He hoped the news this stranger brought was good news and glad tidings, but the sixth sense he developed from years of war gave him an uneasy feeling on the state of his daughter.

King Dabir passed his guards in the throne room who stood ready to take any action if he were to give an order, and approached a cloaked man standing in the center of four of his guards.

"Come closer," King Dabir said as he walked to his throne and sat down.

"I heard you brought news of my daughter Eleni. I do not care for secretive meetings. It is not the way of my people. State your business and be mindful of the words parting your lips."

The cloaked figure walked over to stand in front of the king and removed his hood. A tall, dark, bald, muscular man stood before him.

King Dabir remembered the man. He was one of Arkamun's guardsmen.

"Ruler of these high lands, and king of the great warriors of Ethiopia, there is news of the queen, and it saddens me to say the news is unfavorable."

"Before we continue, state your name to jog my memory and tell me who sent you?" King Dabir asked.

"My name is Berhanua. I am a guardsman in King Arkamun's court. We met briefly before when I was in your kingdom. I have been made aware of your daughter's situation by Queen Meseret, Arkamun's mother. She is in danger, and I come to warn you. You need to save your daughter and return her home where she is safe."

"Safe?" King Dabir yelled. "Why is she not safe! explain yourself, before your head, is removed from your shoulders!"

"It has been brought to my attention that Queen Eleni has been suffering at the hands of King Arkamun. She has been thrown into a life of brutal rapes and beatings. Upon her escape, she was intercepted by Arkamun. If something is not done to stop King Arkamun, I fear Queen Eleni will be killed. Eleni is being tortured at the behest and pleasure of the king".

King Dabir sat back on his throne and stared heavily at Berhanua. He had no words and shook his head in utter disbelief of what he been told.

Before he could form a reply, his wife Queen Abrihet, entered the throne room. Queen Abrihet saw the look on her husband's face and scornfully glowered at the man she immediately recognized in front of her husband.

"What is going on here?"

Queen Abrihet took her seat next to her husband as a young boy around the age of one wobbled over to the throne near his parents.

Berhanua eyed the child who he saw was the spitting image of himself. His eyes locked with Abrihet's, questioning her silently.

King Dabir turned to her solemnly and struggled to speak. "My wife, my queen, there is news of your daughter Eleni."

"Eleni!" Queen Abrihet said in shock. "Tell me... what news of my daughter."

Berhanua gazed back at Queen Abrihet. "I was explaining to your husband, your daughter Queen Eleni is in danger, and he needs to bring her home. There is not much time to spare; something must be done soon."

Queen Abrihet glanced back at her husband. Her eyes bubbled up with tears in the corners.

"What will do you, my husband?" she asked him sternly.

King Dabir took a deep breath, straightening his back against the throne's padding. He gained his composure, his mood changing from sadness to pure anger.

"Those who crossed us will pay with their heads." He pounded his fists on the arms of his throne. "Berhanua you will tell no one of your visit here." He stood, stepped off his throne and paced the room.

"I will assemble my counsel and devise a plan to save my daughter from the hands of your king. He will pay for what he has done to my daughter. I give great thanks to you for the information you provided me. How can I repay you for this information you shared so freely?"

"Milord, saving your daughter from suffering is enough for me. I beg and pray you will hurry in your rescue efforts; I am not sure on how much time Queen Eleni has left. Arkamun tires of her every day. I must return to the white castle, if I do not move in haste, I will be missed.

Berhanua tucked his cloak back over his head and shoulders. He said his goodbyes to the king and queen and hurried out of the castle to retrieve his horse.

Queen Abrihet picked up her son in her arms and followed Berhanua out of the castle into the night. "Please wait, I need to speak with you Berhanua."

Berhanua paused from getting on his horse and looked at her blankly. "There is not much to explain; I see that you have the son you wanted. You and your husband seem to be in a much better place because of it.

"You have to know by looking at him that he is yours." Abrihet reached her hand out touching Berhanua on the shoulder.

Berhanua sighed and circled towards her. "What would you like for me to say? I have a son who you are claiming to be a prince. A child I never knew existed."

"Just hold him." Abrihet placed the baby in his arms.

Berhanua's hand became sweaty from holding the baby. "What did you name him? He is truly beautiful."

"His name is Biniam, after my father."

"Does Dabir know that he is not his son?"

Abrihet shifted her stance and took Biniam back into her arms. "No, he does not know his true lineage. I just pray the child I am carrying now is a son. I will tell him as soon as this baby is born."

Berhanua became quiet. He had a son. "Well, I hope that you at least tell our son about his father one day. I am not sure I will ever have the chance to see him again."

"Don't say that; I believe you two will meet again. There was a moment between us, Berhanua; I will never forget. Even in that very brief moment, I found myself loving you."

"And I loved you as well. Perhaps we will have another conversation in the future. But now I have to return before the other guardsmen realize that I am gone".

Berhanua kissed Abrihet gently on the lips, and then kissed his son on his forehead. "Goodbye for now."

Abrihet stood back and watched Berhanua ride off into the darkness.

Riding fast and hard, he pushed his horse on the journey back to the white castle. Berhanua approached the path and saw all his immediate surroundings were quiet.

I made it back unnoticed.

He slowed his horse down to a trot, riding through the back gates of the castle. He dismounted his horse, tying the reins to the side of the fencing in the courtyard, and headed up the path towards the castle.

A woman screamed in agony from outside of the castle walls. He released his sword from its scabbard and proceeded towards the front entrance of the castle leading into town. As he neared the gates of the castle walls, Berhanua was ambushed from behind.

He struggled to get free and gained his freedom for a moment. Two unknown assailants pushed Berhanua into the wall and tried to knock him down to the ground. Berhanua grabbed his sword off the ground, slashing the neck of one assailant. Spinning around, he tried to locate the other assailant. He did not see him to his right or his left.

Berhanua let his guard down and placed his sword back in the scabbard and moved forward. A sharp pain struck him across his back, and he fell to the ground in pain. He was stabbed from behind with a knife. He tried to whip his sword out again to defend himself, but it was too late. Unable to move and bleeding profusely, the lone assailant stepped onto his back.

"Someone wants to see you," The assailant barked in a sinister laugh. He yanked Berhanua's arms behind him, tying them together, then pulled him up with the coarse rope.

The assailant shoved Berhanua down the path in the direction of the screams. He noticed the figure of a woman under duress, shackled, and visibly beaten off to the side.

A significant amount of blood was splattered on the woman's face preventing him from identifying her. The masked man nudged Berhanua forward again. He glanced down at her feet and saw an ankle bracelet strikingly identical to the one he had given his sister years ago which she swore to him she would never remove.

The painful truth started to set in Berhanua's mind. The unknown woman was his sister. Despair and extreme hostility consumed Berhanua's thoughts and physical being.

"What is the meaning of this madness? You, cowards, dare abuse a woman of this land! My sister nonetheless! Your lives shall be ended! "screamed Berhanua.

"Save your baseless threats Berhanua...." King Arkamun stepped out of the shadows. "Your betrayal has been revealed to me by your whore of a sister. It seems betrayal and deceit are in your family's blood."

"What is the meaning of this, King Arkamun?" Berhanua yelled.

King Arkamun nodded to the men surrounding them, resulting in vicious punches and kicks to the faces of the Berhanua and Ayantu. The King smiled at the specter of his authority and the pain inflicted on the siblings.

"What is the meaning you ask... Shall we begin with the disdain and insolence of your frequent sexual encounters with my mother?"

Berhanua gazed at Arkamun in shock through his blood-soaked eyes.

"You thought it was a secret, Berhanua? I have watched you both engage in your sex acts for several years. Always under the impression, no one knew, I just relished in the thought of your foolish attempt at secrecy. Now I know why my mother began to respond adversely to our usual sexual encounters."

Berhanua turned away from Arkamun's glare in disbelief. He made a choking sound in his throat.

"The queen was mine before she was yours, you fool. She will be mine again once I have disposed of you. The queen will return to her rightful place, as my whore mother and lover, or she will join you in death. As for your sister..."

King Arkamun signaled to his guardsmen. The guards standing at the side of Berhanua, forced his head, making him watch the impending grotesque sight. Another guard removed his knife from the holder at his waist, stepped behind Ayantu, and violently tugged her hair.

He yanked her head backward, fully exposing her throat. Berhanua struggled to fight off his captor, using the last of his energy in an attempt to save his sister. He skillfully and swiftly killed two of his fellow guardsmen as he ran to aid Ayantu. As he drew closer to her, Berhanua was detained and beaten.

Berhanua was restrained and held down on his knees again within arm's reach of his sister. Ayantu made eye contact with him. He could see the fear in her eyes; they both knew she was about to die.

King Arkamun scuffled over to where Berhanua knelt. "It seems you want to save your sister's life. Kiss my feet, pledge your allegiance to me, and I will spare her life."

"As the true and living God is my witness, you will..."

King Arkamun raised his arm, gesturing to his guard. The guardsman plunged the knife into Ayantu's throat, causing it to exit violently through the side of her neck. Her blood erupted, covering Berhanua's face.

Berhanua let out a scream, bellowing from the depth of his soul at the sight of his sister gruesomely killed.

Arkamun smiled as he slinked over to where Ayantu's corpse hung. Dipping his finger into her severed throat, he then tasted her blood.

"I suddenly feel the need to relieve myself." Arkamun proceeded in pulling out his penis, urinating on Ayantu's heavily bleeding and twitching corpse. Arkamun reeled around glaring in Berhanua's direction. "You have suffered a fate worse than death. The last thing you will ever see in my lands is the death of your sister. All those who betray me suffer. You should have been wiser in your actions. Take him to the dungeon at once!" Arkamun yelled at his guardsmen. "I will sell him to the highest bidder. Maybe he will make a better slave than a guard."

Arkamun let out a final crackling laugh and spit onto Berhanua's face as he marched off towards the castle.

Queen Meseret had felt quite weak the last few days and found herself taking more naps throughout the day than normal. She would speak to Berhanua when he returned to the castle that evening. She hoped that he had made it safely, and King Dabir would come for his daughter. Queen Meseret was sound asleep when her chamber door opened, and someone walked in.

The person who entered the room was quiet, but upon sitting on the bed, Queen Meseret was awoken from her slumber.

"Berhanua," The Queen called out.

She began to stir and sat up in her bed. Her vision was out of focus in the dark room, but the figure lit her candle lamp in the corner of the chamber, and started to take form. Queen Meseret realized it was her son.

"Arkamun, what are you doing here?" She pushed back the covers from her bed and sat up on the side of the bed.

"Mother, are you not happy to see your beloved son?" Arkamun asked He came closer to the bed.

Queen Meseret saw the dark spots of blood on his light clothing. She looked up at his face and noticed something dangling from his neck.

"I am always pleased to see you, Arkamun. Why would you say such a thing to me?"

Queen Meseret swung her feet over the side of the bed and approached Arkamun. She gazed at him dead in his eyes and rubbed his face with her hand. She glanced down Arkamun's body and got a better look at the objects around his neck. There were two hands removed from a female's arms.

"What have you done, Arkamun?" Queen Meseret retreated, taking a step back from her son in horror. "Whose hands are those around your neck?"

"Whose hands are these; you ask?" Arkamun laughed sinisterly, a devilish grin on his face. "Oh, Mother. You seem to think you, Eleni, Berhanua, and his whore of a sister who served my former queen would get away with so much."

Queen Meseret gawked at Arkamun with a blank stare. She knew then that he had found out everything, and her life was also in danger.

"What have you done, Arkamun? she asked, repeating herself. "What have you done with Berhanua and Ayantu?"

"What have I not done, Mother? You will be joining them both very soon."

Arkamun took Ayantu's hands from around his neck, clapped them together and tossed them on the bed. He removed his shirt and pants and stood naked before his mother.

"Come to me mother; I want to taste you," he said with a sinister laugh

He approached Meseret, and wrenched her into his arms, and kissed her. Meseret snatched away from her son. He smelled and tasted of blood, and he repulsed her.

"Stay away from me, Arkamun!" she screamed. She tried to make it to the chamber door.

Arkamun blocked her exit, uprooted her from the floor, and flung her down on the bed.

"You will be mine this last time, Mother."

Arkamun forced her face down on the bed. He ripped her gown and robe up over her hips exposing her buttocks. He became aroused immediately and jammed his hard phallus into her anus.

Meseret screamed out in pain. All the past times she had made love to her son did not come close to the pain and despair she felt in those last moments. She struggled to free herself from under his weight, but could not. He drove himself deeper into her, and she could feel her anus tear from the pressure of his thrusts.

"Oh mother, how I missed this, you have kept this from me. How could you take from me what was mine? I told you, you would pay for disrespecting my love," Arkamun whispered into Meseret's ear.

Arkamun thrust his cock into his mother's anus until he reached his climax. He climbed off her, and after retrieving his bloody clothes, he redressed himself. He picked up Ayantu's hands off the bed and hung them around his neck.

Meseret slid herself off the bed and covered herself with her torn robe. In her mind, the rape was the extent of Arkamun's punishment for her becoming involved with Berhanua, and for helping Eleni. She was wrong. Not soon after she regained her composure, Arkamun snatched her hair from behind and yanked her out of her chamber room into the hall.

"I told you that you would be joining the others shortly, and now you shall."

"What are you doing, son? you had your way with me, now turn me free." Meseret's voice elevated.

Arkamun continued to drag his mother by her hair to his private torture chamber which he used to torture his concubines for his pleasure. He opened the door and lunged his mother inside the room, closing the door behind them.

Meseret gazed around in horror at the contraptions her son had collected over the years. She knew her son was not all there in the head, but she never thought he could be as cruel as she now saw.

"Let me go, Arkamun; you cannot do this to me! I am your mother, and Queen Mother," Meseret sobbed.

"Save your tears and your screams, you whore. You have betrayed me for the last time. Now you will pay for your insubordinate actions to oust your king."

Arkamun flung his mother into a contraption and tightened the chains around her wrists. He ripped off her robe, exposing her body. Meseret's ankles were shackled, pulling her legs open.

Meseret knew she would be joining Eleni, Ayantu, and Berhanua in death, sooner than she initially believed. Arkamun moved over to the table in the corner, smiling at all of the devices he had laying there.

"Hmm, what should I choose Mother?" He asked in a cocky tone. "What is your pleasure, you whore?"

Arkamun drooled over his spoils, his eyes widening while he stared at the giant contraption with a cylinder and thick body with claws on the end. Another screw on the other end was used to enlarge the contraption. Arkamun picked it up and spun around in Meseret's face.

"Look what I have here, Mother, this should be fun." Arkamun stood in front of her.

"Do you know what this is mother? Do you know where this is going to go?" He asked, taunting her.

Meseret stared in horror. She had only once seen the pear of anguish. Her father had used it on a man when she was a child. Meseret rested her head on her shoulder and tears streamed down her face.

Arkamun raised his mother's head to his eye level and kissed her. Meseret bit his lip with her teeth, and he slapped her across the face for her disobedience.

"I love it when you fight me, mother. You make things so much more interesting. This should only hurt for a moment."

He laughed as he kneeled and pushed the pear of anguish into her vaginal region. She could feel the claws tearing the flesh from the inside of her. She screamed out in pain. Blood ran down her leg and pooled on the floor.

Arkamun got excited and laughed before licking the blood from her leg with his tongue across his lips. He reached down and rubbed his cock, his erection swelling.

"Shall we continue Mother." Arkamun reached up and turned the screw on the contraption, expanding it more. Meseret screamed in pain again.

"Please stop, Arkamun," she begged.

Arkamun became more aroused with her begging him. He spun the contraption until Meseret passed out. When he was satisfied, he pulled the pear of anguish out from between his mother's legs. Arkamun slapped his mother until she woke up. He licked her flesh off of the contraption as she watched.

"Tasty, Mother."

Arkamun placed the pear of anguish back on the table and released his mother from her chains. She was so exhausted she could not stand and fell into his arms. He dragged her by her shoulders over to the iron chair that was covered with a bed of sharp spikes.

He sat her down in the chair and the spikes immediately began to tear at her flesh. Meseret cried uncontrollably from the pain she felt from the spikes on her back and her thighs. Arkamun smiled again at his mother as he tightened the restraints.

"Arkamun! Please stop! I'm begging you, stop!" she cried.

"Your tears do nothing for me but give me an erection," He bellowed, rubbing his penis again. "You will please me now orally."

Arkamun pushed the stool from under the table in front of his mother and stood on it. He forced his erection into her mouth, rocking his body back in forth, making her suck his cock.

Meseret gasped for breath as Arkamun thrust his penis deeper and deeper into her mouth. Unable to take a breath, she fought the pain as the spikes drew deeper inside her flesh. Meseret could fill the pain seeping into her bones. She prayed silently for this torturous act to be over and that he would give her mercy and end her life.

After what seemed like an eternity, Arkamun climaxed and released his cum into his mother's mouth. Meseret choked and spat the fluids out of her mouth as she gasped for air.

"Awe mother, you pleased me." Arkamun released the restraints on her ankles and wrists, flinging her out of the iron chair and allowing her to fall to the floor.

"Now for my final act," Arkamun said, stepping over to his mother and lunging another contraption to the middle of the room. Meseret knew she was dying. Her body became limp as the blood poured out her. She became more delirious but managed to take one final look up and over at her son's muscular nude body flexing as he rolled yet another bulky device in the room. Stopping where his mother laid, he dragged her by her hair over to the contraption.

"Any last words, Mother?"

Arkamun tugged his mother onto the contraption and screwed the circular vise down on her head so she couldn't move. Between her shallow breaths, she uttered her final words.

"My lasts words for you, my son. Will be me waiting for you to join me in hell!" she screamed between breaths.

"Awe, I thought those would be your words, Mother! I will see you in hell, but not today," Arkamun replied, laughing.

With a swift motion, he turned the vice, crushing his mother's head beyond recognition and silenced her forever. Blood spattered all over Arkamun and splashed on the walls around the room. His mother was dead by his hand. Arkamun redressed himself still covered in blood. He called to his guardsmen to clean up the blood and the mess in the torture room.

"Get this room back into working condition," Arkamun stated as he strolled out of the chamber. "Take this woman's remains and throw them in with our traitor, Berhanua. I'm sure he will be pleased to see his beloved again."

"Yes Milord," The Guardsman answered.

The Guardsman sent for the castle's servants to come and clean up after Arkamun's activities in the throne room. They removed Meseret's body from the room and covered her with a cloth. No one including the guardsmen realized it was Arkamun's mother he tortured and killed.

The guards took the body down to the dungeon where Berhanua was. He was asleep in his cell when he woke to a loud noise outside.

"What is going on?" Berhanua called out, sitting up in his cell.

"King Arkamun sent a gift for you." One of the guardsmen said as they came closer carrying a large covered object.

"Step back from your cell," said the other guardsman

They stopped in front of Berhanua's cell, unlocking it. Berhanua moved back from the cell door, and the guards dropped the large wrapped object on the ground. Berhanua looked down at the pool of blood forming beneath the sheet. He realized it was a body.

"We have brought your whore to see you," said the first guardsman He kicked the body into the cell with Berhanua, slamming the cell door behind them.

"Enjoy your visit," The second guard laughed.

Berhanua paused with fear in his heart. He knew it was his beloved Meseret underneath the cloth. He dropped down to his knees next to the cloth and peeled it back. Overwhelmed with sobs of grief, Berhanua fell onto Meseret's remains.

Arkamun had taken two of the three women he ever loved. Berhanua's heart turned cold. He prayed King Dabir heeded his words and would avenge not only Eleni but Meseret and Ayantu as well.

The next morning, after sleeping for a few hours, Berhanua was kicked awake by the same two guardsmen. He kissed Meseret one last time on her hand and led out of the dungeon to the courtyard.

Berhanua's eyes adjusted to the daylight and he could see Eleni across the lawn standing among other servants and slaves. He also noticed more pale-faced strangers from a neighboring country were at the white castle. They were not there for a social visit. Some of the pale men were shackling servants and guiding them down the stone staircase to the beach below.

Berhanua realized they were being enslaved and taken away from the kingdom. He knew now King Dabir would not make it in time to save his daughter. Berhanua was shackled with the remaining servants and was taken down to the beach. He took a

final glance of the white castle as it disappeared behind him. His life had taken a turn he never expected, but he vowed to himself he would protect Eleni as best as he could. He would not let her fate be the same as his Ayantu or Meseret.

13 Goodbye

Two months past after Eleni's and David's last encounter. Eleni's life in court had declined from being the Queen of Abyssinia to being a prisoner of Arkamun. After her wounds had healed enough to satisfy Hillina, Eleni was taken from the main castle to the stables and shackled to the walls. She had heard from a servant that Queen Meseret had mysteriously disappeared from the court weeks ago. Eleni suspected Arkamun might have done more than make up a story about Queen Meseret running off with a servant.

Eleni was secluded and alone in the stables for many days. Arkamun visited Eleni in the stables, tormenting her with physical abuse and anal rape. But even through her continuous abuse, she remained stable.

During Eleni's seclusion, she noticed her body changing. She recalled that she had not gotten her monthly bleeding since her encounter with David on the night she was to leave Abyssinia.

She became aware she was with child again. Eleni became inconsolable when she acknowledged to herself that she was pregnant with David's child. She broke down in tears, cried and pleaded to the skies through the patched roof above her.

"I cannot have this child in a stable," she cried out loud. Eleni got on her knees, pulling her chains with her and prayed to the one God for her deliverance and freedom from her prison. "Please help me, and help my child," she prayed. Eleni's prayers were answered in the following days. One morning as Eleni lay sleeping on the straw in the stables, the door was opened. It was a member of the Guardsmen who came to fetch her.

"Gather your belongings. I have come to take you to the auction."

Eleni gazed up at him from her straw bed, sat up and slipped on the only pair of satin slippers she owned. They were much fancier than the rags she wore, but it was all she had. The guardsman led her to the open courtyard where there were many other servants lined up in a row.

King Arkamun stood on a pedestal and next to him was a man who looked like he could have come from David's country. Eleni's pulse raced. Maybe this was her chance to get to England.

Have my prayers been answered? Will I find David?

The court clapped and cheered in excitement. King Arkamun raised his hand, quieting the crowd.

"I have gathered you all here to witness this great kingdom of Abyssinia come to terms with the great country of France. You who are lined up in front of all of these people will be my test subjects. You have been procured to be servants for the royal court of France."

Eleni's mouth fell open. Arkamun sold her into slavery as a servant for someone in the royal court in France. She nodded her head in disbelief and began to cry. Her prayers of deliverance were only leading her to another kingdom to be oppressed by another.

Cheers from the crowd rang out again after Arkamun's speech ended. He spotted Eleni in the line with the other servants and wanted her brought to him in the throne room. The guardsman escorted the disgraced queen through the crowd. She held her head low, struggling with the chains at her feet.

Eleni entered the throne room alone, and the door slammed behind her. Arkamun appeared from behind his throne, disrobed and naked. His body was still like a god, strong, muscular and rippled in every direction.

"My Eleni. This will be the last time I will have the pleasure of taking what I told you was always mine." He sang out coming closer to her.

Eleni took a step back toward the door. She knew what was about to happen. In her mind, she only cared about protecting the life inside her. She knew what she had to do.

"Do what you will," Eleni snapped coming towards him. "You are right; this is the last time you will ever have your hands on me."

"Now why could it not be like this when I wanted you as my queen?"

Arkamun grabbed Eleni by the arms. He kissed her neck and snatched the rags from her body. He ran his fingers down the small of her back, then over her stomach.

Eleni could tell he noticed something was different. His eyes narrowed in on her stomach which was swollen and bigger than it had been previously. He stepped backward to get a better view of her nakedness. "What has happened to you, Eleni?" Arkamun looked her up and down in disgust. "Nothing has happened, Milord. I might have gained a little bit of weight." Arkamun was immediately turned off by what he saw. Eleni had never seen him change his mind about raping her. The deliverance she had prayed for had arrived. She knew he would never touch her again. "You disgust me. Leave my presence at once. I shall satisfy my needs with my new bride. You will never have the pleasure of having me touch you again."

Arkamun laughed, heading out throne room. Eleni stood back, relieved, pulling the tattered dress back over her swelling stomach. She swung the throne room door ajar and stepped into the sunlight. The guardsman was waiting to escort her. Eleni was re-shackled and led down the long stone staircase to the lagoon with the other slaves.

Her life as she knew it would never be the same, but in those moments, she still thought of David and what her life could have been if she would have escaped with him.

I wonder where he is now? Did Arkamun do something to him? I have to find him somehow.

Eleni knew her choices cost her greatly. But she did not regret the beautiful moments she shared with David. Nor the little life growing inside of her created by their love. The small dingy pushed up onto shore with a few members of the French crew. They started loading the servants and slaves onto the small boat. Eleni was one of the first to be loaded and sent out into the lagoon.

The ship Eleni boarded was massive compared to David's ship the Lady Fantasy. Eleni followed behind the other servants and crew members up the ladder. The shackles around her ankles and wrists made it a daunting task to climb, but she continued.

Eleni reached the top deck. Glowering around the ship, she saw other men and women in chains doing chores. She also noticed some slave women pleasuring French men with oral sex.

Eleni was disgusted and knew she had walked into another nightmare. She bowed her head as she was led across the deck of the ship.

Before going below, she glanced up and saw off in the distance an African man looking at her. He had to be no less than six feet tall. He had a muscular build, chocolate skin, bald head, and slanted eyes. She believed he could have been a mixed race. He had no shirt on, and his exposed muscles and tight abdomen gleamed in the sunlight from the sweat running down his body. He smiled at her, and to her surprise, had a beautiful white smile that beamed in the sun.

He seems friendly.

Eleni moved along with the other servants who were bound to her. She took one more glance at him and ducked her head down into the large hole in the deck. She climbed down the ladder leading to a narrow wooden staircase that led to the bottom of the ship.

Eleni pressed her lips together and swallowed hard. The stagnant smell of filth filtered through her nostrils. It was obvious the captain of this ship was trying to profit on as many slaves and servants he could hold. There was not much room for any movement. The slaves and servants were packed on top of each other and chained together by their wrist and ankles.

Eleni felt lightheaded and fidgeted with her rag dress. She had never witnessed anything like what she was seeing. Some of the other servants and slaves were sick and downtrodden around her. Some women had given birth and still slept in the blood and bodily fluids after having their babies. Eleni wondered how often, if at all, they were allowed to bathe.

The sanitation conditions were poor. There were few buckets for the slaves and servants to relieve themselves. If those buckets

were not reachable, the people who were farthest from the buckets urinated and defecated on themselves. The stench of urine
and feces made bile rise in Eleni's stomach.

She had never seen such horrendous conditions and hoped her
pregnancy would hold until she made it to the new country to
which they were sailing. She did not want to give birth on a ship
in such condition. Food was scarce on board. Eleni had only been
given water twice a day by a crew member since boarding the
ship. The lack of food and attention led Eleni to be disoriented,
weak, and tired.

After a few weeks, the day came when she was released from
her bondage. Eleni shackles were unbuckled, and she fell into the
sailor's arm who released her. He stood her up on her feet and
led her up the stairs to the deck of the ship.

He sat her down on the floor and handed her a bowl of stewed
oats. Eleni had never eaten anything quite like it, but she was so
malnourished and hungry she drank the oats down like they were
water. The sailor noticed how hungry she was, and refilled the
bowl.

The second helping of the oats soothed Eleni's stomach, and
she felt full. He handed her a cup of some brown liquid. Drinking
it, Eleni noticed it had a strong taste. She was not sure of what
it was but continued to drink.

The sailor took the cup from her and pulled her up onto her
feet. Eleni felt better from eating but was still a little dizzy. She
had drunk something other than tea. The sailor grabbed Eleni's
arm and escorted her across the deck towards the captain's corridors.

The sun's rays blinded Eleni's vision as she moved towards
the captain's chambers. She did not notice all the other crew
members staring at her. The captain had seemed to have taken a

liking to her, judging by the way he ran his fingers through her hair and when he leaned in to smell it

.

Eleni would catch him staring at her when he would sneak down to the bottom of the ship. His stares made her uneasy, as she had seen them before in her former husband. She knew it would not be long before he asked for her.

Eleni and the sailor reached the captain's corridors. He knocked on the door, opened it, and pushed Eleni inside, closing it behind her. Eleni looked around the dark room and saw a single candle lit. The captain of the ship came forward, staring at her. He was a fat tub of lard with greasy black hair and a long beard. He spoke French to her which she understood. The captain came closer and pulled her into him. He pressed his mouth against hers and slipped his tongue into her mouth. She bit him, and he slapped her. The captain let out a laugh as if it was a game to him.

He rounded his desk and poured a glass of red wine into his goblet. "voulez-vous un peu de vin." He spoke in French, raising the glass to Eleni.

Eleni shook her head in response. The captain stepped from behind the desk and approached Eleni. He asked her again, about the wine forcing her to drink it.

"You will have some wine, and you will like it!" He pushed the glass into her face and forced the wine down her throat.

Eleni gagged and forced the captain away from her. She could not keep quiet any further about her knowledge of French or that she was an educated queen.

"How dare you touch me in this manner, Captain. Do you have any respect? Do you know who I am?" She spoke in French.

The captain's eyes widened. He was shocked Eleni could not only speak French but spoke with such authority.

He let out bellow laugh. "I do not care who you were. You are nothing but a slave now, and at the present moment, you are my whore, and you will do what I ask."

Eleni backed her body up against the door. She knew he was right. There was nowhere to run, and she could not escape from this encounter or what he wanted to do to her. She braced herself for what she thought was going to happen next. She knew she would be raped again.

The captain came forward one final time, reaching Eleni at the door. He yanked her into him again her pregnant stomach resting against his chest. He snatched his belt from his waist and handed it to her. He spun around facing the door and dropped his pants down to the floor, showing his hairy naked buttocks.

"Spank me, please spank me!" the captain screamed out.

Eleni's eyebrows puckered.

He wants to be spanked?

Eleni laughed quietly. She had never seen a man want this type of pleasure, let alone for her inflict the pleasure on him. This was something she would enjoy. Eleni tightened the grip on the belt in her hand and swung it down on the captain's bare buttocks. The first smack was soft.

"Harder!" the captain bellowed.

Eleni smacked his buttocks harder the second time.

The captain became aroused with the spanking. He started to masturbate his organ with every smack Eleni inflicted on him. After his buttocks had been red and bruised, the captain stood back off his desk and smiled at Eleni. He was pleased with Eleni's performance thus far and wanted to continue.

The captain took the belt from Eleni's hands and threw it down on the desk. He scooted around to the drawer of the desk and forced it open. He extracted a wooden phallus and handed it to her. She had never seen anything like it before. It was shaped like a penis but larger. Eleni estimated it was about thirteen or fourteen inches in length, and had a thick girth.

The captain's pants still around his feet, scampered back around the desk and assumed his previous position.

Eleni knew he wanted her to insert the phallus into his anal region and move it back in forth in a sexual nature. She moved closer to his pimply behind. Gently she inserted the instrument into his anal hole. The captain let out an erotic moan. She continued thrusting the phallus deeper, and the captain moaned even louder.

Eleni found a rhythm, driving and extracting the phallus in and out of the captain's anal cavity. He moaned in pleasure and rubbed his cock steadily in his hand. Moments later, the captain screamed out in pleasure, releasing his load all over himself and the desk. He stood up and looked at Eleni, seeming pleased with her performance. The captain eased his breeches up and took his shirt and wiped the cum off the desk. He drew Eleni into him one final time and kissed her on the cheek and smiled.

"Merci." He then summoned one of the sailors to return Eleni to the slave barracks.

Eleni dropped the object on the desk and was led back to the barracks. The French sailor shackled her back to her position and left. Eleni broke down crying. Encompassed in her thoughts, she felt a hand grab her shoulder from behind.

A voice cooed to her in French. "It is going to be all right."

Eleni stopped crying and sat up to listen again.

"It is going to be all right," the voice repeated. "You speak French? Who are you?" Eleni's pulse quickened and her eyebrows raised.

"Yes, I speak French! My name is Berhanua. I am also from Abyssinia. I know who you are, Queen Eleni. I am former a guardsman to King Arkamun."

Eleni blinked her eyes repeatedly. "You are from Abyssinia. Do you know English?"

"Yes, I know English, Milady."

"How did you come to be here on this ship, Berhanua? Are you the man I saw days ago on the deck of the ship? Why are you in this part of the ship when the larger men are kept towards the middle?"

Eleni had not recognized him as one of the guardsmen in Abyssinia. She was intrigued.

"Yes, Eleni, I am the same man. I am in this part of the ship because the diseases are killing many of the men in the other part of the ship. They moved me on this side because I am still healthy."

"I see."

"You would not recognize me outside of my uniform. But to answer your question further, I am on this ship because of your former husband King Arkamun, and for the love, I have for two women."

"Which two women are you speaking of, Berhanua?" Eleni shifted her chains and strained to hear.

"The two women are Queen Meseret, and my sister Ayantu, your former servant."

"What! Queen Meseret! And your sister Ayantu! Are you the same man I noticed looking at my Mother and Queen Meseret?"

"Yes... I am that same man. Milady, I feel I owe you an explanation of the events leading me to be here."

"You most certainly do need to explain." She leaned back up against the wood post to have a little more comfort.

"King Arkamun's mother, Queen Meseret, and I have been lovers ever since I was a much younger man. She had been the only woman I ever loved until I met your mother. She found comfort and solace with me after her husband died. We had a close relationship, and I loved her very deeply. I believed our relationship was kept secret for years, only being exposed by one of Arkamun's concubines, when she saw me leaving her chambers one morning. She ran to tell the king immediately, despite me trying to dissuade her."

Berhanua took a deep breath and continued. "Around the same time, it was brought to my attention that you and Ayantu had conflicts. My sister found no solace anywhere else and came to me about the actions she took against you."

"What actions would she want to take against me? I did nothing but told her I did not love her the way she wanted." Eleni's nostrils flared as she breathed harder.

"Milady, Ayantu was the one who showed King Arkamun the letter you wrote to King David describing your plan to leave. King Arkamun read the letter, and that was how he was able to locate you that night when you had made your escape to the lagoon."

Eleni pulled her shackled hands to her back in anger. She now knew the reason Arkamun showed up to the lagoon and why she was not with David. Ayantu had betrayed Queen Meseret and herself in a jealous rage. Eleni felt the baby kick. The kicking made Eleni long for David more.

"After she showed Arkamun the letter describing what you were planning, she was guilt ridden and came to me. Ayantu proceeded to tell me all the horrors you had been suffering. Meseret had also confirmed the story Ayantu told me about your life with Arkamun. I felt obligated to do something about it, so I traveled to see your mother and father telling them of the things happening to you. Upon hearing all I said to him, your father wept and begged for your forgiveness Eleni. He summoned his warrior Council and planned to rescue you. I believe your father intends to kill King Arkamun for what he has done to you."

"My father begged for my forgiveness?" Eleni shook her head in disbelief.

"Yes, my queen. Your father was very distraught and angry. I saw war in his eyes. I also saw the pain of a father who feels he had betrayed his daughter."

"It is of no consequence now. I've lost my life, the love of my life, and I am now a slave. I will never see my father, mother, or homeland again." Eleni bowed her head into her chin and started to sob. "Why could he have not stood up for me from the beginning? My father sold me for jewels, land, and status!" Eleni cried with a bellowing of pain from the pits of her soul.

"I understand your father has done a horrible thing, Eleni. I pray one day, despite our current circumstances, you can find a way to forgive your father. Your father cannot change the past, but rest assured Eleni...you will be avenged." Berhanua became silent suddenly and winced out in pain.

"Berhanua, what is wrong; are you okay?"

"Ayee! I am all right, my queen. I have been having these pains in my head since leaving Abyssinia. I am not sure what is going on with me. Please forgive me.

"Of course, all is forgiven. Are you up to telling me happened to your sister and Queen Meseret?"

Berhanua paused and inhaled deeply. "Eleni, I will not plague you with details on what happened to them. Those visions on how they suffered will be taken to my death. I was unable to save the two women I loved and for that, I am being punished. Just know they both are now at peace."

Eleni knew not to push the subject on what had truly happened to Ayantu and Queen Meseret. She could hear the despair in Berhanua's voice. She understood what he was feeling all too well. Eleni was emotionally drained after the conversation. She tried to close her eyes to sleep, but the discomfort of being shack-led like an animal to the wood post kept her mostly conscious.

Another two days passed, and she was once again released from the constraints holding her captive in the bow of the ship.

They had docked in the Canary Islands for supplies and food.

Eleni had believed she was going to be returned to see the captain again, but she overheard the sickness was spreading on the ship, and the captain had taken ill. A few members of the French crew went to shore for medicine.

Eleni, Berhanua, and other slaves were taken to the deck of the ship and given brushes and rags to clean. She had never cleaned anything in her life. She got down on her knees slowly, which was not good enough for a French soldier watching her.

He knocked her feet out from under her, making her land on her belly. Eleni screamed out in pain and pushed herself up onto her knees, rubbing her stomach. She hoped her baby was all right.

The French sailor seemed aroused by Eleni's actions and would not let her be. As Eleni scrubbed the deck, he came behind her and jerked her into a standing position by her arm. Eleni winced in pain as she was yanked up.

The sailor leaned her to the side railing and started to unbut-ton his breeches with one hand, the other holding Eleni's neck. He wiggled his pants down to his knees and hiked her dress up exposing her buttocks. He was going to rape her out in the open.

Eleni braced herself for his penetration but felt nothing but the cool breeze on her backside. She turned her head and saw Berhanua had wrenched the sailor off her and punched him across the deck. Other crew members tried to get control of the situa-tion, but Berhanua was too strong for all of them.

He flung the sailor who attempted to rape Eleni overboard the ship to his death and knocked down the other crew members who tried to fight him. Eleni smoothed her dress down over her buttocks, and she and a few other slaves threw their wooden cleaning brushes they at the sailors.

Many unchained slaves jumped overboard to their deaths to end the pain and torture they endured. A few even managed to get a hold of the ropes on the deck, wrapped them around their necks and jumped over the side of the ship, strangling themselves in the process. Chaos erupted, and the French sailors lost all control of the slaves. Gunfire rang out, and some of the slaves were shot dead before they stopped fighting the French men.

The sailors regained control over a few remaining slaves, shackling them together and returning them to the slave barracks. Eleni was only able to glance briefly at Berhanua before she was led down into the ship. She did not see the lash taken to Berhanua's back, but heard his moans from above and saw him marched past her bloodied when he was secured in his chains.

The French sailors cut off the heads of many slaves and servants bunked in the slave barracks. Dead bodies were strewn all around them in an attempt to keep the remaining slaves from trying to kill themselves. In many African cultures, Africans believed their death would return them to their homeland and their spirits would be returned to their friends and loved ones.

"Berhanua," Eleni called out. "Berhanua, are you all right?"

There was no response at first. Berhanua took a deep breath and responded, "I have had better days, Milady. I will be fine."

"I wanted to thank you Berhanua. You saved me from being raped and tormented by another man."

"You are welcome, Milady. I could not stand there and allow him to hurt you. I will always be there to protect you," Berhanua whispered.

"I wish there was something I could do to help you." Eleni moved her wrists. Her shackles were not tight, and she was able to slip them over her wrists. Eleni pulled the long screws holding her ankles, and she was free.

Berhanua heard her stirring around and tried to turn his head to see what she was doing. "What are doing Eleni? You are going to get caught and whipped if they see you are free."

"No Berhanua, I am not. I am going to get you some help. They were bringing medical supplies and a doctor back for the captain."

Eleni circled to where Berhanua sat. She leaned over and could see he was bleeding profusely from his wounds.

"If you do not get taken care of, you will die from infection. Can you not see what these sailors have done?" Eleni pointed to all of the corpses scattered around them. "I am going to find the captain. He likes me, and if he is well enough, he will help."

"Be careful, Eleni," Berhanua whispered gently. "If they find you out, they will whip you. And this time, I cannot help protect you."

"I will be careful; you do not have to worry."

Eleni quietly maneuvered her way through the corpses of slaves and the others shackled to the walls. The living slaves stirred and moved in their chains as she walked past them. They too were hoping she would free them.

"Be quiet," she whispered. "If they hear you moving, the sailors will come down here."

Berhanua heard her struggling with the language barrier, and he spoke a few of the languages Eleni did not know. Whatever he had said worked, for the slaves stopped squirming in their shackles, and it was quiet once more.

Eleni proceeded to the ladder. Looking up and around, she did not see any sailors standing guard. She assumed they had bunked down for the night. Eleni used her last strength to climb the ladder to the deck. Her belly was so much bigger than it had been, and she found it harder to move around, she was determined to get to the captain's corridors. Eleni reached the deck and caught her breath. For the first time in weeks, she was able to look up to the night sky.

The sea was calm, and the wind blew around her calling her once again to take the plunge into the sea. Eleni ignored the calls. She knew she had little time to get Berhanua the help he needed. Eleni made her way across the deck to the captain's door. Knocking, she heard him answer. "Enter!"

Eleni opened the door and stepped inside. The captain was lying in bed, and another two men were in the room with him.

"What are you doing here?" He spoke in French.

Eleni came closer, glancing around the room at the other two men. One man looked like he could have been the doctor. He was older, balding and had pale, pasty white skin. The second man must have been his worker. He had caramel colored skin, blond-brownish dreadlocks, green eyes, and bright white teeth.

Eleni lost her train of thought for a moment. The younger man was quite handsome. She focused back on why she was there.

"I need your help, Captain. Your best slave helped save me from getting raped. He was whipped and needs medicine. He did not think you wanted me touched because I was your whore."

The captain sat up further in his bed and pointed to a seat. Eleni bolted over to the chair and sat down.

"You are my little whore, are you not? I did not want you touched by another he was right to step in. If I help you with this slave, what am I to get in return?"

"I will do anything you ask of me if you will help him, Captain. You have my word."

"My precious little whore, that is all I have been waiting for. You will have my help but first, come here, come closer and kiss me."

Eleni had no choice but to join him at his bedside.

He reached over and rubbed her face with his hand and leaned in and kissed her lips.

Eleni despised the captain's lips on hers but suffered through it.

The captain pulled the covers off and exposed his limp penis. He pointed down to it. "You will suck my penis until I have an orgasm, and I will help you."

Eleni shifted her glance, not able to make eye contact with anyone in the room. She felt herself becoming sick and uneasy from having to perform the act of oral sex on the captain. She could smell the stench on his skin. He had not bathed in days.

The young man in the room locked his eyes on Eleni. He nodded his head slightly to the right. He was telling her to proceed, to get it over with.

The captain moved his large frame close enough so Eleni could reach his penis. She closed her eyes and took his penis in her mouth. She envisioned it was David who she was pleasuring. Her mouth moved in a slow stroking fashion, her saliva running down the shaft of the captain's rod.

The captain moaned and rammed her head down deeper on his manhood.

She sped up her movements and incorporated her hands moving up and down his shaft as her mouth sucked.

Her vision returned her to the beach where she and David laid upon the sand and enjoyed their night at the salt springs. Faster and harder she sucked, until the captain, let out a moan and shot his cum into her mouth. Grabbing her head down further onto his shaft, he released his grip on Eleni and laid back into bed.

"Merci vous avez bien effectué."

Desperate to get the captain's cum out of her mouth, Eleni retrieved a cloth sitting on his desk and spit the semen into it. A bottle of wine was sitting on the table. She poured herself just enough to swish it around in her mouth and spit into the napkin sitting on the bedside table. "Will you help me now since I have done what you have asked of me?"

The captain got out of bed, cleaned himself off, and got dressed. "I am going to help you now, but my requirement is for you come to me every night until we reach France. You will no longer be shackled or chained. From here on out, you are my personal whore." He yanked the door open and shouted for a crew member to fetch Berhanua.

Eleni thanked the captain and agreed to the terms of her visiting him every night until the voyage was over.

Berhanua was brought up to the deck. His wounds dressed by the doctor and the young Caribbean man.

"What is your name? "Eleni asked the man who assisted the doctor.

"I am Jamond, miss. At your service. What is yours?"

"I am Eleni. Thank you for your help tonight. It was hard for me to get through that embarrassment."

"There be no problem, miss. I could see you were suffering. I did my best to assist you through it, without being obvious. I only hoped I helped."

"Yes, you did. Thank you again. I shall never forget your kindness."

Eleni left Jamond's side and assisted with Berhanua. He was given fresh clothing to put on and food to bring back his health.

The next months went by in a blur. Eleni was never shackled below deck from that night onward. She managed to bring some order to the ship, and the remaining slaves were treated better. She never had to make love to the captain. She did have to continue performing oral sex and pleasuring him anally, but he was never forceful again towards her.

The tumultuous journey to France from Abyssinia was finally over. The French slave ship made its way into the Port of Caen.

Eleni was nearly nine months pregnant by the time the ship pulled into port. She gave praise to the Creator, he had spared them and brought them safely into France.

The voyage cost many slaves to lose their lives. There were many casualties on the ship due to famine and suicide.

A few women slaves who birthed children on the ship became pregnant again by the sailors who raped them, but in the end, the abuses stopped due to Eleni's control over the captain. Berhanua regained his strength and kept a watchful eye on Eleni.

They had become close friends, and she was thankful for their friendship and his protection. Eleni hoped whoever purchased her would purchase Berhanua as well. She wanted to remain close to him and believed they would have a better chance of survival together than separate.

The ship was unloaded and the remaining slaves were led into town. They were not chained and had regained their health because of the care given in the last months of the voyage. Eleni looked around at all of the faces staring at her. She clutched Berhanua's hand tightly.

"I hope we stay together," she whispered to him as they walked.

"As do I, Milady," He responded.

The people of Caen had never had slaves sold in their village. They poured out of their homes and stores to see the commotion. Eleni, Berhanua, and the other slaves were led into the center of the town and lined up. There they waited to see what fate had in store for them.

14 Revenge

Seven months before Berhanua and Eleni arrived in France...

Abrihet watched as Berhanua race off into the darkness. What she'd shared with him was a weight lifted off her shoulders. In her heart, she knew she would never see him again and retreated into the castle with their son, Biniam in tow. She rubbed her lips, the smell of him still lingering across them.

King Dabir appeared in the doorway with his arms crossed. What reason did his wife have for running out of the castle behind the guardsman?

"What kept you so long, Abrihet? What did you and the guardsman have to speak about?"

Abrihet was going to have to tell Dabir the truth of when they met. She sighed loudly and shifted her son to her other arm.

"I met him the last time he was in our kingdom. When Hillina asked to take Eleni away from us."

"What do you mean you met him when he was here before? How is that possible, Abrihet?"

Abrihet brushed past Dabir back into the castle and let Biniam slide down her arms and scurry off ahead of them.

"You are not going to walk away from this Abrihet. "Dabir followed behind her and snatched her arm, causing her to pause. "I want you to finish explaining yourself."

"What more do you want me to say other than I met him here in our kingdom? I encountered him as he was leaving your chambers."

Dabir crossed his arms, his lips flattened into a line.

Abrihet did not want to bring up the past. She knew uncovering old secrets would spill old wounds. She had a pained expression on her face, and her mouth turned downward.

"I can see by your expression that you know where I am going with this. I know your secret about the contract you set up with Arkamun. I know you were bribed to give Eleni to him for a price. I know you sold our daughter to a monster."

Dabir was quiet. Abrihet's words stung him like little bees jabbing him with each and every word. He dropped his hands to his side and furrowed his brows as he focused on Abrihet.

"What you say is the truth, my wife. I did do these things, and I regret them. But still in all of this, it does not explain your connection with the guardsman."

Abrihet wiped her hand across her mouth. Dabir was not going to let her walk away without speaking the entire truth. She rounded her shoulders and inhaled deeply.

"I do not want to hurt you with what I am about to say, but Biniam is not your son."

Dabir's eyes narrowed as he slammed his fist against the wall, punching a hole through it. He lumbered towards Abrihet grabbing her neck and forcing her back against the wall.

"What do you mean he is not my son? Have we not worked on our marriage? Have I not given you my heart again?" he screamed.

Abrihet sobbed uncontrollably. She wrapped her hands around his wrist and pried his hand away from around her neck.

"Yes, Dabir... You have given me those things recently." She continued to sob. "Let us not forget about all of the nights you left me alone to sleep with your whores."

Dabir pinched his mouth close and retreated a few steps away from Abrihet. "I see now why you needed a moment with the guardsman. Tell me, wife, was he aware he had a child?"

Abrihet wiped her tears and tried to approach Dabir.

"Stay right where you are and answer the question."

"No, he was only told this very night. I had not seen him since we left the white castle."

"Finish saying what you need to Abrihet."

Abrihet told Dabir of how she met Berhanua when he came to their kingdom and of their encounter at the white castle. She told him the truth of how he made her feel abandoned and alone and sought comfort with another. Dabir stood quietly staring at her blankly. Her words stung him over and over.

"I do not need to hear another word. You have told me enough. Please let me be."

Dabir left Abrihet standing alone and marched toward his chambers. Biniam tried to run after him, pulling his leg to be picked up. Dabir paused and kneeled down next to the little boy and glared back at Abrihet. "You stay with your mother now."

Dabir kissed the boy on the forehead leaving him in tears.

Abrihet swooped to his side and gathered him in her arms. "Everything will be all right," she cooed, bouncing him up and down calming him. "Everything will be all right."

Six months had elapsed since King Dabir was told of his daughter Eleni's predicament. His wrath was only equaled by his sorrow. He mourned for a seeming eternity, and his mourning could only be quenched with battle plans to expedite the death of those responsible for the cruel treatment of his daughter. As he mourned, he reminisced on times with Eleni when she was a young girl. He thought about times when he held his precious daughter in his arms, and nothing in the world mattered more than the beautiful child he cradled in his arms.

His relationship with his wife deteriorated after she had confessed to having another man's child. He kept his distance from her once more and sought comfort with the women from his previous affairs. Those nights with the whores did little to help his mood or to take his mind off his daughter and his wife. Abrihet was the one person who could understand how distraught he was.

The kingdom was abuzz with the news of the new prince being born. Dabir was ecstatic and wanted to hold the new baby in his arms. He left his advisers and hurried to Abrihet's chambers and swung open the door.

"You have a fine prince," one of the servants said smiling as she wrapped the baby in blankets.

Dabir moved to the side of the bed where Abrihet laid. She was pale and sweating profusely.

"What is wrong with my wife?"

Dabir's face showed concern. Something was not right with his wife.

"She has been ill, Milord. And having the baby has made things worse. She has a high fever and has lost a lot of blood."

Dabir grasped Abrihet's hand. Her eyes remained closed. Dabir dropped his head onto the side of the bed and began to cry. "What do you need of me?" He asked the servant.

"We have sent for the healer; she should be here soon."

Dabir lifted his head and nodded. "Good, I am glad you sent for her. Please give me a moment alone with my wife."

The servants all nodded and scrambled out of the room. Dabir gazed back at his wife. Her breaths were shallow and labored. He clasped her hand tighter and whispered into her ear.

"Abrihet, please you have to fight. You have to come back for your children and me."

Dabir was not a man who cried, but seeing his wife on the brink of death made him sob.

"I am sorry for all that I have said and done. Please forgive me Abrihet. I will be a better husband, father, and king if you do."

The chamber door swung open, and the healer sauntered into the room. She waved a sage smudge stick around and chanted. She mixed a concoction of herbs and black tar and applied them to Abrihet's head.

"She will be healed," she called out loud, waving her hand above her head and continuing to chant.

Dabir watched in silence as the woman worked on his wife.

For the next few days, Dabir sat by his wife's bedside. All of the planning to retrieve his daughter was on hold. He was not able to hold his baby boy to his chest until his wife opened her eyes. Finally, after a night's rain, Abrihet blinked her eyes open and clutched Dabir's hand. Dabir's head rose, and he glared into his wife's eyes.

"You are alive. I am here."

Abrihet gave him a weak smile and pointed towards a goblet of water on the table. He retrieved it and helped his wife slowly drink.

"Where is my child?" she asked weakly.

"The baby is fine, Abrihet. You gave me another prince."

It was the first time Dabir had acknowledged Biniam as his son since her confession. Abrihet smiled weakly again, reaching out for Dabir's hand. He dropped back down to her side, and they embraced.

The next few weeks moved quickly. Abrihet regained her strength, and her focus shifted to bringing her daughter home. She and Dabir were united again. He accepted Biniam for his son in addition to the new prince they named Sheshy. She moved through the castle with a fury that had not been seen since the kingdom's last battle and joined her husband by his side for the final war council.

King Dabir's war counsel had met on many occasions in the six months since Berhanua had made his visit to Eritrea. In the last meeting, a plan was devised to infiltrate the white castle and kill King Arkamun and everyone who had stood by and watched Eleni suffer. King Dabir had hoped he would reach Eleni before it was too late.

There was little time left before King Dabir, and his army were due to exit the kingdom and bring Eleni home. Word of what happened to Eleni spread. The men of King Dabir's army gathered weapons and awaited their orders. The women of the Kingdom assisted their men to the best of their capabilities to prepare the city for battle. It was an unspoken unanimous under-standing throughout the kingdom: the war was on the horizon and violence was the only response. King Dabir glowered out of his chamber windows down into the village and saw the men and women of his kingdom working hard to prepare.

There has been peace for many years, thanks to my daughter. Maybe this was the awakening needed. I have not seen my people come together in such fashion for many years.

It took Eleni being sacrificed to another land, and for her life to be in danger for his people to come together. King Dabir grew overwhelmed with the emotion of his daughter, and tears welled up in his eyes. He was in deep in thought when the chamber room door opened, and his wife entered the room. Abrihet saw her husband was distraught. Walking behind him, she placed her arms around his waist and pulled him into an embrace.

"My love, what is troubling you?" she asked in a soft tone.

"My wife..." King Dabir replied, grabbing her hands in his. "I was only thinking about Eleni, and what I have done. I remembered when she was just a small baby who I held in my arms. She was the most beautiful little girl I had ever seen. What have I done, Abrihet? Will Eleni ever forgive me for my actions?"

Queen Abrihet released her embrace and turned her husband to face her.

"What you have done has saved our kingdom from ruin. You did not know who you married Eleni off to. I know what I said to you in times past was wrong and I apologize. I know those words hurt you. But now is the time for her to be brought home safely. You will destroy King Arkamun's kingdom, and everyone who betrayed our daughter."

"My wife, you have such wisdom. I only pray you will continue to forgive my actions against you. I have not been the best king I could be, nor the best father. I now realize all my daughter wanted was to remain close to me. I allowed my personal ambitions to supersede the love of my child."

"All of those things are over now. I love you, and we have two little princes that need your love and support. Our actions will be set right when we bring our daughter home, and after punishing the mad king for releasing his brutality upon our daughter. Go now, my husband, and finish making your preparations for this war on the white castle."

Queen Abrihet clasped Dabir's hand and kissed it, and strolled out of the chamber room.

King Dabir took one more look down into the courtyard and watched his people scurry around preparing for their departure. He gathered his composure and proceeded out of his chambers toward the throne room.

King Dabir summoned his battle captain to his throne room to finalize the plans for the mission before their departure.

"You asked to see me, King? "The battle captain asked, entering the throne room. "What will you have me do my King?"

He kneeled in front of King Dabir.

King Dabir slid off his throne and placed his hand on the captain's shoulder.

"Rise, my friend."

The captain glanced up at the king and got to his feet. King Dabir paced back and forth in front of the throne.

Our goal is simple Captain. When we reach the white castle, we will kill them all. They have disgraced our princess, our nation, and our people. Our women represent the mothers of earth, and any violation of them must be avenged without mercy." King Dabir spoke in a calm, yet menacing, authoritative voice. "Have my spies returned, battle captain?"

"Yes, my King. They have returned and provided detailed reports of the inner workings of our enemy. Our spies exposed their military strength and their weaknesses. They confirmed everything told by the defector from Abyssinia."

"Excellent...Prepare the plan of attack and ready our elite warriors. We will paint the streets with the blood of our enemies."

"We must consider the political and economic impact of such an endeavor, my King!" A frantic adviser yelled to the king from across the hall.

King Dabir paused in mid-speech and looked over at the adviser. "I notice you have elevated politics and economics over the honor of our people," King Dabir shouted back.

"It is you who gave her away to this foreign king against our advice, my King."

The adviser scampered across the hall and stood next to the battle captain. The adviser continued with his ranting.

"This foreigner cannot respect our ways if he does not know our ways. It was you, my King, who elevated politics and economics above our people and your daughter. Now you seek to wage war against an enemy of an unknown size and strength, who by your admission, has had spies in our city walls for an unknown period. This enemy certainly knows more of us than we of them. War at this juncture is unwise, my King."

The adviser dropped to his knees when Dabir's eyes deepened, sending chills down the spines of everyone in the throne room.

"You have stood by my side since I began to reign at the age of fourteen. I made many wars for many years, and you advised me wisely in them all. You were present at Eleni's birth when I could not be, nevertheless..."

King Dabir unsheathed his sword from its scabbard and with one swift, graceful, and extremely hostile motion, removed the adviser's head from his shoulders. The chancellor's head hit the floor and rolled across the room, stopping at the feet of another councillor.

"Would anyone else like to engage in political banter? I have a war to finalize and more heads to sever. Either you stand with me, or find yourself joining your fellow headless adviser in the afterlife," Dabir stated in a calm but menacing voice.

Unmoved and without reserve, the battle captain drew his sword and placed it on his chest.

"We stand with you, my King. As you have decreed, we will kill them all."

The battle plans were finalized, the night before the fight. The kingdom spent the evening celebrating with a great feast and music. Men danced around the fire where songs of old and new were sung. Women painted their husbands with striking colors of orange and gold and chanted for their safe return. King Dabir and Queen Abrihet spent the evening dancing around the bonfire until dawn with the people of their kingdom in celebration and prayer.

The day to depart finally arrived. King Dabir glared into the eyes of his men and saw the rage of his nation. They pledged their swords, arrows and knives and he knew they were all prepared to do what was needed, including giving their life to save Eleni from capture. King Dabir mounted his horse and rode back and forth in front of the men.

"You will show NO MERCY! You will take no prisoners, and you will show no clemency. We will completely erase their kingdom, take their treasures, jewels, and livestock, and make their nation a mere memory."

The men cried out in agreement and raised their weapons before they all marched out into the desert from the kingdom. The journey from King Dabir's country to the white castle was hot, sweaty, and a hard thirty-six-hour journey on horseback. It was nightfall when King Dabir and his army of warriors arrived at the white castle. The guards who stood at the front of the gates were taken out in complete silence by arrows King Dabir's archers shot through their hearts from behind.

The warriors scaled the walls and slit throats of men and women who tried to run up the cobblestone road to warn King Arkamun of the imminent danger approaching him. All those who opposed King Dabir and his men were silenced. The white castle was dimly lit and quiet as King Dabir moved from room to room searching out Arkamun. His adrenalin was running with anticipation of facing Eleni's soon to be dead husband.

One floor after the next, King Dabir moved as silent as the night itself. Finally coming to the third story hall, he heard loud moans from one of the chamber rooms. King Dabir and three of his warriors surrounded the chamber room door. Signaling to the others, they broke down the bedroom door and entered.

Arkamun was inflicting his pain and brutality on another woman. King Dabir walked behind him and flung him off the woman by his neck dropping him to the floor. The shock of being interrupted and caught off guard terrified Arkamun, who stood and faced King Dabir. The ferocity by which he had raped and tortured women had all but disappeared in the face of the worthy adversary standing before him.

"Where is my daughter, Arkamun?" King Dabir pushed Arkamun's naked body towards the wall.

Arkamun smiled and picked up his robe off the floor.

"Woman, return to your chambers, no need for my future bride to witness bloodshed." He turned his attention towards the girl still lying in the bed.

"Yes, Milord."

She gathered her dress and robe and scurried out of the room past the other warriors and King Dabir. Arkamun turned his attention back to Eleni's father. "Now continue King Dabir." Arkamun laughed out loud and paced in front of him naked.

"Pick up your sword, you wretched king and fight!" King Dabir said kicking the sword he dropped on the ground in Arkamun's direction.

Arkamun laughed again and continued to antagonize the king with his words. "You have come to avenge your whore of a daughter I see. She was by far my favorite conquest. I loved her screams each time I thrust my shaft into her anus. She would cry for you to come and save her! HAHAHAHAAHAHAAHAHAHA-HAAHAHAAHAHAAHAHAHAHAAHAHA!!!!!!!!!!!! Eleni was only good for my sexual pleasure. I did you a favor. I paid far more for her than she was worth."

His arrogance blinded him to King Dabir's subtle motions as he inched within striking distance.

"Now she will be a slave for the French. I told them of her lusts and desire for violent sexual encounters. I am sure the French are enjoying the whore you created as we speak. HAHA-HAAHAHAHAAHAHAHA!" He cried out, continuing to insult and berate Eleni.

King Dabir's foot movement was quick, and his sword was swift and accurate as he removed Arkamun's leg and arm. Arkamun winced in pain and fell to the floor, blood spattering in all directions.

King Dabir dragged Arkamun throughout the castle and into the courtyard of his kingdom, strapping the former king to the same wood cross he had previously used. The remaining survivors of Abyssinia were gathered there to lay witness to the public display of his ferocity. He grabbed a pot of oil off a nearby fire used for lighting lamps and torches. He lugged the cauldron back towards Arkamun and flung the pot, drenching Arkamun in the oil. He picked up a nearby torch, holding it in his hand.

"Let this be a reminder to those who dare oppose my people and disgrace our women."

King Dabir threw the torch on Arkamun, setting him on fire. He watched quietly as his flesh melted from his bones. Arkamun was baptized in complete pain and suffering in the presence of his future bride and people.

Arkamun's body burned in front of all those who bear witness. King Dabir approached Arkamun's former bride-to-be. She immediately dropped to her knees.

"Have mercy, great King! Please! I did all I could to save Eleni! Please have mercy!"

King Dabir yanked the girl up to her feet by her shoulder and glared deeply in her eyes.

"You did all you could to help Eleni, you say? I do not understand how you helped her, if you were becoming Arkamun's new bride, and had Eleni sent away."

"Please, King, you must have mercy." The girl cried out amidst her sobbing.

King Dabir was now joined by the arrival of his wife Queen Abrihet, who was lowered to the ground in the palanquin by the servants who carried her. Queen Abrihet stepped out of the palanquin, covered head to toe in bright purple silk, reflecting the sun and blinded all of those who looked upon her by the gold glistening around her neck.

She picked up a sword on her approach standing by her husband. A look of vengeance and anger were on her face. She was ready for battle.

King Dabir turned to his wife. "What say you, my Queen? Shall we have mercy on this woman?"

Abrihet approached the girl, grabbing her by the hand. "I see the sincerity in her eyes, my husband. She speaks the truth in her words. She did make efforts to help our daughter." Abrihet stared into the girl's eyes. "However, it clearly shows your efforts were not enough, resulting in my daughter being sent away. You instead you used her downfall to elevate your cause."

Without warning, Abrihet thrust her knife in an upward motion underneath the girl's chin, and the blade burst through the top of her head. Queen Abrihet violently removed the knife out of her skull and kicked the girl's bleeding corpse off to the side.

"What are we to do with the rest of them, my King? "The battle captain joined King Dabir at his side.

"Kill them all. Leave not one of them alive."

King Dabir cut Arkamun's head from his charred remains. "Burn this kingdom to ash, and retrieve all livestock, weapons, gold and jewels." He moved away through the courtyard towards the stone staircase.

"May we partake of the remaining women we might find, my king?" The battle captain called after him.

King Dabir paused, twisting back towards the captain. "Certainly not. We are not rapists, and these wretched women are not worthy to have one of my warriors inside of them. However, I'm sure our lions will enjoy their flesh. If you find any others outside of those, we haven't killed, return them to our kingdom and dispose of them there."

"Yes my king," The battle captain responded.

The fight was over and King Arkamun and all those who did nothing to protect Eleni were dead. There was no trace of his daughter. She was nowhere to be found. King Dabir descended the long stone staircase to the beach with Arkamun's charred head in his hands.

Standing on the sand looking out into the water, he realized he was too late to save his daughter. He did not know where her fate would lead her in France, but in his heart, he knew he would never see his daughter again. He thought about Eleni being loaded onto a ship from where he stood, and the horror and danger she would experience on the voyage. Overwhelmed with grief, King Dabir threw Arkamun's head into the lagoon water and fell to his knees. All of the strength he had saved for the battle left his body. King Dabir raked his hands through the sand and bowed his head in tears.

15 Homeward

David had lost the love of his life and carried that with him on his voyage home. He knew that he would never be the same. The last night he spent with Eleni, he promised her his life, love and marriage. He had let her down. The journey home for him was one of complete agony. He was returning to a wife he did not love and to the unknown condition of his kingdom. This was another secret he kept from Philippa. He could never tell her he fell in love with another woman, and he was going to overthrow her for his true love.

Another secret I shall take to the grave.

Eleni plagued his mind and his dreams. Even when he was awake, he could not push the thoughts of her from his mind. When he glanced at the sky above, the formation of her body would take shape in the clouds. When the wind blew, he swore he could hear her voice calling out to him. He prayed that his pain would ease, and the guilt he felt would somehow displace itself from him.

He told himself when he reached home he would send out inquiries of what happened to his Abyssinian queen. He would never stop looking for her until he knew if she was dead or alive. The amount of blood he saw on the stone stairs worried him. He was not sure if she could survive that. He prayed for a miracle and hoped she pulled through. He promised to the God to whom he prayed, that he would go to his grave searching for his beloved Eleni.

David's ship pulled back into the Canary Islands to restock supplies for the remainder of the journey home. David and the crew were happy to get off the ship and have some decent food. The local tavern on the beach was bustling with sailors and captains who all made port for one reason or another. He moved around the sailors and found a table in the corner. The tavern girl brought over a drink and placed some bread down on the table.

"Can I get you something to eat, sir? shrimp, fish, stew?"

"I think I will take the shrimp please," he muttered. "Oh, and another brew please," he called out to her.

David glanced around the room at all the men who sat laughing and engaged in conversation. He reflected on the last time he was there when the old man told him of the mysterious island. He shook his head and wished he had listened.

"Here is your drink sir."

David raised his head and saw a man setting a cold drink down on the table. He had the same complexion as Eleni; only his hair was dreaded and blond.

"Thanks," David muttered, taking a swig of the contents in the cup. "This is quite good, what is it?" he asked looking up at the man.

"Just something we locals blended up with coconut. I am glad you like it. Say that is quite a locket you have around your neck. Never seen anything quite like it."

David glanced down at his chest. He had forgotten that he placed it around his neck. He grabbed the chain pulling the locket off and clicked it open. Eleni's picture blew out and rested on the table.

The man reached over and held the small portrait in his hands. David noticed that his eyes widened as he gave the picture back to him.

"I know this girl. She docked here not too long ago."

David's heartbeat raced, and he started to tremble as he returned the portrait to the locket. He then pushed out the chair and gestured for the man to sit. The man had glanced behind him before he sat down.

"Please tell me everything you know. I thought the girl was dead. I am sorry for not introducing myself. I am David." David shook the man's hand.

"I am Jamond. Nice to make your acquaintance. The girl's name is Eleni, is it not?"

David nodded. "What happened to her? Where was she sailing to? Who was she with?"

"The girl was on a slave ship heading to France. I was called aboard the ship with the doctor I sometimes assist. The captain of the ship she was on had taken ill, and she tried to help a friend who was with her."

"Is she okay?"

"Yes, the last time I saw her she was fine."

David got the confirmation he needed. Eleni was alive and heading to France. He bowed his head and a wide grin crossed his face. "This is the best news I have heard in weeks."

"I'm glad I could be of service to you." Jamond spun around again and saw the doctor he worked with looking for him. "Excuse me for a moment."

David stared as Jamond walked outside and spoke to the other man. Moments later, he returned to his seat next to David.

"Listen, I have just been informed that I am to travel to France with Doctor Trudel for a few months. We are to leave at the end of the day."

David took the information as a sign of good fortune. He pulled out a pouch of gold coins and handed them to Jamond.

"I am offering this gold to you, for your helping securing Eleni's freedom. If you find her alive in France, please send word to Westminster Castle in England."

"Westminster Castle? Why there?"

"Because I am the King of England. And I want Eleni brought to me there."

Jamond's face reddened from embarrassment. "I am so sorry Milord. I did not realize."

"No need for apologies Jamond. To you, I am just David. Now my friend... listen to what I need to say."

David explained the situation to Jamond and told him what he would be attempting. The two men shook hands and parted ways.

Philippa could not have been happier her husband David was away from Westminster Castle. In the two months that David had been away, Philippa had been able to relax and enjoy her surroundings. Her friendship with Jasper blossomed and she found they spent more and more time together. Many nights she would often sneak out of her quarters in the evening to meet with

Jasper in the stables. He made her laugh, and they would stare up at the stars, talking about all sorts of topics.

Jasper lurked around every corner watching Philippa. He waited for his opportunity to strike. Just like he waited for the chance to poison his father's glass. The night he was to make his move on Philippa had finally arrived.

Philippa ate dinner in the garden alone by candlelight. The night was calm, and the birds sang their love songs deep into the evening. David still crossed her mind. She wondered of his journey and if he was safe. She mainly wondered what would happen when he returned home.

My feelings for him have changed.

She lifted the spoon from the soup bowl to her mouth before placing it back on the side of the bowl. She reflected on previous conversations with Queen Anne and how she had a duty to David to produce male heirs. Their relationship had become only about the monarchy. By her being sexually aggressive with David, caused him to shun her. She would never allow him to see her so vulnerable again. Her heart had hardened against him and in her mind, it was he who had wronged her.

He will pay for hurting me and treating me so poorly. I will never allow him to take advantage of me again.

Philippa finished her dinner and strolled through the courtyard. Jasper found her there.

"Good evening Milady, May I join you?"

"Why of course you may, Jasper. It is quite nice to have some company this evening."

Jasper joined the queen at her side and escorted her through the candlelit garden. "So Milady, why are you out here all alone this evening?"

Philippa blushed. She had waited all day to lay her eyes on Jasper. "I just wanted to eat in the garden and to be out in the fresh air. It gets lonely in the castle when you do not have many friends."

"And do you see us as friends now? I seem to remember you saying that we could not be friends because of your husband."

"I do see us as friends now, Jasper." She grabbed his hand and clutched it. "I feel we have become close to one another. And I value the time we can spend together."

Jasper and Philippa stopped in front of the castle's entrance and faced each other.

"Well, I must be getting to my chambers for the evening. Thank you for the stroll. It was nice."

"I enjoyed it as well, Milady. I will see you again soon."

"Yes, you will. Good night."

Philippa released her hand and moved towards the door. Jasper took his chance and spun her around, pulling her into a lasting kiss. Philippa had wanted the chance to kiss him for so long. She embraced the moment, wrapping her arms around his neck. Jasper released her from his embrace and lumbered off.

"Good night again," he said as he moved into the darkness.

"Good night..." Philippa smiled.

She was starting to fall for the stable hand. What she did not know, was that it was all part of his plan.

In the coming months after Philippa's husband left on his voyage, her body started to feel different. She no longer bled and began to believe she could be with child. Not ready to share her secret with the queen mother, she decided she would seek the advice of the court's physician to confirm what she already believed. She had the guard send word to the doctor and asked him to meet her in one of the vacant chamber rooms in the castle.

After she had finished her meal in the garden, she had her servants remove her plates, and ordered their silence about her meeting with the mysterious visitor. She took her last drink of wine, handed the goblet to the servant girl, and made her way inside to meet with the physician.

"Thank you for coming, I appreciate your secrecy from Queen Anne."

"Of course. Now come my dear, and lay down. So I can get a look at you." He inspected her thoroughly and gave his answer. "Well, Princess Philippa, you are indeed with child. Several months to be exact."

"That is what I believed. Thank you for seeing me on such short notice."

"There is never a need for notice. You are royalty."

Philippa thanked the physician again and placed a large bag of gold coins in his hands. Her heart dropped as he headed back towards the door of the vacant chamber room. She knew she would eventually need to have a child to secure her place in the kingdom. However, she was not prepared to carry the child while David was away on his voyage.

She also wanted David to pay for his mistreatment of her. Making their child hate him would be the perfect plan. All she needed now was someone to support her while she was pregnant, and she decided Jasper would be the perfect choice. She would carry the secret of the truth until David's world was destroyed. She clapped her hands in excitement as she entered her chamber room.

Now what will be the best course of action in making my plan succeed?

Philippa stripped her clothing off and sunk into her tub. She rubbed her swollen belly as she sat composing her plan. The court's physician confirmed she was several months along. She would conceal the true paternity of her child from Jasper, despite the fact the child was David's. She would allow Jasper to sleep with her and when she told him she was with child; he would assume the child she carried was his. She would in return raise her child to believe Jasper was its father. Philippa knew being a hefty woman she was able to conceal her pregnancy from anyone who looked upon her.

Two nights had passed before Jasper put the next part of his plan into action. When the castle quieted down for the evening, he snuck away from the stables, into the castle and found Philippa's chambers. He entered the room quietly, undressed, and got into her bed. He would wait for her to say her goodnights to Queen Anne and head back to her quarters.

Philippa arrived at her chamber room pleased that she had avoided her mother-in-law that evening. She did not want to field questions of why she was out and about the castle so late.

She entered the room, closing the door behind her, and lit an additional candle in the corner. Her tub awaited her, filled with steaming hot water. Her servant was always prompt in preparing her evening bath. It was one of the few moments Philippa found to pleasure herself and think of things outside of being a princess and a future queen. She stripped her clothing, off standing nude, the candle light basking off her skin. She did not notice Jasper was laying in her bed watching her as she stepped into her bath and sunk into the water.

Jasper laid in the bed watching Philippa undress. He became aroused, reached down and began stroking his cock until it became hard. Unable to lay there any further he threw the sheets back off of his skin and walked behind Philippa as she sat in the tub. He kneeled down taking the sponge from the side of the tub, dipping it in the water and releasing water drops down her back. Philippa was startled and turned to see who was behind her. She was about to scream, but Jasper hushed her, covering her mouth with his hand.

"I'm going to release my hand from your mouth, Milady, please do not scream," Jasper murmured.

Philippa nodded, and Jasper released his hand from her mouth. "What are you doing here Jasper?"

"I wanted to see you, Milady." He dipped the sponge in the water again and drizzled water down her back. "I found an opportunity to get into your chamber room, so I did. I wanted to be inside of you. And I believe you want me as much as I desire you."

Philippa was not shocked by his actions. She had flirted with him over the weeks, and they had become close. The kiss he gave her a few nights ago made her feelings for him grow and intensify. She was intrigued by him and also wanted to know what he felt like inside of her. She thought of her plan, which she could now put into action without trying.

Jasper was there in her chamber room. She would have her way with him and get him to release his seed into her.

"Perfect," she mumbled to herself as she washed the suds off her body.

Her devious plan would go as she wanted. Philippa stood up in the tub, and Jasper also got to his feet wrapping her robe around her shoulders. He was not at all attracted to her as he looked upon her nakedness, but he too had ulterior motives for wanting to be intimate with her.

Philippa stepped out of the tub and walked over to her vanity to sit down. Before she was able to brush her hair, Jasper captured her into his arms, pulling her into a passionate kiss.

Philippa felt herself become wet between her legs and moaned in excitement in the embrace. As they continued to kiss, Jasper moved his hand down to Philippa's mound and gently parted her legs. He found her clit and rubbed it with his index finger and thumb making it harder as he intensified his movements.

Philippa broke their kissing and moaned louder. She clutched his arm and pushed his hand deeper into her wet pussy.

"Stoke me harder," she whispered into his ear.

Jasper obliged stroking her clit harder to the point of her almost having an orgasm, and stopped.

Philippa looked at him confused. She did not want him to stop and wanted to release her juices all over his fingers. Before she could compose herself to say a word, Jasper lifted her robust body up at her hips and sat her upon his shoulders facing him, spreading her legs open.

He dug his tongue deep into her pink and moist vagina, lapping the fluids dripping from it. Philippa had never encountered anything quite like what she was feeling. She moaned in the enjoyment of feeling his tongue inside of her, so much so she grabbed his head and forced him into her more. She grinded her pussy in his face until she came.

Jasper continued to suck and lick her clit until Philippa pleaded for him to release her. Then and only then, he lifted her down into his arms and carried her to the bed placing her gently on the sheets. He stood on the side of the bed moving his cock over to her mouth, gesturing for her to open her mouth and receive him. She obliged and swallowed the bulging cock with a sucking motion. She liked the taste of him, for he released precum out of the tip of his cock into her mouth.

Salty and sweet.

She continued sucking and swallowing, making him harder with each motion. Jasper loved the way her mouth moved over his penis. He guided her head into him, and she took all nine inches he gave her. He would plant a seed in her this night, and make her his going forward. His plan was as it should be, seducing Philippa and making a child with her. He would take it all from his brother: his wife, his kingdom, and his children. He fucked her mouth with his penis until he came.

Philippa released his penis when she felt his seed empty into her mouth. The taste of his seed made her more aroused, and she swallowed it without hesitation.

Jasper was a little surprised she did not release his seed into a cloth sitting on the bedside table but took it as a sign he had achieved his goal. He was immediately hard and turned on again.

Jasper leaned Philippa over on the bed and laid down beside her. Rolling on his side, he pulled Philippa on top of his hard massive penis. She rode his cock feverishly as if she would never make love again. She pinched his nipples, making them hard.

He moaned out loud in enjoyment; he had not felt such a closeness since his beloved wife, Faerydae. Could he be falling love with Philippa? She was not a beauty like many other women. But he had to admit; there was something intriguing about her, and he wanted more.

I cannot let myself fall for her.

Philippa continued to ride his penis.

Switching positions, he rolled her onto her stomach and slid his cock into her from behind. He intensified his speed and spanked her bare ass with a loud crack of his hand, as he rode her from behind.

"DEEPER!" she moaned louder begging him for more.

Jasper once again obliged and pushed his penis in deeper, causing his ball sack to bounce and slap her bare ass. Philippa moaned louder and pulled the pillow into her mouth to muffle her cries.

"I'm going to cum, Jasper," she called out loud in a scream.

"As am I, Milady."

Simultaneously, they came together. Jasper released his seed inside of Philippa, and she released a squirting orgasm drenching his penis with her juices. He collapsed on top of her as she fell onto the bed. After a few deep breaths, Jasper rolled off her back onto his side and looked at the silhouette of her body, having enjoyed himself. Running his fingers down her thighs, Philippa turned towards him and kissed his lips briefly. She could taste herself on his tongue and lips and liked how sweet the juices were. She knew David would never be a kind lover like Jasper. She hoped she was not falling in love with him.

"Did you enjoy me, Milady?" Jasper asked curiously.

"Why yes Jasper, I did rather enjoy this moment with you, as much as the others we have had together. You are not like anyone I have ever met. I only hope one day you will be able to confide in me as I with you."

Jasper knew he would not be able to keep the truth from Philippa for much longer, but on this night, he was not ready to confess his true identity. Jasper leaned over and kissed Philippa's forehead.

"I promise I will tell you all when it is time, Philippa. Let us enjoy the rest of this evening in each other's arms and me inside of you." Jasper climbed on top of her again, slipping his hard cock back inside of her.

They made love another five times that evening. Finally, when their bodies could do no more, they both fell asleep in the comfort of one another. It would be the best sleep both of them had in years.

The following morning, the two of them awoke in each other's arms. Philippa had little time to get Jasper out of the castle before a servant brought her breakfast.

"Hide behind the curtain," she whispered as there was a knock on the chamber room door.

Jasper jumped up from the bed and fetched his clothes. He moved behind the curtain as Philippa asked.

"Enter," she called out straightening her sheets and smoothing her hair.

"Good morning, Milady." The servant placed her tray down on the table. "Is there anything else I can get for you this morning?"

"Why no... That should do."

The servant girl nodded and headed out of the room.

Jasper pulled the curtain back just as the door slammed shut. "That was a close call. "He picked up a grape and threw it in his mouth and smiled. "And a good morning to you." He plopped back on the bed kissing Philippa on the lips.

She smiled at him and slid off the bed, slipping her robe over her naked skin. "You need to get going. If someone else catches you here, we could be in a lot of trouble."

"Philippa there is no need to worry."

Jasper chased Philippa around the room before pulling her back into his arms, kissing her tenderly.

"You must want to take me back to bed?"

"That sounds like a grand idea." He smiled and swept her up into his arms and carried her to the bed and laid her down. Just as he climbed on top of her and opened her robe, the chamber room door swung open.

"Oh, Milady, I forgot to let you know a messenger has arrived with news of King David."

The girl stopped in her tracks and saw Jasper laying on top of Philippa. Philippa stared at the girl in horror. Jasper moved off Philippa, recovered his clothes and scaled down the window. He ran back towards the stables naked.

Philippa moved off the bed slowly, retying her robe and came to stand in front of the girl. "I hope that this situation can be our little secret and that you will tell no one of what you saw here today."

"Of course not, Milady. No one could fault you for your attraction to Jasper. He is a handsome, sexy man. All of the ladies think so. I promise I will keep your secret. It is safe with me always."

"Thank you. I do appreciate your discretion."

"Well, Milady, I think you better get dressed. Queen Anne will will want to see you downstairs. Like I said before, there is a messenger here with news of your husband."

The servant girl bowed her head once again and retreated from of Philippa's room.

Philippa stood there silently trying to figure out if the girl could be trusted. She realized if she wanted her plan to work, she had no choice.

She would have to compensate the girl with something for her silence. But now she would have her chambermaid assist her in getting dressed. Philippa called her chambermaid into the room, and she helped her with her gown. After she finished, Philippa took one final deep breath before going in the search of the messenger and Queen Anne.

16 France

The clouds moved across the sky revealing the bright sun sparkling over the castle in the rolling hills of France. Queen Vivienne was awoken from a deep slumber by the passionate kisses of her husband, King Edmond in-between her legs. The slow touches of his tongue caressing her smooth thighs sent shivers down her spine. Vivienne snatched the covers away from her body, letting out a deep moan of pleasure. She exhaled and laid deeper into her pillow, opening her legs wider, allowing King Edmond to continue exploring her inner thighs.

His kisses led him to the sweetness of her flower, and he buried his tongue inside of her until she released her savory juices into his mouth.

The excitement of her climax caused Edmond to release his load into the bed sheets. Vivienne blinked her eyes open. She realized it was her husband who was kissing and licking between her legs.

"Darn," she mumbled under her breath.

Vivienne wished it had been another who had been there with her. She inhaled, dismissing the thoughts of the other man in her mind. She focused on Edmond, who was kissing his way from her thighs up to her belly. He paused and placed his head on her pregnant stomach to listen to the baby inside her womb move around.

"The birth of our child is almost upon us." Edmond continued his kisses up the rest of Vivienne's body, resting his kisses upon her lips. Vivienne smiled widely, kissing him in return. "Yes, it is."

"It is going to be a busy day today." Edmond rolled off the massive feather bed, dressing in a hurried fashion.

"What is going to be so busy about today?" Vivienne turned over in Edmond's direction.

"Because, my love, I received word in the evening last night the slave ship has made port. I am going to the village to see if there are any interesting subjects we might like to purchase and bring back to the castle."

Edmond threw on his boots and buttoned up his shirt. He yanked his coat off of the chaise and threw it over his shoulders.

"A slave ship here? I am coming with you, Edmond." She began to get out of bed and tried to move around.

Edmond dropped his coat on the bed and swung Vivienne's legs back under the covers.

"You are not going down to the port in your condition; you are carrying the king's child, and you need your rest. If I find anything good, you will see upon my return."

Vivienne had no choice except to obey. Edmond pulled the covers back over her.

"You rest my love; I will return to you later. Your lady in waiting Rachelle is awaiting your command for breakfast and a bath." Edmond kissed Vivienne on the forehead and sauntered out of the chamber room.

Vivienne slammed her fist down in anger. She wanted to be at port making the decisions with her husband; she hated giving up control of anything having to do with the kingdom. But she knew Edmond was right; she was in no condition to ride horseback or in a carriage. Vivienne rang the bell in her room. "Rachelle, bring me my breakfast!" she screamed.

Vivienne's chore was done. She had finally conceived a child with the king and won a place in his kingdom which would not be challenged. Her plot of becoming queen was finally achieved.

Edmond made his way out the castle and headed towards the group of his knights and guards that awaited him. The breeze blew cooly over his face, as they headed out towards the Port of Caen. The thought of him becoming a father for the first time excited him. He reflected on how his current situation came to be.

Before Edmond arrived in Naples, he had not heard his brother Charles had waged war upon the country until he pulled into the port. Edmond had been cooped up on the ship for weeks. He decided to take a stroll off the vessel so he could stretch his legs. As he passed people in the market streets, he heard whispers between servants, sailors and those who traveled in and out of the city foretell of the battle happening outside the city walls and heading their way.

Edmond found many residents of Naples leaving the city and fleeing to the countryside. Before the French soldiers arrived killing everyone in sight.

Edmond had always loved Naples; he remembered spending time there as a child with his mother and had always had an affection for the natives of Italy.

He could not believe his brother would be waging a war for a title he actually knew nothing about. Charles was not even born when the promise of the throne was presented to their father. He had hoped he would be back on the ship and out of port before the soldiers made it to the Napoleon city.

Edmond continued to stroll the streets, the scared and nervous citizens of Naples scurrying to get their belongings and flee the city. He too needed to move in haste to fill his stomach and get back to the ship. He stopped in the local pub to get some bread and cheese, and upon entering, he noticed it was quite empty. Only Edmond and the bar owner remained.

Edmond paid for his meal and ate quickly in silence. He returned to the streets continuing his trek back to the port.

Sitting across from him in a carriage was a beautiful brunette woman staring at him. Her hair pulled up to the back of her head, jewels at her neck, and her kind eyes gazed briefly into his own.

"She could not have been looking at me," he whispered.

Edmond felt eyes boring into the back of his neck. He spun around to study the woman once more. He nodded his head in acknowledgment and scurried up the path. Horse hooves clicked on the brick pavement behind him. The lady in her carriage was following him.

"What are you doing?" he asked in Italian as he shuffled over to her carriage.

"I wanted to see where you are on your way to." The lady grinned at him warmly. "You seem like an interesting fellow; I was bored so I thought I would follow you. Do you mind?

"No, I do not mind, Milady. I am always up for the company. I am heading back to the docks."

"Do you have to get back to the docks so soon? could I suggest a place where we might be able to talk and get to know each other?"

Edmond blushed at the offer. There had never been a time when a woman had wanted to get to know him.

"Yes, I would like to go somewhere where we can speak and get to know each other better." Edmond climbed into the carriage.

The woman tapped on the roof, and the carriage rolled off into the night. They introduced themselves and told stories about their lives.

He became engrossed in her every word, the feeling of having someone take an interest him was new and marvelous. He fell madly in love with Vivienne that night.

"I want to confess my feelings to you." Edmond switched sides in the carriage, grasping her hands in his. A subtle kiss turned into a deep kiss, and their tongues met in each other's mouth.

Vivienne saw an opportunity. She reached down and touched Edmond's shaft that became harder with every touch.

Still embraced in a deep kiss, Vivienne undid Edmond's trousers. His cock hardened. Nervously he moaned as they kissed.

"Touch me," Vivienne panted breathlessly.

Feverishly, Edmond ripped the top of her dress to expose her bust line. He anxiously lifted her beautifully formed breasts out of her corset and sucked on her perky nipples.

Vivienne hiked up her dress over her hips and sat on Edmond's lap. She inserted his engorged flesh inside of her. She rode him violently, moving up and down his shaft, her juices puddling at the base of his cock.

Edmond liked her aggressive nature. He shifted in the carriage flipping Vivienne onto her back, raising her legs up over her head and slid into her warm damp entrance. Edmond lifted her hips to his thrusting body until the final threshold of passion overcame them both.

He laid her legs down on the carriage seats and straightened out his shirt and trousers.

Vivienne put her breasts back into her corset, and she her snapped jacket on over her ripped dress. She flashed a grin at Edmond and told him she was in love with him.

He asked her to marry him in the carriage and return to France with him, and she agreed. They got married on the docks of the port that evening and Edmond returned to France with a new bride.

A forceful hand shook Eleni and told her to unlock all of the slaves remaining on the ship. She followed the orders and opened Berhanua's chains first, followed by releasing the others from their chains. She was then told by the French sailors to get them lined up to disembark the ship. Eleni lined all of the slaves up, and they left the ship marching into the village port of Caen.

Eleni stayed as close as she could to Berhanua. She took small steps to keep her balance but was repeatedly propelled forward by a sailor who was walking beside her. She almost lost her balance, but Berhanua caught her before she fell.

"Keep moving, you are doing well," he whispered into her ear, steadying her back on her feet.

Eleni and the slaves marched into the village, many sets of eyes staring at them as they passed. The village was beautiful and reminded her of the white castle. She saw more pale faces than she was she was used to. There were not many who resembled her, and if there were, she noticed they too were slaves.

The French sailors halted the slave party from marching any further and lined them up in the village square one after another. Breaking the formation, one of the lead sailors approached the auctioneer and whispered in his ear.

Eleni surveyed her surroundings and noticed a man standing in the front of all the peasants. His handsome face reminded her of David, and he was dressed like royalty. She wondered who he was, and thought perhaps if she smiled at him, her kind gesture would make him want to purchase her. Eleni let go of Berhanua's hand and glanced at the man again. Their eyes locked, and he smiled back at her.

King Edmond had not thought about purchasing any slaves until he saw the girl standing there. She was so beautiful to him, with her caramel skin and long curly black hair. Despite the fact she was with child, her curves captivated his thoughts as his mistress Mina did. Edmond's thoughts flashed to his wife for a moment. He remembered the many sexual rejections before her pregnancy, which led him to find comfort in another. The girl reminded him of when he first met his wife. There was something about her, and he wanted to know more. He wanted to touch her and smell her hair and woo her.

She was an erotic creature to him. He yearned for her, and his cock swelling in his pants told him so. The way she had looked at him and smiled, made him wonder if she wanted him too. He would bid and win the auction for her. No one else would have what he desired. King Edmond signaled to the auctioneer, and he strolled over to where the king was standing.

"I want the girl standing there." King Edmond pointed to Eleni.

"But your Majesty, we have not started the auction yet."

"I do not care if it has not begun. I will pay you your entire weight in gold for her, "he said forcefully.

"If she is important to you, Sire, I will most certainly take the offer. "The auctioneer smiled as he shook the king's hand.

"Pay the man." King Edmond turned to one of his knights.

The knight dismounted his horse and handed the auctioneer three bags of gold coins.

"She is all yours." The auctioneer signaled one of the sailors to usher over Eleni.

Eleni watched as the transaction occurred. She knew he had purchased her. Her hopes were confirmed when the sailor escorted her out of the line. She spoke to Berhanua quickly.

"I will not leave here without you."

He glowered back at her and nodded silently. Something was wrong with him. That look she had seen so many times on the ship was back. His eyes were glazed over; pupils darkened to a dark black. Eleni felt almost as if it was Arkamun who stared back at her.

Not possible. Berhanua must be having one of his head pains.

The sailor grabbed Eleni by the arm and led her over to the where the man was standing. He was smiling.

"Hello," The man said in his native tongue of French

"Hello."

He grinned, notably excited that she could understand him. "You speak my language."

"Yes, I speak many languages, sir."

"Well, today must have been my very lucky day. I should introduce myself. I am Edmond, King of France. Welcome to my country."

Eleni smiled. She was not too very far away from David's kingdom. He had shown her the maps of his and neighboring countries on his ship. Her hope returned to her. She would see him once again one day, and they could be together.

"I am Eleni. Thank you for welcoming me, it was a very hard journey."

"I am sure it was. Now let me get you back to my kingdom, your new home." Edmond turned to mount his horse.

"Wait, we cannot leave." Eleni grasped his arm, glancing back to the slaves.

One of the knights stepped in between the king and Eleni.

"It is all right Rohan." King Edmond stepped around him, facing Eleni. "Why can we not leave?"

"Sir there are other slaves here who can work hard for you." She faced the row of slaves. The auction had started to get underway.

"I know three other slaves who would work hard for you, please you must purchase them as well." Eleni pointed to the three other slaves.

King Edmond stood and pondered for a moment. He felt the bulge again in his pants.

"Very well, Rohan go and make offers on the slaves she pointed out. Come now, Eleni, you will ride on my horse."

Touching Eleni's arm gently, King Edmond escorted her over to his steed, lifted her up and placed her on the saddle.

Rohan did the king's bidding, and the other three slaves were purchased. Their chains were removed, and they followed Rohan back to where Eleni and King Edmond were sitting on horseback.

"This girl here has saved your life today." King Edmond addressed the other slaves. Two of the slaves did not understand his language but turned to Eleni for meaning. She smiled at them, and they exhaled. She gazed into Berhanua eyes. His eyes had returned to normal.

She had upheld her promise; she did not leave without him.

King Edmond continued to speak as if the others understood him. Once he finished he pulled the reins, and his horse moved into a steady trot back to towards the castle.

Queen Vivienne had been on pins and needles awaiting word of her husband's return. She remained in bed as she was asked and called on Rachelle every few minutes for attention to keep her from going stir crazy.

"Rachelle!" the queen called out. "Bring me my breakfast!"

Her chamber room door flew open, and Rachelle entered the room with a tray of bread, cheese, and jam.

"Where is my tea, Rachelle? I cannot eat this without my morning tea!"

"Milady it is coming. The cook is preparing the hot water for you now."

"Well, since I have to wait, you will have to entertain me until my tea is ready. Come here." Vivienne waved her over.

Rachelle hurried over to the side of the bed where the queen was laying and kneeled down on the floor.

Vivienne rolled over to her side and kissed Rachelle. "I have missed you my sweet, she said. I want you to lick me until my juices flow into your mouth. But first undress. I want to see you unclothed."

Rachelle got to her feet and removed her clothing, dropping it on the floor. Her pale snowy skin shivered from the breeze blowing throughout the room. She moved the queen's bedding out of the way, yanking her gown up over her knees and dove her head in-between the queen's legs. She gently licked on Queen Vivienne's clit making it hard, and the queen began to moan.

Rachelle sucked on her clit and swirled her tongue around Vivienne's moist mound. Vivienne cried out in enjoyment. Rachelle took her fingers and slid two inside of her wetness to pleasure herself. As she moved them in and out, she too started to moan while continuing to give Vivienne pleasure.

Queen Vivienne clutched Rachelle's head, forcing it further into her mound. Rachelle enjoyed hearing the queen's cries. She shoved her tongue deeper into Vivienne's hole, moving it in and out.

Vivienne's moans became deeper and louder. Vivienne screamed in ecstasy and released her juices into Rachelle's mouth.

"Sit on my face Rachelle; I want to taste you."

Rachelle opened her thighs and sat on the queen's face.

"Ride my face," the Queen mumbled between licking.

Rachelle rode the queen's tongue in and out of the apex between her legs.

The queen plunged her tongue deeper until Rachelle shot her juices into her mouth.

Rachelle moved off the queen's face and kissed her forehead as she moved down to sitting on her lap. "I love you, Vivienne. If things were to change, I would not know what to do."

"You do not have to worry, my pet. Nothing will change, you still will be mine. Now please go and get my tea."

"Yes, Milady."

Rachelle redressed and fixed her hair back into the bun that had fallen and headed off to the kitchen.

Vivienne laid back on her pillows thinking about what had transpired. Rachelle was able to bring pleasure she never felt with Edmond. He was a means to an end. Rachelle was still another pawn in the game of chess that Vivienne played. Her thoughts drifted back to the year before her meeting Edmond.

Vivienne's mother had awoken her from a deep slumber, alerting her that her father was murdered in his drunkenness in a tavern fight. He became a drunk after their family lost everything while trying to fund the army of Naples to fight the French army. Vivienne's mother Lady Allegra vowed to get revenge for her husband Lord Nazario Marchesi and recover their losses.

Vivienne was ensnared to do her mother's bidding to conceal the fact that she was in love with the family's stable hand and had secretly given birth to a son. Vivienne was backed into a corner and had no choice but to go along with her mother's plan. Lady Allegra used her contacts and spy's to locate King Charlie's brother Edmond. Vivienne was then groomed for the day she would get her chance to make things right. The opportunity came when Edmond made port in Naples.

The trumpets sounded alerting the castle that the king returned. Vivienne shook the thoughts from her head. She got out of the bed and freshened herself up. She changed into another robe and wiped the juices off her face, away from her mound and removed the sheets from the bed. She then sat at her table eating breakfast as another servant came in and changed the sheets.

King Edmond dismounted his horse, lifting Eleni off behind him. Eleni glanced around at the massive castle. It was quite different than the white castle, not smooth, or shiny just a large rock formation. King Edmond instructed Rohan to take the other slaves and show them where they would be staying. Eleni smiled once more at Berhanua and the others as they were led away. She hoped they would be okay.

"Come with me." King Edmond took Eleni's hand.

Eleni followed behind him as they entered the castle. Eleni jutted out her chin as she saw all the faces watching her. She forced a smile, despite their jeers.

King Edmond stopped dead in his tracks. "You will not treat this woman or the other slaves in the manner of which you have shown at this moment. If I see or hear of it, I will have you killed or thrown into the dungeon."

All of the servants in the presence of the king dropped to their knees and did not say another word.

"Come," King Edmond whispered. He led Eleni through the hall to a large staircase. King Edmond ascended the stairs, stopping at a chamber door and swinging it open.

Eleni followed closely behind. She saw a woman sitting at her table eating breakfast. The woman spun around in her chair and faced them. Eleni noticed that she was also with child.

"Vivienne, this is Eleni." King Edmond smiled. "I brought her here to be a companion for you, especially since you both are with child."

Vivienne eyed Eleni up and down.

Yes, she is with child. She thought to herself, but she knew, being her companion was not what Edmond had in mind.

"Yes, I can see she is with child Edmond, how smart of you to bring me a friend," Vivienne answered sarcastically.

"I thought you might like the company. She will replace Rachelle as your lady in waiting."

"Replace her! You cannot replace Rachelle." Vivienne's voice boomed. "I'm not getting rid of Rachelle."

"Vivienne, she will move back into the kitchen with the cook. I am leaving Eleni in your care, and you will show her the ropes of what needs to be done for you around here."

Vivienne glared at Edmond and Eleni in disgust. She wheeled back around and continued to eat her breakfast.

"If that's all dear husband, I will make sure Eleni knows everything that is to be done."

"Good, dear wife, I am glad you agree. I will now show Eleni where she will be sleeping. Come, Eleni." King Edmond led Eleni farther down the corridor, and up three more flights of stairs.

"This is where you will be staying. "He cracked the chamber room open. The room was modest, with a small bed, a writing table with a chair, a washbasin and a small window looking out towards the water.

Eleni studied her surroundings before smiling at Edmond. "This room is the nicest thing I have seen in a long while, thank you."

"You are welcome." Edmond moved closer to her and ran his fingers through her hair.

Eleni shuddered and stepped backward.

"Forgive me. I should not have touched you so soon. I am so drawn to you."

"You should think of your wife, Majesty. It is wrong to want something you cannot have." Eleni brushed past him and gaped out of the tiny room window.

"But I can have you. Maybe not now, but someday you will allow me to. "Edmond leaned over Eleni brushing his lips against hers in a gentle manner.

Eleni did not want him touching her, but she endured his kiss.

Edmond pressed himself against her; his engorged cock poked through his pants.

"Why did you bring me here, Majesty? Am I only to be an object of your obsession?"

"I brought you here to please me when I am ready for you too. If I must answer your question, yes, you will be my obsession. You and any other woman I want to have. Your choices are far and in-between. Once you have your child, I will have my way with you."

Eleni was now aware of why she was purchased. She was to be the king's whore.

"I understand." She glanced off into the sunset.

King Edmond stepped behind her, resting his hand on her shoulder. "I did not mean to scare you or want to hurt you. It is better for you to know now what you are to me. You are my exotic little creature. I will leave you to get settled." King Edmond kissed Eleni's shoulder leaving her alone in the darkness.

Eleni was going to have to escape, but how and when? How would she get away from here with her child? There was little time to prepare.

Her belly, feet, and thighs had swollen in the coming days. The baby would come any day now, and it was a day she was excited for.

The sexual encounter she would have to endure after the birth was not something she was looking forward to.

King Edmond found his way to her chambers on a nightly basis. Eleni would catch him watching her and masturbating, in anticipation of what was to come after she gave birth. He would sometimes ask her to play with herself and to stick her fingers in and out of her mound.

Sometimes she would please herself doing so, but often she would play along to get him to leave her chambers.

Finally, two nights later, the much-needed break from King Edmond came. He had left the castle to attend to village business and would be away for a week.

Eleni breathed a sigh of relief. She was able to move about the castle without his eyes gazing upon her at every turn. She enjoyed her work a little more and was excited to see how the French kingdom celebrated the harvest. The night of the harvest ball was upon the kingdom and with King Edmond away, she was left only to prepare Queen Vivienne for the ball.

Eleni knocked on Queen Vivienne's door.

"Enter," a voice called out from the inside of the chamber room.

Eleni opened the door and quickly entered, slightly bowed as she closed the door with her foot. She dragged the bucket of warm water behind her over to the tub and poured it in.

"It is time for your bath, Milady." Eleni poured jasmine oil into the water and swirled it around with her hand.

"How funny," Eleni muttered under her breath.

"What is so funny?"

"I was thinking about my past life. It was not so long ago I had a chambermaid who prepared my baths for me, and would put healing oils into my bath water."

"I find that hard to believe, Eleni," Queen Vivienne said with a little laugh. "You have such an imagination, girl. Everyone knows slaves have never been royal. I forbid you ever to speak of such foolery again in my presence. Next thing I know you will be talking to me as if I am on the same level as you."

Eleni fixed Vivienne with a cold look.

"I am the same as you, Queen Vivienne. I was married to a king and a princess in my home of birth. The only reason I am in this country is because of my husband." Eleni's voiced trailed off, and she quieted.

Queen Vivienne disrobed and sunk into the warm bath, the water swirling at the nape of her neck.

"Why did your husband send you here, Eleni?"

Eleni leaned over the tub and poured a little more jasmine into the water. She picked up the sponge, dripped water over Vivienne's shoulders, and began to bathe her.

"My husband sent me here because I disobeyed him, in his eyes. He wanted me to take his cruelties and suffer. I fell in love with another man who came to my country on an expedition."

"What type of journey?" Vivienne asked. She snatched Eleni's wrist spinning her around the tub to face her "What kind of expedition Eleni!"

"From what David explained to me, they were traveling to find India. Unfortunately, they ended up in my country of Abyssinia."

"Well, now that is quite a story, Eleni." Vivienne laughed "I cannot help but believe you made all of that up in your head to amuse me. So tell me who is this David you are speaking about?"

"It is not a story," Eleni got to her feet to gather Vivienne's robe. "David is the king of England. If all went well, I would have been his wife. That is why my former husband was angered and banished me from the white castle."

"Well Eleni, I have to admit you made my evening with your tale. You and the king of England in love and let me guess the baby you are with child with belongs to him?"

Eleni evaded her question and held out the queen's robe. "Milady, let's finish getting you ready for the ball. I am not going to go into any more detail about my life since you believe I only tell stories for your amusement. I will finish with one more statement. If I am a silly slave or servant, how is it I can speak several languages including your native tongue of Italian and French. Can other slaves do it? Do other slaves hold themselves as I do?"

Vivienne's eyes dropped. She had never thought about Eleni being well educated. Eleni spoke the truth in her statement.

"I am sorry if I inflicted any pain on you. It was not my intention Eleni," Vivienne said. "I believed you were telling me a tale. I have never heard of any of the things you have described to me."

Eleni looked at her quietly and continued to dry the queen off.

"I accept your apology Milady. Let's finish getting you ready."

17 Birth

Eleni finished preparing the queen's hair and makeup and got her dressed for the ball. King Edmond had been called away suddenly and left Vivienne in charge of the kingdom. Vivienne viewed herself in the mirror and saw her swollen belly.

This baby will be here anytime.

"That will be all Eleni. Please leave me."

Eleni bowed, leaving her alone in the chamber room.

Vivienne brushed down her gown with her hands, took one more glance in the mirror and headed out her chamber room to face the nobles and the rest of the guests Edmond had left her to entertain.

Vivienne often wondered about these sudden meetings that took Edmond from court. She felt that their relationship had been strained as of late. She pushed away all thoughts of him taking a lover. She would not allow herself to believe that he would find solace in the arms of another woman because Edmond had been so enamored with her.

"He would never take another to his bed," she whispered to herself.

An announcement was made of her arrival, and she entered the room. As Vivienne passed her guests, they all smiled and bowed and curtsied. She hated them all: In her paranoia, they were plotting to steal her spot as queen.

She knew that the nobles never wanted Edmond to marry her. She was always worried that someone would be her demise. Vivienne toasted to her husband and explained his absence had to do with treaty issues. Edmond had given his regrets that he could not attend their annual ball but sent his well wishes to all those members of the court.

As she glared around the room, she noticed whispers between the women. Some laughed and some sneered at her. The thoughts of what Edmond was doing crossed her mind again. The toasts of the evening were over, and the ball went on as planned. Vivienne was bored out of her mind by the endless dancing, laughter, and drinking. All of it made Vivienne want to vomit.

Tapping her fingers against the armrest of her throne chair, she decided that she had had just about enough of all the commotion and wanted to go up to her chambers. She signaled for her adviser to come forth and whispered into his ear that she was going back up to her room to rest.

"Make sure that the ball ends smoothly and that everything is accounted for after the festivities are finished."

"Yes, Milady," he answered.

Vivienne got to her feet. She felt quite uneasy. A sharp pain radiated down the left side of her body. She leaned back, placing her on the arm on the chair, and regained her strength. Inhaling, she stood up straight, proceeded down the throne steps and moved slowly out of the ballroom.

Vivienne made it as far as the hall before another pain shot down from her stomach to her leg. Clutching her stomach, she winced in pain. She needed to get to her room and lay down.

She continued to move down the hall, resting against the wall between steps. A servant passed her.

"Is everything all right, Milady?" he asked on the way back to the kitchen.

"Yes I am fine, Vivienne answered. "Go about your business. I am just taking my time."

"Yes, Milady. "He continued to walk towards the kitchen.

Vivienne was left alone in the hall again. Coming to the stairs, she started to climb, managing to make it to her wing when she collapsed on the porcelain floor. Vivienne felt a liquid running down her leg.

She snatched her gown up over her ankles and saw blood dripping down her leg onto the steps beneath her. She tried to crawl the rest of the way to her room, but the pain in her stomach rendered her from moving further.

"Someone, please help me," she called out frantically. "Please someone give me a hand," she screamed out again.

Eleni had been finishing up her cleaning in the queen's room when she heard the calls for help. She ran out into the hall and saw Queen Vivienne curled over on the staircase floor. Eleni hurried over kneeling beside Queen Vivienne and called out for help.

"Berhanua," Eleni called out. "Berhanua, come quickly."

He appeared at the opposite end of the hall.

"It is the queen Berhanua, please help me get her up and into her room."

Berhanua dropped his bucket and rags he was using to clean the back flight of stairs and ran over to assist Eleni. Berhanua drew Vivienne up into his arms and carried her into her chambers, laying her down on the bed.

"Go and get help Berhanua," Eleni told him. "Do it now, do not linger, there is no time."

"Right away, mistress," he replied and left to find some others to help.

Vivienne let out another scream.

Eleni went to the bedside and unlaced Vivienne's gown. "We have to get this off of you Milady." She cut the delicate gown with a knife she had in her apron pocket. Eleni sliced the bloody dress off Vivienne's body and cut the corset off her as well. She was down to her smock which Eleni then shimmied up over her waist. She peeled the top cover off the bed and pushed the queen further over so she would not fall. Eleni worked quickly through the large quantity of blood. If the baby was not delivered soon, the infant and the queen herself could die.

Berhanua came back with a couple of the other French lady servants, and Katlego, another slave who also worked in the castle. The French servants mostly ignored Eleni in all other circumstances, but in this case, it was Eleni who was telling them what to do.

Word was sent to the doctor, but he lived so far out in the countryside it would take him some time to arrive. Eleni knew the queen did not have long to survive.

Eleni had seen deliveries in her kingdom when she was younger, and she knew enough about them to spring into action. Eleni touched Vivienne's stomach, and the Queen winced out in pain.

"We have to get this baby out, Vivienne!" Eleni yelled, parting Vivienne's legs open.

"Eleni, the baby is too early."

"I understand the baby is too soon, Vivienne. But if we do not get this baby out now, you both will die."

Eleni reached in-between Vivienne's thighs and pressed her fingers inside of her to see if she could feel the baby. She found that the baby was in a breached position.

"I'm going to have to turn this baby into the right position for it come out. This is going to hurt, Vivienne. "Eleni grasped the door stop and placed it in Vivienne's mouth. "Bite down." Vivienne bit down on the door stop and clasped one of the servant girl's hands.

With no hesitation, Eleni pushed her hand into Vivienne's vagina and angled the baby's body so the head would face the right direction. "You are going to have to push now, Vivienne." Eleni removed her hand from inside the queen and shifted to the center part of the bed.

Vivienne trembled. "I cannot do this," she cried out. "I cannot have this baby! It is too soon."

"You will and you must, Milady! Push," Eleni ordered. Queen Vivienne focused and pushed on command.

"Push again," Eleni hissed.

Once again Queen Vivienne pushed.

Eleni exhaled when she saw the head of the baby between Vivienne's legs. "One more time, Milady. Push."

Eleni caught the baby in her arms. She saw that the baby was blue and not breathing. She immediately flipped the baby over and hit it firmly on the back. The baby took a breath and regained its coloring. She wrapped the baby in a sheet and handed her to the queen.

Queen Vivienne smiled taking the child from Eleni's arms. She placed the baby on her breast, the baby latching onto her nipple.

"Thank you, Eleni. The baby is so beautiful." Vivienne smiled, looking down at the little bundle in her arms.

"You are welcome, Milady." Eleni scooted off the bed, removed the bloody sheets and towels from around Vivienne and handed them to Katlego. An hour passed and just before Eleni was going to dismiss Berhanua, Katlego, and the other servants, Vivienne called out to her.

"Eleni, there is something wrong with the baby. She is not breathing." Vivienne removed the baby from her breast in a panic.

Eleni spun around and took the child out of the queen's arms. The baby's colored drained, turning blue again and struggled to breathe. She turned the baby on her side, hitting the child's back. Breast milk trickled down the baby's chin to the floor. Eleni worked feverishly, but the child did not regain consciousness. The baby died in her arms.

All the servants in the room fell silent. Queen Vivienne knew that something was wrong.

"I cannot hear the baby cry!" Vivienne said in a panic. Eleni what is wrong with my baby! I want to see the baby!"

Eleni handed the little princess to one of the other servants and moved to the side of the bed where the queen was laying. She sat down and clasped the hand of the queen.

"Milady, I am so sorry, but your daughter..."

"My little girl! What is wrong with her! I want to see her! Give her to me now!"

"Milady, I do not think that you want to see your baby like this. She was born to early and too soon. She was not strong enough to survive."

"What do you mean that she is dead Eleni?"

"I am so sorry my queen; you really should not see her like this."

"Eleni! You cannot keep her from me. Give me my baby! "Queen Vivienne's tone turned cold.

Eleni hesitated for a moment but swiveled around to the other servant who was holding the child in her arms. "Let the Queen see her child," Eleni said to the woman.

The servant woman handed the baby wrapped in sheets over to Eleni, and she placed her into Queen Vivienne's arms. The Queen focused on the small frame of her daughter. The baby was blue in color, and her eyes were closed. Vivienne kissed her daughter on the forehead and covered her face with the sheet she was wrapped in.

Vivienne gained her composure and was to back to the emotionless woman Eleni had known. She signaled the other servant in the room and passed the baby to her. "Take this child and burn it. Upon Edmond's arrival, I will inform him that we lost our daughter. I want the rest of this room cleaned up."

"Yes, Milady," the servant woman said, leaving the room with the baby in her arms.

"As for the rest of you get this room cleaned up. Eleni prepare me a bath so I can get this filth off me."

Eleni stood, glancing at the Queen with sorrow. It was hard for her to imagine that she would just ignore the fact that she had lost a child.

"Stop staring at me Eleni, and do what you are told."

"Yes, Milady." She turned away and looked down at her stomach and rubbed it. She understood what Queen Vivienne was going through. She left the queen's side briefly and went to gather water for her bath. Eleni helped Vivienne out of the bloody sheets and into the warm bath water. She washed her hair and rinsed the blood from her body.

Vivienne dropped her head to her chin and began to sob. "My daughter," she said in-between her sobs and tears. "My little girl is dead."

"Milady, she was much too young to survive. I did everything I could to save your little girl. If nothing had been done, your husband would have lost you both."

"You did this to me!" Vivienne roared, splashing water on Eleni from inside the tub.

Eleni wiped the water off of her face with a clean edge of her dress. "Milady, I did nothing but try to help you. You were in distress at the top of the stairs. Do you not remember?"

"I remember not asking you for anything. You have done nothing for me but cause me trouble. Get out of here Eleni! I do not want any more help from you this evening. You have cost me enough."

"But, Milady, I do not want to leave you in this condition."

"I can take care of myself. Leave me! Leave me now!"

Eleni handed Queen Vivienne her towel and left the Queen's chambers with Berhanua and the other servants who were still cleaning up the evidence of her delivery.

Berhanua took Eleni's hand and led her into the hall away from peering eyes and ears.

"I have not seen much of you since we came here." Berhanua stroked Eleni's face.

She gazed up him and gave a weak smile. "I know, the queen has had me busy, and I sleep away from all of the other servants. I have not had the chance to sneak away to find you or any of the others. How are you faring here in this kingdom?"

"These people in this country are no different than the slave traders who brought us here. We keep our heads down and do what we are told. A few of the other slaves and servants have been hung or sent to the executioner because of their actions. Eleni, I implore you to do what you can to survive. I fear that you have angered the Queen and in her grief, she may try to harm you. Please try not to upset her any further."

"I will try not to anger the queen any further. She is filled with grief, not just from the death of her daughter, but I fear, from other things as well."

"What do you mean, Eleni?"

"Berhanua, the king has taken an interest in me, more of a sexual nature. She could have found out about his interests, but I am not positive. There also have been whispers around the castle of King Edmond's absences. No one knows for sure, but I believe that there is more going on with Queen Vivienne and King Edmond than I even knew. All I can tell you is to keep your ears open, and all things will be revealed in time."

"Be careful around this king and queen, Eleni. I cannot protect you when they keep you away from me."

"I promise I will try, Berhanua. I will do my best."

Berhanua stroked Eleni's face once more and leaned down and kissed her softly on the forehead.

She cared for Berhanua but was not sure about her feelings towards him. After all, he was part of her reason for being sent to France. Eleni pulled away from Berhanua to walk back to her quarters.

"I will see you," she said as she left.

"Yes, you shall." He smiled and hurried away to finish disposing of the evidence the Queen asked to be destroyed. Berhanua had the baby's remains burned with the sheets, her ball gown, and towels in a fire outside of the castle walls.

A few nights had passed since Queen Vivienne's daughter was born and died. Eleni did her best to please the queen even though she was blamed for the young princess's death. Even in pain, Eleni worked long hours scrubbing, cleaning, and doing what she was told. She obeyed every command hoping that the queen would ease her punishment that she inflicted on her daily.

Queen Vivienne's anger mounted in those following days and continued to spread. Every person she passed in the hall or came into contact with felt the iciness of her mood and demeanor. She spent a lot of time alone trying to come to grips with the grief she felt as well as the thoughts of her husband's whereabouts. She tried to regain her strength and ease the pain from her delivery. But when she thought about her husband's escapades it upset her.

The pain she felt did not subside completely because of the anger and rage consuming her. She had wished Edmond had been at her bedside, and for a moment wished she had not pushed him away. Vivienne had received word that her husband King Edmond was due back at the castle in a fortnight.

What would she tell her husband? Would she tell him the truth about the baby dying? Would she pretend to continue with the farce of being with child? Vivienne knew she had to provide a child to the king. Her life as queen depended on it.

King Edmond found his time away from the castle always to be much needed. Mina was a light in his life and seeing her kept him from having impure thoughts of Eleni. He found happiness where his wife seemed to remove it from his life when he was around her. He was able to be himself. The whispers around the castle did not concern him. He never wanted to be king and was only thrust into it because his brother had died.

The morning King Edmond was due to depart from his country cottage house and return to the French kingdom was one of passion and delight. Edmond and Mina spent the week horseback riding and made love in the woods and swam in the nearby stream. There was not a care in the world, and all was well when

Mina was by his side. The sun came through the shutters on the window and bathed Mina and Edmond in sunlight. Edmond was awoken by a soft sucking in between his legs. The passion of the oral pleasure placed Edmond in a state of perpetual animation or an altered reality of sorts.

He was so engulfed in the awesome feeling of Mina's lips and tongue caressing and massaging his cock that he did not know for sure if he was in a dream or awake. As his consciousness began to catch his suspended state of blissful animation, he realized that he was not only awake but was awaken in a fashion that he had only dreamed about before. His heart raced with every passing second of oral pleasure. Each second felt as if they were minutes as the seductive, and hypnotic motions of Mina's mouth intensified with every moan Edmond made.

Mina herself became more aroused listening to Edmond's moans and whispers of pleasure resulting from her fervent desire to please him. As she pleasured him, she thought back to when Edmond shared with her that he wished to be awoken with oral pleasure as it were a dream of his, and how she wanted to become the woman of his dreams.

Every pleasurable jerk of his body increased her desire to continue pleasing him. She glanced deep into Edmond's eyes, visually showing him her willingness.

The excitement combined with the passion of the moment brought Edmond to near climax. He was caught between the pleasure of releasing and the sadness of the moment coming to its conclusion. As Edmund reached his peak after a seemingly endless seven minutes of oral pleasure, he released his life-force into Mina's mouth, and she received every drop as if it were delicious honey from the fountains of heaven.

Edmond's body completely relaxed as if he were in a coma from the pleasure and intensity of releasing his seed. Mina's flower had now become an ocean of erotic and orgasmic juices and without hesitation, she mounted Edmund's face to ride his tongue. Edmond quickly dived into the moment and attempted fervently to provide Mina with oral pleasure in the similitude of how she pleasured him. He grabbed her hips, taking control of her motions to form a rhythmic serenade between his mouth and her flower, in an epic duet of harmonious oral bliss.

Mina's nature rose as she felt his tongue reach the depths of her inner being. It was as if Edmond's tongue had become a hand gently and seductively reaching through her flower petals and caressing her heart and soul.

Mina shed tears as the beauty and passion of the moment caused an eruption of orgasmic fluids to flow like fountains of legend. She temporarily lost control of her body as the depth of the orgasm took control of every fiber of her being. After consecutive orgasms from oral pleasure, Edmond sought to be inside of Mina, and she accepted the invitation. Both of their sexual organs had increased exponentially in sensitivity as they simultaneously orgasmed after a short, but extraordinary four strokes.

They connected on a level unknown to them both. And they were now tied together for the rest of their natural lives by the most intense sexual experience they both had ever encountered. Falling into each other's arms, they lay as the morning hours passed by. Mina closed her eyes and drifted off into a blissful sleep.

Edmond shifted his body to face her. He wanted to observe her in her natural state. Her long blonde hair fell over the covers down to her waist. He loved looking at her little pink nipples that were still hard as she slept, and her slim frame outlined the silk sheets covering her. After slipping out the bed, Edmond quietly exited the cottage door and walked naked down to the stream to bathe. The sun had shifted from the east and now beamed down onto Edmond's head. He loved being at the cottage. It was where he stayed briefly as a child after being sent from court.

"A lot of fond memories." He walked into the cool water and began to swim.

Not long after, Mina blinked her eyes open to find Edmond gone. "Edmond!" She called out as she looked around the room, and over to the window where she saw him swimming in the stream. She kicked the sheets off and headed out to join him in the warm sun and fresh water. Mina walked into the water, her nipples perking up and becoming harder the deeper into the water she waded. Swimming up behind him, she wrapped her hands around his neck and her legs around his waist.

He spun her around and kissed her gently on the lips.

She parted her lips inviting him to enter with his tongue.

He obliged and allowed his tongue to enter her mouth and move around freely. He lifted her thighs around his waist and opened her flower once more. Their love making continued as the fresh stream water circled them.

Mina ground her flower upon his cock as he held her by the waist, pulling her down into him harder. The quiet around them was broken by their moans and intense screams of passion. Edmond released his life force inside of her with a fierceness that Mina herself could feel. She answered that feeling with her juices that warmed his cock dripping down from the inside of her over the head of his cock into the water.

They kissed passionately once more and released each other from their embrace. Edmond gently put Mina down in the water allowing her to catch her balance. They both sauntered out of the water hand in hand standing naked on the stream bank.

"I have to get back to the kingdom." Edmond kissed Mina on the forehead and retrieved his clothing. "I hate leaving you here alone, but I will send the carriage to come back for you the day after tomorrow. We have to be careful not to be seen with each other."

Mina took Edmond's shirt from him and slid it over her body. "I understand. "she closed the opening, tying the strings. "I want to come back to court tomorrow. I do not like being away from you too long."

"You do not have to worry my love. I will arrange to see you again after the queen gives birth. I am sure we will have time to find time in each other's arms once again. Two more nights here at the cottage will not hurt you." Edmond finished putting on his boots on and kissed Mina tempestuously.

"I cannot wait. "Mina took Edmond's hand and placed it in between her legs. "My juices continue to flow waiting for you to take me in your arms again, and thrust your manhood inside of me."

Edmond's cock became enlarged again from Mina's juices on his fingers. He removed his hand from between her legs and tasted her sweetness on his lips, rubbing his tongue to get the full flavor. She felt so good to him. He looked forward to making love to her again and putting his head between her supple thighs.

Edmond shook his head. He had to get back into being a married man and a king. "Now you must give me my shirt back." He untied the strings from around Mina's neck then pulled the shirt back over her head. He finished dressing; buttoned his coat and mounted his horse. "I will see you soon my love." Edmond blew a kiss at Mina as he rode away.

"Yes, you shall. I love you Edmond!" she called after him.

Edmond turned and smiled back at her, gazed at her naked body then continued the overnight ride back to his kingdom.

The beatings that Eleni took in those following days took a strain on her, and her pregnancy. She was in the end stages and due to give birth at any time. Typically vigorous and able to work through any adverse condition, Eleni felt her body begin to give out due to the amount of work she was given.

"One more night," she said to herself.

She hurried out of the castle into the cold wind and howling rain to dump the queen's waste bucket. A storm was sweeping into the kingdom. Lightning and thunder pounded in the distance. Eleni looked up into the sky and saw the lightning strike overhead.

Let me hurry.

She scurried down to the hillside to the moat and emptied the bucket. As she ascended the slope back to the castle, she felt a pain in her stomach that knocked her off her feet.

Gaining her composure, she felt a liquid run down her legs. She pulled her dress up over her thighs to see what it was she felt. A clear liquid pooled at her feet.

Eleni knew she was going to give birth that night. She grabbed the bucket in her hand and pushed her dress down over knees. She maneuvered the best she could with the intense pain shooting through her stomach as shuffled back to the castle in the pouring rain.

18 England

Philippa sat at her vanity staring at her reflection in the mirror. She received word by messenger that David had made a stop in the Canary Islands. He was alive and continuing with his voyage to India. For her plan to work, Jasper had to believe the child she was carrying was his.

Philippa's mother in law, Queen Anne was suspicious about her whereabouts in the kingdom. She felt that Philippa was hiding something from her and cast spies throughout the palace to gather information.

Philippa finished preparing herself for her outing in the forest to meet Jasper. She had been alerted of Queen Anne's directions by one of her loyal servants. Philippa kept Jasper at a distance because of the spying. It had been a little over a week before they were able to coordinate to see each other again. She decided before her ride that she would tell her mother in law of her pregnancy to throw her off the trail of the rumored affair that she was having with the stable hand.

She left her chambers and headed straight towards Queen Anne's room. She knocked once, no answer, then again, and still no reply. She then headed down the flight of stairs to the courtyard.

"Philippa, my dear, where are you on your way to?"

Philippa spun around at the castle door and faced Queen Anne. "I was trying to find you, Your Majesty."

"Philippa, what have I told you about calling me, Your Majesty? I have always told you to call me queen mother." Queen Anne scurried towards Philippa. "What did you need to see me for, my dear?"

"There was something I wanted to speak to you about in private Queen Mother."

"Why of course, my dear."

Queen Anne gestured for them to enter the throne room. She swung the door open and escorted Philippa into the chamber.

"Now Philippa." Anne closed the door behind them. "What is it that you need to tell me?"

Philippa grasped her hands together and then rested her hand on the back of the throne.

"Queen Mother," she started calmly. "I am aware that you have had spies following me to find out about my whereabouts and what I have been doing. Do you deny this.?"

Queen Anne blushed in embarrassment. How did she find out about her plan?

"Well, no, I cannot deny that I had people looking into your wellbeing. My dear, I knew something was wrong that you were not telling me. I had been alerted about a mysterious visitor in the kingdom, and you were sneaking away from the castle at all hours. I assumed you must have found comfort in someone's arms since your husband, my son, has been away."

Philippa shifted nervously. How could Queen Anne know of her affair? She and Jasper had been so careful. She would have to tell half- truths to protect them both.

"Queen Anne, I assure you that I love your son very much. I would never do anything to compromise his position or mine, or this kingdom. The mysterious visitor you speak of was the court physician. I was coming to find you to tell you that I was with child. My outings outside of the kingdom were simply to get some fresh air and exercise as the physician ordered. There are no other mysteries or anything for you to solve. I can tell you it is safe for you to call off your goons from following me throughout the kingdom."

Queen Anne stood quietly looking at her daughter- in- law. "Congratulations on the child, Philippa," Queen Anne said taking Philippa in her arms and embracing her. "I promise I will call off my goons as you put it, and there will be no one else following you around the castle. Now you must get some air on your afternoon ride, and as soon as you return, you must retire to your chambers and rest. I will have your meals sent to you, having an heir is a dangerous thing, and I will not be held responsible if you do not follow my orders and end up losing your child."

"I promise that I will rest after my ride." Philippa kissed Queen Anne's on her shoulder then brushed past her out into the courtyard. "I shall see you later in the afternoon."

Philippa was pleased that the encounter with Queen Anne was over. The secret of her pregnancy was now spilled, and hopefully, no more spies would be following her around the castle. Her horse was saddled and waiting for her at the stables.

Jasper was thoughtful. I am so in love with him.

Hoisting herself onto the saddle, she rode out of the kingdom to the spot in the forest where they always secretly met. The day was a bright one, and the sun's rays beamed down onto Philippa's head, making her sweat underneath her riding hat. The week that passed was a long one. She missed Jasper and longed to be with him. They spoke about everything, and the way he made love to her made her lady parts tingle.

Philippa became saddened as she rode. She knew that her visits with Jasper would become scarce when David arrived back into the kingdom. She loathed his return. Her ride the rest of the way into the forest was peaceful. She listened to the birds singing sweet songs above her, the wind blowing gently, cooling her off.

Philippa arrived at her destination in the forest. She rode into the clearing, slowing her horse to a slow trot, and noted that Jasper had set up a blanket with their favorite foods positioned on it. His eyes were closed, and he was fast asleep.

Jasper awoke when he heard the horse's hooves of Philippa's horse slow and came to a stop. He smiled at her. A large grin appeared on her face, and she waved back at him. Jumping to his feet, he trotted over to where she sat on the horse. He took the reins from her and led the horse over to a tree, securing it.

"Well, hello there," Jasper smiled at Philippa, and she shyly glanced at him.

"Well, hello. I have missed you, Jasper. It has been quite a while since I last saw you."

"It has not been that long, Philippa," Jasper said. "But I can admit to you that I missed you as well."

"Well since you have missed me as well Jasper, then please help me down from my horse so I can embrace you as I desire."

Philippa started to slide her body down off the saddle, and Jasper stopped her, slid his hands up her legs and under her dress.

"I do not want you to move Milady; I want to show you how much I have missed you."

Philippa shifted in the saddle of the horse as Jasper continued to rub her bare legs and thighs with his hands. He then moved down to the boots she was wearing, unlaced them, and threw them down to the ground. He removed her stockings next, exposing her bare feet. Her feet were well kept and were quite lovely. He had never noticed them before in past encounters. Jasper got to his knees and rubbed her right foot gently, kissing her toes and the center of her foot.

"What are you doing, Jasper?" She was caught off guard by his actions. He continued to surprise her every time they were together.

"Let me continue, Philippa. Let me please you." Jasper sucked on her big toe.

Philippa felt a chill run up her leg, straight to her moistness. Juices formed and dripped down her leg. Jasper then moved his arm up her legs again and felt her moist juices on his hand.

"Are you ready for me to be inside of you?" Jasper asked, pausing from his toe licking.

"Yes, I am so ready for you." Philippa panted and held back her moan. She was desperate for him to remove her from the horse and to take her right then and there. "Jasper, please take me now!" She squirmed from his toe sucking and rubbing in-between her thighs.

"Not yet." He released her toes from his mouth and kissed up the thigh of her right leg. He then spread her legs as wide as he could in the saddle. He got to his feet and kissed Philippa on the lips. He licked her lips with his tongue, moving her mouth open gently and allowing his tongue to slide in and out of her mouth intertwining with her tongue.

Her arousal grew, and she wrapped her legs around his waist. They kissed one another passionately, their tongues once again dancing inside of each other's mouths. Jasper broke from their kiss, moving to Philippa's neck licking and sucking it softly. He then moved down to her chest, bursting her gown and corset open, exposing her supple shapely breast to the forest's air.

Her velvet peaks stiffened and Jasper licked her pink nipples making them become little hard mounds that he then twisted with his thumb and index finger. Philippa moaned louder when he did this. He was driving her crazy, and she could not take any more of his teasing.

"Jasper, please take me now," she pleaded.

He smiled and moved his mouth over her nipples biting the left one with his teeth.

"Now for my final act before I take you to the blanket. Lean back on the horse."

Philippa adjusted herself one last time. The horse was becoming impatient with her shifting and tried to move. Jasper, however, steadied the horse and calmed him down.

"Whoa, boy."

He broke from the moment, petting the horse's head. He picked up an apple from the basket and fed it to him.

"There you go; boy you deserve a healthy treat for standing here this long."

Philippa thought that she was off the hook and once again tried to get down off the horse.

"Where do you think you are going, Milady?" Jasper stopped petting the horse and sat Philippa back onto the saddle.

"I thought with you taking care of the horse and all I could get down."

"I am not quite done with you yet, open those legs back for me. I want to get a better view of you."

Philippa obliged and raised her gown over her knees. The fabric of her dress rested at her mid-section preventing Jasper from noticing how pregnant she was. She opened her legs as much as the saddle would allow.

Jasper wiped the juices of the apple on his breeches and kneeled back onto his knees in front of Philippa. He once again positioned himself so he could kiss her thighs. Licking them softly, he moved his head from one thigh to the other until he reached the moistness in between her legs. She was indeed ready for him. His licking persisted up to her wet spot, resting on the little pink nub and playing with it, with his tongue.

Philippa's toes curled as tingles shot up through her legs. Jasper liked the response he was getting from tasting her and continued to plummet his tongue further inside of her until she grabbed his head trying to get him to stop.

"Jasper, I am going to explode, please let me off this horse and take me now."

Jasper removed his head from between Philippa's legs and lifted her into his arms, carrying her over to the blanket underneath the tree. Jasper laid her down on the blanket, untied his breeches and removed his shirt. He kneeled down on the blanket next to Philippa, leaning over her and kissing her passionately.

He moved his hands to open her legs once more. She once again obliged him and spread her legs open. Jasper traced his hands underneath her dress and up her thigh once more playing with her hard mound.

Philippa's moaning and shallow breaths gave him the signal she was ready. Jasper tried to lay on top of her, and Philippa placed her hands against his chest, preventing him from resting on her.

"Let us do something a little different. Help me to my knees."

Jasper looked a little confused but helped Philippa up onto her knees. She shifted around facing her back towards him and lifted her gown exposing her bare behind.

"Now, you will take me from behind. And ravage me."

Jasper smiled letting out a brief laugh. He placed his hands on her hips, digging his hard cock into her moist and wet treasure from behind.

"Jasper," she cried out in a whisper. "Jasper, make me yours." She sucked in a deep breath as she rocked to his rhythm.

"My darling, I want to you to be mine forever."

"And I shall be," Philippa answered through a loud moan.

They moved their bodies together in a hypnotic rhythm until they climaxed. Jasper slowed his movements and withdrew from her. She pushed the crinoline on the underskirt of her dress over her buttocks and turned to face him resting on her knees.

"My darling, I have something that I need to tell you," she said softly and shyly, playing coy.

"There is no reason to be frightened you can tell me anything, Philippa." Jasper grasped Philippa's hand as he laid on the blanket. "What it is that you need to say?"

"Well first I need to tell you, I received word that David is alive and has made it to the Cannery Islands."

Jasper shifted uncomfortably on his side. He did not like hearing anything about David. It angered him when Philippa mentioned his name. He knew when David arrived back in the kingdom that he would have even less time to spend with Philippa. They would have to find an alternative place where they could meet discreetly.

"Is that all you needed to tell me about Philippa?"

Philippa clutched his hand a little tighter, forcing a slight smile. "No there is something else I had wanted to say to you. I am with child Jasper. You are going to be a father."

Jasper sat up straight and smiled at Philippa. He kissed her again deeply.

"Are you happy?"

"I am jubilant; I hope that it is a boy. But even if it is a girl, that would give us the excuse to try again for another child."

"Jasper, you must understand, I will have to continue to produce heirs for David. I am not sure on how much time we will be able to spend together before he comes home. We conceived this child our first night together, which was three months ago. I hope we can conceive again before David returns.

"I would not worry about such things right now Philippa. We will find time to be together, even if David is back in the kingdom."

The day faded into evening, and the sun started to set behind the clouds.

"I must be getting back to the castle; it is getting late." Philippa got to her feet, strapping herself back into her corset. "Please tighten this for me."

She turned her back towards Jasper.

Jasper rose and began lacing her corset. He kissed the nape of her neck gently. "Are you sure you have to get back so soon?"

"Yes, my love, unfortunately, I must. Queen Anne will be on the lookout for me especially since she now knows that I am with child. I wish I could stay here with you longer my love, but we will have many more opportunities to spend with each other before David returns."

Jasper finished lacing Philippa's corset and spun her around towards him and lingeringly kissed her.

Philippa's face reddened and released his lips from hers. "Jasper, I must get going. You cannot continue to kiss me like that. I will never want to leave, and would desire for you to take me again."

"Well now. "Jasper smiled, drawing Philippa closer again.

"I must continue to kiss you as I do, so you will not leave. We have not had much time today; you have not even eaten the food I worked so hard to prepare."

Philippa glanced at the food they had not touched. She sighed back at Jasper.

"You are right. We must enjoy our meal together. After that, I must get back to the castle."

Jasper was happy he won her over to stay with him. Whatever time he could continue to have with her added value to his plan. The two of them ate lunch together laughing and enjoyed each other's company. She helped Jasper finish clearing their afternoon meal. Philippa gathered her belongings, and Jasper escorted her to where her horse was waiting. Jasper helped Philippa up into the horse's saddle, untied the reins and handed them her. She yanked back on the reins, circling the horse in the opposite direction. She glanced back at Jasper, blowing him a kiss as she sped off in the fading daylight.

The remainder of the princess's pregnancy was in seclusion. She had many complications, in the coming months, keeping her in the castle and her visits with Jasper to a minimum. He would see her as much as he could in the evening when the castle was quiet. Sometimes sneaking up the castle wall or stairwell when no peering eyes were around. Queen Anne kept a watchful eye on Philippa during her pregnancy. Philippa was rarely alone. The weather went from the warm summer to the dreary, dark and cold winter.

David still had not made it home from his voyage, and there was a growing concern for his safety and his whereabouts as the months continued to pass. Philippa was due at any moment, and

Queen Anne could see that David would not be there for the birth of his child.

Philippa awoke that morning from a sweet dream and the day seemed to take shape as a happy one. The sky was a bright blue, the sun was shining, and even though it was winter, a warm breeze that came through the window.

Tired of her seclusion, she asked the queen mother if she could take a stroll out in the courtyard. She was tired of being cooped up in her chambers, day in and day out.

Queen Anne obliged her and warned her to be careful. Philippa took her ladies maid, Chelsea, with her. Putting on her robe and slippers, they slowly made their way out of the castle and into the cold air of the courtyard. The weather had not changed drastically enough to produce snow, but the frost had caused all the trees to lose their leaves and the flowers to die until next spring.

"Chelsea, I am going to sit for a while I think. You can leave me here. When I am ready, you can walk me back inside." Philippa eased herself down onto one of the multiple stone benches in the courtyard.

"Milady, I do not believe that is a good idea for me to leave you here, the queen mother would be angry."

"Chelsea, who is going to be your queen?"

"You are, Milady, but still, think of the baby and your health."

"I will be okay. If you want, take a walk around the castle, and when you are finished, I shall be ready to return to my chambers. I implore you to do this for me. I just need a moment to myself, and remember, I am going to be your reigning queen."

"Yes, Milady," Chelsea answered, speeding away. "I will not be gone long."

"Take your time." Philippa turned her back on the lady's maid. "Finally peace," she said to herself. She pushed herself off the bench and stood.

Philippa moved slowly throughout the courtyard to the place where she and David last saw each other and had their sexual encounter. She glanced around to make sure she was alone, then rubbed her belly talking to the life inside of her.

"This is where your father and I conceived you, this very spot." She touched her hand to the tree.

Philippa gazed up at how high it extended into the sky. Tears crept into her eyes. She had wanted so much for David to have loved her. But that would never happen now. Jasper had her heart, and she wanted to give him a child of his own.

Lost in thought, she continued her stroll through the courtyard when a pain struck her in the stomach. Grabbing her belly, she managed to get back to the bench and sit down. She took a few deep breaths and gained her composure as Chelsea came back to escort her back to the castle.

"Are you ready to go back inside?" she asked, helping Philippa up on her feet.

"Yes, I think I am," Philippa panted.

Another sharp pain shot through her stomach and her back. Philippa lost her balance from the pain and fell to her knees.

"You must get someone to help us, Chelsea," Philippa cried out.

"Will you be okay for a moment? I will find someone to assist me."

"Yes, please go and hurry back!" Philippa screamed out.

Chelsea ran off screaming for someone to come and help. As she approached the castle, Jasper saw Chelsea out of the corner of his eye and heard Philippa's screams off in the distance. He dropped his rake into the hay and trekked from the stables.

"What is going on? Is everything all right? Is there a raid?" he called out meeting Chelsea in the path.

"No, the princess, she is in trouble. Please, you must help me and get her back into the castle. The baby, she and the baby are trouble."

Jasper's face turned a ghastly white, and he ran behind Chelsea, finding Philippa, doubled over in pain. Without hesitation, he lifted her up in his arms and carried her behind Chelsea back to the castle.

As they approached, the castle staff saw the commotion and a servant ran to tell Queen Anne about her daughter- in-law. Jasper carried Philippa up the stairs and into her chamber room. He whispered to her that everything was going to be okay, and he loved her and the child. Philippa managed to squeeze out a small smile at him, letting him know she understood.

He gently placed her down on the bed, and as he was about to hurry out of the room to remain out of sight, Queen Anne entered the room frantically. She ordered Chelsea to send word to the physician and ordered the other servants to prepare for the delivery.

"You, young man," she called out as Jasper tried to walk out of the room unnoticed. He circled as realized she was speaking to him.

"Yes, Milady," he answered, turning and dropping down to one knee.

"I wanted to thank you for assisting the princess; you could have very well saved her life and the child's."

"I did what I believed to be the right thing, Your Majesty. I am just a humble servant of your kingdom," he answered with his head still bowed.

"You may stand and face me, my boy. I am truly grateful for your service." Queen Anne touched him on the shoulder. Jasper lifted his head and looked deep into her eyes.

"Have we met before, young man?"

"I do not believe so if we had it would only be in passing. I work in the stable, and I saddle the horses for the court."

"You seem familiar to me somehow. I guess that could be the case. I have not been on a horse for some time. Tell me your name so I can refresh my memory on who you are."

"Yes Milady," he said pausing. "My name is Jasper. Your late husband allowed me to stay in the kingdom and work. It was after the raids that I came to your palace."

"Yes, I believe you are right, Jasper. I do remember you coming here around that time. Well, it is nice to make your acquaintance once more."

The queen set her attention back to Philippa, sitting next to her bedside. The color in her face started to drain, and she continued to pant in a lot of pain.

Jasper excused himself from Philippa's chamber room and asked Chelsea to give him updates on the princess's condition.

The birth of the child was a long one. Philippa had been in labor over twenty hours; the court physician was worried that she and the baby could perish if she did not deliver soon. Against the advice from the Queen Mother, the doctor sought help from an outside midwife known to the kingdom for her magical and medicinal practices to assist in the delivery of the baby. Upon her arrival, everyone in the room except Philippa was taken aback with her limp, grayish-green locks, droopy skin that sagged around her eyes, and long brittle yellow fingernails. The woman came next to Philippa's bedside and clutched her hand.

"Can you help me?" Philippa cried between her labored breaths.

"Of course, I can, Philippa. But if I do, there will be future consequences for your actions you have put into play, my dear," She whispered into Philippa's ear. "The secrets that lie within this room shall be revealed someday. If you are okay with this, then we can proceed."

Philippa looked downward and furrowed her brows. She understood what the midwife meant. The threat was not enough to allow for her life or the baby's life to be ended, so Philippa accepted the woman's offer.

"I accept all future consequences," she whispered back into the woman's ear.

The woman smiled at her and announced to everyone in the room. "She shall live and the baby too."

The midwife began mixing herbs, and some other liquids in a small chalice then handed it to Philippa. She stared at the goblet's contents, then drank the substance. Her pain subsided, and the baby shifted in her stomach, and she felt the urge to push.

"I need to push!" Philippa screamed.

The physician stepped in glancing at the midwife first, then over at Philippa. He pulled up Philippa's gown, feeling in-between her legs. It was a miracle. Whatever the woman had given the princess had worked. The baby was in the correct position and was ready to be pushed out. The physician gave Philippa the command, and she pushed.

"Once more," he called out.

She obeyed, and within a couple of minutes, she had given birth to a healthy son.

"A boy!" the physician called out, handing the baby to Philippa.

Queen Anne gushed with joy and ran over to Philippa's side to get a closer look at the baby.

"His name shall be Stephan," Philippa said, rocking the baby in her arms. She looked up at the midwife again, and another chill came over her body. "What can I do to pay you for your kindness?" Philippa stared at the midwife, who continued to smile at her.

"Nothing needs to be done highness; all is well," she said as she gathered her belongings. "I have done this service for the crown. You need your rest. I have left you with a few more herbs for pain. Warm them in water and drink all the contents. Your strength will return in a few days, just remember what I said and all will be well. I must go."

Before the woman could leave the room, Queen Anne took her hand and placed a bag of gold coins in it. "I know that you said that you did not need any payment, but I insist."

The midwife looked at the bag of coins and bowed. "Thank you, Milady," she said and curtsied. "I must go now."

"Of course." Queen Anne opened the chamber room door. "Thank you again."

The midwife bowed her head and hurried out of the chamber and Queen Anne closed the door behind her.

Jasper was a nervous wreck as he waited to hear about the condition of Philippa and his child. He overheard the other servants saying the labor was long and that Philippa was not doing so well. Jasper was concerned for the wellbeing of his child since the baby was coming so much earlier than anticipated.

Jasper could not wait for the chance to hold his baby in his arms and complete his infiltration back into the kingdom. He paced steadily in front of the castle wall waiting to receive news about Philippa and the baby. As he begun to make his next pass around the drawbridge, he saw an older woman approaching from the castle. She stopped in front of him and smiled, her appearance transforming into the beautiful younger face Jasper had seen once before. It was Sema, his wife's teacher of the dark arts. Jasper believed she had been burned alive with Faerydae for practicing witchcraft. He was wrong.

"What are you doing here at this castle? I thought you were dead."

Sema chuckled loudly and adjusted her bag around her hip. "That is what I wanted you to believe. I have been watching you all this time Jasper. You have brought death to your wife, and your misgivings with the princess will have consequences. You shall answer for that day in the forest. The day that your wife tried to assist you, and you allowed us to be captured."

Jasper was dumbfounded. He thought his plan was solid, but now understood she saw right through him.

"I know who you truly are," Sema continued. "All has been foretold, and your actions will catch up with you in the future."

"What have you done, Sema? What have you done to Philippa and my child?"

Sema smiled and proceeded over the drawbridge passing Jasper. She swiveled around one last time.

"I have done nothing more, then facilitate the beginning and the end of you and your precious Philippa. The secrets that lie with you both shall come to the light in the future." And with the end of her sentence, she disappeared.

Jasper tried to process what had happened, and what Sema had said to him. He was unable to give the conversation any more thought because he heard the horns blowing outside of the castle.

"An announcement," he said to himself.

Jasper took off in a jog in the direction of the horns. As he approached the main entrance, a crowd of peasants gathered to hear the awaited announcement. All of them waited in anticipation.

Jasper hoped that everything was okay. In what seemed like a long while, he stood there becoming more nervous. Finally, the steward announced the Queen Mother, and she appeared at the window. The peasants and the court cheered below, and Queen Anne raised her arms to quiet down the crowd.

"To my great court and countrymen and women. I know many of you had heard of the difficulty of the delivery of Philippa's child, but I am pleased to announce that all is well, and you now have a new prince and future king."

The crowd went mad with cheering, and Queen Anne had to quiet them down once more.

"May I announce to you my grandson, Prince Stephan," she said reaching down and picking up the baby in her arms.

Jasper smiled. It was the first opportunity to see his son.

Philippa had told him he had to keep up the charade of the child being David's until they could be together. He wanted so badly to have been by Philippa's side and to hold his child.

"I will see them both," he mumbled under his breath. "Tonight I will sneak in to see them both."

He took one more glance at his mother holding his son and parted from the crowd back to the stables where he belonged. Nightfall finally had come, and Jasper got his chance to sneak into the castle to see the baby and Philippa.

He had a new son and his brother's wife. Jasper's plan was moving forward as it should. He waited until the cover of darkness and scaled the wall up into Philippa's chamber room. He peered through the window making sure the room was emptied of servants and the queen mother. When all was quiet, he made his way into the chamber.

Philippa lay on the bed eyes closed, the baby nearby in the crib. Jasper moved his way over to the bed leaned over and kissed her gently on the lips. Philippa opened her eyes and gave Jasper a half smile.

"What are you doing up here?" she whispered, still weak and tired from the delivery.

"I had to come and see you. If I did not come in the night, I am not sure when you would have been strong enough to leave the castle surroundings. Are you all right? How are you feeling?"

"I am tired," she sighed, then shifted on the bed trying to find a comfortable position.

"Stop moving and relax Philippa. You will wear yourself out. I will not stay long; I just wanted to hold the baby and see you."

Philippa obeyed Jasper's request and relaxed back into the pillow. She grabbed his hand and pulled it to her lips kissing it softly.

"I thank you for coming to see me, Jasper. I wished you could have been with me during the delivery."

"As do I. I waited for word on you and the child like everyone else. I am so pleased that we have had a son." He clutched her hand in his.

Philippa turned her head in the direction of the cradle. "The baby is in his cradle. Go ahead and get a look at him."

Jasper stood up from Philippa's bedside and walked over to where the child slept in his crib.

"Please do not wake him. His crying will alert the wet nurse. If you are caught in here, it will be death for you and me."

"You do not have to worry, Philippa; I will not wake him." Jasper leaned in watching the baby sleep.

"Come back and sit next to me my love." Philippa reached out her hand.

Jasper left the sleeping baby and returned to Philippa's bed-side.

"We do not have much time before I will be checked on again. I just wanted to tell you something I have been keeping to myself for some time Jasper. I think this is the right moment for me to share it with you now."

"What is it that you want to share my love?" Jasper assumed he knew what she was going to tell him.

"After the events of my delivery and my near death, I could not go another day without telling you that I love you. I am in love with you Jasper, and not David nor anyone else can keep us apart. I want us to be together. And I am ready to do what it takes for you to be king. As you know, I was born into royalty before I came to England and married David."

"Yes, I am aware that you were a princess before coming here."

"I am the only child born to my parents and the sole heir to the throne of Portugal. Upon my father's death, I will ascend the throne and become Queen of Portugal as well as the Queen of England. I am willing to leave England and divorce David. We can then be married, and you shall be crowned the King of Portugal."

Jasper smiled, at all he had heard. He never considered leaving England and becoming King of Portugal. It would be a valid solution if his plan did go as he wanted. He was confused about his feelings towards Philippa. He was not sure he if he was in love with her. His plan to regain the throne had always been more important than any feelings he had. It was too important to abandon.

"I love you too." He leaned into kissing her once more. He was not able to get another word in before they both saw a light from underneath the chamber room door.

"You must go, that will be one of the servants or Queen Anne checking on me."

Jasper stood and headed back to the window. He turned once more to Philippa before he slipped out into the night. "I shall see you again my love," he said, climbing out of the window scaling the castle wall back into the darkness.

The sails dropped, the sea calmed to barely a stir and the Lady Fantasy pulled her massive body into Ellesmere Port. Two years had passed, and David and his remaining crew were home.

David's coronation was the week after his arrival back at Westminster Castle. He was officially sworn in as the King of England and Philippa was crowned his queen.

David found his strolls in the outskirts of the kingdom the time for thinking. He mainly thought of his plan to rescue his beloved and how he would get her back to England. The information that Jamond shared with him about Eleni being alive was enough for him to keep living. He hoped that Jamond would send word when they were safely out of France, and he could retrieve them both and bring them to safety. Philippa interrupted his solitude and thought with her yelling.

"David," she called out to him as she approached him from off in the distance.

He spun around in the direction Philippa was coming and met her in the courtyard.

"Philippa, what are you doing out here? You should be resting."

"David, I am fine, I have rested, and truly there is no need for you to worry about me. As I explained to you before you left on your voyage, I told you I would be your wife and have children with you to fulfill my duties as your queen, but everything else is off limits. I have no desire to be anything more to you."

"Philippa, it was never my intention to have hurt you. I would like for us to try to get along for the sake of our son, and any future children we might have. I hope you will forgive me for my previous actions."

"David I appreciate all you have said, and I will take your words into consideration. I however only came to let you know a messenger on horseback has arrived in our kingdom demanding to speak only to you. He said that he had word on a situation you inquired about when you first came home. Do you care to fill me in on what this situation is? Is there a need to worry about our son.?"

"No, there is nothing you need to worry yourself about, Philippa. I had made some inquiries about a situation that occurred while I was away. This situation has nothing to do with anything here in the kingdom. I thank you for coming to find me; that was very kind of you."

David kissed Philippa on the cheek, brushed past her and hurried back to the castle. Could it be the information that he was waiting for? Could Jamond have sent word like he promised? If Eleni were alive and brought back to England, he would dissolve his loveless marriage to Philippa and send her back to Portugal. David would bring the guardian law back into power and send his son away from the court. He would allow Philippa to have limited visitation to their son because he was the sole heir to the English throne. He then would make Eleni his wife and queen, and they would start their life and family together.

Philippa was left standing in the courtyard with no words. She did not know the David she had just encountered. It was the first brief conversation the two of them had since he arrived back at home. Everything he said to her was something she had wanted to hear him say from the first moments they met. She was still in love with him but felt guilty for admitting that because of how much she loved Jasper and the plan she was putting into place to leave England.

Where are these feelings coming from? How could she still be in love with David? Everything she had told Jasper was the truth, she loved him and wanted David to pay for hurting her. Should she confess Stephan's true paternity to Jasper? Philippa was not sure what her next step should be. She could only hear the voice of the mystic woman in her head.

"The secrets that lie within shall be revealed someday" She was frightened to think what those words could mean.

David made it back to the castle out of breath, excited, and nervous about the news the messenger had brought with him. He sped into the throne room where his mother was entertaining the man. He knew that she would be trying to get information as to his visit and why he was there. David hoped that the messenger did not crack under the pressure from his mother.

"Mother, I thank you for keeping this young man engaged, but you can leave us now." David strode deeper into the room.

Queen Anne and the messenger turned towards David.

"My son, I am pleased you arrived. I was just having a conversation with this young man, asking him what brings him to our home."

"I'm sure you were, Mother. Now if you excuse us, I would like to have a private conversation with this young man."

"Well if you do not need any assistance, I shall leave you both to your conversation. I will not be far if you need me, David."

"Thank you, Mother." David extended an arm in the direction the two men should walk. The messenger walked deeper into the throne room, across to another room. David closed the door behind him.

"Please sit down." David offered a chair to him.

The young man appeared nervous but took a seat as the king asked of him.

"What information have you obtained of the whereabouts of Queen Eleni? Is she dead or alive?"

The messenger pulled a letter from his bag and handed to David.

He tore open the letter reading it thoroughly. A wide grin crossed his face. He slammed his fist into his father's desk and let out a laugh. Jamond had sent word that he had made it to France. Eleni was indeed alive.

19 Betrayal

Rain soaked and in pain, Eleni made it up the dirt bridge back to the castle. She struggled to open the castle door, dropping the bucket she carried in her hands on the floor of the doorway. She screamed out in pain. Katlego, another slave, who also assisted in the queen's delivery, heard Eleni's screams as she scrubbed the floors nearby. Dropping her scrub brush back into the bucket as the second round of screams sounded, she ran over to the castle entrance to assist her friend. Speaking in their native tongue, she asked if Eleni was all right and helped her to her feet.

"Please get me to my room," Eleni responded through the pain.

Katlego nodded in understanding, wrapped one arm around Eleni's waist and wrapped one of Eleni's arms around her neck balancing Eleni's weight against her own. Walking slowly, they made it to the base of the staircase and started to ascend the stairs to her room.

Rachelle, who happened to be passing through the corridor, heard the commotion and Eleni's screams, decided she would alert the queen. She spun around back towards the kitchen to put down her basket of fruit. When she entered the kitchen, the cook was busy kneading some bread.

"I thought you were taking the fruit out to the stable hands?" the cook asked curiously.

"I will, after..." Rachelle's voice trailed off.

"After what?" the cook asked.

"Nothing..." she rested the basket of fruit on the table. "That bitch of a slave is going into labor." Rachelle sighed.

"Well now, she's in labor?" the cook responded still kneading the bread at the table.

More servants bustled in and out of the kitchen preparing for the evening meal. Their conversations and laughter annoyed Rachelle further.

"Yes! she is in labor, I heard and saw her out in the corridor." Rachelle slammed her hand down on the wooden table. "She does not deserve to have a baby. That slave girl has been nothing but trouble for me since she came here."

"Oh Rachelle, you need to stop being so angry about the king's decision to remove you as the lady in waiting. You should not say such things. It is a horrible thing to say about her not deserving her baby."

"Well, it is true. She does not deserve it. Besides, I can be as angry as I want to be. It is because of her I am unable to see the queen. My life is no longer the same."

"Well what do you expect to do about your current predicament, Rachelle?" the cooked asked.

"I'm going to get her out of this kingdom, and out of my life if it is the last thing I do!"

The cook stopped kneading her bread and frowned at Rachelle. "And how do you plan to go about getting her out of the kingdom?"

"Well, to start I am going to tell the queen of what is happening. The rest will come to me in time."

"You should not start things you cannot finish Rachelle. Be careful of the game you are playing; you could get that girl hurt or killed."

"Do not worry about me, if she gets killed, it will be of her own doing. Besides, what harm can come of alerting the queen of what is going on in her castle?

Rachelle smiled at the cook and untied her apron, throwing it down on the table and leaving the kitchen to find the queen. She had searched the upper and lower halls before she decided to go out into the rain and head to the chapel. She roamed the court-yard. The rain had died down to a drizzle. As she approached the chapel, she ran into the queen coming out of the chapel door. Rachelle was excited. It had been weeks since she and the queen last saw each other.

"Your Majesty," she called out as she approached the queen.

Queen Vivienne swirled around and saw Rachelle standing there.

"What are you doing out here? you should be back in the kitchen preparing the evening meal for the court."

Rachelle's excitement waned when she heard the queen's tone.

"Are you not happy to see me?" She stepped forward to stroke the queen's face.

Vivienne slapped her hand away. Rachelle pulled her, hand back towards her massaging it in pain.

"I'm sorry for touching you, your Majesty." Rachelle winced.

Vivienne adjusted her dress and glared up into Rachelle's eyes. "Of course, I am happy to see you, Rachelle," She kissed her and released her hand.

"However, this is not the time or place for personal encounters. If I needed you for anything, I would have sent someone to fetch you. You, however, have still not answered my question as to why you are seeking me out."

Rachelle perked up with the little attention Queen Vivienne had shown her. "I was looking for you to notify you about the commotion I saw earlier. Eleni, the slave girl, was screaming and was being led up to her room with the other slave woman. It looked as if she was going to give birth."

"Hmmm well, well, well... Rachelle, I will have to see about this situation. Thank you for informing me."

"Do you have to return to the castle so soon?" Rachelle was desperate to keep the queen's attention.

"I have things I must do, Rachelle. But I promise we shall see each other soon. I never go back on my word."

Vivienne pulled Rachelle into a gentle embrace, kissing Rachelle on the lips. Rachelle's stomach churned with butterflies.

"Come to me later this evening when everyone is asleep, Rachelle. I will show you my gratitude for your information. "The queen passed by her, leaving Rachelle standing in front of the chapel as the rain started to pour again.

Queen Vivienne sauntered alone to the castle entrance, removing her hood upon entering the castle. She approached the stairs and climbed them to the tower to Eleni's room. As Vivienne approached the door in the tower, she could hear screams coming from within. With no hesitation, Vivienne opened the door, covering her mouth in horror from all the blood she saw pooled on the floor.

Eleni was still drenched from rain water, blood running down her legs. Katlego was moving about the room frantically trying to get Eleni situated. She handed the queen a bowl with water in it. Queen Vivienne scowled at her.

"What am I supposed to do with this?"

Eleni looked blankly at her. "She handed it to you so you can assist in delivering this child, she cannot deliver it on her own. I will walk you both through the process."

"Walk us through the process? You mean for me to assist in delivering your child? I am a queen; it is beneath me to do such a thing."

"Milady, there is no time," Eleni screamed out in pain, feeling the pressure of the baby crowning between her legs. "This child is coming now, so you will be in this room and help us or get out." Eleni took a deep breath between pants. She spoke something in her native language to Katlego, who moved over and spread Eleni's legs wider. With the nod of her head, Eleni knew the time had come for her to push the baby out.

Queen Vivienne stayed rooted in her spot in the room. She stood in silence with the bowl in her hand as Eleni talked Katlego through the process and worked to get the child delivered.

Katlego gave one last command in her language. Eleni obeyed pushing one final time. The child was born; Katlego pulled the baby the rest of the way out, cut the umbilical cord and handed the baby to Eleni.

Eleni looked down with tears in her eyes. She had given birth to a little girl. She held her baby daughter in her arms. A beautiful daughter created from the love between her and David. How she wished he could have been there for that glorious moment to see their precious child.

The baby girl was born with a full head of dark blonde, reddish curls, a light tan complexion, and her eye color was the same sparkling blue her father David had. She continued to look over her daughter, finding she had a heart shaped birthmark on her shoulder. Eleni took the birthmark as a sign.

She will be blessed!

She had given birth to a miracle child. Her many prayers to the creator were answered. The baby fussed and cried. To Soothe her, Eleni put her to her breast so she could feed. The baby quieted and suckled at her breast. Eleni glanced over at where Vivienne still stood and smiled.

Vivienne glared at both Eleni and the fair headed little girl she held in her arms.

"How could a baby be born to someone with a complexion like Eleni's be so fair?" She said to herself. Vivienne's mind whirled with an idea. The thought of revenge plagued her mind for the loss of her daughter.

It had only been a few nights since Vivienne had lost her daughter. She had convinced herself that Eleni was the one at fault for killing her. It was as if the perfect plan and opportunity were laid at her feet. King Edmond was away dealing with issues from other nobles in the court and the uprising due to famine, and Vivienne had secretly had her baby disposed of, so there would be no discovery. Her plan was genius.

This slave girl did not deserve a baby. Especially one who looked as fair and beautiful. Eleni would never be able to prove the child was her daughter. No one would believe her if she tried. Edmond would fall in love with the little girl. She would be their daughter.

Vivienne knew from the moment she saw the infant; she would claim Eleni's baby as her own. The child she held in her arms would become hers and Edmond's princess, their daughter Sabine. Vivienne stepped closer to the bed where Eleni laid.

"May I hold her Eleni?" Vivienne asked, holding out her arms for the baby.

Eleni smiled and handed the baby to the queen.

Katlego came around from where the queen stood and started cleaning up Eleni, and gathered the bloody sheets and towels used in the birthing process.

"She is beautiful, is she not?" Eleni asked.

The queen stepped back and rocked the baby gently in her arms admiring how fair she was. "Yes, she is quite beautiful Eleni," she answered steadily rocking the baby. "Have you decided on a name for this child?"

"Yes, I shall call her Gwenaelle meaning holy and generous. She shall be generous to all those around her, and raised in the faith."

"Well, Gwenaelle is quite a name, Eleni."

Eleni laid back into the bed and winced in pain. She was feeling tired and sore from the delivery.

"Are you all right Eleni?" Vivienne asked coming closer to Eleni's bedside.

"I am fine, I am in a little pain and quite tired after the delivery."

"Well, let me go and get you something for the pain." Queen Vivienne handed Gwenaelle back to Eleni. "I shan't be long," she said, walking out of Eleni's tower room.

"Yes Milady, and thank you." Eleni kissed her daughter on the forehead.

Queen Vivienne had not been gone very long when she returned with a cup of warm liquid. "Drink this down," she said offering Eleni the cup.

"What is this liquid, Milady?" Eleni asked.

"It is something that will take away your pain, a home remedy of sorts." She forced the cup again into Eleni's hand.

Eleni hesitated before finally drinking the contents. She felt fine for a moment but began to feel woozy. She looked around and called out to Katlego, but the queen had sent her away. Glancing back in the direction of the queen, she noticed that the queen's demeanor had changed. She looked at Eleni with a cold blank stare.

"What have you done to me?" Eleni asked trying to get out of the bed.

Queen Vivienne pushed Eleni back into the bed and covered her with blankets. "Nothing more than you deserve, sweet Eleni. You need to rest. Your baby will be here when you awaken from your nap."

"No, I am not tired, and I am not leaving my child in your care," Eleni stated, starting to drift off to sleep.

"Your daughter shall be here when you awaken."

Eleni tried to speak once more, but the overwhelming need for sleep overcame her. She fell back into the pillow into a deep sleep.

Queen Vivienne stepped into putting her plan into action. She picked up little Gwenaelle and headed out the room.

"You shall be my daughter now, precious one," she said, talking to the baby. She headed to her room first and rang the bell for the kitchen staff. She knew Rachelle would come running. Not long after she rang the bell, there was a knock on her door.

"Enter." Queen Vivienne rocked her newly claimed daughter. "Rachelle, this is my little girl, I wanted you to be the first to meet her."

"She is beautiful Milady." Rachelle came forward, smiling. She leaned over to kiss Vivienne on the lips. "I know you wanted me to come to you tonight, would you like me to come sooner?"

"Well, Rachelle, I have to admit these last few days have been tiresome, and I think I have over-exerted myself. I shall spend this evening with my daughter. I did not want you to think I had forgotten about our arrangement."

"No, Milady! I understand, I have missed you and your company and wanted..." her voice trailed off, as she tried to hold back the tears.

"Your desires do not go unwarranted, precious Rachelle. When I have need of them again, I shall call on you. I wanted you to see the baby, and to tell you my dinner needs to be served in the royal chambers tonight. The king is due to arrive at any time, and I want him to see me rested and well when he returns."

"Yes, Milady." Rachelle tried to kiss the queen once more and this time, it was followed by a slap to the face.

"Do not ever think you can kiss me again without me asking you or giving you permission!" The Queen shouted. "Get out of my room and do what you are told."

Vivienne took her new daughter and put her in the crib in the room prepared for her arrival. She knew she had to get rid of the servants who witnessed the birth of her biological daughter.

As little Sabine slept, Vivienne paced the room back and forth, piecing together the next part of her plan. The woman who had been helping Vivienne through delivery pain and the grief of losing her daughter stepped out from the shadows. She approached Vivienne from behind placing her wrinkled, bony hands upon Vivienne's shoulder.

"What is troubling you my queen? Are you still having pain? Do I need to mix another potion for you, my dear?"

"No Sema, I am fine. Tell me, upon your travels have you come up with a spell to rid a person of demons surrounding them?"

"There are many demons my dear. You need to specify what you require, and who are these demons?"

"These demons are the ones who witnessed the delivery and death of my biological daughter. And the woman who is at fault for all of it. Help me be rid of them."

"There is one who can assist you with your problem. He is here in the Kingdom residing in the body of one of your slaves."

"Who is this person?" Vivienne spun around, and Sema had disappeared.

Who was the old woman speaking of? She thought long and hard and remembered the male slave who was in her room when she delivered. She yanked open her chamber room door and called out to the guard outside her room.

"Bring me the male slave, my husband, brought into this kingdom some days ago."

"Yes, Milady." The guard moved hurriedly to retrieve Berhanua.

Queen Vivienne closed the door behind her and clapped her hands. "I will get everything I want, and I shall have my revenge on Eleni," she said smiling.

Moments later, the door sounded with three knocks. Vivienne opened the chamber room forcefully to see a tall and handsome dark-skinned man standing before her. She had not looked at him closely before, but she had to admit, if only to herself, that he was handsome. Muscular, bald, and beautiful.

"Come in." Vivienne exhaled as she gestured for him to enter the room. She closed the door behind them and took a seat at her table by the fireplace. Berhanua stood silently in front of her.

"Do you understand my language?" the queen asked.

Berhanua nodded.

"Good," she responded. "It seems as if you and Eleni are quite educated for slaves. Speak freely; you do not have to stand there like I am going to bite you." She chuckled.

"Why am I here your Majesty? what is it that you require of me?"

The queen shifted in her seat, cocking her head to the side and gaping at Berhanua's body.

Such a beautiful specimen of a man.

"You are here because I am in need of a person who can be discreet and solve a few problems for me."

"What type of challenges do you have Milady? How can I resolve them? You are a queen of this kingdom; you have all the power in your hands."

Vivienne winced out in pain grabbing her stomach from the delivery of her daughter. She picked up a chalice from the table drinking the remaining contents Sema had mixed for her earlier that evening.

I just want to forget it ever happened. Eleni is the reason my baby is dead.

Vivienne focused her attention back on Berhanua. He was smart as well, and she enjoyed the way he conveyed his words. "Well-spoken slave, I do have the power. But the situation I need to have taken care of requires secrecy and the utmost privacy. If you can follow through with what I ask of you. The reward will be great."

"What is it, you believe I want?" Berhanua asked crossing his arms.

"You want your freedom and Eleni's."

"Do not tell me it is not true slave. I have seen the way you look at her when you believe no one is noticing. You have the look of love written all over your face".

"I care for Eleni, your Majesty. I still, however, do not understand why you have brought me here or what I can do for you."

Queen Vivienne stood up from her seat and started to walk around the room. "There is much you can do to assist me." She continued pacing. "I need you to dispose of the servants who were in my room the night I gave birth to my biological daughter."

Berhanua's face dropped, and a frown appeared. "Why would you want those servants disposed of Majesty?"

"Because slave, no one can know I lost the child."

"I have already destroyed all of the evidence Milady. No one would ever know."

A noise came from the adjoining room, then a baby's cry filled the air. The queen left Berhanua standing where he was and went to the fetch the child. She and an older woman joined Berhanua back in the room, Vivienne carrying a baby girl in her arms. Berhanua started to put the pieces together in his head of what was happening.

The queen wanted to dispose of those who knew the truth. She had taken someone's child and claimed the baby as her own. He was aware that the only other woman pregnant in the castle along with the queen was Eleni. And he now saw that Queen Vivienne had claimed Eleni's child as her own.

"You see slave, this is my daughter now, her name is now Sabine. No one will ever know the truth of how she came to be here. "With your help and Sema's, you can have what you want, and I can have what I want."

"Whose child are you holding your Majesty?"

"I think you already know whose child this is. She no longer has a child." Queen Vivienne sat back down on the chair and unlatched the bodice of her gown allowing the child nurse on her swollen breast.

"What if I decide not to help you, your Majesty."

She rocked the baby in her arms and ran her fingers through the little girl's soft curls.

"If you decide not to help me, slave, death would become your punishment. You have already destroyed evidence for me. I could easily say you plotted with your dear Eleni to kill my child and myself."

Berhanua had no choice and was backed into a corner. If he did not do what the queen asked of him, he would be killed. Death would be a relief for him. He would be able to join his sister and his lover. Before he was able to give his answer, Sema stepped toward Berhanua placing her hand upon his chest. She mumbled a few words causing his head to pound in an immense amount of pain. Berhanua dropped to the floor screaming.

"What are you doing to me?"

Sema continued to chant loudly until Berhanua passed out. She then faced Vivienne and cackled.

"The person you have been waiting to speak to will be with us shortly."

Vivienne and Sema waited in silence for Berhanua to awaken. His body twitched and shifted on the floor in convulsions and then fell still. His eyes opened, his pupils rolling to the back of his head before stabilizing. He regained consciousness and got to his feet. When Vivienne looked into his eyes; she could sense that she was looking at a different person.

"Awe... You have awoken me; I have heard everything you said. I will do what you ask of me Majesty."

"Good... awakened one, now as I was saying previously, I want the other three women servants beside you and Eleni, who were in my chambers the night of my misfortune disposed of. I do not care how you dispose of them. Their bodies are not to be found, all I ask for is proof of death by bringing me two sets of nipples from the French servants and place them in the boxes that are sitting on my table." She turned in the direction of the table.

He shook his head in agreement his eyes slanted into narrow slits, and the wide sexy and mysterious smile crossed his face. Arkamun had been resurrected. He grabbed the two jeweled encrusted boxes off the table and placed them into a satchel.

"I will personally see to it that there is no evidence of Eleni ever giving birth in her chambers or elsewhere."

Vivienne ran her hand down his cheek and smiled at him flirtatiously. "Now go and wait in the adjoining room and I will call for my French girls to come to me. There is no time to waste. The King will be returning to the castle soon."

Again Sema disappeared into the night.

Arkamun bowed his head and moved into the adjoining chamber as Queen Vivienne asked. She then rang her bell and the guard at the door entered.

"You rang the bell, my queen?" The guard asked, entering the room.

"Yes, I did, please bring me the servant girls Morgaine and Neva. I have some things I need to discuss with them in private."

The guard bowed his head and obliged her orders. Vivienne closed the door behind the guard with her foot. She rocked Sabine in her arms and placed the sleeping baby back into the cradle in the chamber room where Arkamun hid.

"Keep her quiet," the queen said to him as she moved back to the front room and laid across her chaise.

A few moments later, another three firm knocks hit Vivienne's door. "Enter." Vivienne swiveled her body around on her chaise so she could see the servant girls enter the room.

"You sent for us?" Morgaine pulled Neva into the chamber room behind her.

"Yes, I did. Close the door behind you and come closer. I have something I would like to discuss with you."

Neva slammed the door shut behind them, and the two girls strode closer to the queen.

"Now you two can stop there."

"Yes, your Majesty," both of the girls answered in unison.

"I am sure you both are wondering why I have called you to my chambers on this very night," Vivienne said with a smile.

Both of the girls looked at each other, Neva speaking up first.

"Yes, we both were wondering why you asked us here? We had hoped you had recovered from your terrible loss of the princess."

Morgaine, finding her voice, interjected into the conversation.

"Yes, we both had wondered if you were okay, we did not say a word to the other servants about what happened here."

Vivienne shifted on her chaise and crossed her arms." Well, I can assure you both, I am well. I thank you for your concern about your queen, but my misfortune is not why I asked you two to come here."

Morgaine and Neva looked at one another, confused.

"So why did you summon us? And why are we here Your Majesty?" Neva asked.

"You are here, my darlings because I know a secret about the two of you."

The girls looked at each other, confused again, then back at the queen.

"What secret could that be?" Morgaine asked.

Queen Vivienne let out a loud laugh and clapped her hands together in enjoyment. "I have seen how you both have been looking at my dark man slave, and I get the distinct feeling you both would like to know how his hard cock would feel inside of your little pink pussies. That, my darlings, is the secret."

Neva and Morgaine stood quietly. They had never heard the Queen speak with such vulgar language, and she was indeed right about their secret. They both had seen the dark male slave around the kingdom and castle. His half nude body aroused them both as well as half of the French servant women of the court. No one, of course, would dare say they were curious about him or wanted to see more of his body.

"How did you come into this knowledge, Your Majesty?" Morgaine asked.

"It is my job to know everything going on in this kingdom and castle; I have eyes and ears everywhere. So I take it with the silence of both of you ladies; my previous statement was correct. You are indeed curious about my dark and handsome man slave."

Neva took a deep a breath and crossed her arms over her chest, rubbing the sides of her breasts.

"Yes," she replied. "Yes, we are curious about your man slave, but none of us servants would ever dare..." her voice trailed off. "None of us servants would cross you, Milady, or take a chance in speaking with him."

"Oh, I am very aware my darlings; none of you would cross me, you two helped me in my time of need, so I found this time to be appropriate to reward you with a gift."

"A gift?" Morgaine asked. "What type of gift, and what did we do to gain such a reward?"

Vivienne slid her legs off the side of the chaise, standing up to approach the girls. She paused in front of Morgaine and took her hand.

"The gift, my sweet Morgaine, is a night for the two of you with my dark man slave. I want to reward you both for your help in delivering my child. I want you to experience all there is to experience with a man."

She let go of Morgaine's hand and waddled around the room. "I want you to feel his cock inside of the depth of your oceans, and for both you to be brought to eternal bliss with him and each other. Does this not sound like an enjoyable time?"

"Yes Milady!" they both answered excitedly.

"I want you both to be in my elite group of friends, and we can share and compare experiences together. I would like for you two to become more than servants. I would like for you two to become productive members of the court. The opportunities for you both are endless."

The queen continued her conversation with the servants, and Arkamun heard every word she spun into a silvery lie. The plan was set, he was to sleep with these women, have his way with them, and end their lives. To regain control over Eleni, he would do this. As he listened, he heard a faint sound coming from the cradle. The child had started to stir about the crib.

He turned sideways reaching his arm into the cradle soothing the little girl back to sleep before she cried out.

"You were the reason for your mother's demise. She could never produce and heir for me, but she could produce one for that bastard, King David."

Arkamun released the grip on the crib and turned towards the queen who was now back in front of him.

"I take it you heard everything you are to do with those servant girls?" She brushed past him, taking the baby in her arms.

"Yes, I heard everything Majesty."

"Good, I have drawn a map to the cottage I will be giving you as a reward for your obedience. It is far from the castle, and you can take Eleni there when the job is done."

Arkamun snickered and nodded his head.

Vivienne kissed her daughter again and put the baby back down in the wooden cradle. She then walked over to Arkamun, tipping his chin up with her index finger to look into his eyes.

"You will not fail me slave, or it will be the end of you and the one you hold close to you."

"Yes, your Majesty." He looked down deeply into her eyes. "You shall also rid me of the other slave woman upon bringing me my evidence. Kill her or take her with you; I do not care, as long as she is out of this castle.

"Yes, your Majesty."

"Now, you need to get going and started with tonight's adventures. I have been alerted that King Edmond will be arriving mid-day tomorrow, and all requirements need to be done before he makes his way back here to the castle."

Arkamun bowed one final time and left the chamber. He went back to his room and gathered the supplies he would need to make the lengthy walk to the cottage the queen had deeded to him. He did not trust her but was willing to do her bidding if this could lead to his regaining control over Eleni. He made it out of the barn, the cold air engulfing him as he headed out into the night. He approached the castle's stone wall from the left to avoid detection by the guards patrolling the gate around the moat.

Arkamun hid behind a tree and peered around to assure he had not been seen. The shadow of the night cloaked him in darkness. When the guards changed their positions and the coast was clear, he threw his bag over the gate into the sandbank below and scaled the wall. As he moved quietly, Arkamun stayed off the main road as she instructed. Doing so, protected him from the road bandits he had managed to sneak past unnoticed. Not many people were accustomed to seeing his kind in France, and he did not want to stir up any trouble or waste time while trying to achieve his goal.

After what seemed like an eternity, Arkamun arrived at the cottage, which in his eyes was more like a shack. It was small covered with straw and made with mud and stone at the base. It was still dark and was only illuminated by the glow of the full moon overhead. Arkamun checked his surroundings, making sure no one was in the clearing of the cottage before he proceeded inside. Upon opening the door and walking inside a cloud of dust blew out into his face. The cottage had been abandoned and unused for some time.

He wondered how Vivienne knew of this place. Once the dust settled, he stepped inside and saw a stove, a pot for cooking, blankets, and two flimsy straw mattresses on the ground. Arkamun threw his bag down on the ground of the cottage and walked back outside to find wood to start a fire. Upon his gathering wood, he noticed two little beady eyes glowing at him in the dark. Without hesitation or a sound, the wolf charged at him missing his target.

Arkamun dropped the wood he carried into the grass and assumed a defensive stance. The lone wolf tried to attack him a second time, this time, Arkamun snatched the wolf's head with his bare hands, breaking its neck with a twist of his muscular arms. He had not had the opportunity to hunt with such fierceness since before his death in Abyssinia.

This wolf will make a royal feast tonight.

He dragged the dead wolf closer to the light so he could skin the animal. Once he had finished, he returned to the cottage retrieving the cauldron so he could gather the wolf meat to prepare a stew. Arkamun added all the ingredients needed for his dinner and returned the pot to its place in the cottage, and awaited his guests to arrive.

Neva and Morgaine left the queen's chambers feeling excited. They would have their night with the Abyssinian slave and then inducted into the queen's elite group. They could not stop smiling and giggle about their good fortune. The queen was so generous, in purchasing them seductive robes to wear to their engagement. She also treated them to a bubble bath and had their hair and makeup done for the evening. After they were primped and pampered the servant girls were met by a carriage at the castle wall to take them to their destination.

Clasping each other's hands and smiling, they giggled again and entered the carriage and sat down as the footmen held the door open for them. Once they settled into their seats, the carriage pulled off from the castle wall into the dark forest.

"Well, this is quite the adventure," Morgaine said to Neva, still clutching her hand.

"It is quite the adventure; I am curious about how the dark man looks in the nude. I was told by some of the other servant women that have seen him bathe that he has a massive cock, a lot bigger than we should expect." Neva laughed.

Morgaine smiled in return at Neva and the two of them busted out in laughter. "I am sure he is quite the marvel Neva, as are you," Morgaine said feeling a little frisky from the wine she had before leaving the castle. She leaned over and kissed Neva on the lips.

Neva had never been kissed by a man nor a woman before, so to see Morgaine become aggressive made her slightly nervous. She pushed Morgaine gently off her.

"Oh, Morgaine, what are you doing? You know I have never been with anyone. We should take it slow and wait until we reach our destination."

"Neva, I am sorry I had forgotten and got caught in the moment... it must be the wine that is making me feel so... but you are so beautiful... and I have always wanted to..."

"Wanted to do what Morgaine?"

"Neva, I had always wondered what it would be like to kiss you and taste you, and touch you, and now I am getting my chance to fulfill that desire."

Neva's cheeks turned red from blushing. She did not respond to what Morgaine had confessed to her. Instead, she got quiet and shifted her glance to look out of the carriage window. The mood in the carriage changed, and they rode the rest of the way in silence.

Arkamun's eyes opened, from his brief nap, to find his body covered in blood from the encounter with the wolf and a strong smell of stew cooking in the cottage. Walking inside, he saw that stew had finished cooking and was ready to eat.

Hmmm, dinner.

He scooped a heaping serving into the bowl on the little wooden table by the hearth. He barely had a chance to assess his surroundings and finish eating when he heard the clicking of hooves in the dirt road leading to the cottage. He retrieved his bag of knives by the door, removed them and placed them in strategic locations around the room for easy access.

He did not know which knife he would need first and how long it would take to complete the task, but he would not leave it up to the real Berhanua to regain control to finish it. Berhanua was always weak in his mind. So caring, loving and compassionate. He would never complete the task the Queen had given him.

Arkamun finished cleaning the blood off his hands and chest. He peered out the window near the door as the carriage came to a stop in front the cottage.

The two women exited the carriage and walked up the cobblestone path. Three knocks softly hit the wooden door. He swung the door open, stepped back and allowed the women to enter the cottage. The two women smiled, crossed the threshold and closed the door behind them. Arkamun gestured for the women to sit down, in front of the fire. They both obliged and sat down warming their hands against the tall flames burning underneath the cauldron.

"Are either of you two hungry?" Arkamun asked in French.

"Hmmm, no sir, we have already eaten. But we both thank you for your offer," Neva said nervously. "I'm Neva, and this is Morgaine. She pointed to the girl next to her.

Arkamun glanced at both women and was immensely aroused. They were both beautiful specimens. He smiled widely about what the night would bring. Thoughts of how he would kill them both excited him. But for now, he would play nice, giving the ladies the treats they desired. And when they least expected, he would take what he needed from them.

"What is your name?" Morgaine asked feeling a little more comfortable in her surroundings.

"My name is Arka..." he paused before he released his full sentence. "My name is Berhanua."

"Well, it is nice to make your acquaintance, Berhanua. We often wondered if you spoke French like the slave girl we have seen around the Queen. It is nice to know not all of your kind are savages," Morgaine said excitedly.

"My thoughts exactly," Neva interjected. "Will you tell us about more about where you come from?"

"There is not a lot about my life you two would be interested in." He stood to untie his trousers, tossing them to the side of the cottage floor, exposing his muscular naked body to the both of them.

"I am sure what you see before you piques your interests more than my previous life before I came to your kingdom."

He stood naked before the two girls; his cock hardened from the breeze blowing through the cottage window encircling it.

Morgaine and Neva looked at each other excitedly and then at the large protruding organ in front of them. They had never seen skin so smooth and dark before, his muscles moved and flexed with every step he took.

Morgaine wasted no time, standing up in front of him. She untied the robe she wore and dropped it down over her shoulders, exposing her breasts. She was aroused and turned on by the handsome specimen standing before her. She walked over to where he stood, pulling him closer to her and forcefully pushed his head down to lick her hard pink nipples.

He obliged her command taking one her nipples in his mouth, tracing it with his tongue. She moaned out in pleasure, grabbing his left hand pushing it between her thighs to rub her hot and wet clit.

Neva was infatuated with what she saw happening but was a little apprehensive to get in on the action. She too stood up removing her robe and joined Morgaine at her side. She hesitantly kissed her on the lips.

Morgaine was surprised by Neva's kiss because of her shyness and the earlier rejection, but when she realized Neva was not pulling away from her, she allowed her tongue to find its way into Neva's mouth kissing her deeply.

Neva's body relaxed and embraced Morgaine's tongue in her mouth. She kissed her deeply in return, wrapping her hands around Morgaine's head. The moment seemed to last forever but was broken when Arkamun released his grasp on Morgaine's nipples and leg.

He stood up once again, shifting his attention towards Neva. She was the one he desired the most, mainly because she was weaker than Morgaine. She would be his first victim of the evening. Grabbing her by her hair and breaking the embrace she still shared with Morgaine, he yanked her curls from behind, tugging her so hard she stumbled backward.

Neva regained her balance and turned around to face him.

"On your knees," he said in French.

She obeyed his command and slid down on her knees to the cottage floor.

Arkamun walked in front of her and stood. "Take my cock in your mouth and suck it hard," he spoke again.

Neva was excited about this; she had never touched a man's penis, let alone a slave's. She once again obeyed him and did as she was told.

Morgaine was getting a little jealous of the attention he was paying to Neva, so she walked over to where he stood and tried to kiss him.

He refused her, wrapping his hand around her neck and threw her to the floor.

"Stay there until I say you can move," He growled.

She did not ask any questions. She ignored his command and joined Neva in sucking his hard cock. The two of them took turns pleasuring him and kissing each other in-between. The scene brought memories to his mind of a past life. Arkamun shut his eyes to remember how much he enjoyed having women at his beck and call, and he would find that pleasure again when the transition into the vessel he occupied was complete.

"Now stand up," he said, releasing them both from their knees. Neva and Moraine both stood as Arkamun asked.

"What would you like us to do now?" Neva grasped Morgaine's hand resting it on her breast.

"I am going to take both of you, and you shall both take each other. Once that is done our night together shall come to a close."

He separated Neva from Morgaine and kissed her passionately before dragging her down to the blanket he had spread out the floor. He laid down on his back gesturing for both of them to join him.

"Get on top of me," he ordered Neva.

Neva became nervous again, but Morgaine looked at her and smiled gesturing to her it was okay. Neva did as he asked and kneeled down to lie on the blanket as well. Before she could get comfortable, he had rolled over, wrapped his hands around her hips, and sat her on top of his hard cock. She winced in pain before relaxing again and allowing the pleasure to follow.

"Morgaine come and stand over me," he said before she could lay down on the other side of the blanket.

She did as she was told and stood over his head as he began to please her orally.

Slowly and deeply, Neva rode his cock and he licked and sucked Morgaine's clit until she released her juices into his mouth. Neva found pleasure in what she was feeling as well. She had never experienced a man before, and the sensation as she climaxed caused her to tilt her head back, riding him harder until she collapsed on his chest.

Arkamun felt somewhat pleased but was not satisfied. He was disgusted with Neva's performance. Pushing Neva off him, he stood up, snatching Morgaine from beside him and flung her into the cottage wall. He forced his penis inside Morgaine pumping her buttocks profusely. The rage he felt inside came to the surface.

Rough sex was the type of sex he remembered and enjoyed. Not the tender, loving sex he assumed Berhanua had with his lovers.

Morgaine tensed up from the pressure of his roughness and tried to move away from his grasp and hard thrusts.

"Please stop, you are too rough," she called out in pain.

"Shut up you whore," he said. "This is what you came here for is it not?" he continued thrusting himself deeper inside of her.

Morgaine turned her head to the side and glanced at Neva.

Neva could see that Morgaine was in pain and tried to assist her. "I think she has had enough, you need to stop," she said, approaching the two of them.

Arkamun turned his head towards Neva, as he continued to Morgaine's head down against the cottage wall with his right hand.

"I am the only one who can determine who has had enough, little girl. You should stay out of my way, or I could become angrier than I already am."

Neva knew he was serious, and stepped back in caution, dressing again with her robe.

After he had climaxed, Arkamun released Morgaine, who then ran over to pick up her dress and joined Neva on the other side of the room.

"We have gotten all we desired from you, sir; we will be going now." Morgaine tried to brush past Arkamun with Neva and head for the door.

He blocked the door from either of them exiting. "Not so fast." He said taking a step in their direction, flinging them back from the cottage door. "Where is it that you think you will be going?" he said continuing to lumber towards them as they stepped back towards the fire.

Before either of the women knew, he had retrieved a large object from a hidden location in the cottage. They realized now that he was coming towards them with a large knife.

20 Buried

The two dead women lay next to each other on the bloodied cottage floor, Berhanua laying between the dead bodies. He was awoken by the sound of a wolf's howl off in the distance. He sat up looking around the cottage in disbelief. He knew he was ordered by the queen to kill the young women, but he could not remember anything that took place the night before. Bile rose in this throat, and he ran out of the cottage and vomited on the tree outside.

Still in disbelief over how brutally the women were attacked, he had no choice but to finish the task given to him by the queen. He walked back into the cottage, selecting the sharpest knife in his bag and moved over to where Neva laid. He kneeled down, mounting her, sitting on her waist as he worked to her remove her nipples. Berhanua placed her set into a box labeled with her name.

"The queen's prize," a familiar voice echoed in his head as he continued cutting her flesh. "She shall be pleased with me," the voiced echoed again.

Berhanua dropped the knife on Neva's body and grasped his head with his hands. He shook his head feverishly trying to get rid of the voice. After a few moments, Berhanua gained his composure and moved off of her body to place the box with her flesh by the cottage door. As he was bending down to put the box in the bag, visions, of the previous evening flashed in his mind. He could see clearly the women pleasing him orally and intimately.

He reflected on how they placed their mouths against his penis and body, sucking and licking him, and he initiated them into sucking and licking each other. He took Neva first, then Morgaine from behind, on top, and every position imaginable. But as the vision became clearer, he could see the figure of the man was not him, having sex with the women in such a brutal fashion. It was the face of his adversary and oppressor. It was none other than Arkamun's.

Berhanua stumbled backward; the vision fading as he fell over Morgaine's body onto the floor. What he had seen was so confusing. Was he going crazy and losing his mind? Was the vision he just saw real?

"It cannot be," he said out loud, holding his head in his hands. "I must be going crazy." He sat back on his heels taking a few deep breaths, composing himself. "Get yourself together, man," he said shaking his head one final time before standing. "Arkamun is alive and well, and not floating around inside of you. Get this task done so you can get back to Eleni."

Berhanua returned over to where Neva laid to dispose of her remains. He removed the robe from over her head and saw how brutal he had been to her in her final moments. Seeing her disfigured face disturbed him greatly. The cuts and the flesh removed from her face were not actions he would have employed in his right mind. Had the queen drugged him? What had come over him?

He was so confused by the scene around him. Were his hands this capable of being so evil? Berhanua shook the thoughts from his mind again, and his stomach churned.

He looked closer at her remains. She had a stab wound starting from the back of her head, the knife blade exiting through her right eye. He could see that she had died in pain. Neva's other eye was open as well as her mouth. It appeared as if she died screaming out for help. Berhanua closed her remaining eye and adjusted her mouth, so it too was closed.

He leaned closer, rubbing her blonde, blood-ridden hair through his fingers, and rubbed her blood-stained face with his hand. He said a prayer in her ear. Before he could conclude the words of the prayer, Berhanua's head suddenly pounded immensely again, his eyes rolling to the back of his skull. Arkamun once again possessed his body. He looked down at Neva and smiled.

"Awe, there you are my precious," he said out loud.

He leaned down and kissed her passionately on the lips. Continuing to smile, he picked up his knife, kissed Neva one final time, before removing her head from her shoulders.

"Thank you for the enjoyable evening," he said.

He held Neva's decapitated head in his hands, before tossing it into the fire. He returned to where the rest of her body laid. Knifing body parts one by one, he removed her limbs from her torso and those were also tossed in the fire. He continued in this fashion with the mutilation until flame consumed her entire body. The smell of flesh circulated in the air of the cottage. Arkamun became aroused again with the dismantling of her body. He had the sudden urge to relieve his sexual tension building up inside of his body. He glanced over to Morgaine's body still resting on the floor where he knifed her down that evening before she could escape into the night.

"Awe, there you lay, my lovely little thing." He dropped the knife down by his feet and knelt next to Morgaine's body. Arkamun fell to the floor hitting his head.

A few minutes had passed before Berhanua awoke again from the darkness that consumed him. This time, when he awoke, Berhanua noticed Neva's body was gone, the cottage smelling like burning flesh. He stood up rubbing his head and staggered over to the door. He opened it stumbling out onto the cobblestone pavers. The wind blew through the cabin, blowing out some of the stench.

The sun had not risen yet, the forest still dark from the night's sky. It would be fading soon, and the sun would be rising. He had to hurry to finish his task and return to the castle. As he got to his feet, he could feel a presence lurking to take a hold of him, to possess him.

He stepped away from the door again back into the fading night and rounded the back of the cottage. He pondered about these mysterious events happening to him, trying to understand what they meant. As he meandered out in the night, he recalled a conversation he had with the elders' of the kingdom in his homeland when he was younger. The elders had told him of such events happening to others.

They had explained and warned him when a person died in a tragic way; sometimes their soul refused to cross over to the afterlife. The spirit would refuse to die and seek to overtake a person they held in captivity for a time and deemed worthy to be an inhabitant. When a person was selected, a mark was branded on that person, but the location on the body part would be different for each vessel.

The elders' words pounded in Berhanua's head. He nervously searched his body for such a mark. He found nothing on his arms, legs, back, or hands. The last place to check was his feet. He sat down in the darkness outside of the cottage, the glow from the fire within illuminating his skin. He looked down at his feet covered in dirt.

He glanced around to find something to clean them with and noticed a barrel with water in it sitting off to the side of the cottage. He retrieved the water from the barrel, splashing it down on his feet. Once they were clean, he stepped into the grass, sat down again and peered at the soles of his feet. The right foot was clear, but when he looked closely at his left foot, he saw the brand. Placed in between two of his toes a black tattoo with a small incantation to invoke a spirit into a living breathing soul.

The vision he had seen earlier, now made sense. King Dabir had kept his word. Arkamun's body was dead, but his soul wanted Berhanua. He did not know how long he could fight off his arch enemy's takeover. He would most certainly try to protect his soul and keep his humanity, but with him already blacking out, it was only a matter of time before Arkamun had complete control.

Berhanua looked up into the early morning sky. "My Savior, I beg of you. Please allow me to make it back to Eleni to warn her. I care for her and cannot bring any more harm to her. I promise you I would not kill anymore after this. Please allow me to warn her," he prayed out loud.

Berhanua fell to his knees and continued to pray silently. When he finished, he stood once more and returned to the cottage. He took a deep breath and entered back through the doorway. As he crossed over the threshold, he felt Arkamun's spirit circling to overtake him again. He felt like he had no control over what was happening, his head pounded, and ears rang like so many times before.

Berhanua tried to fight it and screamed as the pain stretched through every part of his body. When the pain subsided, Arkamun had once again made his transition; Berhanua was now under Arkamun's control again.

"Now where was I?" he said as he walked back over to where Morgaine laid. Arkamun dropped down beside her body and rubbed her hair with his fingers. He leaned in to smell the brown locks falling past her shoulders on the floor.

"Hmmmmm, jasmine. Eleni used to wear this particular scent." He smiled as he played in Morgaine's curls.

He had broken her neck that evening, but now she looked as if she slept. She was beautiful even in death. Her face still adorned with makeup. Her eyes were closed and painted with a blue shadow. Arkamun's arousal returned, and the more he gazed at her, the harder his penis became. He laughed out loud again, reliving the night's events, the two little servant girls he had seduced, and killed for the Queens Vivienne's benefit.

"Hmmm, Queen Vivienne," Arkamun said out loud. "She is a woman who deserves me to fuck her senseless," he told Morgaine's corpse.

"What is it you say Morgaine? You want me to do what with you? Awe... I hear you; I can accommodate that beautiful."

He leaned down and kissed Morgaine on the mouth. He then climbed on Morgaine's body, sliding his trousers down and thrusting his shaft inside of her cold flesh until he climaxed.

Arkamun relieved himself of the sensation he was feeling and moved off of the body. He felt his strength leaving him, and he knew that until the transition became complete and Berhanua was dead, he would have limited ability to what he could do in the vessel he controlled.

"Soon," he said. "Soon I will have complete control." He laid back on the cottage floor. "Time for me to go to sleep so that I can regain my strength. Berhanua you can now come out and clean up my mess as you have always done for your king."

Arkamun then slipped out of his body. Berhanua regained consciousness and looked down at himself to find his pants were open. He glanced over at Morgaine's body lying next to him to find she was completely exposed. He was overcome with guilt. Arkamun had gained control over him and had sex with a corpse.

Feeling disgusted and sick to the stomach again he jerked his pants up over his thighs and ran out of the cottage again into the night. Berhanua fell to his knees in tears after he emptied himself, and looking up to the starlit sky, he prayed once more to his Savior and his God.

Berhanua finished his second prayer, wiped the vomit from his face, and trudged back through the grass to return to the cottage to finish the job the Queen gave him. He stepped over the threshold, wondering if Arkamun's spirit was lurking to return. This time, he felt nothing around him and was able to observe the state of the cottage. He saw blood from the bodies spreading across the floor. He gathered straw in the nearby barn to absorb the bloody mess.

He finished removing Morgaine's nipples, placing those into the other box, and wrapped her torso in the wool blankets where she laid. He moved her remains out of the cottage dropping them into a large hole he had dug in the tall grassy knoll. The hole was so large it almost consumed his tall six-foot frame.

"Almost complete." He brushed the dirt from his hands and returned to the cottage gathering the last of Morgaine's remains. He would dispose of it by feeding it to the wolves. As he cleaned, he thought about all of the times back in Abyssinia where he had to come to Arkamun's aid covering up for his king. He was once again cleaning up after his king's mishaps. The only difference was now Arkamun inhabited his body to do his evil deeds.

He wondered how King Dabir killed him? Was it a violent death? And when would he try to make his next appearance? He finished burning the rest of the bloody straw on the fire, and the smell of burned flesh throughout the cottage disappeared.

Good... I cannot have Eleni coming here smelling such filth.

Berhanua worked hard to restore his surroundings to its previous condition. He poured scented oil into the cauldron, hoping to mask the remaining smell of burnt flesh. He scrubbed every nook and corner until the cottage looked normal again. When he was done cleaning, he observed himself. He was covered in dirt, mud, sperm, caked blood and straw. Berhanua sought out a stream to cleanse his body. There was one not too far from where the cottage stood. He stripped off the blood-soaked and dirty clothing and tossed them into the stream.

"Away with you," he said out loud as he dove underneath the fresh water.

He rose out of the water and cleansed himself with the soap Eleni had made for him. How he wanted to confess his secrets and looked forward to sharing the cottage with her. The sun peeked over the dark sky, and Berhanua had to return to the castle. He swam to the edge of the stream and hurried up the embankment.

Berhanua redressed himself and picked up his bag with the trinkets for the queen and the food for the wolves. It was going to be a long trek back to the castle. As he paced himself, he sent out a wolf call in the forest. They answered and gathered around him forming a circle. The wolves were hungry and nearly starved.

Before he could even have pulled out the food for them, they started to come closer snapping at him.

"Whoa, Whoa, boys," he said unwrapping the burlap cloth. "I got what you want you right here." He tossed the limbs in the animals' direction.

The Wolves fought amongst themselves over the remains, but the bigger alpha wolf settled the dispute between the smaller two ones and got them to stop fighting. Berhanua finished emptying the burlap cloth and sent the Wolves running back into the woods.

He washed his hands in the nearby pond and continued towards the castle. The sun rose overhead. He thought about how he would tell Eleni about what was lurking inside of his body and in his very soul.

Would she stay with me, even if she knew?

He would tell her the truth when they settled into the cottage. It was hard enough to keep the secret about her daughter not being dead. Berhanua made it back to the castle in a timely manner, long before all the other servants in the castle awoke from their slumber. He moved quietly into the back castle door and up the stairs to Queen Vivienne's chambers. He knocked on the door as quietly as he could so he would not alert the guards.

Vivienne heard the knock on the door. She kissed the sleeping baby in her arms and placed her in the crib next to her bed. She tried to block out the horrid delivery and the death of her little girl and enjoy her stolen baby.

"Enter," she answered sauntering towards her chamber room door. Berhanua moved through the door and knelt before the queen.

"Have you done everything I have asked of you?" Vivienne crossed her arms over her breasts.

Berhanua glanced up at her from his kneeling stance. "It is done, your majesty."

"Did you make sure the ladies had a good time and an evening they would never forget? You may stand now slave; I want to hear the details."

Berhanua leaned over his bag and retrieved the two boxes the queen had given Arkamun before getting to his feet.

"These are for you, Your Majesty."

Queen Vivienne clapped in excitement and took the boxes from Berhanua's hands.

"Do these boxes contain what I asked you to put in them?"

"Yes, Your Majesty, you can take a look if it pleases you."

"I will take a look at the contents later. You, however, still have one more job for me to do for me before all of your tasks are finshed. Have you taken care of the slave Katlego.?"

"I planned on taking her with me when I left this kingdom. She would be permitted to stay with Eleni and me at the cottage as you instructed."

Vivienne shifted her stance when baby Sabine stirred behind them in the crib. Her attention diverted, she went to the child's side and patted her on the back. She quieted and fell back to sleep, and Vivienne turned her glance back towards Berhanua.

"Oh, my little slave, you do not understand. I have changed my mind. I simply cannot have anyone who was in the room during my delivery or Eleni's delivery live. You will take care of her as well; you will kill her and leave her body in the woods behind the castle. After you have done this final task, you will await Eleni in the front of the castle. Slave, do these last things I have asked of you and your debts will be paid. You will be allowed to live in peace with your slave slut Eleni away from my castle and kingdom. My husband will be returning to the palace soon. You must be gone and have completed your task before he does. Go now and complete what I have asked of you. We shall not meet again, and I thank you for my gifts. I shall add them to my chest of secrets."

Berhanua bowed his head like he was going to leave the chamber room to enter back into the hallway. He dropped his bag by his side and tried to calm the pounding in his head. But instead of leaving, Arkamun regained control and quietly walked in the queen's direction. He came up behind her and spun her around.

"I know you wanted me as much as I you," he whispered. He forced her into a passionate kiss sticking his tongue down her throat.

Vivienne resisted at first and tried to push his large muscular frame away from her. "Let me go," she sought to say as he muffled her voice with his mouth and tongue. But as the kiss continued she relaxed allowing him to continue. They clinched each other into a deeper embrace. She released herself from the embrace wiping her lips with her hand.

"Who do you think you are a slave?" she crossed her arms.

"I am no slave queen. But I am, and will always be a king."

"'A king! Slave, you sound as crazy as Eleni seemed saying she was a queen." Vivienne retorted laughing out loud.

Arkamun took a step closer her forcing her arms down and lifted her off the floor closer to him.

"You will listen to me woman, I am a king. King Arkamun to be exact, and I will be back to take what I want."

Arkamun kissed her again passionately, taking his hand and moving it slowly up the center of her leg. He ignored that she still bled from her delivery.

"I will be back for what is mine." He scuffled out of the room.

Vivienne rubbed her lips, still tasting him on her. She did not know what to expect from him next, but liked his controlling manner and was excited by for his return.

Arkamun moved swiftly down the staircase, pleased to be back in control. His transitions into Berhanua were becoming easier. While in spirit form, he studied everything about this foreign land: The people, the stories, the roads. It was a new playground to him. He saw how the people of this country slept, played, and entertained. He knew he would be able to manipulate the queen and have her under his thumb.

Once Eleni was out the kingdom, he would come back for her, seduce her and do as he pleased with her. He always kept his promises, and she was no exception.

"Now on to find this Katlego," he cooed. He came to the bottom of the staircase and out to the courtyard where the chicken coops were located. It still was very early, and he believed that Katlego would be out by the chicken coop gathering the eggs for the kitchen staff to prepare breakfast. He was not wrong in his guess; he could see her gathering eggs in the distance, placing them gently in the basket by her feet.

Arkamun knew he had to move quickly. He would overtake her and be fast about it. His palms were relaxed as he removed the knife that rested in the scabbard by his side. Slipping his sandals off his feet, he moved quietly on the dirt ground until he stood behind her. He inhaled, and with the quick movement of his hand, he swiped the blade of the knife across Katlego's throat, blood pouring out the gaping wound he created. She struggled to take a breath and dropped the eggs out of her hands. They broke on the dirt below her as she wrapped her hands around the wound in her neck.

She managed to turn around to see her assailant who still stood behind her. Katlego's eyes widened with despair and horror as she looked upon what she believed to be Berhanua's face. She tried to produce the words but was unable because of her severed vocal cords. Her eyes darkened, and all she could only see was the grinning face looking down at her. A few tears welled up in her eyes and she glanced up at the bright morning sky, mouthing a prayer as she started to slip out of consciousness.

Arkamun continued to smile down at the body lying under him. Three dead bodies in a span of hours, he was on a roll. He clapped his hands in the enjoyment.

"Now to move this body," he muttered to himself.

He did as the queen instructed and moved Katlego's body into the forest behind the castle. He called the same wolves that Berhanua fed earlier that morning. The wolves knew what the call meant and came running out of the woods into the clearing. They were a little frightened at first to proceed to where Katlego laid. But when they sensed things were safe, the wolves dragged her body behind them back into the opening of the forest.

Arkamun kept a few feet of distance behind the wolves. He watched in amusement as the wolves tore the flesh and bones from Katlego's body.

His excitement waned once he lost sight of them. There was only a bloody mess that remained. "Berhanua should have quite a time cleaning this mess up," he said out loud. "I shall allow him out to handle it." Arkamun slumped down underneath the closest tree, closing his eyes and retreating once again into spirit form.

Berhanua awoke again on the ground in the clearing of the forest. He was not sure how he arrived there but realized once again Arkamun had overtaken his body. The spell Arkamun had cast was almost complete. He was slipping further and further out of control.

He would have to tell Eleni as soon as he could, so she could be warned about what was lurking inside of him. Berhanua looked around surveying his surroundings. He was not far from the castle walls and saw traces of blood leading from the castle chicken coop into the forest not far from where he sat.

Berhanua did not have to guess at what happened. He walked a little deeper into the woods to confirm his suspicions. He followed the trail of blood until it tapered off leaving the remains of Katlego spread around before him. The site saddened Berhanua. His hands were used to take yet another life.

Berhanua made his way back to the castle's stables to retrieve a shovel to clean up the mess left for him after Arkamun's tryst. After retrieving the shovel, he hurried back to the clearing of the forest where Katlego laid. He dug a deep hole off the path, hidden from plain sight and not easily spotted by one riding horseback.

He moved her body into the hole in the ground, and he inspected her body closer. Wolves had ravaged her. He wondered if those were the same wolves he had called upon before. Once he finished, he lit a fire and burned the areas of the ground where blood spilled.

Berhanua made it to the chicken coop and lit the entire area on fire, making it seems as if it were an accident. He could not leave evidence of murder nor could he leave evidence that could be traced to him. He knew the smell of smoke would have the servants running in search of water to extinguish the flames. The commotion would give him enough time clean himself up and wait for Eleni at the front of the castle.

"My final task is complete," he whispered. He dropped the torch on the chicken coop and headed back to the castle the same way he came.

Eleni awoke from her slumber with a headache, and she knew she was drugged by the Queen the night before. She searched around her room expecting to see the precious face of her little girl Gwenaelle; she had given birth to only hours before. The room was dim and quiet. Eleni pushed herself up into a sitting position and forced herself out of the bed. Her legs were limp under her, her strength was all but gone, but she still wanted to see her baby and hold her in her arms once more. She stumbled over to where the baby should have been slumbering, and looked down into the wooden crib. Its contents empty.

It was as if there was never a baby there at all. Eleni's focus shifted around the room, everything used for the delivery was gone, her simple room was back to how it always looked. All was in its place, and it seemed like she never gave birth.

An old woman that Eleni had seen around the castle entered the room. She tried to force Eleni to drink a warm liquid she brought with her in a chalice. Eleni spat the liquid back in the old hag's face, and the woman slapped her with her bony hand.

"Drink this down slave," she hissed and forced the contents of the goblet into Eleni's mouth. She held Eleni's mouth closed with her wiry hand. The cup's contents made Eleni feel tired, confused, and dizzy. She fell back into bed in an unconscious slumber.

Eleni slept for another night in a deep sleep and awoke with her strength returning the next morning. Realizing once again her baby girl was nowhere to be found, Eleni was determined to find her daughter and seek those out who were responsible for taking her. She slid out of bed, grabbed her tattered gown, dressed and left the tower to find her daughter.

"Gwenaelle, Gwenaelle," She called out as headed down the narrow staircase to the lower hall to the queen's chambers. Eleni reached the queen's door and pounded on it.

"Queen Vivienne," she called out. "Milady! What have you done with my baby!" She screamed. There was no response.

Eleni kept pounding on the chamber room door. Before she could head to the next hall on the floor below her, the queen's guards surrounded her grabbing her by the arms. They did not speak a sound, but the force they used to lift her small frame was enough to subdue her.

"Let me go!" she screamed. She struggled to free her arms from the men who dragged her down the stairs to the entrance of the castle.

Queen Vivienne stepped out in front of her and grinned. "My dear Eleni, what seems to be the problem? Why are you making all this noise? I could hear you screaming throughout the castle."

"Your majesty, my daughter Gwenaelle, what did you do with her?"

"Your little girl died during the night while you were sleeping," Vivienne answered slyly.

"You are lying. I held her in my arms; she was perfect!" Eleni screamed. Eleni struggled to free herself from the guard who captured her.

"No one is lying to you, Eleni; your delusions are the reason why I had to keep you subdued. You see, my daughter is alive and well; it was yours who died in delivery."

Eleni could not believe what she was hearing. The queen had surely lost her mind.

"Your daughter?" Eleni said questioning the queen. "Your little girl died in delivery, Katlego and I delivered your child, Your Majesty."

"No Eleni," Vivienne was still smiling. "You only imagined that happened. Katlego and I delivered your baby, and unfortunately, she died in the night as you slept. I am truly sorry for the loss of your baby."

Eleni struggled and tried to break free again from the guards. She could not believe what she was hearing. The queen had indeed gone mad.

"Where is Katlego, Your Majesty? She will tell you what happened. Please bring her here to stand before you. She will explain everything."

Vivienne paced back in forth in front of Eleni, folding her arms in amusement. "Katlego, was taken care of, as you will be, Eleni. After this conversation, we shall be forever parted. I have no more use for you. And you will not remain here to tempt my king, or draw his attention from his daughter or me. But I am a kind queen so I will allow you to leave here with the other man slave. Never to return, or I shall be forced to deal with you in a harsher fashion."

Eleni knew she could not fight the queen or the guards who held her; she would have to try to reach the king somehow. Would he believe what his wife was capable of? Would he believe her story? That the baby Vivienne had was not of his blood. She would try to remain out of sight, and when the opportunity presented itself, she would get the king's attention. She could use his infatuation for her to her advantage, and when the time was right, she would expose the queen.

Vivienne slowed her pace and stopped directly in front of where Eleni stood. Her eyes darkened as the blood drained from her face.

"Get her out of my sight," Queen Vivienne told her guards angrily. "Get rid of her and every trace of her."

Vivienne stepped closer to Eleni's face and stared deep into her eyes. Eleni saw nothing but blackness. The queen had won this round. She would have to find another way to see Edmond. The tears from Eleni's eyes streamed once again. She was leaving without her child, her only remaining piece of her true love David.

Eleni was tossed out of the French castle by the guards. She pleaded to Queen Vivienne to give her baby daughter back. All the members of the court who laid witness turned a blind eye and the servants she had once served next to laughed and threw fruit at her. She was forced over the bridge and thrown onto the dirt road with only the clothing on her back. She fell to her knees, weeping uncontrollably.

Berhanua finished jotting down the letter he wanted to give Eleni, telling her everything. He watched from the side of the castle waiting for the perfect moment to come to her aid. When the servants were done throwing fruit and jeering at Eleni, he went to her side and helped to her feet.

"Come away with Eleni." He extended his hand lifting her to her feet.

"Berhanua, my daughter," Eleni mumbled between sobs as Berhanua helped her up and started to lead Eleni away from the castle towards the forest. He rubbed her shoulder and tried to comfort her.

"She cannot be dead Berhanua." Eleni turned her face once again towards the castle.

"I know it hurts my Eleni; your daughter is with the Creator. There is nothing you can do; she is dead."

Eleni stopped walking and jerked away from Berhanua's arm wrapped around her shoulder.

"She did not die Berhanua! The queen has my daughter," Eleni cried out.

Eleni rubbed the back of her neck, her posture sagged.

"Eleni, your little girl died after you gave birth. She died while you were delirious with fever. That is why the old woman who sat with you continued to give you a medicine so you could sleep."

Eleni shook her head with disbelief again as they continued down the path deeper into the forest.

"Berhanua, you are telling me lies," she called out as she followed him. "I do not believe you when you tell me my daughter is dead. I cannot believe this; I have to find out what happened to my daughter."

Eleni spun around and headed back towards the castle. Berhanua swiveled around and ran behind Eleni, knocking her to the ground. They both struggled with one another until Berhanua got the upper hand, sitting on her small frame holding her down. He wrapped his hands around her neck until she was unconscious and stopped moving. When he was satisfied she would not budge, he moved off her body. He picked her up, swinging her over his shoulder and continued to walk deeper into the forest towards the cottage.

Jamond had made it to the castle right as Eleni removed. He saw her forced down the path into the forest by a large, dark-skinned man. He bypassed the castle heading directly down the road behind Eleni. Staying covered by the brush, he followed the dark-skinned man carrying Eleni to a small cottage. He kicked the door open and took Eleni inside. Jamond hid behind a tree close to the cottage and tried to peer inside. The man tied Eleni down with rope and gagged her mouth with a cloth.

He would have to wait for the cover of darkness to release Eleni from her bondage.

Jamond rested his back against the tree and waited for the opportune time to strike. The moon rose in the dark sky and a bright glow gleamed out of the cottage window. Jamond had dozed off and woke up to Eleni screaming. He flipped over and crawled closer to the window, remaining unseen. He peered through the window and watched the dark- skinned man strike Eleni across the face numerous times.

Jamond wasted no time in pulling his knife from his bag. He jumped to his feet, kicking the door, in and striking the dark-skinned man in the back. The man spun around screaming and punched Jamond in the face, knocking his knife to the ground. Jamond's blonde dreadlocks flung behind him as he fell to the floor. He struggled over to the knife and turned on his back as the dark-skinned man plopped down on him.

"Jamond, get up Jamond!" She screamed, struggling to free herself.

Jamond blinked his eyes open and grabbed the knife. He pushed himself onto his knees then his feet and came in the direction of the dark man.

"You have not had enough had you?" The man yelled coming towards him again.

"You will not lay another hand on her!" Jamond yelled. He held his knife out in front of him and lunged towards the man, plunging the knife into his neck.

Eleni freed herself and stood over Berhanua as he fell to the floor. His eyes returned to the normal color and pupils decreased. The monster that had beat her disappeared. Eleni dropped to her knees beside him.

"What happened to you Berhanua?" she whispered, "How could you do this to me?"

Berhanua coughed up blood through his mouth and gasped for air. He managed to pull the letter out of his pocket and push it into her hand.

"I am so sorry, Eleni, please forgive me. I have written it all down. Your daughter is not dead. Read my letter; it will tell you everything."

Berhanua coughed two more times closed his eyes and died.

"You are now free my friend, Rest well my sweet Berhanua" Eleni kissed him gently on the forehead and clutched the letter in her hand. She got to her feet and circled towards Jamond and hugged him. "Thank you for saving my life Jamond. Why are you here in France? And how did you find me?"

"Eleni, I was sent to here France to find you."

"What do you mean you were sent here to find me?"

"Eleni, you must come away with me. David sent me to find you. He wants me to help you get to England."

Eleni covered her face with her hands. David had not forgotten her. He was alive and knew she had lived. She had so many questions to ask Jamond. Eleni hugged Jamond once more and smiled.

"You must tell me everything. I want to know everything."

"In due time Eleni. Now you must come away with me."

Jamond and Eleni hurried out in the night sky. They had little time to secure a ship and get out of the Port of Caen. For a few brief moments, Eleni imagined how her life would be with David. She would reunite with him in England, and she would have the opportunity to tell him about their daughter. They would have to devise a plan to rescue their child from the hands of the evil Queen Vivienne to have their happily ever after.

ABOUT THE AUTHOR

Devin Devonne was born in Chicago Ill, relocating to California with her mother when she was five years old. Assimilating in the southern California life she grew up loving the beach and warm weather. She has always been a hopeless romantic and can be found watching old musicals such as Brigadoon, Seven brides for seven brothers, South Pacific and many others.
Raised in culture she found herself loving all aspects of the

arts. She is an accomplished musician, cook, writer and seamstress (loves vintage clothing).

www.ingramcontent.com/pod-product-compliance
Lightning Source LLC
Chambersburg PA
CBHW021429240626
47153CB00001B/87